2-11-20

1

PATHS TO FREEDOM

THE MALLORY SAGA
BOOK 2

PAUL BENNETT

Printed in the United States of America

First Printing, 2019

Hoover Books

mallorysaga@gmail.com

Table of Contents

List of Characters

Bold=historical figure

Italicized=appeared in Clash of Empires

<u>Mallory Town</u>

Liam Mallory – youngest son of Thomas and Abigail

Rebecca Jameson– Liam's wife

Albert Jackson (Jack) – twin son of Liam and Rebecca

Liam Caleb (Cal) – twin son of Liam and Rebecca

Daniel Mallory – eldest son of Thomas and Abigail

Deborah Mallory – Daniel's wife

Bowie Rhys (Bo) – son of Daniel and Deborah

Abigail – daughter of Daniel and Deborah

Ethan – son of Daniel and Deborah

Elizabeth Clarke (Liza) – daughter of Thomas and Abigail

Henry Clarke – Liza's husband

Thomas Joseph – son of Henry and Liza

Meagan Jane – daughter of Henry and Liza

Jonas Lapley – early settler

Hannah – Jonas wife

John – son of Jonas and Hannah

Ruth – daughter of Jonas and Hannah

Anne Webb – widow

Josiah – Anne's oldest son

Samuel – Anne's youngest son

Crane family: early settlers

Richard & Hilda – William, James, Susan, Lucy, Marsha, Robert

Bert Sawyer – runaway slave

Reverend James Grantham – minister

Micah Townsend – former soldier-works for Grantham

Gerald Brightman – another Grantham henchman

Timothy Winslow – brewer

Glyn Mulhern – former soldier, companion of Liam and Wahta

Jack Tomlinson – teamster

Bartholomew Morgan - shopkeeper

Boston

Marguerite Edgerton – works for Revere

Paul Revere – silversmith, Sons of Liberty

Dr. Joseph Warren – physician, Sons of Liberty

Sam Adams – politician, Sons of Liberty

William Dawes – tanner, Sons of Liberty

John Hancock – prosperous businessman

Militia

Martin Lake – former soldier

Steven McKay – Woburn militia

Robbie Bayliss – Woburn militia

General William Heath – Brigadier

General Artemus Ward – Commander Massachusetts Militia

Salem

Dan Sinclair (Big Dan) – warehouse owner

Beth Winslow – tavern owner

Captain Felt – Salem militia

Colonel Pickering – Salem militia

Reverend Barnard - minister

<u>Native Americans</u>

Wahta – Mohawk companion of Liam and Mulhern

Mishka (Turtle) – Terrance Justice, captured and adopted Ojibway

Pucksinwah *– Shawnee chieftain*

Chiksika – eldest son of Pucksinwah

Catahecassa - principal chief of the Shawnee

Hokoleskwa – Shawnee chieftain

Shemeneto – Shawnee chieftain

Takoda – Pawnee holy man

Morning Dew – Crow widow

Badger – young Crow warrior

Makya – Shoshone guide

Kariwase – Oneida chief

Waneek – wife of Kariwase

Mingan – Ojibway

Soyechtowa (Logan) *– Mingo chief*

<u>British</u>

Colonel Whitby – ambitious officer

Sergeant Paul Kelleher – gregarious Irishman

General Thomas Gage – commander of British forces

Thomas Hutchinson – Governor of Massachusetts Colony

Colonel Leslie – seeker of weapons

Corporal Charles Buxton – keeper of horses

Corporal Stu Laing – partner of Buxton

Sergeant Jack Collard – jailer

<u>The colonial frontier</u>

Two Birds Ouellette – Fort Pitt tavern owner and trader

Joseph Clarke – Albany, father to Henry

Gabe Emerson – mountain man living with the Crow

David Rollins – Whitely Creek, looking for help

<u>Waiting in the wings</u>

George Washington – soon to be named Commander of the American Army

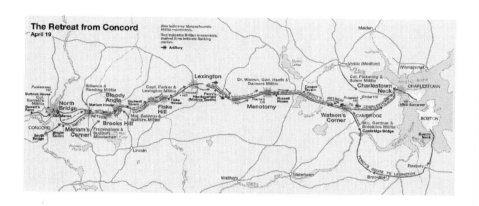

Map of the British retreat – Battle of Lexington and Concord April 19, 1775

Map used by the kind permission of "Minute Man National Historical Park, National Park Service"

I highly recommend a visit to this historic site.

Prologue

Mallory Town – February 1767

Reverend James Grantham closed his Bible, and raised his hands toward the ceiling of the new church. His benediction praised God for the work He had begun in this frontier village. With the French no longer a threat and the pacification of the native tribes in the area, Mallory Town was growing by leaps and bounds. New settlers were arriving every month; some with plows, others with a trade, and some with only the clothes on their backs, but all needing salvation, or God's guidance.

As he stood in the door to greet the parishioners leaving the church, he could not help but notice that, once again, some did not attend. He resolved to have another talk with Daniel Mallory and Liza Clarke about their wayward brother, Liam. He knew that it would be futile to confront Liam, or the unmarried mother of his children, Rebecca. His last attempt seemed only to further the distance between him and Liam. He recalled the last words Liam spoke as he discourteously ushered the Reverend from their cabin: "I will worship who I will and where I will, so save your damned judgmental preaching."

'Judgmental indeed', Reverend Grantham thought to himself, 'who was this ignorant backwoodsman to jeopardize the souls of his children? I will hold them up to the entire community as faithless examples of the devil's work! Once they feel the wrath of God in my sermons, we shall see him and his sinful woman soon come crawling to the church, begging for forgiveness. Time for them, and the rest of this flock of sheep, to recognize their true shepherd.'

Boston – The Green Dragon Tavern – 1767

The Green Dragon Tavern patrons gathered for a pint, or two, and for news, and rumors concerning the right of the Crown to tax the colonies without their consent. Sam Adams, a politically active member of the first Massachusetts House of Representatives, slammed his mug down in outrage on the table, exclaiming to all, "This is just another example of Parliament and the King exercising a right that they do not possess. Taxation of British subjects, even those in the Colonies, without representation is unconstitutional, and must be rejected and repealed!"

In 1765, Parliament passed the Stamp Act, (imposing a new tax on every piece of printed paper they used), to help recover the costs of the French & Indian War. Following the lead of Virginia, many of the other colonies banded together and declared that the Stamp Act was illegal, as it was promulgated without the consent of the taxed. Parliament repealed the act a year later, but insisted that the Crown had the right to tax the colonies. In 1767, the new Townshend Act levied a duty on tea, glass, lead, paper and paint.

The reaction of Parliament and King George III to this, and subsequent actions in the colonies, further widened the gap between the Crown and its subjects, and eventually led to the garrisoning of more British troops in Boston to quell the growing unrest. During the next decade, the Boston Massacre in 1770, the Boston Tea Party in 1774, and finally the Declaration of Independence in 1776 were but a portion of the fuel that fed the flames of revolution.

Mallory Town – April 1767

Rebecca tried to stifle a groan as she rose from their bed. She was pretty certain that she was pregnant, but this time was different from when she carried the twins. With Jack and Caleb, she did not suffer from morning sickness; however, for the last week she was ill every morning. Not wanting to disturb or worry Liam, she tried to hide the nausea and dizziness, but this morning he woke to her groaning. "Are you alright?" Liam asked as he rubbed the sleep from his eyes.

"Oh, I'm sorry. Yes, my dear, I'm fine," Rebecca answered, "I must be a little sore from chasing the twins. You go back to sleep for a bit. I'll get breakfast going." After checking the twins, she took a bucket outside to get water from the well.

About halfway to the well, Rebecca doubled over, fell to her knees, and vomited. As she started to stand, she felt a pair of hands helping her to rise. "Oh my, Rebecca," said Liza with a smile on her face, "are you pregnant?"

"I believe I am, though I didn't have the morning sickness with the twins," she replied.

"Well, you were fortunate," Liza said. "I suffered every morning for a month or so with both of my children. You look a little pale. Why don't you sit for a minute? I'll fill your bucket."

Donehogawa's village along the Mohawk River – July 1767

Donehogawa survived a plague of dysentery that ravaged his village just a couple of years earlier. It left him in a weakened condition, and this summer's fever proved too hard to resist. The venerated chief of the Wolf Clan died peacefully in his sleep, his wife Onatah beside him. Wahta and Pierre kept vigil outside the lodge, letting their last moments together be private.

The elders of the Bear and Turtle clans arrived to prepare the body for burial. They carried Donehogawa's body to the village's communal longhouse, entering through the east-facing door; they placed his feet facing the western door to prepare the deceased for the final journey. After condolences were offered, the body was carried out the western door to the freshly dug grave. The people of the village all attended Donehogawa's burial; he was beloved for his wisdom and compassion. The family of the deceased would be taken care of during the ten day mourning period, at the end of which a large meal would be prepared for the village. During this period, Donehogawa's family would give away all of his possessions. They presented Wahta with Donehogawa's favorite war lance; Pierre, his medicine pouch. They also gave to Wahta the chief's finest wolf pelt to give to Otetiani to remind him of his Wolf Clan father.

Chapter 1 1767 – Discord

Mallory Town
Thursday, October 15

Liam gazed down on Rebecca's sleeping form. The pre-dawn light outlined her extended belly. "Only a few months and we'll have another child," Liam whispered, "you sleep a bit longer. I'll make breakfast today." Climbing out of bed and grabbing his tunic, he crept out of the room. He could hear the twins beginning to stir, but decided to let them be until they made it known they were unhappy. He stepped outside, and took in a lungful of the chilled early morning air. Stooping to pick up the water bucket, he noticed a rather large man sitting against the well.

"Wahta, my brother," exclaimed Liam, "it is indeed a happy sight that greets me this morning."

"Snake Slayer, I was wondering how long I would have to wait for a cabin dweller to awaken," Wahta replied, "I was getting lonely, with only a pair of eyes watching me. Who lives in the god house, watching me the whole time I sat here?"

"Imagine it was the preacher, Mr. Grantham. He takes a lot of interest in what happens in the village, especially the arrival of a savage like yourself," chuckled Liam. "I don't like him much. He's too full of himself; reminds me of some of the British officers we worked for. Come, you can help me with the boys while I make breakfast. Rebecca will be so pleased to see you."

After breakfast, Wahta retrieved his saddlebag and removed a wolf pelt. As he handed it to Liam, he bowed his head and said, "Receive this, Otetiani, from your Wolf Clan father."

Liam, holding back tears, took the pelt and replied, "Thank you, Wahta, my brother. I wondered why you carried my father's war lance. I reckon he and Colonel Washington are the two finest men a man can meet, and call them their friend. Another fine man, though – how is Pierre? I am saddened he is not with you."

Wahta burst into a big grin and chuckled. "Pierre said to tell you that he is getting too old for long journeys, but I do not think that is the reason. He has taken Teeyeehogrow's Abenaki widow as his wife, and is content with her comforting ways. He also said to tell you to listen to the buffalo dreams."

Liam clapped his brother on the back. "When I'm here with my family, the buffalo does not visit. He only comes to me when I am troubled. Except for that overzealous preacher, I am a very happy man."

Wahta rose from the table and with a grin, said, "I must go find Mulhern, just to hear the little Irishman talk. I have missed that."

Sunday, October 18

Reverend James Grantham's home church (in Marblehead, Massachusetts) sent him to the frontier, his mandate that he bring to the western settlers the beliefs, and tenets of the Puritan ethic – though in his mind, the mandate came from God, and thus could not be denied, or ignored. He had struggled since his Mallory Town arrival in December of the preceding year. There were many people in this settlement who had lived too long without the guidance of Scripture and, more importantly, the guiding hand of a godly man. His sermons became thinly veiled attacks on anyone who would not bow to his understanding of the will of God, Liam and Rebecca in particular.

For Reverend James Grantham, his was not only a battle for souls – it was a battle for control of the life of the village. He had begun to see the village as his own, and while he preached the Puritan ethic, his real ambition and goal was to make this a village destined to be formed and controlled by him. His latest sermon took aim at the merchants who did business with flagrant sinners.

Reverend Grantham walked to the church to prepare for the service. It would begin in two hours, "still time to add more grief to the Mallory's", he mumbled to himself. Across the village square, he noticed Henry, his son Thomas, and young Samuel Webb preparing to go hunting. "Ignoring the Sabbath, are we, Mr. Clarke?" Grantham said to no one. "I saw you pretending you didn't see me. Well, Mr. Clarke, a time of reckoning lies in our future. Mark my words, but I must take it slowly. I think breaking the Sabbath just became a far more serious sin," he hissed as he continued his walk.

"All right boys," Henry said to Thomas and Samuel, "you head on over to the gate. Timothy should be there too. I'll meet you there in a few minutes. Need to speak to your Ma, Thomas."

Thomas shook his head, saying, "Come on, Samuel. My Pa wants to grab a smooch with my Ma."

Liza stuck her head out of the door, and taking Henry's hand, she grinned and commented, "Sorry, no smooching on the Sabbath. What would our dear preacher say about that?"

"You're likely to find out if you go to church this morning," replied Henry. "Grantham saw me as he headed over to the church. I reckon he's working up a Sabbath-breaking sermon just for me, but you'll have to listen to it." Henry smiled at his wife and kissed her.

Liza broke off the embrace; her hands on the sides of his face. She spoke very intently. "Reverend Grantham is no laughing matter. That bit last week about doing business with sinners, what if that type of thinking takes hold? It sets a very bad example, if you ask me. Doesn't sound much like what Jesus taught."

"I know," said Henry, "time for a town meeting, I think. I'll talk to Daniel, and Timothy, see what they think."

Tuesday, October 20

Liam kissed Rebecca before heading out of the cabin. He placed his hands on her belly, "The little one must be sleeping in this morning."

Rebecca smiled, "She does seem to be less active than the twins were. Maybe she knows how energetic the boys could be and she's just sparing me this time around."

"How do you know it's a girl?" he asked as he paused in the doorway.

"I don't, but since we already have the two boys, I will think of this baby as a girl until we know for sure," she answered, "now, go, Henry and the others will be waiting."

She watched Liam walk away, the smile disappearing, she gasped, clutching her belly as a spasm coursed through her body. She hadn't told anyone about these sudden onsets of pain, thinking that they were just the little one moving around. It wasn't like anything she had experienced with the twins, but she told herself that this was different, that there was only the one baby this time, and there were bound to be dissimilarities in how this baby moved.

Jack and Caleb, now almost five years old, looked up from their breakfast at the sound of their mother's groan. "Are you all right, mama?" asked Jack.

"Is it time for the baby to be born?" asked Caleb excitedly.

"I'm fine, and no, it is not time for that," Rebecca replied, "we have a few months yet before your sister arrives. Now, finish your breakfast and get to your chores. Please bring in some more firewood first, it is rather chilly today." She watched as they scurried out of the door, noticing how much lower leg was showing out of the bottom of their trousers and that Jack's arms were longer than the sleeves of his shirt. "Time to visit Mr. Morgan's store, though it's impossible to keep up with growing children," she said smiling.

Bartholomew Morgan, born of solid Puritan stock in Salem, Massachusetts, finished sweeping the nightly deposit of dust and dirt from the steps leading to his General Store. As he turned to enter the store, Micah Townsend called out to him. "Mr. Morgan, a word, if I may?"

Townsend, a former aide to General Jeffrey Amherst, was used to carrying out the more distasteful orders of his superiors. During the recent troubles caused by Pontiac's rebellion, he was tasked with pacifying the tribes, using whatever means necessary; including the supplying of whiskey while delivering only a part of promised gifts, or eliminating the more hotheaded warriors. The desire to be noticed, to succeed whatever the cost, drove Townsend. His subsequent dismissal from the army when Amherst was replaced left him rudderless. Until, that is, he met Reverend Grantham, a most ambitious man, using the guise of religion; the power of the pulpit to wrest control of Mallory Town. It came naturally for Micah to join forces with Grantham. God, instead of whiskey or murder was his new weapon.

"Why, certainly, Micah. What can I do for you?" replied Morgan.

"It's what you can do to help our community resist the ways of the devil," said Micah with a feral smirk. "With your impeccable Puritan heritage, going back to Edmund Morgan, may he be at rest in the bosom of Christ, you should be outraged at the blatant sins of Liam Mallory and his Jezebel. Have you given any thought to what Reverend Grantham said about doing business with the evil doers?"

"I have, Micah, I have," answered Morgan, his hand stroking his chin in thought, "it will be a hard thing to deny the Mallory family, but God's will be done. May this be the way to their salvation?"

"Ah, good day to you, then," said Micah, "I will leave you to your daily commerce."

Micah strode to the church where he knew Reverend James Grantham watched and waited – 'watching over everything that goes on in this village and waiting for my report,' thought Micah, 'well I mustn't keep the good reverend waiting too long.'

Reverend Grantham opened the door to the chapel and bade Micah to enter. They entered his office, a small room behind the chapel. Offering Micah the only chair, Grantham stood by a small window that gave him a fine view of the village center. "So, how did your talk go with our good brother, Mr. Morgan?" asked Grantham.

Micah cleared his throat and replied, "Just as you thought. He sees the wisdom of your sermon; as the will of God, and he will abide with that. However, I'm not sure the others will be so easy to convince."

Grantham, his gaze set firmly on the sight of six months pregnant Rebecca, making her way to Morgan's General Store, turned suddenly to Micah, and sternly replied. "You let me worry about the others. You just do as you're told. Keep up your subtle sowing of discord. Stick to the plan, your devotion to this endeavor will reap great rewards. Great rewards, indeed."

****

Bartholomew Morgan saw the will of God made manifest as he watched Rebecca enter the store. "Good morning, Mr. Morgan," said Rebecca as she let her hood down, "I find myself in need of a few yards of linen. Those boys seem to grow overnight."

"I, I am sorry, Miss Rebecca, truly I am," stammered Morgan, "but I am duty bound to God's sacred word, and must refuse you service of any kind. So, if you will please leave, and may you come to see the grace God has for you." The immediate shock Rebecca felt was fleeting, and she was able to compose herself before answering.

"I see, it is the will of your God that you cannot sell me a few yards of linen. Seems a trifling matter for God to be so involved, but as you said, you are duty bound to James Grantham, and so I will leave until such time as common sense returns."

Rebecca made it to Henry and Liza's cabin, collapsing on the bench outside the front door. A sudden pain shot through her swollen abdomen. Her gasp brought Liza to the door. Before Liza could ask, Rebecca – unable to hold back the tears – between sobs described Bart's rejection. She continued after a moment to regain her composure, "and that's not all of it. Seems I'm the cause for many a gossip, and wary glances. The looks of pity, and even hate. It just doesn't seem real. What have I done to merit such feelings?" She held her stomach as another wave of pain struck.

"Rebecca, dear, we need to get you home and to bed," said Liza. She turned back into the cabin. "Thomas, go find your Uncle Liam. I think I heard your father say something about clearing some land south of town. Tell him to get home quick, I think Rebecca is in labor." Helping Rebecca to her feet she thought, "And it is way too early for that."

As Liza put her arm around Rebecca's shoulder, she noticed Susan Townsend walking toward Jameson's bakery. "Can you walk to your cabin?" she asked.

"Yes, the pain has gone. I am worried though, the baby can't be born yet," Rebecca replied.

"Now, don't you fret, let's get you home and comfortable," Liza said waving her free arm to signal Susan.

****

Susan, the wife of Micah Townsend, lately found that she was torn between her husband's ambition, and what she quietly felt about how her husband, and Reverend Grantham ridiculed Liam and Rebecca. She knew Rebecca to be one of the sweetest people she had ever met; though Susan felt that Liam was somewhat gruff in his manner, he was no more so than any other man, especially one who had lived his whole life on the frontier. Micah would not be dissuaded, however, having coming under Grantham's spell.

Micah was drawn to Grantham because he was ruthless in both the pursuit of his goals, and in the manner he controlled people, just like General Jeffrey Amherst (Micah's former commander in Quebec). One night, after Micah came home drunk, Susan heard him as he fumbled around getting undressed for bed, "Do you need any help, husband?" she had asked, "This drinking is unseemly. I wish you would stay away from Reverend Grantham."

"Shows how little you know, woman," he said pointing his finger at her, "old Reverend Grantham is gonna take care of me once we get rid of the Mallory's. He says for me to keep sowing discord among the villagers, spreading the goodness of Reverend Grantham, and King George, and when we get control of the village, I'll be his right hand man."

Yes, Micah has changed a lot since he entered, and left the army, but I have not, thought Susan to herself as she headed over to see what Liza wanted.

****

Thomas didn't ride his mare, as he knew that he could run the distance in the same amount of time it took to saddle her. He sped through the southern gate and headed for the field being cleared, about half of a mile from the gate. He found his uncle with Wahta and Mulhern; after having attached one end of a chain to a pair of harnessed work horses, they worked to secure the other end around a tree stump. "Uncle Liam," Thomas called out after catching his breath, "My ma says to get home quick. Aunt Rebecca is in labor." Mulhern wordlessly hastened to unhitch a Shire horse for Liam, who mounted quickly and urged the animal into an immediate gallop. As he approached the cabin, his mind in turmoil, he heard Rebecca's screams. Liam leapt from the startled horse, who galloped away toward the stable.

Bursting through the cabin door, he saw that Rebecca was attended by Liza, Susan Townsend, and Margaret Jameson. Seeing Liam, she tried to muster a smile, but another spasm tore through her and she screamed again. Liza took Liam's hand and led him outside. "She's in a bad way, brother. If the baby is born alive, it will need a lot of care, but we'll do the best we can. For now, bring us another pail of water, and then please stay outside. I see Wahta and the sergeant coming along, they will keep you company."

The stillborn baby girl arrived three hours later, followed by an unceasing torrent of blood that could not be staunched. Rebecca looked up weakly, her face pale and sweat-covered, and whispered, "Liam." Margaret waited until Liza had removed the child's body from the room, and then went to prepare Liam before bringing him in the cabin. Sitting next to him, she took his hand and said, "The baby was stillborn."

Liam gasped. Holding his head with both of his hands, he asked, "Rebecca?"

"We can't stop the bleeding," Margaret replied, her tears now starting. "She is leaving us, Liam."

Liam stood, sobs racking his body. Wahta held him, his own eyes full of tears, until Liam could compose himself. Liam steeled himself, and entered the cabin.

At Rebecca's side Liam knelt on the floor, his hand caressing her face. She opened her eyes, smiled, and in a weak voice said, "Kiss me one more time." Liam placed his lips on hers, felt her quiver slightly, and she was gone.

****

There was no shortage of tears as they prepared Rebecca's body for burial. Liza, Deborah, Susan Crane, and Rebecca's mother, Margaret washed the body clean dressing her in her best dress. They wrapped the lifeless child in a linen shroud, and placed her in Rebecca's arms. Hilda Crane and Hannah Lapley took charge of the after funeral meal, organizing the many offers of help. Thomas, the oldest of the children kept his younger siblings, and cousins out of the way as best he could.

Liam felt devastated. Wahta and Mulhern stayed by his side, their own grief held in check while they tried to console him, though neither of them spoke much. What was there that they could say? Jack and Caleb came to the bluff overlooking the river where their father sat with his friends. He took one in each arm and started rocking back and forth, trying to find the words, trying to explain what happened without understanding why it happened.

Following the funeral the next day, Rebecca, and her daughter were buried between the graves of her father, and Liam's parents. Daniel presided over the graveside service; there was no thought at all to include Reverend Grantham. Most of the villagers attended the burial, as Rebecca was much loved by the older settlers as well as the new ones. However, a notable number of villagers were conspicuous by their absence at both events. These were the families who most adhered to the Will of

God as pronounced by the good Reverend. A notable exception was a contrite, remorseful Bartholomew Morgan.

When Daniel finished his prayer, the crowd slowly dispersed, many of the villagers coming up to Liam offering words of condolence, most knowing that the fine quality of their words fell on deaf ears. Morgan approached Liam extending his hand, "I would not blame you if you refused," he said with a slight tremor in his voice, "I am so sorry, Mr. Mallory. I am so, so sorry."

Liam grasped Morgan's hand with both of his, and struggling with his emotions replied, "I think, Mr. Morgan that you are under the sway of an evil man, but I hold you blameless."

Tears coursed down Morgan's face, "Thank you Mr. Mallory. It is you who needs comforting, yet you comfort me. If there is ever anything I can do for you, or your boys do not hesitate to ask."

Finally, Liam stood alone by the grave, only Wahta nearby. Liam spun around at the sound of someone approaching. With undisguised hatred in his voice, Liam warned Grantham, "That is far enough preacher, I have no need of your comfort or words. Be gone from my sight."

Grantham stopped, and held his hand out in an apparently peaceful gesture. "Liam, I only..."

"I said, none of your words. Be gone before I help you meet your god," Liam snarled as he pulled his knife from the sheath on his belt. Wahta grabbed Liam and pulled him back. Careful not to impale himself, he shook Liam's wrist until the knife fell to the ground.

Once he was out of danger, Reverend Grantham snarled his reply. "This is not over, Mallory!" He strode away, to the waiting Micah.

****

Micah Townsend, former Major on staff with Governor Amherst, had been a model soldier, and officer. His rise in the ranks was due solely to merit, as he performed his assigned tasks with unfailing success, often beyond expectations. When Amherst was recalled, Major Townsend was devastated; he greatly admired the general, and his style of overhanded leadership. Because he could not bear to return to England, he resigned his commission, and joined his wife Susan with her family in Mallory Town.

Upon meeting Reverend James Grantham, Townsend quickly recognized in him the qualities he admired in Amherst, and sought his patronage.

At the same time, Grantham saw that Townsend's eagerness caused him to be easily manipulated. Micah could be influenced to assist the reverend in his conversion of Mallory Town from godlessness to the religious conduct that would accompany his own economic prosperity. Not that God or religion had any real meaning to Grantham, except as means to an end.

"My dear Micah, I think it time to step up your activities. It won't take much to push Liam into a fit of fury Just be sure you are ready for him."

"I'll be ready for him, make no mistake about that," replied Micah.

"Just be sure he is dead. We are close now to having this village in our palms," said Grantham, "like clay to the potter, ready to be molded to our vision. A village totally beholden to God and the Crown, and a village beholden to me... to us, for the prosperity sure to come, and of which we will take the lion's fair share."

****

For a week, Micah followed Liam, looking for the chance to draw him into a fight, but Liam was either with Wahta, or with Mulhern; most of the time with both of them. It was improbable that a confrontation would happen during either daylight, or when the odds were stacked against him. Changing his tactic, he watched Liam's cabin door while he hid in the nighttime shadows of the barn that sat in the middle of the village square.

That Liam no longer slept more than a couple of hours was obvious. Every day he was increasingly surly. Not sure that he was able to deal with the twins, he had asked Liza and Daniel to care for them until he could. Earlier this night, he argued with Wahta and Mulhern, eventually loudly suggesting that they fuck off, and leave him alone. He lie down to try to sleep. Because the buffalo dreams had returned, once again sleep did not last long. Liam rose from his pallet heading out to walk the town's perimeter.

Micah heard the argument coming from Liam's cabin. He watched the Mohawk and the Irishman head toward Mulhern's cabin on the other side of the square. This could be the night, he thought; wait a couple hours and see if he takes one of his walks, this time without his companions. Micah raised his collar against the nightly chill, and waited. When he saw Liam emerge from his cabin, Micah quickened his pace as he moved out of the shadows, and caught up to him.

Liam was aware of Micah even before he left the safety of the shadows, he kept his hand on the hilt of his knife as Micah approached. "Mallory," Micah called out, his knife out, ready for the plunge he was about to make, "sorry about your wife dying, must be hard on your bastard children losing their ma like that."

Liam was unlike any foe that Micah had ever faced. His knife hand had just started to move when Liam's hand flashed out with such speed that Micah barely saw the razor sharp knife before it sliced through his throat, cutting through arteries, and windpipe.

Liam jumped back, avoiding the squirting blood, and Micah's falling body. For a brief moment, Liam stared at his trembling knife. When he raised his head to look for a place for the body, he saw Wahta running to him. Together, they carried the corpse to the rear of the tavern, and laid it behind a stack of empty barrels. Now that the threat passed, surging adrenaline gave way to calm assessment of the reality of the situation. Liam told Wahta, "My brother, I cannot ask you to go with me, but I need to leave here tonight."

"I will wake the little Irishman, and meet you by the canoes," Wahta replied. "Talk with your brother."

Daniel awoke to a hand covering his mouth. Peering in the darkness, he saw Liam, and inhaled the unmistakable odor of blood on his brother's hand. He cautiously rose from his bed, being careful not to disturb Deborah, and followed Liam outside. After he glanced at the blood stained tunic and sleeve, Daniel asked, "What is the trouble, Liam?"

"I have killed Micah Townsend. He called my children bastards and spoke poorly of Rebecca, and then he came at me with his knife, so I killed him. The good preacher told me this wasn't over yet. That may well be, but I won't be around for any more of it. I'm afraid I leave you, and the others in a tough spot, and trust you with the well-being of my boys. Tell Liza I am sorry, and that I'll write when I'm far enough away."

Daniel grabbed his brother in a farewell embrace, and said as he pulled back, "If I were you, I'd head to Two Birds to get supplied, and then go west; find that buffalo herd you keep dreaming about. Don't worry about us, or your children, little brother. I pray the Almighty to keep you safe, and that you find peace."

Liam nodded his thanks, and turned to meet Wahta and Mulhern who waited with the canoe. He clambered aboard, and they pushed off, silently gliding into the river's current. The nearly full moon provided enough light for them to navigate, their three paddles barely making a ripple.

Fort Pitt

 Within a few hours, they were beaching the canoe outside of Fort Pitt, home of their friend, Jimmy Two Birds Ouellette, owner of The Two Birds Tavern, and proprietor of the largest trading post on the frontier. Wahta and Mulhern headed to Two Birds' warehouse to begin loading up supplies after picking the locked door, while Liam went to the tavern to wake Two Birds. Two Birds remained silent as Liam described the recent events while they walked to the warehouse, breaking his silence to groan when Liam mentioned Rebecca's death.

They approached his warehouse to unlock the padlocked door, but found it unlocked, the door wide open. Two Birds turned to Liam. "I take it that my favorite Irishman is traveling with you?"

Mulhern emerged with a sack of flour. "Tis amazing what skills come back to you after all these years."

The three travelers loaded the canoe as full as possible, and made ready to depart. Two Birds pulled Liam aside. "It appears that things may heat up between the British and the colonists. From what I've heard from you and others, the good Reverend Grantham is in deep with the British. If I send word to Daniel, do you think he would pass it on further east? I dare not trust the army post, and Colonel Washington will want to hear about doings here at Fort Pitt. The army has been taking in much more ammo and ordnance than what they need for this garrison. My guess is that it is for Fort Detroit – or even worse, that ammo could be for the Delaware, Mingo and Shawnee."

Liam nodded, and replied,"I'm sure Daniel will find someone to deliver the message. The tribes have been peaceful, but that's sure to change as more settlers push west. The Shawnee in particular won't take kindly to settlements along the Ohio. Tell Daniel that he can send messages for me to Fort Detroit, and Fort Michilimackinac. I reckon I'll still be in that area for a few years before crossing the Mississippi." Liam shook Two Birds' hand, and boarded the canoe. The trio headed out toward the Ohio River. Their plan would see them follow the Ohio then head inland north from the mouth of the Licking River, and through Shawnee territory. Their immediate destination was Fort Detroit, then the La Grand Traverse area in the Michigan Territory. Mulhern had made it known that he wanted to visit, and possibly settle among the huge white pine trees that stretched for miles in that seemingly endless forest. After that, nothing was set –though Liam still dreamt of the buffalo, and the thought of finding the herd in his dreams was a strong factor in his ability to cope with his tormented mind.

Mallory Town

Feeding the village uproar over the apparent murder of Micah Townsend, Reverend Grantham announced that Micah's body would be displayed for a full day outside of the church, despite the protests of Susan and her family – he would give the eulogy at noon the following day. Daniel, Henry, and Timothy tried in vain to have the body enclosed in the casket, but Grantham declined to even see them, only sending word for them to be sure to attend the funeral.

The Mallory clan entered the church. It seemed that nearly everyone from the village was there; the Mallory family sat in the last row of pews. The church was abuzz with the whispers of the villagers. Some turned to pointedly glare at them. Reverend Grantham entered a few moments later, stopping first at the casket kneeling before it, his hands clasped in a prayerful manner. Almost as one, the crowd bowed their heads. Their collective 'Amen' resounded through the room as Grantham rose. He ascended the short staircase leading to the raised pulpit, and gazed down on his flock. As he opened his Bible, Reverend Grantham spoke, his voice low.

"My children, it is always a sad occasion when a fellow soldier in Christ's Army is taken from us. How much more so when the taking is in such a brutal, savage manner?"

Grantham raised his voice while he continued to speak, its volume steadily increasing. "Micah Townsend was a soldier of Christ, and before that he was a loyal, and brave soldier for our earthly master, King George III.

"I traveled here under the mandate of God, and of King, to turn this frontier into a bastion for Christ, and England. I came to lead your efforts to rid this village of sin, and to purge it of its sinful leadership. Micah Townsend shared my love of God, and King, and he worked tirelessly to further the goals of eliminating sin in our village – but now, this kind, and loyal man will not see the results of his work for God."

His voice now raised to a furious pitch, Grantham continued to inflame his audience. "No, he was cruelly, and shamefully slain by the chief of sinners, Liam Mallory!"

At this, he slammed his fist down on the pulpit. The crowd began screaming for justice. Daniel stood, and called loudly for quiet, but the noise of the congregation turned mob was overwhelming. Thomas, who stood just inside the door, raised his father's pistol, and fired it into the air. The boisterous crowd turned, as their voices quickly became quiet Daniel walked up the aisle toward the podium, "Liam did not murder Micah Townsend," he said, "It was a tragic event to be sure, but Micah taunted Liam by besmirching the memory of Rebecca, drawing a knife as he spoke, attacking Liam. The attack came when my brother was alone, which was highly unusual. Sounds more like Micah was stalking my brother."

"A fine speech," responded Grantham clapping his hands, "one worthy of a loving brother, but if he is innocent, why did he run? If he is innocent, he would have found justice here. If he is innocent."

"Justice here," countered Daniel, "after you've driven your flock of sheep into a pack of ravening wolves? Your mandate, as you call it, is nothing more than maneuvering for power, no matter how you coat it with scripture or loyalist fervor." With that, Daniel turned and headed to the door. His family, and friends followed him, but the majority of the villagers remained in the church.

Stirred to bloodthirst, they angrily shouted. "Murderer!" "Coward!" "You'll burn in hell!" Meanwhile, Reverend James Grantham smiled and, closing his Bible, headed down the stairs.

Pausing at the casket, he said, "Rest in peace, my dear Micah. You did well, my son."

Chapter 2 1768/1769 - Travels and Turmoil

March 1768

Winter camp along the Licking River

At first, the three travelers had no thought of a winter camp, but two near-blizzards in late November convinced Mulhern of the need to lay low until spring. They made camp near the confluence of the Licking and the Ohio rivers. Now early spring, they prepared to begin their journey overland through Shawnee territory, on their way to the Lake Michigan region of the Ojibway.

Glyn Mulhern, fifty-eight years behind him as best as he could recollect, felt these years as he struggled to help load the canoe for the short trip across the Ohio. He rolled his shoulders after setting down his pack, his fingers and the old wound in his upper back each stiff with the cold.

"I'm telling you, lads," he spoke to Liam and Wahta as he sat on a boulder that had recently emerged with the melting snow, "this is the last journey for me. I pray the good Lord, and all the saints to keep me joints working."

Wahta chuckled as he approached Mulhern, and replied, "Come, little Irishman, mama bear will help you into the canoe."

Mulhern smiled, and playfully slapped his hand away. "Oh, keep away from me, you freak of nature. How a man can walk about in this weather practically bare chested is beyond me."

Since they had decided to camp over the winter, most of their time was spent hunting and trapping, improving their miniature longhouse, and poring over the scantily detailed maps they got from Two Birds.

Now, Liam heard Mulhern groan as he clambered out of the canoe. As he pulled the canoe up onto the rocky beach on the north bank of the Ohio, Liam felt a familiar sense of guilt momentarily surge within him. These feelings had been an occasional topic of discussion while they waited out the snow now. Although Liam was uncomfortable about having dragged his friends away from civilization's comforts, he eventually had to admit that Mulhern, and especially Wahta, never would have let him leave without them. That knowledge alone was such a comfort that Liam's dreams, once they left Mallory Town, became less tormented.

Over the years, the three of them had become as close as brothers. Wahta and Liam from Liam's adoption as a Mohawk, and now the same closeness had developed with the affable Irishman. Yet, despite Liam knowing that he journeyed to his destiny, and that his path was west of the

Mississippi, the three now took a several hundred mile detour north, so that Mulhern could see some big trees. They had a vague idea where the Shawnee built villages, but were bound to follow the trail the tribes used as they traveled to and from their hunting ground south of the Ohio, so the chance of passing through undetected was remote. In addition to the Shawnee, other tribes which might not look kindly on their presence, the Miami, Mingo, and Delaware also frequented this part of the river. The weather favored them; even though the spring sun brought greater warmth, the snow was still deep enough to discourage travel, which, they thought, lessened the chance of meeting a hunting party. However, the winter had been so severe that very little hunting had occurred, and the native hunting parties were forced to start earlier than they would normally.

Mallory Town

June 1768

Thomas and his band of sibling and cousin followers were making their daily patrol around the inside perimeter of the village wall. As usual, the twins, Jack and Caleb, marched side by side while the rest, Meagan, Bowie, and Ethan were in a somewhat single file formation. The only cousin who did not take part in what she termed a 'silly walk', was four year old Abigail. When they reached the main gate, Thomas stopped and glanced down the road, his sudden shock, and amazement evident when he saw a troop of red-coated soldiers heading for the village. They were led by an immaculately attired officer on the most beautiful horse Thomas had ever seen. Shaking himself out his reverie, he corralled the children and marched them back to Liza and Henry. "Pa," he exclaimed as they reached the cabin, "there's a company of British soldiers on the road, headed this way."

"Go and fetch your Uncle Daniel, and tell him to meet me by the main gate," Henry told his son, "and then you hightail it back here and stay with your ma."

Two Birds had arrived in Mallory Town with his news about the munitions stockpile. Although Daniel hadn't been entirely convinced that the British were making preparations for possible hostilities, he sent the message on ahead to Washington anyway. Now, he had second thoughts about British intentions. This was the first time a patrol bothered to stop at their town; that was cause at least a case for curiosity, if not for concern. As he approached the gate, he saw Henry and Timothy waiting for him. Glancing back at the church, he wasn't surprised to see Reverend Grantham standing in the doorway.

The British officer ordered his men to stand easy and then rode in through the gate, his horse high stepping, and a proud tilt to its head, its long mane interlaced with red and gold ribbon. As it came to a halt, the officer dismounted and removed his Grenadier helmet. He held his hand out to Daniel. "Major Charles Whitby of His Majesty, King George III's 44th Regiment of Foot, at your service."

Daniel shook his hand and replied, "I'm Daniel Mallory, and this is Henry Clarke and Timothy Winslow."

Whitby took a step back to raise his hand in a salute. "Your reputations precede you sirs. I've heard some amazing things you and your scouts did during the last war. I imagine that some of those tales are at least partially true. A true honour to meet you, I am sure."

"Why, thank you, Major Whitby, for the sentiment, but we only did what needed to be done, nothing more. Excuse me for any presumption on my part, but why are you here with a patrol troop?"

"Well, we're not really here in the strict sense of the word," replied Whitby, "this is merely a stopping point. Our mission is to visit the various tribes we come across, and deliver the kind wishes of King George III. So to not alarm the good folk of this village, my troops will bivouac outside the wall, and we'll be off at first light tomorrow. However, I will require a place for tonight, and stabling for Rubicon."

"We'd be pleased to have you as our guest," answered Daniel, "so, I better go warn the womenfolk."

Whitby laughed and said, "Oh, one more thing, can you direct me to Reverend James Grantham. I've heard some good things about him and would like to meet him."

"If I'm not mistaken, you can see him in the doorway of the church just over my right shoulder," Henry replied, his face showing his disgust at the mention of Grantham.

"Thank you," said Whitby, "I will see you for dinner then." He strode away leading Rubicon toward the church. He tied the reins to a hitching post and while stroking the horses nose said to him, 'Well, old Rubicon, there doesn't seem to be any love lost between the Mallory's and the good reverend – just as we were led to believe. They will be formidable foes, but less so without Liam in the picture. Let's go see what kind of mischief we can plan.'

****

"My, that is good," said Major Whitby as he drained the last of the ale in his mug, "this must be the work of Mr. Winslow, if I'm not mistaken. I wonder, would it be possible to procure a keg, it would be a boon to have after being in the saddle all day?"

Timothy raised his mug in salute and replied, "Normally I would be happy to oblige, but am almost out of the last batch. The next one will not be ready for another week or so, but I can send you a keg with my compliments with the next delivery I make to Two Birds at Fort Pitt."

"That is most generous of you," answered Whitby, "I look forward to it."

The meal with Major Whitby had gone as well as could be expected, though there was an undercurrent of tension as he continually espoused the duty and benefits of remaining loyal to the Crown. It seemed to Daniel that Whitby was probing for evidence of their level of adherence to the loyalist cause, and while there was plenty of good natured banter about life on the frontier, Daniel and especially Henry held back from revealing too much to the inquisitive Major.

Long after Whitby had retired to the quarters made available to him, Henry was still fuming about the attitude of the British, "If half of what I hear from folks coming from the east is true, we're going to be in for a struggle. Mark my words, it will be a bloody one." Daniel nodded in agreement, and not for the last time wondered if they were strong enough to resist.

As Major Whitby led his troops southeast, the sun just peaking over the tops of the trees on the east bank of the Kiskiminetas River, Daniel turned to Henry and asked, "Do you believe his story about a mission to the tribes? To me, his visit has more to it than just that. This was a show of power, or I'm sorely mistaken."

Henry finished lighting his pipe. "Oh, I think they're wanting to make sure the tribes remain loyal, but I also think there's something afoot between that Major and the preacher. They were together for quite a long time, and I don't rightly believe they were quoting scripture verses to each other."

"Aye, I reckon you have it," said Daniel, "we better keep a closer eye on Grantham, and we also need to pay a visit to our Oneida friends to hear what they have to say about Major Whitby."

****

Major Whitby sat astride Rubicon atop a small knoll and watched his troops cross the Kiskiminetas at the ford south of Mallory Town. The sunlight reflecting off the ripples in the river lulled him into thinking about the meeting he had with Reverend Grantham. A most satisfactory meeting it was, due in the main to the fact that they shared similar character qualities.

Charles Henry Whitby's ambition, and his desire for adventure, led him to volunteer for a post in the North American colonies. He saw his first battle action at the siege, and ultimate victory, at Fort Louisburg in Nova Scotia. His horsemanship and leadership abilities were quickly recognized;

he was rewarded with this post as commander of the regiment, and sent to Fort Pitt as part of the garrison there.

However, his strongest personal quality was his unquestioning loyalty to the Crown. It was a family quality, handed down through the generations, back to a distant cousin of Henry VIII. When he met Reverend Grantham, he recognized a like-minded soul, and knew at once that he could use this man. He didn't necessarily care for or need the God element – but he knew that Grantham's use of God and religion was an effective tool in maintaining order and keeping the flock loyal. Whitby couldn't predict if at some point – soon or in the future – hostilities would erupt between the colonies and the Crown, but he wanted to be prepared.

The sound of a braying mule snapped him out of his reverie. When it balked at crossing the river, the animal was pulled from the front by two infantrymen and pushed from behind by two more – the waggoneer cracking his whip just missing the two who were pushing. But, the mule would not budge. Whitby trotted down, pulling his saber out of its sheath. "Get that mule and wagon moving! We mustn't keep the natives waiting for the trinkets King George has generously provided," he said as he poked the mule in the arse with the point of his sword. The startled beast lunged forward – pitching the two infantrymen who were pulling on the reins into the water – and hurriedly scampered to the other side.

Oneida camp along The Allegheny

The troop marched all day under a cloudless sky with nary a breeze to offset the heat of the sun. It was getting on toward late afternoon when the Seneca scouts hired by Whitby reported back to him that there was a fairly large encampment of Oneida and some Mingo just a few more miles down the track that paralleled the river. As they drew nearer, the sergeant in charge of the scouts approached Major Whitby and saluted. "Sir, seems we've had a bit of luck. The Mingo War Chief Logan is in the camp."

Whitby returned the salute and replied, "Well, that is indeed fortunate. I thought we'd have to travel much further than this before we found the one man I need to talk to. Sergeant, have your scouts keep an eye on the camp, and report back any movement in or out of it. We'll set up our camp here. I will visit our erstwhile allies come the morning."

Soyechtowa, the son of a Cayuga chief and his Oneida wife was known to the whites as Logan. He and a band of followers from some of the Iroquois Nation tribes had moved to the Ohio Country and took the name of Mingo. His importance to the British and to the colonists was driven by his desire for peace. Peace that would only come, he was convinced, by adapting to the white man's ways. It was known by the British in Fort Pitt that Logan was in the area; hence the patrol led by Major Whitby. Leaving most of the troop in camp, Whitby brought only the standard bearer and an interpreter when he entered the Oneida-Mingo hunting camp soon after dawn.

Chalahgawtha

Shawnee Village on the Scioto River

Liam and Mulhern walked single file behind Wahta, following a hunting trail flanked by a creek swollen with snow melt on one side, and by a thickly wooded ridge on the other. The trail showed recent use, evidenced by the snow packed down from the passage of many feet, and the frequent patches of mud made by the warming sun. An occasional gust of wind brought the smell of wood smoke ahead, and Wahta now heard voices. He stopped and held his hand up to signal the others. They resumed their walk cautiously, until they came to a clearing where the ridge sloped down to meet the creek. The Shawnee hunter tending the fire saw them, and yelled for his companions. Soon, seven Shawnee armed with knives and hunting bows approached the travelers.

Liam stepped forward with his hands raised, palms facing out, and in passable Shawnee spoke to the group of hunters. "I am Liam Mallory, Otetiani to the Mohawk and Snake Slayer to others. My companions and I are searching for the village of Pucksinwah. We mean you no harm."

The Shawnee lowered their weapons, but kept their arrows nocked. The apparent leader approached Liam and said, "We have heard of you, Snake Slayer, but it is we who should be claiming to mean no harm. You are outnumbered; why should we be wary of you?"

Liam allowed a slight smile before he replied. "You say you know of me. If this is so, then you should also know my companions: Wahta, my Mohawk brother, and Sergeant Glyn Mulhern. Together we have fought many battles, defeated many foes. Do you want to die today, or live to tell your children and grandchildren that you met such men?"

"It is as you say, Snake Slayer," answered the Shawnee named Taregan, a smile spreading across his face, "indeed, my sons are here with me now, so they will know I did not falsely brag about this meeting." At this, the other Shawnee relaxed. Soon, the three were seated around the fire enjoying fresh venison and that was an improvement over the dried version they had been eating.

Taregan licked the meat juices off of his fingers, pointed to Liam, and asked, "Why is it you seek Pucksinwah?"

Liam reached into the shoulder pouch he carried and pulled out a very distinctive Shawnee-made necklace. "I wish to give this to him," he said as he handed it to Taregan.

Taregan's eyes widened as he held the necklace, recognizing what it was. As he handed it to Liam, he said, "I will not speak of the dead."

****

Rather than spend the night with the traditional enemies of the Mohawk, Wahta convinced Liam and Mulhern to put a few miles between them and the hunters. Taregan had told Liam where he could find Pucksinwah; they were in luck, as the chieftain was nearby in the village of the principal chief, Catahecassa. The chiefs were gathered together to talk about the white man's incursion into Shawnee lands. The village, Chalahgawtha, was situated on the Scioto River near Paint Creek, the creek they had been following. The next morning, as the sun broke the horizon, Liam, Wahta, and Mulhern stood on the wooded hillside looking down at the village just now coming to life with the dawn.

A Shawnee woman dropped the water skin she had just filled and ran back to the village, loudly warning of strangers coming down the hill. The village soon erupted into a flurry of activity, as warriors gathered their weapons while dogs yelped their displeasure at the intrusion. One warrior stood out from the rest; he waited at the bottom of the hill, the rest of the Shawnee fighters arrayed behind him. Liam hailed the leader. "Greetings, Pucksinwah, esteemed war chief of the Shawnee. We come in peace, and wish to speak with you." Before Pucksinwah could answer, the group of warriors behind him made way for three elder chiefs, Hokoleskwa, Shemeneto and the principal chief of all the Shawnee, Catahecassa.

Oneida camp along The Allegheny

The Mingo war chief was for the most part a peaceful man who longed for his people to survive the influx of white settlers. To him, the only way to do this was to adopt the white man's ways, to forego the nomadic hunting life and adapt to a more sedentary way of life. That the British had come to see him and offer their help against the colonists spoke volumes to Logan, but he could not be swayed by the arguments put forth by Major Whitby – a situation that Whitby had not foreseen. Not that Logan's rejection bothered him all that much; after all, there were plenty of other war chiefs who would be more than happy to take up the hatchet on behalf of the British – especially with the promise of new and better weapons, weapons that even now were being delivered to Fort Pitt from the British Governor in Canada.

Whitby took one last look at the encampment and said to his standard bearer, "Logan may have his peace for now, but I doubt he will have it for long. There's war in the air, can you smell it, corporal?"

Fort Detroit and beyond

As Pucksinwah looked at the necklace, sadness filled him, but he had known that Huritt was bound for a violent death ever since he followed Chogan on the path urged by the French. Pucksinwah had tried to dissuade his sister's son from going on the raid that led to Chogan's death and the eventual revenge sought by the three men sitting across the fire from him. "While my heart is heavy, I am glad that you came to tell me of his death," he said placing the necklace back in the pouch. "You need not fear any retaliation. The matter is ended."

Liam nodded. "That is good to know. We will be traveling through Shawnee land on our way to the big dunes on Lake Michigan. Now, we will sleep with both eyes closed during our journey."

Pucksinwah and the other chiefs burst out in hearty laughter. Catahecassa, still grinning, said, "You will be in no danger from Shawnee, but who is to say how the Ottawa, Ojibway, and the others will react to your presence."

Mulhern, after Liam translated what was said, responded, "They bloody well better get used to it, I plan on living out my days on that lovely shore."

They stayed in the Shawnee camp for two weeks, during which time Liam talked with the chiefs about the possible future of those people already prospering in this land of plenty, along the banks of the Scioto and Ohio rivers. Already there were more and more white explorers and trappers on the Ohio. Their defeat saw many French withdraw to St. Louis on the Mississippi River. Still, many sought out the fabled cane lands of Cantuckee, regardless of the danger from Shawnee, Miami, and others who felt the pressure of white settlements newly established south of the Ohio.

Wahta was something of a novelty to the Shawnee, particularly the children who had never seen one of their people's traditional enemies. Most of the warriors accepted him because of his reputation; though some resented him being in their camp, no one dared speak that resentment aloud. He accompanied a hunting party, but held some of his prowess in check so to avoid any jealousy in a situation that could erupt if he was not careful. When the hunters returned to camp, all he had to show was one turkey, while the others brought in four deer and a small bear.

Mulhern was content to rest while he regained his strength for the next part of the journey. His many old wounds bothered him more than ever before, a sure sign that he was getting too old for this type of life. He did have some impact, however, on one Shawnee; the seven year old son of Pucksinwah, Chiksika, who learned many colorful Irish phrases from the feisty old soldier.

As Liam and the others were preparing to leave, Pucksinwah came to them with a welcome surprise – four horses trailed behind him. "These should help speed you on your travels," he said, handing the reins to Wahta. "I ask for no payment or trade for them. After all, I came into possession of them by raiding a white settlement."

His comment earned a big chuckle from Liam. "We thank the chief for his generosity. These will indeed be a great help, especially for Mulhern, though now I suppose he'll complain about how sore his arse is."

Mulhern grinned and said, "Aye that I will. Ahh, don't look so surprised that I understood what you just said. What do you think I've been doing the last couple of weeks? That young son of Pucksinwah is a good teacher, so my Shawnee is much better now."

Wahta laughed and replied, "We know that Chiksika is a good student as well. We have heard him speak some of your language." At that, the three mounted up with Wahta leading the pack horse and rode off. Chiksika stood at the end of the village; as Mulhern came level with him, Chiksika said, "You take care, you fecking bogtrotter."

****

They made as good a time as one could expect given that early March meant the trail was a muddy track, and the creeks and rivers ran high with snowmelt. After leaving Chalahgawtha, their first encounter was a band of Ottawa just a few miles south of Fort Detroit. The Ottawa were on their way to the fort to receive promised gifts from the British. The three travelers joined them, sensing there was no hostile intent given that the Ottawa were accompanied by their women and children. "Now, isn't this a sight?" queried Mulhern. "Last I remember of this place we were fighting to keep the Ottawa out of the fort."

Liam, lost in his own thoughts, grunted in reply. Wahta looked at the Ottawa and replied, "I think I may have fought with one or two of them myself."

"Will we be staying long? I know we've only been away from the Shawnee town for a few days, but my arse is killing me," asked a grinning Mulhern, "and I could use a couple days to recover."

****

Major Gladwin was busy reviewing the paperwork involved with the gifts for the visiting Ottawa when he was interrupted by his aide. "Excuse me, Sir, but there are three men claiming to be friends of yours waiting outside. Two white men and an Indian, I think he's a Mohawk."

"Well, see them in, Corporal," said Gladwin, chortling. "And, yes, he is Mohawk, and trust me, you do not want to face him in battle."

"This is a most unexpected and most welcome surprise," exclaimed Gladwin as he rose from his desk and greeted the three friends, "what brings you out to the last bastion of civilization?"

Liam took a moment to form his reply, "Well, Major, it's partly running away from tragedy and sorrow, and partly so the good Sergeant can settle up by the big dunes in Ojibway country."

"The good Sergeant should have no trouble with the Ojibway," replied Gladwin, "they've been peaceful ever since Pontiac's defeat. You may even run into a former colleague of mine. Captain Justice, who was the former commander of Fort Michilimackinac, was captured when the fort was overrun. As most of the prisoners were killed, he was presumed dead. Word has come to me, however, that he survived, and has been adopted into the tribe. As to the other reason for your journey, I received a letter a couple weeks ago from a Reverend Grantham alleging a very serious crime was committed by a Liam Mallory, and that I should arrest him should he venture here."

Liam reached to draw his knife when Gladwin stretched his hands out and said, "There's no need for that, Liam. I don't know this Grantham character, but I do know you, and arresting you is not something I care to do. The circumstances must have been extreme for you to act in such a manner. Cold blooded murder, as Grantham calls it, is not in your nature."

Liam returned the knife to the sheath on his belt, his shoulders sagging as he sighed in relief and then recounted the events leading to Grantham's request for his arrest. His voice cracked when he spoke of Rebecca. Major Gladwin took Liam by the shoulders, his voice compassionate as he said gently, "I am so sorry. You are welcome to stay as long as you like." He then called out to his aide, "Corporal, see that their gear is stowed in the emptiest barracks we have, and tell the cook that we have three guests for dinner tonight."

"One more thing," he continued as he handed the letter from Reverend Grantham to him, "please use it to start a fire, or perhaps to wipe your arse on your next visit to the latrine."

****

The travelers spent the winter at Fort Detroit, repairing gear and occasionally joining an Ottawa hunting party bringing in venison. The rains of March and April finally subsided, and the springtime weather brought a longing to be moving again. Major Gladwin supplied them with flour, sugar, tea, and a large sack of oats. The Ottawa women took the meat, cut it into thin slices, dried it over a fire until brittle, pounded it into small pieces and mixed it with fat and pounded berries. This would keep for quite a while and provided the travelers with a meal that could be eaten anywhere.

By the time Liam, Wahta, and Mulhern walked their mounts through the main gate of Fort Detroit, the trail they would follow had dried, and the countryside abounded in new growth.

Mulhern regained his strength during the visit and was looking forward to being out on the trail again. Not yet astride his horse, he reached into his saddle bag to retrieve a flask, and handed it to Major Gladwin. "It's only fitting Major, me lad, that we have a nip before we depart. After all, this good Irish whiskey came from your private store."

Gladwin took the flask and raised it, saying, "To your good fortune, Sergeant Mulhern." He took a sip and handed it back.

Mulhern responded by standing at attention and saluting the Major. "Aye, but you're a credit to the army, sir. I'm glad I had the chance to serve with you, if only for a short time."

Liam and Wahta were already mounted and watched the two old soldiers say farewell. Finally Wahta exclaimed, "Is the wee Irishman going to mount his horse, or does he need Wahta's help?" Mulhern winked at Major Gladwin, replaced the flask in the saddle bag and with the agility of a younger man leapt upon the horse. With a chuckle, he said, "Does it look like I need your help?"

Wahta came alongside, reached over and clapped Mulhern on his shoulder, "Snake Slayer, I think the wee Irishman is ready."

Grand Traverse Bay

Late Spring 1769

The countryside around Detroit was mostly woodland, dotted here and there with small lakes. As it was also very flat, they made good time reaching the rolling hills north of the fort. They camped alongside a small creek, and established the pattern for their journey north. Mulhern organized the site, while Liam and Wahta used the last of the daylight to hunt. When they returned, Mulhern had a fire going and a spit ready for whatever game they brought in. Soon the smell of roasting meat and the sound of juices hissing in the fire mingled with the rumblings of empty bellies.

From the information they received at Fort Detroit, they turned northwest when they reached a large bay that was part of a huge lake named by the French, Lac des Hurons for the number Huron who lived along its shore. They wanted to avoid contact with them – not that they thought the Huron would cause them trouble, but because Wahta was uneasy about encountering any of the Mohawk's historical enemy.

The woodlands gradually changed over the next few days from the deciduous oak, maple, and birch to stands of immense white pine. The stream they were camped alongside teemed with trout. Mulhern returned to the camp from what he termed the perfect spot for fishing with five trout. He set them down next to Wahta. "Now, it would be a fine thing for you two to check your muskets," he said, "we're about to be visited, and I dunno if it's merely a social call or if we're in a spot of trouble."

Terrance Justice, former Captain and commander of the British garrison at Fort Michilimackinac, stepped out from the group of Ojibway hunters who surrounded the camp of three men and four horses. As he approached, he couldn't help but laugh at the sight. It was apparent by their demeanor that these three would not be easy victims, no matter that the Ojibway outnumbered them four to one. He turned to the leader of the hunters, speaking in the Ojibway dialect of the Algonquin language, and told him to lower their weapons; he knew these men.

"Bugger me sideways if it ain't Liam Mallory and friends," he called as he moved closer, "greetings and welcome."

It took Liam a moment to see that this Ojibway was indeed a white man, but Wahta knew right away. "It is the captain from the fort where the two lakes meet."

"Captain Justice? We heard that you might still be alive," said Liam while extending his hand, "I'm sure there's a tale to tell."

"I am, indeed, and yes, there is," chuckled Justice, "though now is not the time. I see you are already settled for the night. Our hunting camp is about two miles north of here, right along the lake shore. You can't miss it, if you would care to join us tomorrow. We will swap stories then."

Mulhern replied, "Speaking for me, I welcome the chance to talk with anyone other than my two rather laconic friends."

Wahta looked at Mulhern and asked, "What does the wee Irishman mean by laconic? Is that a word that means beloved, or perhaps wise?"

Liam answered, "No, my brother, it just means we don't talk a whole hell of a lot, and the wee Irishman finds that a hardship."

He then turned to Justice and said with a big smile, "We gladly accept. It will be nice to eat something not cooked by the good sergeant here."

****

The next morning, they entered the Ojibway camp, a temporary one used in the spring for hunting and for the good fishing in this inland lake. Numerous drying racks sat about the campfires for the bass, walleye, and perch that were found there in abundance. It was also a prime spot for geese, and many of the women busily plucked the downy feathers that would be used, among other things, to staunch wounds. The sounds of yelping dogs and the cries of children – neither sure of the strangers – brought Captain Justice out of his wigwam. Though he was not the leader of this band, it was decided that he would be the one to greet the visitors.

"Welcome to our camp," he said pointing to a grassy meadow, "you can hobble your mounts over there; plenty of grazing available, and a nice little spring for them to be watered from."

They left the horses, now hobbled and grazing contentedly, and walked back to the center of the camp. Seemingly numberless large pines towered over them. "Ah, this is certainly a lovely place," Mulhern said quietly, intent on not disturbing the songbirds as they serenaded the sun rising over the lake.

They rejoined the camp, and were handed bowls of a hearty fish stew for their first meal. They sat around a small fire while they ate. "I imagine you are more than a little curious as to my situation," Justice said between mouthfuls. "When Fort Michilimackinac was overrun, I was taken captive with a few others. The first few days were sheer hell. As we traveled to the village of our captors, we were made to run a gauntlet whenever we came upon another village. I was the only one who survived, which surprised and impressed the chief of the village. After I recovered from the wounds made by clubs, willow branches, fists, and whatever else they hit me with, the chief adopted me.

"I am now called Mishka; that means turtle in English. I guess I resembled one during the last gauntlet as I wound up crawling at the end with my head sort of tucked in to protect it from any more blows. Anyway, I am now a warrior in the Salteaux band of the Ojibway. Quite a change from the prim and proper Englishman I used to be, but to be honest, I don't miss my old life – though it is a little troubling that it is known down in Detroit that I am still alive. I'm sure the army would like to cashier me for losing their fort so easily."

"As to that," responded Liam, "Major Gladwin told me he believed the rumors of your survival but he was not going to alert his superiors of that. In fact, he is reporting that the rumors are false, so you are safe to enjoy your new life."

Mishka tipped his bowl to drink the last of his stew. He smiled. "I always liked that Major. Now, pray tell, what are you doing back in this part of world? I thought you would be back home raising hell with the tribes around Fort Pitt, or regaling your children with tales of your many deeds."

Liam's face went from a grin to a grimace of pain at the mention of his children. He recovered quickly, and relayed the reasons for their journey west. Mishka put a hand on Liam's shoulder and responded, "Of all the buggered and bloody fools in this world, it is my experience that religious leaders can be the worst kind. Believe what I believe or be damned; what a load of shite. I am sorry for bringing it up, but I had to know. My chief needs to know what your intentions are; he's a peaceable sort, but not too keen on whites settling down here."

"Not to worry, me lad," replied Mulhern, "my companions are merely humoring an old man and his wish to die in a place of his own choosing. I will be the only settler; Liam and Wahta, at some point, will be moving on. When we were here last, I fell in love with the land near the Grand Traverse. It is my plan to live close to those big dunes. I hope this will not be a source of contention – I've grown weary of fighting."

Mishka stood up, "I will speak to the chief of this. He was with Pontiac during the fighting at Fort Detroit, and witnessed firsthand your fighting abilities. He respects and admires those qualities in a man, regardless who or what they are. You are free to wander the camp, but do not try to leave yet. My guess is he will want to talk it over with the elders before deciding what to do. I wouldn't worry though; like I said, he's a peaceable man at heart."

In the end, and even though the chief and the elders agreed that Mulhern posed no threat, it was the children in the camp who swayed their decision. They followed Wahta around whenever they could, awed by his size and reveling in the attention he paid them. He played ball with them, swam in the lake with them, and told them stories about life in a Mohawk village. To Liam's credit, and to the surprise of Wahta and Mulhern, he too spent time with the children, even fashioning a few crude toys, such as whistles and animals carved out of wood. So it was – three weeks later, when the Ojibway broke camp to return to their main village in the north, the three travelers went with them.

Six days later, Liam, Wahta, Mulhern, and Mishka left the Ojibway group. The Ojibway village was a little further north situated on a peninsula that separated Grand Traverse Bay from Lake Michigan, while the four travelers were headed west to the big dunes. Mishka had the blessing of his chief to help with the building of Mulhern's cabin. That evening, they were seated around a campfire on the bluff overlooking the lake. Having turned around occasionally to glance back at the towering pine trees, Mulhern gazed across the lake, soaking in the last of the day's sunlight. "Aye, this is a good place to stay and rest me weary bones."

Chapter 3 1770 – Conspiracy

Mallory Town – late winter

Hearing the screams of children, Liza stepped out of the cabin. For what seemed to be a daily event, her nephews Caleb and Bowie - who had become inseparable companions over the last couple of years - found the trouble they sought(adventures, they called them). Today's 'adventure' involved chasing their cousins around the yard with sticks they pretended were muskets, while screaming, "You'll not get away, we will track you."

Rebecca's death and Liam's departure made the last two years especially challenging for both Liza and Henry, and Deborah and Daniel. Although the twins, now seven years old, at first overwhelmed by their mother's death, gradually emerged from their grief, and surrendered at last to the warmth and love of their extended family. They missed Liam, too, of course, but they were used to him being away for long stretches, and they knew not to expect him to return.

Jack was timid but calculating. Caleb continued to be rambunctious and outgoing, even more so since he found a kindred spirit in Bowie. They weren't mean or vicious in their actions; besides not being in their characters, which would not have been tolerated. Although their primary motive was to have fun, they also took on the protection of their siblings and cousins. Understandably, then, when Thomas and his best friend, Sam Webb, approached them and pointed toward the main gate, the twins immediately stopped chasing six year old Abigail and four year old Ethan, to join Thomas and Sam for their daily patrol around the outside perimeter of the town.

****

Jimmy Two Birds had not visited Mallory Town for a couple of years, due both to his business and to a short illness. Once rotund, he was now much thinner, but not in a haggard way. Indeed, he looked and felt better than he had for years.

Halting his horse at the top of the ridge, he looked down to see the children, and thought with surprise how much they had grown. A huge smile played across his face as he watched Thomas squatting on the ground pointing to an animal track while apparently explaining it to Caleb and Bowie.

Glancing away to Mallory Town, he was stunned by the growth of this once-small trading post. The original walls he'd helped build were gone, having been removed to make room for the many new settlers finding their way west. The new walls, necessary according to Daniel and Henry, were almost at the limit of their expansion possibilities, due to the terrain and to the rivers at the town's north and east edges. Farms stretched as far as he could see on the opposite sides of both rivers. Outside the walls stood a mill and blacksmith shop; the interior contained the new church, general store, and many newly-built living quarters (two more under construction). After one last glance at Thomas and his two recruits, now undertaking their perimeter inspection, he urged his mount down the hill and toward the gate.

****

Liza hugged Two Birds. "This is a most wonderful surprise. It has been too long since you came to call. We heard that you were ill. You look like you've recovered."

"I have," replied Two Birds while taking a few small packages from his knapsack to hand to Liza. "Some small tokens for the children. Are Daniel and Henry about? I bear news they will be interested in."

"They are across the Allegheny, helping the Lapley's clear boulders from a field to build a new barn," she said, "but I expect them back before dusk. Can you stay for supper?"

"Yes, indeed. I may be skinnier now, but that hasn't put a damper on my appetite," he chuckled. "Perhaps I will take a stroll about the town; so much is new. I see that Timothy has expanded his brewery to include a tavern. I think I may visit there first."

Liza laughed, "Oh yes, you must do that, though be prepared for a possible tongue lashing if any of the faithful see you coming out of that den of iniquity."

"So, the good Reverend Grantham continues to mold his followers in his own image. More's the pity. Doesn't that loud-mouthed distorter of the truth realize that ale is one of the more precious gifts the Good Lord bequeathed to mankind?"

Liza's smile faded as she answered, "That man is a curse on this town. I will let the menfolk know you are about when they return."

****

Daniel, Henry, and William Crane sat in Timothy's tavern with Two Birds. Timothy joined them, bringing a cask of ale and five mugs. He had dismissed his staff after bolting the front door, so that they could freely discuss Two Bird's news about the weapons.

"It's not just the weapons. We've heard rumors about them for a while now," Two Birds said. "A couple of nights ago a corporal had a bit too much to drink, and told one of my barmaids about the deals being made with the Indians. He thought that the colonists had better watch their steps."

Henry took a long drink, the cream like foam resting on his upper lip. He wiped his mouth with his sleeve and said, "My God. I was so hoping that we wouldn't go through that again. I still have nightmares of fighting with them."

"I think we all have that problem," Daniel replied. "We need to be prepared in any case, starting with stepping up our patrols, and expanding their range. We also need to get word back east. William? Would you be willing to take a letter for Colonel Washington to him? It's a long journey, perhaps as far as Virginia."

"Gladly," William said as he refilled his mug. "I better have a couple more of these now, might be a while before I'll be swilling Master Timothy's concoction again."

Boston- late winter

The wind blew in from the ocean. The falling snow swirled in miniature cyclones around the legs of those venturing out on this stormy night. Sam Adams pulled his cap down to keep it from flying off in a sudden gust of powdery wind. In a way, Adams thought, this bitterly cold night held one advantage; not many British Regulars were on patrol. The winter had been mild until mid-February, when it seemed the weather gods began to make up for lost time. The region was in the throes of a nor'easter that had already dumped eighteen inches of snow on Boston. Most of the shopkeepers had closed; the streets saw no one other than those seeking the companionship of likeminded men and a pint or two of ale.

The public house Green Dragon Tavern-owned by the Saint Andrews Lodge of Freemasons-was also a gathering place for the nascent Sons of Liberty. The Lodge's Grandmaster, and many of its members, met frequently to discuss ways to counter what they saw as unlawful mandates from the London Parliament.

Starting in 1764, in direct response to the enormous British debt incurred in the French and Indian War, Parliament passed new taxes and tariffs to raise revenue, all to be borne by the colonies. The Sons of Liberty took the view that Parliament had no right to pass legislation that concerned the colonies, unless the colonies were represented in the Parliamentary process. Their petitions, letters, and pamphlets had been somewhat successful. Some of the more egregious laws were revoked-in

1766, their efforts led to the repeal of the Stamp Act of 1765. However, London continued to insist that it had the right to legislate colonial matters without colonial input.

In order to make the point, Great Britain dispatched four regiments of Regulars to Boston to enforce British will. Boston was now under occupation, many of the British troops now quartered by mostly reluctant private citizens. Tensions understandably ran high; any British soldier's seemingly improper behavior was described in a somewhat exaggerated manner, to sway greater public opinion to action against these violations of their liberties as British subjects.

Fort Michilimackinac – early summer

The former commander of the garrison fearing recognition, Liam, Wahta, and Mishka approached the fort cautiously. Mulhern remained at his cabin, in the care of an Ojibway widow. Happy in his new surroundings, he was adamant that he did not want to explore, and was content with his newly-sedentary lifestyle.

As Mishka dismounted he commented, "I believe I will stay here while you two go ahead."

Liam nodded, and he and Wahta continued to the fort. The garrison was somewhat undermanned but busy, while three large wagons (holding crates of muskets, and barrels of lead and powder) were unloaded. After tying their horses to a post, they entered the headquarters and gave their names to the commander's aide. He disappeared into the inner office to announce them to Captain Higgins, who could be heard to bid them enter.

"Liam Mallory," said Higgins, "your reputation precedes you, as does your companion's. What brings you here?"

Liam shook Higgin's hand, "Curiosity, for one thing. Been wondering how the fort fared after the unfortunate events a few years ago. The other reason is to see if there have been any letters for me."

"As a matter of fact, one arrived last month," Higgins replied as he opened a drawer in his desk, retrieved the letter, and handed it to Liam. "Major Gladwin forwarded it from Fort Detroit. I guess I shouldn't have been surprised to see you, but in my experience mail like this is often delivered but rarely picked up, there being too many hardships in this wilderness to guarantee one's survival."

"You have that right, Captain, though there are those among us who have the ability to survive," answered Liam. "I thank you for holding onto my letter despite the odds. We noticed you have a pretty small number of troops for this post, and yet there seem to be enough fighting supplies for three times that number. Forgive me if I'm butting into army doings, but part of that ability to survive is to have a good grasp of what's happening around him."

"No need to apologize, Mr. Mallory," said Higgins, surprised by the sagacity of this backwoods braggart, "but I assure you there is nothing for you to be concerned about. The Quartermaster has obviously made a mistake, and I expect I'll receive a request to send it all back. Now, if that is all, I have other business that I need to attend."

Ushered out by the aide, they were surprised to immediately face an armed squad of troopers – surprised until they were told to mount and get out, under the orders of Captain Higgins.

****

Wahta remained quiet until they left the fort. When they reached the other side of the gate, he turned to Liam. "They have a lot of weapons for such a small group of soldiers, and that Captain Higgins spoke much, but not much truth. I wonder why that is, Snake Slayer."

Liam grunted, "It can't be good. We shall speak of this with Mishka."

They made camp that night among a stand of birch reflecting the moonlight, giving the copse a slightly eerie glow. Mishka and Wahta went about camp chores preparing their dinner, while Liam sat off alone on the other side of the fire. He took the letter from his deerskin pouch. He had thought about reading it earlier in the day, but was afraid of its possible contents.

The pain he had suffered over the years sometimes returned; his buffalo dreams would then return, and haunt his nights to display a frightening fate. Other visions, though, usually woke him, and they soothed him. He steeled himself and began to read.

March 6, 1770

Liam,

I hope you are well and are out of the reach of Grantham's seemingly long arm. He has made it known that he will reward anyone who brings you in; your condition doesn't matter.

The town continues to grow. As we discussed before you left, we have rebuilt the walls to accommodate our new residents. There was quite a bit of dissension as to the need for the walls, as many do not feel there is any danger nowadays. Fools all.

Your children thrive. Jack and Caleb are growing fast, and though they miss you and Rebecca, they are happy enough. Jack has taken a keen interest in learning to read, and spends a great deal of time with Liza for that. He is also learning about the plants Pierre taught Liza to use for medicines. He may turn out like Pierre, wouldn't that be a blessing? Caleb, on the other hand, is more like you, and spends all the time he can on adventures with my Bowie. Rest assured that we will turn that spirit of adventure into something good. Lord knows we need more trained woodsmen.

There are rumors out of Fort Pitt of some unrest among the tribes, and that the army is stockpiling weapons. The question is, are those weapons meant for the army, or will they be used as enticements to the tribes? I fear that London's new laws and tariffs may bring trouble ahead. The residents here are somewhat divided, between those who adhere to obedience to the King and those who do not. We plan to increase our patrols of the area as a precaution, and have sent William Crane to deliver the news from here to Colonel Washington.

Again, please take care. Reverend Grantham has stepped up his preaching on the subject of the importance of following the dictates of God, of which he deems himself God's true and only voice. It should come as no surprise that he is of the group loyal to London.

Daniel

Liam chuckled as he read about his boys, but the rest made him uneasy. He folded the letter, returned it to the pouch, and turned his attention to Mishka. "Have you noticed any soldiers visiting the villages around here?" he asked, "There's quite a cache of weaponry in that fort, too much for that small of a garrison."

Mishka gingerly pulled a piece of the cooked rabbit off the spit and handed it to Liam. "Not that I'm aware of in this vicinity. If there had been, I'd know. My adopted father, Mingan, keeps his eyes and ears open to the doings of the other members of the Three Fires, the Potawatomi and the Ottawa."

"I don't like coincidences; my brother Daniel wrote that Fort Pitt is rumored to have been stockpiling as well. And, before I left Mallory Town, British patrols were nosing around Mingo and Delaware villages. My guess is the tribes are being swayed to side with the Redcoats if things go to hell between London and the colonies."

Mishka, a look of confusion on his face, replied, "I can see how that would be a cause for concern, but that doesn't really hold out here. There are not that many white settlers around, and I don't think the army would be fighting any engagements on this frontier." He paused for a moment, and then with a big grin said, "Perhaps they anticipate strengthening the garrison just in case some enterprising backwoodsman and a huge Mohawk decide to take the fort away from them."

That had both Liam and Wahta laughing. Wahta reached over and pounded Mishka on the back, causing him to lose the grip on his piece of rabbit and send it into the fire. "They need many more guns for that," Wahta said, handing Mishka another piece of rabbit.

****

They broke camp early, and returned to Mulhern before nightfall. The next morning as they were packing up the camp, Liam with a mischievous grin, turned to his three companions and said, "You know? That Higgins has pissed me off; he reminds me of too many officers we had the privilege to serve under. He didn't sound all that convincing about those weapons. He is a poor liar. I do not fancy being lied to, and I figure we're the only ones out here to do something about it."

Mishka looked at Wahta. "He's not kidding, is he?" Wahta laughed, but before he could pound on Mishka again, Mishka moved behind his horse.

****

Mulhern listened to Liam's plan. Pointing his finger at him, he said, "You're daft, lad. Jesus, Mary, and Joseph, not only that, but that Momma Bear is daft as well for agreeing with you. I thought better of Mishka, but it's apparent you've made him daft, too. I only have one question, you daft bastard. When do we leave? Aye, you heard me right. Listen, lads, I figure I have one more adventure left in this old body. I'm going a bit loony, old Nekemos won't let me do anything around here. Besides, this Higgins and his guns could spell trouble between tribes, and I kinda like the place peaceful. But, most importantly, who is gonna keep you three from mucking this up?"

Mallory Town – early autumn

Henry put the musket he was cleaning down when Liza joined him at the table. Liza wanted to continue their earlier conversation since the children were asleep. "You're sure that they are ready for this?" she asked. "They are still boys."

"It's time for them to learn, and we are short of trained trackers and scouts." he answered. "Besides, they'll enjoy it, and Daniel is the best around. Yeah, it is time for Thomas and Samuel Webb to help patrol." They quickly looked up when they heard Thomas, who was supposed to be sleeping, give a whoop of joy from the loft. "Go back to bed, Thomas," pronounced his father. "We'll be leaving at first light."

Daniel divided the patrol into two teams. Henry, Timothy, and Jonas Lapley would head south along the Kiskiminetas River, crossing the ford a few miles down. They intended to scout the area east of the river all the way to the Mingo village where Logan lived. Daniel took James Crane and the two boys, Thomas and Sam, to cross to the north side of the Allegheny and proceed northeast toward the area the Delaware and Seneca used as temporary hunting camps. They planned to avoid any contact, and certainly confrontation. Both teams' primary purpose was to identify anything suspicious occurring in the various camps and villages close to Mallory Town; the other purpose was to train two very excited fourteen-year-old boys.

Liza, Deborah, and Sam's mother, Anne, watched their husbands and sons march away, and then continued their own tasks of the day. As Liza passed by the church, she glanced at the window. She thought she saw Reverend Grantham duck back out of sight. "Nosy as a cat and evil as a snake," she thought to herself. That momentary anger was immediately replaced by happiness as she spied her nephews, Caleb and Bowie, carrying on Thomas' daily patrol without him. "Before you know it, they'll be going out for real. I hope they have it easier than we did, but it sure doesn't look like it will be in the near future."

****

Reverend Grantham's recent sermons mostly extoled King George III, and exhorted his flock to see the King as God's anointed - any disloyalty to the King was thus both treason and heresy. As he sat at his desk, his hands clasped together, he contemplated the parchment before him, which concerned a committee he planned to form. Its agenda was the suppression of disloyalty to British rule. For now, he could do nothing to bring the miscreant rebels to heel — but soon, he thought to himself, he would have the resources to do so. While he waited for their arrival, he would strengthen the hold he had on the diehard Loyalists in the town, and continue his efforts from the pulpit to sway as many of those who were undecided.

A troubling detail remained: the best time to implement his plan. Now, an idea emerged. These extra, extended patrols could be the means to an end. He rose and entered the next room, where he shook the snoring Gerald Brightman, a tall, thin former minister who now worked for Grantham. Brightman had been defrocked by his congregation after his involvement in a brothel knife fight. As well as losing his profession, he lost two fingers on his left hand and the sight of his right eye. Belying the gruesome appearance, Brightman was soft-spoken, unfailingly polite, and a shrewd judge of character and events.

"Gerald, wake up," Grantham said shaking Brightman a little harder, "I have a job for you."

Brightman sat up, his eye patch askew and lying on his forehead. "Ah, my good man, let me throw some water over my face, and you'll have my undivided attention."

"Very well, and for God's sake, put that patch where it belongs," replied Grantham.

Two cups of tea and a loaf of fresh bread later, Brightman mounted to ride to Fort Pitt. "Just for my own satisfaction, repeat back to me the message," ordered Grantham.

"I'm to report to Major Whitby and tell him to meet you tomorrow at the usual place. You have a plan to take Mallory Town and want to discuss it," replied Brightman.

"On your way then," said Grantham as he backed away.

****

The next morning Grantham mounted his favorite horse, and left the fort at a trot. He was confident that his leaving wouldn't arouse suspicion; he rode out at least twice weekly. He followed the semblance of a road until he had long passed the last farm, and then found the game trail that led through the woods and down to the river. Below, he could see Whitby, seated upon a boulder that sat partially in the river. Grantham made his way over, and after dismounting tied his horse to a birch sapling.

"Good morning, Major," hailed Grantham.

"There is nothing as peaceful as sitting next to rushing water," said Whitby. "Now, what is this plan of yours?"

Gerald Brightman had taken a room for the night at Two Bird's tavern. After much flirting with the bar maids and many mugs of ale, he procured the services of a lady of the evening. As a gatherer of information, Two Birds instructed the girls to do what they could to gain confidences, especially of soldiers and strangers. In due course, during some delightful persuasion, Brightman revealed that Whitby was to meet with Grantham the next morning. Jimmy Two Birds, already suspicious of the Major since the arrival of the extra munitions, now felt even more distrust. Having followed Whitby out of the fort, he watched the two men meeting at the river.

Fort Michilimackinac – early autumn

It was the second night of their trek to the fort; the clear, dark sky meant a chilly evening and morning. I'm surprised that this place isn't covered in a deep, snowy blanket, thought Mulhern as he moved his gear closer to the fire. It seemed like every joint in his body had been jarred out of place. Two days in the saddle after months of lying about was taking its toll.

"Is the wee Irishman warm enough?" asked a smiling Wahta.

"Ah, don't be a worrying about me," groused Mulhern, "is that steam rising off the top of your bald head or are your brains evaporating?"

Laughing, Wahta replied, "I have missed you, Mulhern."

"I don't mean to break up this touching reunion, but is everyone clear on their part of the plan?" asked Liam.

"We go in tomorrow night. It would be nice if we could pull this off without having to fight our way out, but I doubt it. I want Mulhern to stay back with the horses, bringing them up to us after we spring our surprise."

"I didn't come along just to nursemaid nags," Mulhern argued.

"Look, Glynnie, we all have heard you moaning and groaning for two days. You just don't have the reflexes to get stuck in a fight," reasoned Liam.

"Lad, I do believe that is the first time you called me by my given name. I hope you're not going soft on us now. I'll hold onto the horses, but if the fight comes to me, I ain't gonna just stand there like a fool. Now be a good lad, and put some more wood on that fire," Mulhern said, wrapping his blanket even tighter around his shoulders.

****

Private Wilkins stood post at the farthest end of the fort. "Nothing down here but storage sheds and a livestock pen, and nothing to look at from here, either," he thought, his mind drifting from the boredom of the duty. His daydream ended when he was startled by the voice of someone outside the small gate. "Hoy there, soldier, be a good soul and kindly open the door for me," said Captain Terrance Justice.

"What's the password, Sir?" asked Wilkins seeing in the torchlight a man in the tattered and worn uniform of a British Captain.

"How would I bloody know? I'm Captain Justice, and I've been on a bit of a jolly holiday for the last six years. Now, open the bloody door like a good boy."

Liam and Wahta remained hidden in the scrub brush dotting the landscape. Behind them, Mulhern stood just inside of the woods, holding the horses ready while he loaded his musket. When

Liam saw Mishka enter the gate, he and Wahta raced forward to join him. Private Wilkins had just enough time to salute when Mishka pulled his war club out from under his coat and rendered the surprised Wilkins unconscious. Grabbing the torch, Liam told Mishka, "Right, tie and gag him and take his place. Wahta, let's go."

They ran across the compound, keeping to any shadows they could. A heavy wood beam secured the storage building's double door. With a grunt, Wahta lifted it out of its brackets and gently laid it down. Once inside, they used the torchlight to scan the room.

Setting the torch in a bracket on the wall just inside the doors, Liam and Wahta piled casks of gunpowder in the middle of the floor. They pried the lid from one, and poured the powder over the pile and on a stack of musket crates, leaving a trail to the entrance. Liam grabbed the torch and stepped outside; looking around, he saw no one. He motioned for Wahta to start back to the gate, and returned inside. He thrust the torch into the pile of powder at his feet, hearing it hiss as it followed the path laid out for it. He burst through the door and ran faster than he had in a while — he was gasping for breath when he reached the gate.

While Liam dashed toward the gate, an officer stepped out of his quarters to see him running across the yard toward a gate that should not have been open. At the same time, an earth-shattering explosion lit the sky with a brilliant flame, followed by a series of smaller blasts as other parts of the warehouse succumbed to the fire.

It took Mulhern a moment to gain control of the four startled horses; once they quieted down, he mounted and rode to the gate. Liam, Wahta, and Mishka watched the inferno for a few seconds, but then Wahta saw the squad of armed troopers headed their way. They backed out of the gate heading for the cover of the brush when a shot whistled over their heads. Liam whispered, "Hold your fire. When Mulhern gets here I'll fire one shot to keep their heads down while we mount." Mulhern brought the horses up as close as he deemed safe and called out, "Get your hairy bollocks over here!"

They crawled over to the sound of Mulhern's voice and proceeded to mount up. The sound of a fired musket and the thud of the bullet as it hit Mulhern shocked them into action. Liam and Wahta returned fire while Mishka took hold of Mulhern's reins; they started up the slope and to the safety of the woods. The soldiers halted when two of their number was hit, giving Liam and Wahta time to turn and gallop into the dark.

Mulhern was sitting against a tree when Liam and Wahta rode up. "Wahta, ride up to the top of that hill and keep an eye on things while we take care of the sergeant," Liam said as he dismounted.

"Bloody hell, Liam, got it in the same damn shoulder as before, only this time in the front."

"It could have been a lot worse," said Mishka, "any lower and he'd be in trouble. We'll have to dig out the slug at some point, but I've plugged the hole with goose down, that'll have to do for now."

"We'll wait for Wahta to tell us how many are coming after us. I think they'll be doubly angry, that was quite an explosion, and now they know Captain Justice is still among the living," Liam told them. "I think it would be best for you, Mishka, to get Glynnie to Mingan's village. Wahta and I will make sure that they follow us."

Wahta returned about ten minutes later to report that there were six troopers on the way. After they helped Mulhern onto his horse, they rode deeper into the woods. Mishka led the way, angling a little south to reach a creek that they could use to disguise their trail. Their horses confidently they rode into it, and followed its meander west. When they reached a granite outcrop leading back to the woods, they exited the creek without leaving any evidence of their passing. That night, they camped without fire in a small valley, and debated their next course of action. Getting Mulhern to Mingan's village, always the priority, became more urgent when he became feverish. "If we follow this valley, we'll reach a small bay that connects to Grand Traverse," Mishka said, "there's a good chance I can trade for a canoe. There's an Ottawa village near that beach."

Liam looked down at his friend. "Fancy lying down in a canoe rather than sitting up on horseback?"

Mulhern shivered and pulled his blanket tighter, grimacing from pain. "I'd prefer me own feet to bouncing my arse to bits. Just don't be expecting me to paddle."

"This is a good plan," Wahta said between bites of pemmican. "Momma Bear and Snake Slayer will take your horses. British soldiers need to think they are following four."

Mulhern cackled, "Well, would ya listen to that? Momma Bear is getting smart in his old age." They all burst out laughing, which gave Mulhern a coughing fit that sent searing pain to his wound. "Oh Christ that hurts, oh Jesus, Mary and Joseph! Get me flask from my saddlebag; I need a nip."

The Patrols – early autumn

The first thing Timothy noticed as they approached the Kiskiminetas crossing spot was the fresh tracks left in the drying mud of many horses crossing the river—tracks made within the last two or three days. "Looks like they're keeping the boys from Fort Pitt busy," he observed.

Jonas Lapley dismounted to take a closer look. "I'd guess eight to ten riders. They crossed over; they ain't crossed back."

Henry nodded in agreement with his friend's reading of the ground. Jonas was the son and grandson of farmers. He and his wife, Anne, and children, Ruth and John, were among the first settlers to arrive after the trading post reopened. Theirs was the first farm in the community, and they had become leaders in the town. Jonas was one of the more vocal opponents of Reverend Grantham and his oppressive view of God. Jonas was raised as a Quaker, though nowadays he was also a realist. He believed firmly that peace was a state of being that often required bloodshed.

"It seems we have a trail to follow," said Henry, "let us see what our friends from the fort are up to. I don't rightly think they're just exercising their horses." They entered the river; it was belly deep on their mounts this early in the spring, and it was cold (as they soon learned as it lapped up past their knees). The tracks emerged on the other side leading them east along a well-used path. Many tribes, as well as the increasing number of settlers and soldiers all traveled this trail to ford the river.

They rode through the morning, stopping once for coats as a heavy, chilly mist descended upon the valley. By mid-afternoon they were soaked, and decided to set up camp in a dell hidden from view. The mist and drizzle finally cleared out while the sun remained high in the sky, its radiant warmth causing steam to arise from their damp forms as they sat around their small fire.

"It's only half a mile to Logan's village," Henry said, "We've enough light left to have a look see."

Timothy set the small water filled kettle on the fire; next to him lay a freshly killed and butchered brace of rabbits. He retrieved onions, carrots and turnips from their supplies and began cutting and adding them to the kettle. Looking up at Henry, he directed him: "Take Jonas with you. Dinner will be waiting for you. And remember what Daniel said, avoid contact and confrontation."

"Come on, Jonas," Henry chuckled, "we better hurry. Old Timothy will have eaten our portions and drunk all the ale if we don't."

Jonas led the way as they climbed out of the valley's bowl and down the opposite slope to the trail below. As they had expected, the troopers had ridden down into the village. Hidden in a stand of oak and maple, they had a good view of the town below. Logan's village contained many tribes: Delaware, Seneca, Mingo, and a few Huron all made this a more or less permanent home. A stream divided the settlement. Wigwams, log houses, and two longhouses sat on one side, and the other side was devoted to farms and orchards.

"I don't see any Redcoats," Jonas said, "they must not have stayed too long. I put their tracks as being no more than a day old."

Henry patted his friend on the back and chortled, "Must be the farmer in you to be able to read dirt like you do. Not much more we can do today. That stew should be just about ready; time to head back."

Plates of stew and mugs ready for ale were indeed waiting for them when Henry and Jonas returned to the camp, so they set to immediately. In between bites, gulps and belches, Henry and Jonas told Timothy what they had seen, and their analysis of the situation in Logan's village. "Now I know Daniel said to just observe, but this is the best chance we're gonna have to maybe finding out something important," argued Henry. "We know that soldiers from Fort Pitt have just visited Logan. Logan is listened to and respected by many; besides, he knows us, so the meeting will be peaceable."

Timothy shrugged his shoulders in resignation. "All right, we'll talk with Logan—but I urge caution. Let's watch his village for a while before we head in. I know you said that there weren't any soldiers, but let's make sure first."

****

Logan called to one of the young men working in the field with him and told him to take over. "Looks like we have more visitors today," he said pointing to the three riders entering the village. "I know two of them, from Mallory Town." Logan crossed the creek, taking the time to rinse off the dirt from his hands and arms, and waited for the visitors to make their way over to him.

"There's Logan," said Timothy, "coming across the creek. You'll like him, Jonas. He's a farmer, at least he is now. Not your typical tribal leader, that's for sure."

"Ho there, Henry and Timothy," Logan welcomed them, "it has been many moons since we have crossed paths. What brings you this far east of your home? Am I correct in thinking it has to do with a troop of soldiers who came to see me just the other day?"

"Logan, honored war chief of the Mingo," answered Henry, "thank you for your gracious welcome. You are as far-seeing as usual, though we didn't know of the army patrol until we came across their trail two days ago. When we found that it led here, we figured it would be a good idea to find out why. We have been hearing some disturbing news concerning the army trying to make allies with the tribes in the area. They promise to supply them with muskets and ammunition in the event there is conflict between the army and the colonists."

"Come, we will talk while we refresh ourselves," Logan replied, indicating that they should follow him to his cabin. "I can offer you buttermilk, tea, coffee or water."

"Thank you, I think coffee would be just the thing," answered Henry, "I've come to prefer it to tea."

They entered Logan's home, where his wife bid them sit while she brought them all cups of coffee, a bowl of brown sugar, fresh bread, butter and honey. Logan waited until his guests had fixed their coffee and bread before reaching for the sugar. "I really enjoy the taste of coffee, especially as it gets sweeter as you drink it. That's why I don't stir the sugar; just let it dissolve slowly. Now, as to my business with the British.

"My father was a good friend to a white man, and he learned a lot from him. I think the most important thing he learned, and which he passed on to me, is that the white man is as numberless as the stars in the sky, and that they will continue to seek new land. That, I think you'll agree, is an important lesson to learn. That is why I live in a cabin rather than a wigwam. Take a look around you. You'll see a home that any white settler would be comfortable in.

"Now, I have not abandoned my people, or our history and traditions, but I am aware that if we are to have a future to keep alive our history and traditions, then we must learn to live with the whites; that we must live like the white man without becoming a white man. There are many who feel I am a fool, a coward, for not fighting. There are some, and Pontiac was one of these, who think if we unite, we can drive the whites back to the ocean. That effort, as we saw, while a noble idea, was and is doomed to fail.

"I will not fight. I will continue to seek peace and will continue to show my people the way of peace. You'll find that there are many here in this village who would normally be at each other's throats. There are some from the Iroquois nations, and there are some from their enemies—the Huron, the Delaware—and yet here they co-exist. So, I will tell you what I told the British; I will not be involved in the coming conflict; and yes, there will be one. But, be forewarned, my people must be left alone to pursue a peaceful existence. If they are not allowed that, then I will be involved. I may have taken up the plow, but I can still wield a war club."

Henry stood up and reached over to shake Logan's hand. "We thank you for your hospitality, and for your candor. Let us hope that we can remain as friends. I cannot speak for everyone in Mallory Town, but as far as I'm concerned, I look forward to being at peace with our good neighbors in this village." Ruefully, Logan slowly shook his head.

"I know that there is some trouble; yes, I know about the good Reverend Grantham. My people trade with you, and with our mutual friend in Fort Pitt, Two Birds. Not only do we gather goods we need, but we also gather information. Reverend Grantham sounds like a very ambitious man; I do not envy you the confrontation that is coming."

****

Thomas and Sam grinned as their canoes cane alongside each other. They were beyond excited to be included in a scouting mission. Daniel signaled to James that he would beach just beyond the island they were approaching. As Daniel guided the canoe past the island, he noticed that Thomas was visibly distracted by the sad memory of that awful day when Albert Jameson died saving him. The raiding party assembled on this island prior to their attack on Mallory Town.

"Thomas," called Daniel, "lesson number one: when on a mission like this, don't let your mind drift. So, if you don't mind, please start paddling again. I want to land over on that rocky beach."

They pulled the canoes up into the scrub brush, and hid them as best they could. Daniel called Thomas and Sam over to him. "All right, boys, on a scout like this it is important to remain quiet and hidden. The hidden part is the tricky one to master, but a good way to begin is to take advantage of whatever the terrain offers by way of concealment." He looked off toward a small valley up ahead. "You see that valley? It's almost perfect for us. The hills on either side are heavily wooded, and the creek is shallow enough so to not pose any problems. 'Course, I have an advantage being how I know this land hereabouts, and have used this valley many times. It runs almost due north for a few miles, and then as it rises it turns northeast. We'll have to leave the valley at that point, and head northwest. I want to check on a creek that runs toward a Seneca camp. We will still have the cover of the trees, but we'll have to cross a couple of bare hills before we reach where we're headed."

A steady rain fell as they traversed the valley; while it was irritating, Thomas and Sam managed not to complain even as water dripped off their hats and managed to find a way to streak down the back of their necks and under clothing. This did not deter Daniel, and occasionally James, from stopping to show the boys any interesting plants or tracks that they came across. When they left the valley the rain lessened, but was replaced with a dense fog. "We're lucky," said Daniel, "this fog will help keep us hidden until we reach Buffalo Creek. We'll make camp when we reach that. It'll be a short hike tomorrow to the Seneca camp."

The younger men awoke the next morning before the sun climbed above the trees that concealed their campsite. It had been a fitful night for both of them, due to both their excitement and a persistent drizzle.

"Come on, sluggards," teased James, "Make yourselves useful. Fill our water skins, and clean out the cook pot. Be sure that if you relieve yourself in the creek, you do it downstream from where you're filling them."

"James is pretty funny. Make sure you pee upstream," Sam said to Thomas as they made their way down the gentle slope to the creek. The mist rising from the creek spread out in a smoky haze through the early morning rays of the sun that rose no more than knee high. "You know, he wasn't joking," Thomas said quickly as Sam began to urinate upstream from where Thomas was cleaning out the cook pot. Sam, a sudden flash of recognition crossing his face, nodded at Thomas and moved to the other side of him. Suddenly, a loud musket blast from somewhere on the other side of the creek caught their attention, and also that of Daniel and James. Bursting through the trees came a running buckskin-clad Negro, who without hesitation plunged into the creek. The water was cold, rising quickly from ankle deep to thigh deep, and the current was swift, but he managed to make his way almost to the other side when an arrow caught him in the upper back. He lurched forward from the impact, but regained his balance and made it to the opposite bank. Thomas and Sam started to run over to the wounded man. Daniel and James clambered down the hill. "Get back boys," yelled Daniel, "take cover in the trees."

Out of the trees ran six Huron braves, one aiming his musket at the prone figure on the opposite beach. Daniel fired his in the air to draw the Huron's attention, and yelled out in Huron, "Ahanu, hold your fire!"

The Huron warrior pulled his musket up from the black man, and now aimed at the white man. Ahanu took a careful look at this white who spoke Huron, and finally burst out in laughter. "Daniel Mallory, most honored enemy and friend. It has been many moons since we spoke last, and now I find you near my camp. Let us talk, there is much here that is curious."

Daniel waved his hand and replied, "Let me get my horse. This water is too cold for me."

Ahanu chuckled, "Too cold for anyone except those who flee."

While Daniel crossed over to meet with the Huron, James and the boys tended the wounded man. "It looks like the arrow isn't too deep. You were lucky," James relayed to the Negro, "do you speak English?"

"Yes, sir, I speak English," the Negro replied, grimacing as James pulled the arrowhead from his shoulder, "name is Bert Sawyer."

"Well, Bert Sawyer, I am going to need my kit, and then we'll see about cleaning and plugging up this hole in your back. Sam, run up to the camp and fetch my knapsack," James ordered. "Thomas, bring over that water skin."

****

Bert sat against a tree, his left arm in a makeshift sling. He focused on the two men discussing his future, their conversation muted. A runaway slave, he wasn't sure what would be worse, being taken by Indians or by whites; either way, he did not expect much kindness or gentle treatment. He watched the Huron pointed at him, the anger on his face evident even at this distance. The white man, however, seemed to have the upper hand, and now the Huron pointed at something lying at the edge of the shoreline. Bert could not see it until Daniel rode over, bent down from the saddle, and lifted up an iron kettle, which he handed to Ahanu. The Huron warrior gave a yelp and rode back across the river joining the rest of his men.

Daniel returned to the group, dismounted and announced, "Well, we are out of danger. Now, how is our guest doing? He cost us a good kettle, though I'm inclined to think we made a good deal. One kettle for not handing over this would-be horse thief." He walked over to Bert and knelt down, placing a hand on Bert's uninjured shoulder, smiled, and said, "This is a tale I have got to hear. But, first, let's get back up to the camp and get you something to eat. You look a tad peckish."

Bert was ravenous; hunting the last few days had been fruitless. Thomas gave him a hunk of bread, some pemmican, and a mug of tea to wash them down. While he ate, he tried to make sense of the men who now owned him. *No, not owned!* He would never again be a slave, to anyone. These white men were somehow different. They were treating him well, and it didn't seem that this was a prelude to harsher handling. *How much of my past should I reveal?*

****

James and the boys grabbed their muskets and headed into the woods. Earlier, Ahuna mentioned to Daniel where some turkeys had been feeding, so with luck they would have fresh meat. Daniel sat down across the campfire from Bert.

"I imagine you're a bit worried, or maybe scared." He rose and, carrying a musket, approached Bert. "I apologize; very rude of me. Let me introduce myself." He reached down to shake Bert's hand. "Daniel Mallory at your service, such as it is. My companions and I live in a settlement a day's march from here. We're out keeping an eye on things. The frontier isn't a tame place, even in peace time. While we won't force you, I strongly suggest that you accompany us. They told me your name is Bert Sawyer." He took a look at the musket he was carrying, admiring the evident quality of the weapon. "I believe this is yours, Bert," he said, handing him the musket, "that's quite a nice piece. Yes, I sure am looking forward to hearing your tale."

Bert laid the musket across his lap and pointed to some letters nicely etched on a brass plate attached to the stock. "This here gun belonged to my former master. SJT it says. Simon James Turney is his name. He's not a bad man, treats his slaves better than most. I worked in his lumber mill, cutting timber. That's why my name is Sawyer. When times were slack in the mill, Master Simon would take me hunting with him. He taught me how to shoot, and how to ride. He trusted me, so when I got a little older, he let me go out hunting alone using this here musket."

Bert paused for a moment, took a sip of tea, and—his voice cracking a little—continued. "I never met my pa. My momma was carrying me when they were sold to different masters. Master Simon bought my momma and me a couple years later. We was told a few years back that my pa was killed for trying to escape. When the slave hunters caught him, they beat him pretty bad. His master had him flogged; he died under the lash. My momma's heart was broke, and she died not too long after. As she lie dying, I made a vow. I would be free; no man will have a claim on me. I planned ahead; gathering supplies and money, and waited for my chance.

It happened like this. Master Simon was getting old, and it soon became clear that he no longer had the strength to run the plantation. His wife had died years ago, and their only surviving child, a son, lived in England and had no interest in living in the colonies. Master Simon's brother was the only one he could count on. Brothers they may have been by blood, but they were nothing alike. Master Edward is a brute, and has always shown me nothing but scorn, and over the next several months his treatment of me became harsher. Next time I went hunting, I didn't go back."

Daniel stirred the ashes of the fire, nodding his head as Bert told his story. When Bert finished, Daniel stood to build a new fire. "I reckon the others will be back soon with something to cook. We'll take it easy for today, and start back to Mallory Town tomorrow. So, rest up for now, though I do need to know one thing. My Huron friend told me you tried to steal his horse. Is that true?"

Bert stared at the ground while Daniel spoke, but he raised his eyes to respond. Smiling, Bert answered. "Yes, sir, I did. I would have made it too, 'cept as I was leading the horse away from their camp, your friend came out from behind a tree he was pissing on. I don't rightly know who was more surprised."

Mallory Town

The five adult members of the patrols sat with Liza and Deborah around the table in Daniel's cabin. The two boys were relegated to the loft, and hung over the railing to hear the conversation below. Next to Daniel sat a visibly nervous Bert. He just couldn't shake a feeling of dread, despite the kindness shown to him by all in this room. Daniel noticed his discomfort. Placing his hand on Bert's shoulder, he said, "You have all heard about our guest. I know he's feeling frightened at what we decide to do. The mere thought of returning him to slavery has not once crossed my mind. No man deserves that fate. So, I say this, Bert has worked in a lumber mill; we have need of more help in that area. Bert also knows his way around the countryside; we can always use more men for our patrols." Daniel paused for a moment, taking the time to scan each face. Not seeing any sign of disagreement, turned to Bert and said, "Bert, what say you to becoming a part of our little community as a free man?"

Bert exhaled a huge sigh, got to his feet, and with tears in his eyes, said, "Mast--. I mean Mister Mallory, my heart is so swelled up. I knew you was good people, I so believed it. There ain't enough thanks in heaven for how I feel."

With shouts of exclamation and encouragement, they all made Bert welcome. Daniel raised his hands for quiet. "Now first off, my name is Daniel; don't rightly know how to respond to that mister stuff. And, second, while you're healing up, you should take the time and get used to your new surroundings. I'm sure that Thomas and Samuel would be more than happy to serve as guides."

****

Thomas and Sam took Bert on their daily perimeter patrol, showing him the musket slots along the wall. They were joined by Bowie and Caleb, both of whom couldn't help but stare at this brown man. "Boys," scolded Sam, "Quit your staring. Ain't polite. I know old Bert here is a mite darker than you or me, but he's a man like us just the same."

"I guess not too many Negroes come here," said Bert as he followed the troop up the ladder to one of the block houses.

"One or two trappers but they never stay," replied Thomas, "though my pa and Uncle Dan knew one real well. He was a runaway too. Got adopted by the Mohawk and fought alongside my folks in the war. He was killed saving the life of Colonel Washington."

****

Gerald Brightman sauntered over to the church, smiling politely and greeting those he met along the way with a cheerful voice. He was always amused by, and never failed to stop and watch, the children's patrol. The children were, not surprisingly, wary of this scarred up man and kept their distance from him, avoiding eye contact. All except Thomas; he was not afraid to stare him down.

"I suppose that's to be expected from the son of the leading rebel family," Brightman thought. Having taken advantage of a warm morning to read while sitting in the sun, and before visiting Reverend Grantham, Brightman took one last look back at the nearby blockhouse. He thought to himself, sometimes one can gain knowledge from the written word, but sometimes knowledge just comes, unexpected, and in such a manner as to make one believe in God or fate.

Reverend Grantham looked across at his smiling henchman, and couldn't help but smile himself. "This is indeed remarkable information. And you say, you got it quite by accident?" Grantham stood up and walked over to the window.

"So, our good friends—the Mallory's and the Clarke's— are not only harboring a runaway slave, it seems that they have done so in the past as well. Oh, this will be very useful, very useful indeed, Mr. Brightman. It looks like tomorrow you'll make another visit to Major Whitby. I need some time to think how best to utilize our knowledge of this darkie."

Chapter 4 1771 – Finding and Losing

Mallory Town – Late Winter

It was just around Christmas when Bert began working in the saw mill. His shoulder had healed enough for him to swing an axe, and to pull the huge crosscut saw. This time of year most of the work was cutting timber for firewood, but there was also a stockpile of replacement posts for the stockade fence. They were expanding the wall to now enclose the stock paddock, and both the saw mill, and grist mill would soon be within the walls as well. He was adjusting to his new life, becoming accustomed to having his own cabin, and having some control over his daily activities. He was also becoming used to the fact that not everyone in Mallory Town was pleased with his presence. He tried to understand why, even to the point of attending a Sunday sermon at the church. One of the things Bert noticed soon after his arrival was that there was an ever growing divide between those who went to Reverend Grantham's church and those who did not. The church was pretty full when Bert entered. He stood inside the door for a few seconds, noticing the back pew was mostly empty, walked over and sat down. The congregation was at prayer, so with heads bowed and eyes closed, at first no one seemed to notice the late arriving worshipper. It didn't take long, however, once the man seated across the aisle saw him, and began whispering to his neighbors; pointing at Bert with an accusing finger.

Reverend Grantham was about to begin his sermon, and like most of his sermons it didn't matter what Biblical passage he referenced, the subject always returned to obedience, when he heard the murmuring, and saw people gesturing at the rear of the church. Upon seeing the cause for the disturbance, Grantham abandoned his planned homily. His calculating mind was quick to grasp this golden opportunity to take the next step in his plan.

"My children," Grantham began, waiting for the murmurs to quiet, "I see we have a guest with us this morning. We welcome you, Bert, to this house of God, for indeed God welcomes all who come to Him. I can tell that there is some surprise, and a little discomfort to have a Negro in our midst, but my dear children did not our Lord say, 'Suffer little children, and forbid them not, to come unto me: for of such is the kingdom of heaven.' And what is the Negro if not like a little child? They are but ignorant savages, not so very different from the beasts that they share the jungles of Africa with. Ignorant of all morality, engaging in all manner of licentiousness and promiscuity. It seems to me, and to all who endeavor to please and obey God, that we do the Negro a mercy by taking them away from the evil that once was his domain. We do the Negro a mercy by replacing his godless existence, his darkened and damned soul, with the light of Christ, and with bringing them to their rightful place, in the eyes of God, into the world of the white man." He paused for a moment, scanning the crowd. Every eye was on him, an occasional head was nodding agreement. When his eyes came to rest on Bert he had to smile, the darkie couldn't bring himself to look up. 'Well, Bert my friend, you have no idea how happy you have made me today,' he thought, 'it's almost a shame how unhappy you're going to be.' "It does sadden me, however," Grantham continued, "when those to who we have extended the hand of peace, the love of God, a sense of purpose and belonging, turn their backs on God and his perfect plan. The Apostle Paul says in Ephesians 5 verse 6, 'Slaves, obey your earthly masters with fear and trembling, with a sincere heart, as you would Christ.' And Peter tells us in 1 Peter 2 verse 18, 'Servants, be subject to your masters with all respect, not only to the good and gentle but also to the unjust.' How much plainer can God make it? If you are called into slavery, as the Negro has been, then obedience to your earthly masters is not only right and just, but it is commanded by God. So, what about our duties and responsibilities? How does the good Christian behave toward this subservient race? As I mentioned before, Christ taught us to suffer not the little children but to teach them, and what is one of the most important lessons we can teach? Obedience. Obedience. Obedience to God, obedience to those whom God has placed above you. Sometimes that lesson is hard to learn; hard to accept. Sometimes harsh methods of teaching are necessary. Not that we seek to cause pain, but rather out of love and caring we lead them to the bosom of God's love, and to the knowledge of their place in the realm of man. Amen."

Grantham descended from the raised pulpit beckoning Brightman to follow him. "Keep an eye, oh sorry, poor choice of words," chuckled Grantham, "I need to know the best time to put things in motion. Follow our darkie friend; determine our best chance for success. Once I know that, one more ride to Fort Pitt for you, followed one week later by Judgement Day."

John Thompson had had his doubts about having a darkie working for him in the saw mill, but since Mr. Mallory owned the mill, there wasn't much choice in the matter. At first he bullied Bert, never leaving him alone, critical of everything Bert did. Gradually, however, he recognized that Bert knew what he was about, and left him to his tasks, and while he was still gruff, he was also more likely to offer some praise though Bert wasn't overly fond of the 'Good work, boy'. Thompson was sharpening the teeth of his favorite saw when he was startled by the approach of Gerald Brightman.

"Tedious work, sharpening is," said Brightman.

"Aye, tedious it is," replied Thompson, "but necessary. Ordinarily I would leave this for Bert, he has a fine touch for putting an edge on, but he has other duties this morning."

"The darkie is the reason for my visit, Mr. Thompson. He must not have any other duties tomorrow; he must be here, in the mill, and alone. The Reverend wants to have a few words; a lesson in obedience, I expect," Brightman said in a somewhat light-hearted tone, "so make sure he is here. It would so please Reverend Grantham and me to find you so, shall we say, obedient?"

The last few weeks, for Bert, had been both confusing, and to some extent, satisfying. His one and only experience with the church, and Reverend Grantham was certainly not what he had expected. His only prior exposure to the teachings of Jesus had come from a few of the elderly slaves, and what he gleaned from them was nothing like what he heard from Reverend Grantham. Who was he to believe, uneducated slaves or a man of God? Then there was the vast difference in how Bert was treated by Daniel, and his family and friends, and by the townsfolk who followed Grantham. At least at the mill he was treated, if not kindly, then with some respect. Today's task even took him away from the mill for a few hours as he was asked to stay and help with replacing a section of the wall near the canoe landing. He found that he enjoyed being part of a team, and was made to feel a part throughout the day's activity, and the good-humored banter.

That night he had supper with Henry and Liza, and when Henry left to check that the gates were closed for the night, asked Liza what she believed. "Now that's a question people have been pondering for centuries," she said sitting across the table, her hands folded in front of her, "even Christians have a hard time figuring out what to believe. Maybe that's the way the Good Lord intends. Maybe it isn't supposed to be easy, or even have only one answer. I've known godly folk from all sorts of churches, and some, like our friends the Mohawk, from no church at all. Course, now, there are those who want you to think they are godly, perhaps even think they are the only correct followers of God. I fear they are incorrect, and I am fearful of their intent. I have an idea that God wants to be found by each of us. I find God in the fields, in the plants He gives us to use; in the forests, and the animals He gives us for food. I find God in you, Bert, the greatest gifts God gives us, are, each other, and knowing right from wrong. God is all around us, Bert."

Bert got up from the table, and made his way to the door, "Thank you, Miss Liza. I appreciate your words. It's a hard thing to understand. People tells me that Reverend Grantham is a right smart man, but when he says I am not a man, I believe he is wrong, and somehow I am going to prove it." As he stepped through the doorway he turned and said, "Gives my regards to Mr. Henry, and thanks for the supper."

"You are welcome any time, Mr. Sawyer," Liza replied.

****

Daniel was tired, and not for the first time, was beginning to feel old. He bent down to lay another log on the fire groaning out loud when he stood up. Deborah was already asleep, but she had left him some stew, and a loaf of bread. He could hear one of the children mumbling in her sleep as he sat down. It had been a long day, beginning before dawn as he took Thomas and Sam out on patrol. They'd been hearing rumors of a band of Seneca prowling about which was unusual, and worth investigating. They did find an abandoned campsite but it was hard to tell who may have used it, though it appeared to only be a couple days old. It was not an entirely fruitless venture, Daniel thought, Thomas and Sam are progressing well. Liam would be proud of them. Remembering the letter Henry had given to him when Daniel brought Thomas home, he pulled it out of the inside pocket of his coat, and while he ate his stew, he read:

Mulhern's Cabin – Winter 1770

Daniel,

Not much to do around here for the time being. Never seen so much snow as what blows in from Lake Michigan. It is beautiful country nonetheless, but you know me and extended periods of inactivity. The buffalo dreams return, so to the longing to be on the move. But for now, we are comfortable. We built a small longhouse for Mulhern, and we all fit in nicely. We've added a couple more to our group, a former soldier, now an adopted Ojibway warrior, Mishka, and a rather lovely Ojibway widow, Mitena. She has taken charge of Mulhern. I've never seen him happier. He has recovered from the wound to his shoulder, oh, you don't know about that, do you? Well, let's just say that if anyone mentions a munitions dump at Fort Michilimackinac having exploded under suspicious circumstances, act surprised. I don't mean to sound glib, it was a serious situation that needed fixing, and almost cost us Mulhern. And it is yet one more reason for me and Wahta to move on, but we can't bear to leave Mulhern. We don't know how much longer he has, though I suspect he is healthier than he has been in a while; at least given the noise he and Mitena make at night. Go ahead and smile, brother, I am.

Things are quiet among the tribes. The Council of the Three Fires, the Ojibway, Ottawa and Potawatomi, seems to have enough respect that peace is maintained. We hear of some disturbances farther north but they are beyond our reach at present.

I am sending this letter, and ones to Two Birds, and Liza with an Ottawa group who are headed to Fort Detroit. They will give them to Major Gladwin who will send them on to Fort Pitt. You can use the same route, in reverse of course, for any replies. I expect I'll be here for many months. *However, it would be wise to not use Michilimackinac for posting any letters. Somehow I don't think I'd be welcome to retrieve it.*

Give my boys a hug, if they allow that sort of thing.

Liam

Daniel laughed as he put the letter back in the envelope, leaving it on the table for Deborah to read in the morning. "Liam my brother, why does it not surprise me that you blew up a fort? We're getting too old for that sort of activity and I'm sure Mulhern voiced his objections," Daniel muttered as he walked to the bedroom, "though it appears he went along and that doesn't surprise me either."

"Husband," Deborah asked sleepily, what doesn't surprise you?"

"A letter from Liam," he yawned as he answered, while donning his nightshirt, "you can read it in the morning. Go back to sleep, sorry I woke you." He kissed her on the forehead, turned away and fell asleep.

"Well I wanted to also inquire as to what are you getting too old for," she said to his sleeping form, "but I guess I'll have to wait to find out. Good night, my love."

****

As part of his contribution to the safety of the villagers, Bert's day began with a walk around the perimeter of the town, looking for any sign that anyone or thing (there were a few black bears in the area) had approached the walls. As he made his way to the new section he had helped with yesterday, he saw Richard Crane the blacksmith already at work. "Good morning, Mr. Crane," said Bert, "you up and at the task early today."

"Now how many times have I told you, call me Richard?" joked Crane, "yeah, just putting the finishing touches on our little surprise. See here? I made the handles to look like a hitching ring. You here to help out again today?"

Bert leaned his musket against the wall of the trading post, and bent down to look at the handles that would slide this section of the wall vertically; a hidden gate that only a few knew about. "No sir, Richard. Mr. Thompson over at the sawmill says he needs me to sharpen blades, so I'm heading over there now. If I can I'll come by later."

Bert was working on a nasty burr on the blade of an axe, and didn't notice the two men enter the mill. Motioning Brightman to get behind Bert, Reverend Grantham stepped out of the doorway shadow, and walked over to Bert. "A pleasant morning to you, Mr. Sawyer," Grantham said with a smile that held no warmth, "or should I just call you 'runaway'?" Before Bert could reply, Brightman knocked him unconscious. Two other men entered, and between them they carried Bert over to a small wagon, dropping him none too gently in the wagon bed, covering him with a canvas tarp and sacks of grain.

****

The rider asked the first person he saw where to find Daniel Mallory. His mount had clearly been ridden hard, and was lathered in sweat. He dismounted, wiping the sweat and grime from his face. Thomas led him into the Trading Post. In a breathless, frightened voice pleaded, "You've got to come help...my, my village, Franklin...under attack."

Daniel helped him to sit down calling for Henry and Liza. With a mug of cold water to help settle him down the rider began again, "A band of Seneca has surrounded our settlement. Up the Allegheny about five miles from here. I don't know how long they can hold out, we're a small group; four families. Please, you've got to come!"

"Thomas, go out and ring the bell. We need to muster the militia," ordered Daniel, "I figure six to eight of us to go, and the rest to man the walls in case this is a diversion."

Ten minutes later the town square was filled with men, and a few women, muskets at hand. Daniel gave them a rundown of what was happening, "I need two volunteers to come with me, Henry, Timothy, and Jonas Lapley who I just volunteered." Several hands went up including Thomas' and Sam's, but in the end Daniel chose James Crane and Josiah Webb. He then looked around, and shouted, "Has anyone seen Bert Sawyer?" He turned to Henry, "I expected to not see any of Grantham's flock, but I'm concerned that Bert didn't answer the bell."

"He may be over in the mill, and couldn't hear it," ventured Henry, "though I doubt that. The bell carries a ways."

Richard Crane came over to Daniel and handed him Bert's musket. "I saw Bert early this morning. He left this leaning against the building when he headed over to the mill."

A look of puzzlement, and concern crossed Daniel's face. Why would Bert seemingly disappear? It didn't make sense that he would simply take off, especially without his musket. He looked at Richard and said, "I'm leaving you in charge. Make sure the walls and block houses are manned until we return. Also, have Thomas and Sam do some looking around. I fear that the good Reverend has something to do with Bert's disappearance."

"Someone else is missing," said Timothy, "I was just over at the Post, and that rider from Franklin is gone."

"It's a good thing we know where we're going. We don't have time to look for him. Something about this has the hairs on the back of my neck standing up. We'll need to be alert for the unexpected," said Daniel, "let's get mounted up. The sooner we find out what's going on, the sooner we can get back here."

****

It was during the excitement and the gathering of the crowd that the rider chose to make himself scarce. He had done what he was hired for, and was now waiting in the church to be paid. "You know, I've a mind to ask for more. Seems I've come to realize what your scheme is Reverend Grantham," the rider smirked, "yep, I've put the pieces together. First, there's that troop of Redcoats I saw getting ready to march, then there's that ploy to get the militia out of the way. I reckon you plan to takeover this town, and I'd like to share in the spoils."

Grantham smiled as he looked over the rider's head, nodding his own slightly. Excusing himself, explaining that the money was in the next room, and they would talk about an arrangement, Grantham left the room. The rider, his thoughts on the good time he was going to have when he got back to Fort Pitt, didn't hear Brightman, and could only desperately claw at the knotted rope that was now squeezing his life away. Brightman threw one end of the rope over a ceiling beam, pulled hard and hauled the rider off of his feet. He watched in amusement at the rider's macabre dance; his feet jerking around, stopping suddenly, his head slumped at an odd angle and finally a heap on the floor as Brightman let him drop. "Well, Reverend," sighed Brightman spying Grantham with the mill manager entering the room, "another sinner sent to hell. A tedious task but a necessary one, wouldn't you say, Mr. Thompson?"

John Thompson stared in horror at the sight before him. He placed his kerchief over his nose to blot out the stench of voided bowels. "Yes, a necessary one," he blurted out just before vomiting on the floor.

"I see you understand. I am glad. I didn't want you to become tedious to us," replied Brightman, "now help me with this unfortunate reprobate. We've already made a hole for him out back." They picked up the rider's body, and made their way to the back door to a secluded garden area behind the church. Thompson stopped suddenly causing Brightman to drop his end of the corpse. "Oh, you noticed that there are two holes. I always like to be prepared, but it seems I won't need the second one. Today."

In a corner of the garden stood a small six foot by six foot shed that was used by the gardener to keep his tools. It was currently empty of all the gardener's implements, having been temporarily converted into a jail cell. Bert was still a bit groggy but was slowly coming back to consciousness. He lay on the floor, his hands and feet bound and his mouth gagged. His head hurt as did his side and the right side of his face. He could taste blood from the tear in his cheek where he had bitten himself while being kicked. He sat up and once the dizziness passed he looked around. As his eyes adjusted to the gloom he tried to remember what had happened. He recalled waking up as he was being lifted out of the wagon and being rewarded for it by being kicked and pummeled into unconsciousness again. The next thing wasn't clear, he thought he had heard bells or maybe it was only one. His glance around the room revealed nothing he could use to cut his bonds. He did notice that what little light that filtered through, came in by way of a couple of gaps in the back wall. He scooted over to the openings, moving slowly so as to not jar his head. He looked through and saw two young girls placing fresh flowers on some graves.

Daniel and Deborah's daughter, seven year old Abigail, and her cousin, eight year old Meagan, each placed a wreath of fresh flowers on the graves of Rebecca, her father Albert, and Orenda. As long as they were available the girls would gather wildflowers for the graves. When the flowers were done for the season, they would keep the sites decorated with pine cones or branches. "Come on Abigail," urged Meagan, "your ma said to hurry back."

Abigail looked at her cousin, and put a finger to her lips, "Shh, did you hear that?"

Meagan shook her head, "Hear what?"

"That," replied Abigail as the sound of someone banging came from the shed. Abigail ran over to the wall with Meagan yelling for her to stop. They now heard what sounded like someone trying to talk, but it was muffled, and they couldn't understand the words. Holding hands they ventured over, and peered in through the crack in the slat.

Bert tried to smile, but the gag, and the soreness of his mouth made him grimace instead as he saw Abigail's eyes peering back at him. "It's Bert," shrieked Abigail.

"Quiet Abby," said Meagan, as she took a look. Bert mumbled something and a few seconds later Meagan recognized he was saying 'get help'. "My pa, and some of the others have gone away," she told Bert, "but my brother Thomas is still here. I will get him. Oh Bert, everyone was worried about you, but things will be better now."

Deborah and Liza were preparing the evening meal while Caleb and Bowie regaled Jack, and the younger Ethan with their version of the militia muster. Abigail burst into the cabin ahead of Meagan and said, "We found Bert and he's all tied up and hurt." They sat the girls down, and got the whole story.

Liza realized at once that getting Daniel, and the others out was just a ruse for something still to come. "Caleb, Bowie," she said, "run to the Webb's, and fetch Thomas and Sam, quickly now."

It was decided that Thomas and Sam would rescue Bert that night, taking a canoe across the river, and then to the Lapley farm where they would pick up the militia's trail in the morning. Liza and Deborah put together some food and drink to last them a couple days while Jack, using the meager description of Bert's condition, packed up a couple poultices for bruising, and a mixture of wild cherry bark and pennyroyal to be used as a tea for pain. Sam ran through the description of the shed, "we're gonna need something to bust through that wall."

Jack walked into the room with the bundle of herbs and said, "Stop at the mill and grab a saw. An axe would be too loud."

Wanting to be included in the rescue adventure, Bowie and Caleb handed Bert's musket, powder horn, and ammunition pouch to Thomas. Thomas looked at his three cousins and said, "You men are in charge until we get back. Keep the women and children safe." Then with a hug from Liza, and Aunt Deborah, Thomas headed out the door. Sam gave a final salute to the three smiling militiamen, and followed Thomas into the night. They made their way, staying in close to buildings, to the mill. The night sky was overcast so there was no moonlight. Thomas and Sam knew their way around the compound better than most, but inside the mill they would have to risk lighting the small lantern they brought. Fortunately Bert kept the tools all arranged in a tidy manner, so it only took a moment for them to find two hand saws. Sam blew out the candle as they left the mill. They were now in the open, crossing the common area of the village. Walking slowly they kept glancing around for any sign of movement and were startled by a dog. They looked at each other with sheepish grins, and continued across.

Bert was beginning to think things through now that the throbbing in his head had subsided. He had to keep from moving too quickly though, as that would set off the drummers for a few heartbeats. He figured that whoever came to rescue him would most likely not be using the front door of the shed, that being too visible from the church. So, with as much movement he could stand he began pushing out the cracked slat, lying on his back, kicking with his bound feet. He had made some progress when he heard someone lifting the locking bar to the door. He shifted quickly to block the slightly protruding slat, lying crossways with his back to the intruder, feigning unconsciousness.

Brightman opened the shed door and shining his lantern on the prone figure on the floor, chuckled, "Still not back with us? My companions are to be commended on their excellent work." He walked over, nudging Bert with his boot, "Well, Mr. Sawyer, I had brought you some food, but I don't think you'll need it in your condition, and certainly not after tomorrow. Do you know what your future looks like, eh, Mr. Sawyer? You see, the good Reverend has been waiting for someone like you to come along. Someone he could use to further his plans. It could have been anyone, but the fact that you're a runaway slave; well that was just sweetener for the pot. Tomorrow, British troops, commanded by Major Whitby will enter Mallory Town, under orders to seize a runaway, and to conduct an investigation of those accused of aiding and abetting said runaway. Very tidy, and much easier with Mallory out of the way; permanently if things go as planned. As for you, I'm not certain. Whitby will either make arrangements for you to be sent back, in less than luxurious accommodations I'm sure, to your master in Virginia, or he may just hang you as an example. If I was a betting man, I'd wager on hanging; much less trouble that way. Plus the added advantage to having a visible coaxing to obedience. What all this means is that the British will gain an important outpost that will give them control of the upper Allegheny region, and our esteemed Reverend will gain a town of his own. Don't let the religious aspect of his character fool you. He no more believes most of what he preaches than I do. Man of God, my aching arse! He's nothing more than any of the other greedy bastards since the time of Cain. If it's any consolation, though I doubt it will be, Mr. Grantham actually feels slavery is abhorrent and should be abolished. Rather ironic, don't you think? I suppose that along, with being a pragmatic business, politics is also an ironic one."

Brightman nudged Bert again, "I know you're awake, not that it matters, though I appreciate you being so attentive an audience. One more thing before I go. I imagine the two young girls who saw you earlier have by now instigated some sort of rescue." Bert stiffened and groaned, lashing out with his feet trying to trip Brightman. "Easy there, Mr. Sawyer," Brightman responded as he moved away, "let me finish. I will do nothing to stop it, and will see that there is no pursuit until tomorrow. However, at that time I will do my duty, and see that you are captured. Truth is, Mr. Sawyer, I rather like you, and want to give you a chance; not much of one, but a chance nonetheless. I'll leave you now. In a way I hope we never meet again."

Bert waited for a few moments after Brightman left, and began working on the slat again. He had an opening of a few inches as the bottom of the plank finally came loose from the base it been attached to. He was about to kick at it again when he heard Thomas calling his name. A feeling of relief overcame Bert as Sam started sawing. He used the gap to angle the saw so that he was cutting upwards and in a few minutes the hole was large enough for Thomas to reach in, and cut the bonds on Bert's hands. Bert immediately removed the blood, and mucus saturated gag, muttering a thank you as he took the knife from Thomas and cut his feet loose.

****

Daniel and company had crossed the Allegheny using the town ferry. There had once been a bridge but with larger boats coming down the river, they dismantled it. There was a larger bridge planned, but work had not begun on it yet. They stopped at the Lapley's farm and picked up Jonas. From there they struck west along a track that more or less paralleled the river. A mile or so before reaching Buffalo Creek, Daniel called a halt, sending Jonas up ahead to scout the crossing. The settlement was located about half a mile west of the creek but both Daniel and Jonas knew that the crossing was an ideal spot for an ambush. The Allegheny curved south at this point following a line of hills; hills that were heavily wooded. The track at this juncture was more like a ravine as both sides were lined by the tree covered hills.

Mulhern's Cabin - mid-November

Mulhern pushed away the cup of wild cherry bark tea as he was hit with another coughing spasm. He wiped his mouth on an already sodden rag, "Damn tea is supposed to help this cough not provoke it," he said to Liam, "how's Mitena doing?"

"She's doing just fine, as I've told you half a dozen times already," smirked Liam holding Mulhern's head up so he could drink more of the tea. "The Medicine Man and the mid-wife are with her. You just lie back and relax."

Mulhern took a sip, chuckled and said, "Kind of ironic, me dying here while my woman gives birth."

Liam felt his friend's forehead and reached for the basin of cold water. He wiped down Mulhern's head and face, and with a light hearted tone that belied the sadness he felt said, "Yeah, well seems the Good Lord likes a joke or as my Mohawk father would say, 'The Great Spirit likes to balance things'."

Mulhern grabbed Liam's hand, pulling him close, "Liam, promise me this. If it's a boy, name him Gordon Liam Wahta Mulhern. That'll be easy, but if it's a girl, you promise me now, if it's a girl, I want her to be named Rebecca."

Liam recoiled slightly when Mulhern said her name, but he quickly recovered and realized how much he loved this old man. "It will be as you say, Glynnie. Now get some sleep."

"I'll sleep when I'm dead, and that'll be soon enough," he said, "where's Momma Bear? I have things to tell him."

"I'll fetch him. If you're gonna stay awake, drink this tea," Liam said handing the mug to Mulhern, "I think Wahta is out scouring the countryside for more wild cherry bark."

Liam and Wahta returned to find Mulhern in a fitful sleep, his breathing, a wet, raspy sound. From the other side of the long house came the squealing sound of new life. Mulhern opened his eyes at the sound and asked for a drink of water. A few minutes later the mid-wife came over, and handed the small bundle to Liam. Not able to hold back his tears he gently pulled down the cloth. "Glynnie Mulhern, meet Rebecca, your daughter."

Mulhern, with the help of Wahta, sat up and gazed down on his first born, tears rolling down his smiling face, "Ah, Becky sorry I won't be around, you're sure to be a beautiful lass." A sudden fit of coughing had Mulhern doubled over until it subsided. Exhausted, he lay back down, but before nodding off beckoned to Wahta, "Now listen carefully my savage friend; Momma Bear needs to keep watch over our cub."

Wahta laughed, "How will Momma Bear watch our cub without the little Irishman? I will do my best."

Mulhern slept for a few hours during which time Mitena and the baby came over to sit and wait with Liam, Wahta and Mishka. Wahta and Mishka were talking quietly; Liam was holding Rebecca, gazing at her big, bright eyes, and was overcome with a feeling of peace; in those eyes he could see happier times. They were all startled when Mulhern sat up, and in a rather lucid voice said, "Ah, there you are, Colonel, old son. Come to help me pass on? Well, then." He lay back down, and was gone.

Chapter 5 1771 – Treachery

Mallory Town

Bert clutched his aching side, but the pounding in his head brought on by the short trot to where the canoe was stashed had him falling to the ground. Sam reached down and helped Bert back on his feet, "Only a few more steps to go, can you make it?"

Bert leaned on Sam's shoulder and gasped, "Yes, I'll make it." Thomas steadied the canoe while Sam helped Bert climb in. When they were seated, they pushed off for the short pull across the river. Once across they had to walk about a quarter of a mile to the farm house. There was a well-worn path that ran from the river to the house, but they decided to stick to the woods that bordered the farm.

Hannah Lapley, her hands setting bread dough for the morning, heard a knock on the door. Hushing her children, she quickly wiped off her hands. Grabbing the musket she always kept handy she opened the door. "Sorry to barge in on you like this, Mrs. Lapley," Thomas started to say.

"My Lord in heaven! Come in," Hannah said and then turning to her daughter, "Ruth, get some water to boiling. We've a hurt man here."

Bert awoke after a restful night thanks to the ministrations of Hannah, and two cups of pennyroyal-wild cherry bark tea for the pain. She had applied one of the poultices Jack had made up to Bert's bruised ribcage; securing it in place with a linen bandage. While she was pretty sure no ribs were broken, she couldn't be sure that there might be a crack or two. One thing she was sure and adamant about, Bert was not fit for travel. Not until he could walk t without getting dizzy after a dozen steps. When Bert's eyes came into focus he saw sixteen year old Ruth sitting in a chair next to his cot. She was startled when he opened his eyes as she had been staring at him while he slept. Bert cleared his throat and said, "Not seen too many negroes, have you?"

Embarrassed at being caught she flushed red and stammered, "Oh, I am so sorry Mr. Sawyer. I didn't mean nothing by it."

"Call me Bert, I 'spect I'd stare too," he chuckled and that started his head to pounding.

Ruth went quickly into the kitchen and brought back another cup of the tea. He drank it gingerly because it was very hot, and because of the bite mark in his cheek. The pounding gradually receded from the staccato beat of a marching army to where it matched his heartbeat and he soon drifted off back to sleep.

****

Brightman made sure that only the faithful manned the main gate that night. Of course, that meant taking Richard Crane out of the picture. Brightman rubbed his left hand, wincing at the bruising already forming on his knuckles. "Bastard Crane sure has a hard jaw." he said to the guard, "Now, you know what to do? When the British arrive, probably just before dawn, you open the gate, and get out of the way." He headed to the church, needing a drink and some sleep; the drink to fortify himself for when Grantham discovers his prisoner has gotten away, the sleep, for the long days ahead. He walked into Grantham's office, poured a large whiskey, and sat on the couch he had been using for a bed. Looking across the room he stared into the eyes of Richard Crane, his hands and feet bound to a chair, and his mouth tightly gagged. Raising his glass in a toast, Brightman said, "I must say, Richard, next time we tangle I'll know better than to use my fist." Crane tried to yell but all that came out was a muffled cry. "Now, now, Richard," replied Brightman, "please try to remain calm and get some rest. Tomorrow promises to be very entertaining."

Major Whitby rode through the gate, resplendent in his finest redcoat, and tricorn cap. At his throat was a beautifully engraved gorget. At his side, hung a sword that had been handed down father to son for three generations. Behind him, setting up camp, were the two companies of his regiment chosen for this assignment. The 160 men would be encamped in 32 tents; the Major would be housed in the town. A detail was even now replacing any of the settlers manning the walls, while another was going building to building gathering the residents, and confiscating weapons. A third group, a mounted patrol, rode to the outlying farms bringing everyone into town.

Reverend Grantham and Brightman stood outside of the church while Whitby dismounted, "Good morning gentlemen. Our plan moves ahead; my congratulations on smoothing the way. I'll address the townsfolk shortly. As you can see, my men are already gathering them."

"Very well major," answered Grantham. Turning towards Brightman he said, "Go and fetch our runaway. Time to let the people know who's in charge as we decide the Negro's fate."

"Ah, yes, well you see Reverend, your runaway has, well, has run away in a manner of speaking. Through the back wall of the shed; no doubt with help from his friends," said Brightman calmly, a small smile playing across his face.

"You find this to be humorous, you fool? Just when were you going to inform me of this little problem?" fumed Grantham.

"I reckoned that right about now was a good time," replied Brightman, "I also reckoned they couldn't have gone too far. Your runaway is a bit beat up, and most likely could have used some medical attention. My guess is that they headed to the Lapley farm figuring to catch up with their patrol today. Poor sods; that patrol should be taken care of, right about now as it happens."

"As soon as my mounted patrol returns," interjected Whitby, "Mister Brightman will accompany them to the Lapley's, and do what is necessary to return the negro and his accomplices; alive if possible. I do so look forward to hanging the lot of them."

****

When they were about two miles from the village of Franklin, Daniel called a halt making sure everyone had their muskets loaded and ready. Jonas pointed in the direction of the besieged village and said, "What is the one thing you can rely on in an Indian attack? Fire; they always use fire as a weapon. I don't see any smoke, and that has me thinking we should be a little more cautious in our approach."

"I agree," said Henry, "something about this whole rescue doesn't seem right. I remember the messenger's horse, it had very distinctive markings." Henry scratched his head and exclaimed, "I just realized where I've seen it before. The last time Two Birds came to visit, he rode that same horse. I imagine it's the one he keeps for his, or his customers use. What if that messenger came from Fort Pitt, not from this raided village?"

Daniel thought for a moment, doubt now taking hold, the full understanding of what was happening hitting him suddenly. "Jonas, take Josiah with you, and scout ahead," he said, "my guess is we were lured out of town, and there's an ambush waiting for us."

Josiah Webb, oldest son of Seth and Anne, was not the most skilled woodsman, being more attuned to life as a farmer, but he took part in the regular patrols, and while he was an eager student, he knew he would never be as good as the men he rode with. One of the reasons that was so, is that he tended to let his mind wander, as he was doing now, even humming a little tune as he walked behind Jonas. "Young 'un, if you want to live, cease the noise," whispered Jonas, "get down, and be still. See that pile of boulders ahead? We're just gonna set here for a bit, and keep an eye on those rocks. If I was planning an ambush that is the spot I'd do it from."

Settling themselves on an oak tree covered hill, they were soon rewarded with the sight of a band of Seneca warriors taking positions in the strewn rocks below. Motioning for Josiah to quietly make his way back down the trail, Jonas took one last look, and saw the unmistakable red coated uniform among the Seneca. They quickly made their way back to Daniel and the others. "We were setup, that's for sure, and there's at least one British soldier with the Seneca just waiting for us," reported Jonas, "we would be hard pressed to survive the cross fire they have ready."

As he looked around at the faces of his companions, Daniel could see the concern on each one. The fact that they had been lured away from town to be killed in an ambush was one thing; the fact that their loved ones were now in some sort of danger was another matter altogether. A heated debate followed, some wanting to head back to the town immediately, others wanting to gather more information before heading into an unknown situation. In the end it was decided to go back by way of the Lapley farm, gather what information they could, and then decide on a course of action.

****

Brightman led the six mounted troopers off the ferry, and galloped toward the farm house. Before they reached it, he halted the men. Not wanting to be guilty of underestimating his foe, he dispatched two of the troopers to watch for anyone coming from the west. He dismounted, directing the four remaining troopers to search the barn and two sheds, and approached the house.

Hannah stepped out of the door, raised her musket, pointing it at Brightman, "That's far enough. What is the meaning of this?"

Inside the house, Bert, Thomas, and Sam were climbing down into a cellar below the kitchen. The trap door entrance was disguised to look like the surrounding flooring, and which was covered by the table used for food preparation. Once they were safely out of sight, Ruth and her brother John closed the trap door, pushing the table back into position.

Brightman put his hands out, drawing back his overcoat to show that he was unarmed, at least he wished to appear that way; the pistol tucked into his belt out of view, but readily accessible if needed. "Now Mrs. Lapley, there is no cause for the musket. I have been ordered by Major Whitby to apprehend the escaped runaway slave Bert Sawyer, and we have reason to believe that he and his accomplices may be here. I'm also charged with inquiring as to why you and your children did not show at yesterdays required meeting with the new shall we say, regime, in Mallory Town?"

"Bert and his friends are not here now. They stopped for an hour or so, then continued on. I didn't ask where they were headed, so you can call off your search and return to your masters. I do not recognize their authority, and I'm sure my husband doesn't either." She then turned to go back in the house, but stopped when she heard the sound of a pistol being cocked.

"I am truly sorry to have to do this ma'am, but I insist on searching your house," Brightman said reaching for and taking the musket away from Hannah. As he started through the door, his attention was drawn to the unmistakable sound of musket fire, and the shouts of the two troopers he had left watching the western approach.

****

The patrol backtracked until they came to a path leading to Jonas Lapley's farm. From there it was a two mile ride through a landscape dotted with the stumps of the oaks and maples used by Jonas for his buildings. Jonas led the way stopping when he reached a meadow that would soon be covered in wildflowers, and the sound of droning bees, dismounted, calling for Daniel and Henry to join him. He motioned them to follow him to the far edge of the meadow where a row of boulders formed a wall separating the meadow from cropland. He pointed in the distance to the two British cavalrymen riding across the field, and who were coming towards them.

Josiah also saw the horsemen, and thinking he might be needed ran across the meadow to the stone wall. One of the British soldiers saw him, pulled his horse to a stop, and grabbed his musket. As he aimed and fired, his partner set off back to the house shouting a warning. The shot struck the rock in front of Josiah sending a shard flying past his face. Jonas fired back and knocked the trooper from his horse as the ball battered his shoulder. At the sound of the musket fire, the rest of the patrol joined at the wall. Timothy went to check on Josiah who seemed to be a bit in shock after being shot at.

"I can't figure why the British are here," began Daniel, "but by the looks of it they're looking for something or someone."

"Whatever the reason, it seems our arrival has changed their plans," replied Henry.

Brightman saw one of the men go down, but could not tell who was firing at them. He yelled for the rest of his men letting, Hannah's musket fall to the ground, remounted, and told them to follow him. He knew, just knew it had to be Mallory. "I fear our ambush did not succeed," he said to the sergeant in command of the patrol, "let's fan out and see if we can drive them back." Just then a shot rang out from the farmhouse, throwing Brightman from his horse as it was hit in the neck. The sergeant halted the troop, and rode back to help Brightman, hauling him up behind him. "Change of plans, sergeant. Head to the ferry, we have enough of a head start to get across the river to deliver the good news before Mallory can get to us."

****

The room was full of tension and incredulous disbelief that the Mallory patrol survived the ambush, seemingly without a loss, according to the reports from the sergeant and Brightman. Grantham sat down after pacing around his office, his knuckles white from clenching his fists, both of which he slammed down on the desk. "How in the hell did this happen?" he snarled.

Whitby looked up from the report he received earlier about the mood of the townsfolk, and replied, "We'll figure that out in due time. What's important now is how do we deal with the situation? I'm thinking we have three options; we can do nothing about Mallory, but that doesn't solve anything; we can send a large enough force to rid us of the problem, but I'm not ready to sacrifice the lives of my men, yet. Not until we try option three, which is we send them a request to parley."

"Parley? Are you serious? We need to send them to hell," snapped Grantham.

"Temper, temper Reverend. I want to talk first, so that is what we are going to do," answered Whitby, "I suggest that as a just reward for having botched his last assignment that we send Brightman over with a white flag. Tell Mallory that it would be advisable to meet with us, say tomorrow at noon, outside the main gate."

Grantham looked over at a very tired and now somewhat riled Brightman, "You heard the Major. Take my horse since you managed to get yours shot out from under you."

Bristling with anger as he left the room, Brightman was still attentive enough, while closing the door, to hear Whitby say something about taking measures to ensure that Mallory and his gang were taken care of at the so called parley. He wanted to stay and hear more but Whitby's adjutant was coming over to the church, so he was obliged to make his way to the stable without knowing what those plans were. As he led his mount down to the ferry he came to the realization that he was beginning to, grudgingly he told himself, admire Daniel Mallory, and was starting to wonder if the good Reverend and Major Whitby had committed the cardinal sin of under estimating their foe.

****

The Lapley farm house was filled with the sounds of happy talk and laughter while they sat for breakfast the next morning. Everyone had been too tired last night to really enjoy the events of the past few hours, but now they all had tales to tell, and more importantly, plans to make. Thirteen year old John Lapley was the center of attention as he received praise for his courage, and some light hearted comments about how come he shot the horse instead of Brightman. Even Josiah Webb joined in, having recovered from almost being shot. James Crane was sitting outside watching the approach of a rider bearing a white flag, "We got company coming. Looks like Brightman and he's alone."

Daniel and Henry stepped outside to await Brightman. Josiah and James mounted up and rode toward the river to see if anyone else was coming. Jonas and Timothy stood on either side of Brightman as he dismounted; both had their muskets ready to fire. Thomas, Sam, and Bert stayed out of sight with Hannah, Ruth, and John in the kitchen. "Say your piece, Brightman," said Daniel, "and know this; if any harm comes to our families, or friends in town, we will not be merciful in our revenge."

Brightman smiled, "As to that, no one has been harmed; a little inconvenienced perhaps. What Major Whitby and Reverend Grantham need to know is what your intentions are, so request that you meet with them at noon today outside of the main gate. I suggest you do that. I'm afraid that they will progress beyond the mere inconveniencing of your family and friends if you do not. I also suggest, and this is coming from me, not Whitby or Grantham, that you come to this meeting expecting some duplicity from Whitby. I don't know what they have planned, just that they do not intend for this peaceful parley to be peaceful."

****

In the end, and after some discussion, they decided that Jonas would stay at the farm with his family. Initially Daniel wanted Bert to stay behind as well, but Bert could not be persuaded to stay, saying, "Those are bad men we be up against, and not to be trusted." He hoisted his powder horn onto his shoulder, lifted his musket and continued, "You may need me."

They rode along the Allegheny as it made a turn southward, making for a spot where it was fordable. The water was cold and belly high on the horses but they made the other shore without incident. Another advantage to crossing here was that they would be hidden from view of the town by a low ridge studded with boulders, and shrouded by some willows growing along the water's edge. Except for Daniel and Josiah, they dismounted, loaded their muskets and placed themselves to cover the parley. Daniel, with Josiah carrying a piece of white linen tied to his musket, rode a little further until the ridge dwindled and opened up to farmland. Here they paused and Daniel spoke, "Now, whatever happens, you need to remain silent, I'll do the talking. You stay alert, and if I say run, you hightail it out of there. Understood?"

Major Whitby rode out of the gate, Reverend Grantham at his side, and one trooper behind them holding aloft a white flag. Out of sight one mounted contingent waited behind the open gate, and another was already poised outside the walls on the north side of the town. "This should be interesting," said Whitby, "I see only Mallory, and one other coming to meet with us. I guess the others are up in those rocks. No matter, they'll scatter and try to run once I have Mallory, easy pickings for my men."

"The only advantage we have, young Webb," Daniel said to Josiah as they made their way to where Whitby and Grantham were waiting, "is that we know that they are going to try something. Keep your eyes on the gate. I reckon there are a few troopers looking for a signal to charge out." Reaching the waiting party from the town, Daniel and Josiah reined in their horses. Josiah watched nervously as Whitby came alongside him.

"I'm glad you decided to meet with us, Mr. Mallory," Whitby said as he sidled up next to Josiah's horse, "although I don't know why you came armed? This is a peaceful parley, Mr. Mallory."

"That's rather funny, coming from someone who just yesterday took over our town while sending us into an ambush. I am warning you major, nothing better happen to our families," replied Daniel.

Whitby reached into his jacket, pulled out a dispatch, and began reading:

From Headquarters of the Commanding General

At your earliest secure the upper reaches of the Allegheny River using whatever means and resources at your disposal.

Signed,

Thomas Gage

Colonial Commanding General

"So you see, Mr. Mallory, I have all the authority I need to do what I have done. As for you? Well, it seemed prudent to get you, and the other potential troublemakers out of the way. However, I underestimated you. I assure you, that won't happen again." Whitby unsheathed his sword and brought the hilt down on Josiah's head rendering him unconscious, and slumped in his saddle.

The corporal threw down the white flag, and he headed toward Daniel. The troops galloped out of the gate, and from around the corner. The group from the gate headed to the parley, the others went to take care of the rebels in the rocks. Grantham grabbed the reins of Josiah's horse, and galloped back to the town with the unconscious rider. Daniel raised his musket to take a shot at Whitby, but instead, using it as a club on the charging corporal, knocked him off of his mount. Whitby seeing an opportunity charged at Daniel. Daniel knew he had only one chance to avoid the charging Whitby. He pulled back hard on his reins causing his mount to rear, front hooves flailing at Whitby's horse, causing it to pull up sharply. Whitby was thrown back and then forward, slamming his nose into the horse's neck, the sound of breaking cartilage and bone eclipsed by his scream. While Whitby was occupied with staying mounted, Daniel regained control of his, and sped away to the ridge, three British troopers on his heels.

"Come on Daniel," shouted Henry who then turned to his companions, "Make sure of your shot, and reload quickly."

Bert and Thomas scrambled down the hill, kneeling behind the stump of an oak, watching Daniel get closer to the safety of the rocks and trees. Seeing one of the British troopers almost abreast of Daniel with his sword poised to strike, Bert rose to his feet, took aim and fired. The shot hit the trooper in the leg, passing through it, and into his horse, felling it, and in the process taking down the trooper behind him. Thomas took aim at the remaining soldier but pulled up when he saw the other group rapidly bearing down on their position. "We best get back to the others," he said to Bert, "we're gonna be a bit outnumbered in a minute."

Whitby looked down at the front of his blood splotched uniform, pulled a linen kerchief from his pocket holding it to his throbbing, bleeding nose. The sound of the unfolding skirmish brought his eyes up in time to see Bert's shot and the sight of that damned Mallory getting away. He had given orders for his men to pursue, capture, or kill the rebels, but not to go further than the river. He anticipated some resistance, but was confident in the men under his command, and was sure of the fighting capability of a British soldier versus frontier rabble, even if it is Daniel Mallory. He reflected that he would soon be rid of the Mallory's one way, or another. Unknown to even Reverend Grantham was that in the latest dispatch from Boston were new orders for Whitby to report to Gage's staff as Lt. Colonel. His momentary revel was interrupted by the blast of massed musket fire. The seven rebels were now clambering down the backside of the ridge, the carnage from their volley such that there was no more pursuit. Six British soldiers lie on the ground, four of them dead. The four unscathed troopers halted, and once they saw that their foe was leaving, tended to their wounded.

Brightman climbed down from the blockhouse chuckling at the bloodied nose the rebels had given the British, literally and figuratively. No longer was he an insider since being relegated to the simple role of an enforcer. Brightman was rapidly losing his zeal for the good Reverend. As such, he didn't think it a dereliction of duty to go see Liza and Deborah to tell them of the parley's outcome, and to warn them that very soon things might get harder for them.

Anne Webb burst into Liza's cabin, eyes reddened from shed tears, "They've taken my Josiah. He's to be tried as a spy and rebel. They're gonna hang my boy. Do you hear me? They're gonna hang my son!"

Liza put down the letter she was hoping to get out to Daniel and took Anne in her arms, a fresh bout of sobbing; her shoulders heaving into Liza. "Boys," she called to Caleb, Bowie, and Jack, "go on outside, but stay by the cabin." She had a sudden thought of the danger she was about to put those three and just as suddenly dismissed the idea...yes, much too dangerous. "Tell me about Josiah," she said to Anne, "and be strong. Don't give Whitby, or Grantham any sign of weakness to prey on."

"He was captured, knocked unconscious, and brought back into town. They have him bound and gagged over in Grantham's office. Whitby came in with a bloody face. It looks like his nose is broken." Anne stopped talking, a fresh bout of tears cascading down her face. Wringing her hands, she continued to speak, "He has issued a notice that Josiah will be tried in one hour. What are we going to do? Indeed, what can we do?"

Liza left Anne and the children with Deborah, and Margaret Jameson. Bearing a poultice for bruising, and some pennyroyal tea mix for pain, she stopped in front of Whitby's quarters informing the sentry that she wanted to treat the Major's injury.

"It's alright private," Whitby said in a stuffy voice, "after all, it was her brother gave me this. Do come in, Mrs. Clarke. I imagine you're here not only to restore my good looks, but to talk about the prisoner, what's his name again?"

Liza followed him into the room, and told Whitby to sit. "His name is Josiah Webb," she said somewhat forcefully as she twisted his nose, setting it back to its original position, "oh, yes, this might hurt a bit." Whitby tried to scream, but only managed a high pitched squeal that brought the sentry into the room. Whitby held his hand up signaling that he was not in danger as Liza took her hands away from his face. "There, that should do it," she said handing him the poultice, "this will help with some of the bruising and swelling, but you'll still be sporting a couple black eyes. I'll make you a cup of this tea while we talk about Josiah."

"There's not much to talk about, I'm afraid, Mrs. Clarke, though I do thank you for your medical expertise. The boy will be tried, and I daresay found guilty of being a spy, and a rebel against

King George III. As I explained to your brother, I have all the authority to do as I see fit to quell any rebellious activity in this area. Now, and this is a bit of irony, it is your brother I want to hang, not that young boy, but your brother is not here. I cannot think of how conflicted you might feel about that, glad that Daniel is not swinging from a gibbet while at the same time consoling the young lad's mother. All of that notwithstanding, you need to put away all thoughts of rescue, or retaliation in any form. I've kept Grantham at bay regarding the treatment of those he deems troublesome. That can be changed. I hope I have made myself clear, and now I must ask you to leave. I need to change into a clean uniform for the trial."

****

Brightman caught up with Liza as she was walking back to her cabin, a mixture of anger and sadness coming through as she talked to herself. "What do you want?" she barked at Brightman.

"I understand how you feel about me, Mrs. Clarke," he replied, "but we need to talk, somewhere out of sight, and I suggest we have that talk now."

She nodded, sensing something different about Brightman. He seems less sure of himself, she thought, as she headed toward her cabin. She would talk with him, but not alone. Deborah looked up as Liza walked in followed by Brightman, and was reaching for the musket propped up against the wall behind her when Liza spoke, "It is alright, Deborah. Mr. Brightman has something to say. Where are Anne and Margaret? They should be here as well. Unless I miss my guess, our Mr. Brightman has had a change of heart regarding his loyalty to Reverend Grantham."

"I will get them, they went to my cabin to bed down the children there," said Deborah as she got up to leave.

Brightman walked over to the table and sat down, "You are a very perceptive woman, Mrs. Clarke. I hadn't thought my feelings showed. I must be getting soft. I've spent the last ten years hiding my feelings, a necessary habit in my line of work, and yet you have read me like the proverbial book."

Liza went to the cupboard, grabbed a jug of ale, filled two mugs and handed one to Brightman. "A toast then," she said raising her mug, "to your change of heart."

He raised his mug in reply, and took a long drink, "I am honored. This is Winslow ale if I'm not mistaken. I appreciate the gesture. When the other women return we can begin planning, however, I must make it clear that there is nothing we can do about the boy."

"My boy?" said Anne as she walked through the door, "Are you saying we cannot save him? Then why are you here if not to try and rescue Josiah?"

"I'm afraid, Mrs. Webb, that they have him well guarded. They learned well from Sawyer's escape. There will be no rescue this time," he replied gesturing for them all to sit, "but, we can, if we are careful, get word to Daniel, and work with him on taking the town back. At present, any kind of assault will fail. There are just too many soldiers for Daniel and the rest to deal with."

"What other option do we have if an assault won't work?" asked Deborah.

"Mr. Brightman said that at present it won't work," remarked Margaret, "what do you know that we don't, Mr. Brightman?"

"More than what Whitby suspects I know. One of my many nefarious talents is the ability to open sealed dispatches in a way that doesn't make it appear to have been opened. Whitby has been promoted to Lieutenant Colonel, and has been ordered to report to General Gage in Boston. It also said that the garrison here can be reduced to the bare minimum. Part of the garrison is going to the big island upriver tasked with setting up a post there. The rest of the command is returning to Fort Pitt. What I don't know is when, but I'm pretty sure Whitby will stay here with the bulk of his command while they build a camp on the island, and that Grantham, once he finds out, will try to stall Whitby's leaving for as long as he can. Though I don't think Whitby cares too much for Grantham, or his hold on the town. This whole ploy was a steppingstone for Whitby; just a way to get noticed by the high command. He seems to have a knack for self-promotion. Apparently he sends regular dispatches to his superiors filled with his exploits and plans. They can't have known yet how this plan turned out, but they certainly knew about it, and approved it." Brightman paused for a moment to take a drink as he looked around the table at the four women, and was happy with the determined look on their faces. Anne still emitted an occasional sob, but that was to be expected he thought to himself.

In the end they decided that at the first opportunity Brightman would take the letter that Liza had finished, adding the new information about Whitby, to Henry and Daniel. He figured it wouldn't arouse any suspicion if he left the town, it was, after all part of his job to keep tabs on the whereabouts of the rebels. As for the women and their families, they would be conspicuous by their absence at the trial and the execution. Anne balked at this but Brightman convinced her that she should remember her son in ways other than seeing him like that.

****

Major Whitby looked out from the table where he sat presiding over the trial. He was not surprised at the absence of the Mallory faction, but he was puzzled that Anne Webb was also missing. He sensed the influence of Liza over the weaker Anne and wondered for a moment if things would have been different if Anne's husband was still alive. Well, with or without her presence, her son was going to hang.

The trial was being held in the church but since it was technically a military matter, Reverend Grantham was relegated to the front row as a spectator. This also meant that Brightman need not be concerned that he would be asked to take part in hanging the prisoner, so he just stood to the side as close to the front as he could manage while he watched the faces of the townsfolk as the trial progressed. He wanted to see if there was any sense of dissension among some of Grantham followers.

Josiah said not a word during the proceedings, his hate filled gaze moved back and forth between Whitby and Grantham. He knew he was going to die. The hope of rescue had been replaced last night with a stoic acceptance after a short visit from Brightman who had browbeaten the young private on guard into giving him a few minutes alone with the prisoner. He explained the situation to Josiah, and passed on his mother's last words to him. When Whitby pronounced the expected verdict of guilty, and that the sentence of hanging was to proceed immediately, Josiah's knees buckled a bit, but he caught himself and shook off the hands of the soldier who grabbed him to keep him from falling. He looked up at Whitby and spoke for the first time, "You had better learn to sleep with your eyes open. I will be avenged. May God have mercy on your soul, if you have one?" With that, the guard hit Josiah with the butt of his musket, catching the same spot he had been hit by Whitby. He went limp from the pain, and had to be carried out to the gallows.

Because Grantham insisted that the hanging be done so soon, there had been no time to build a proper scaffold. A large oak that had survived the settler's axes was chosen, the rope swinging ominously in the breeze from a stout branch. Whitby was thrilled with the location, especially since it was outside the walls, and the grisly sight of their comrade will be visible across the river. He doubted that this display of unfettered authority would do much to alter Daniel's plans, but it would almost certainly further intimidate the populace of the town, and that, at least, should please the good Reverend.

The only thing Josiah could do when he was asked if he had any last words was to stare blankly ahead. It was with some difficulty that they had roused him to this level of consciousness after the second blow to his head. Not even when they placed the noose around his neck did he utter a sound, but when Whitby began to back his horse away from the one Josiah sat upon, he spoke his last words, "Samuel will come for you." With that the soldier holding the reins to Josiah's horse let go of them slapping it on its rear. Josiah's body twitched three times while it swung back and forth, and then was still.

Grantham grinned at the sight, but soon backed away as the bowels and bladder of the lifeless body emptied itself filling the air with the stench of shit and piss. He approached Whitby and said, "Remember, we agreed that the body would stay hanging from that tree until the crows have had their fill."

"Oh yes, I remember. I will be placing a guard to keep anyone from trying to take it down," Whitby retorted, "Mind you; the guards will not interfere with the crows."

****

Deborah ate the last of her porridge, looking over at Anne who was trying to hide her grief behind a sad smile. When the squeal of an unhappy child in the other room caught her attention, she left Anne in the kitchen, going into the front room to break up whatever it was that young Ethan was doing to his sister Abigail, and their cousin Meagan. Liza and Margaret were over at the Cranes talking to Richard and Hilda, and the three older boys were doing their morning chores, so no one saw Anne leave the cabin by the back door. Lifting her eyes above the town walls, she was greeted by the grisly sight of just Josiah's head, being pecked at by a crow. She put her hand in her mouth to keep from screaming. Racing across the compound, and through the south gate, she approached the tree. The guards had orders to keep everyone away from the tree so they stepped in front of Anne who fell on her knees and pleaded to be let through.

Jack came out from the shadow of the chicken coop and saw Mrs. Webb running to the gate. "Aunt Deborah," he said panting from his run to the cabin, "Mrs. Webb is going to the tree."

"Oh God," she blurted, "get Caleb and Bowie, and take the other children over to the Cranes. Tell Aunt Liza that I've gone after Anne." While she waited for the boys, she put on her moccasins, not having time to change from her nightgown and robe into her usual daytime dress. She stepped back into the front room in time to see the three boys herding their charges toward the Crane's cabin, and taking a deep breath to compose herself, headed to the gate.

"My boy! My Josiah! What have they done to you?" Anne sobbed as Deborah bent down to cradle her in her arms, and to turn her away from the gruesome sight of her son.

"Guarding a bloody corpse all night, and now a sobbing woman", thought the private as he took another pull on the skin of ale he'd been drinking. "Hey now, what's this?" he muttered, catching a glimpse of Deborah's slightly open robe.

"Come on Anne, let's go back," she said while keeping a firm grip on Anne's arms, lifting her to her feet. With all of her attention on Anne, Deborah failed to notice the leer of the guard reaching down to lend a hand, "Thank you, private," Deborah said thinking it was odd that the guard smelled of ale, and she started Anne walking with a gentle nudge.

Liza met them as they came through the gate, "Here, I'll take her," she said, "You can meet us at the Cranes after you change."

Deborah smiled, "Yes, it has been a busy morning. I'll be over soon."

****

Private Higgins scarcely acknowledged the relief crew before he was scampering through the gate, slowing down when he saw that Deborah was now alone, and heading to her cabin. The fact that the reason he was in the army was to escape a charge of rape did not occur to him as he followed her, reaching the door just behind her. Deborah turned when she heard the door scrape the floor as it opened, and was about to speak. Higgins rushed in, clamping his hand over her mouth, whispering into her ear, his breath stinking of sour ale. "Ain't you a lovely piece," he said as he shoved a bandana into her mouth, and threw her to the ground. He came to rest on her back, pulling her arms back in order to tie her hands together. Deborah tried to buck him off, but he was a heavyset man keeping her pinned to the floor. She turned her head watching in horror as he began undoing his breeches when her eyes were drawn to the sight of her son Bowie with knife drawn, rushing into the room, Caleb and Jack right behind.

The British soldiers were used to seeing the three boys as they wandered about the compound, their usual routine of patrolling the walls often brought out some good natured joking, even an occasional lesson on marching, so it wasn't out of the ordinary for the three to be out on their own. They were on the way back to Bowie's cabin to see if there was anything else they could do for Deborah, but as they had chosen to walk the wall's perimeter they were unseen by Higgins. "Why's that Lobsterback following your ma into the cabin?" Caleb asked.

"I don't know, but I don't like it," Bowie answered as he pulled out the knife he always kept hidden in his boot, "come on!" They sprinted out of the shadow of the wall, Bowie in the lead. Bowie peered into the window seeing his mother lying on the floor with a gag in her mouth, the soldier setting on her back. He shoved open the cabin door. The first thing he saw was Higgin's bare arse seemingly suspended in mid-air, followed by the look of total shock on Higgin's face as Bowie's knife sunk in. He rose up backhanded Bowie across the face, and was starting to take the knife from his buttock when Jack and Caleb jumped on him. Jack had Higgins around the head while Caleb tackled his legs. Caleb bit Higgins on the hand reaching for the knife, and pushed the blade further into the wound.

Higgins screamed, "I'll have your bloody bollocks for that!" as he reached down to pluck Caleb off his leg.

Bowie, his upper lip split and bleeding, the taste of copper on his tongue, had come to rest near his mother's face. He pulled the gag from her mouth, sat up to get back into the fray, and said to her, "Be right back, you start hollering for help." He threw himself into the exposed back of Higgins, knocking him to the floor. Jack was able to roll away but was quickly back pummeling Higgins about his head. Caleb was lying stunned across Higgin's feet having been thrown as the soldier was falling. Bowie grabbed the knife and pulled it out of the wound, and with Jack's help rolled Higgins over. Seeing Higgin's now flaccid penis he gave thought to cutting him there, but instead brought the hilt down across Higgin's face, knocking him senseless. He then cut the rope that bound his mother's hands, and was immediately pulled into a sobbing embrace.

"Oh Bowie, Caleb, Jack" she cried, "I don't know what we'd do without you boys." She pulled Jack and Caleb into the embrace, the four of them stunned from the event. A British soldier burst into the room followed quickly by Whitby and Liza all of them having been alerted by Deborah's cries for help.

Whitby quickly sized up the situation, and told the other soldier, pointing at the prone figure of Higgins "Get him out of here, now. Take him to the infirmary." Turning to Deborah he said, "Mrs. Mallory, you as well as the boys, will remain here in your cabin, until a formal inquiry is made."

"A formal inquiry? That man tried to rape me," she replied.

"That will be determined, Mrs. Mallory. Until such time, and for your protection, I am placing a guard on this cabin," he said as he closed the door behind him.

"I don't understand," Deborah said to Liza, "why is he acting like it was anything other than a rape?"

"Oh, I'd wager a wagon load of hides that he sees this as another chance to flaunt his authority. We will need to prepare ourselves for a far different outcome than we expect from this formal inquiry," Liza replied, "now, are you alright? Did he?"

Deborah shuddered but then with a smile answered, "No. Thanks to these brave boys, I mean men, I was spared that."

Liza turned to look at them, "Yes, they are men now, and have wounds that need tending. Jack, go get what we need."

Chapter 6 1771 - Deliverance

Lapley Farm – 2 days later

Thinking it was best, Daniel sent Samuel along with Henry to the Oneida camp along Buffalo Creek. Samuel had watched from the rocks as his brother was first taken by the British, and then in disbelief and horror yesterday as Josiah was hanging from the large oak that grew between the town walls and the river. It took more than just verbal persuasion to convince him not to do anything rash. He saddled his horse, not really knowing what he was going to do, only that Whitby and Grantham needed to die. Bert grabbed him from behind pinning his arms while Thomas yanked his feet. They managed, after a struggle, to manhandle Samuel back into the farm house where they threatened to tie him to a chair, and leave him there. He stopped his thrashing about and looked at Thomas, "You know I will not give up my vengeance, but I will wait for the right time, no matter how long. As long as I have breath left in my body, if it takes the rest of my life, Whitby and Grantham will die. Now please let me down." He smirked and said, "I see it took two of you to hold me down. Good plan. I can whip any one of you."

Daniel poured himself another cup of coffee, returning to the table where Henry, Timothy, and Jonas were continuing to discuss their options. Samuel and Bert were tending the horses while Thomas and James Crane were watching the approach from the river. Daniel sat down, "The way I see it is that we need to know more of what is going on before we can decide on a plan of action. We should concentrate on that aspect first. Maybe we could..." He was interrupted by Brightman being shoved into the room by Thomas, his musket in Brightman's back. Startled as he was by that, he was plumb stunned when following Thomas he saw his son Bowie, and Liam's twins, Jack and Caleb.

"What in the name of all that is holy is going on?" asked Daniel, "what are you doing here, Brightman? Why are the boys with you?"

"First, Mr. Clarke? Can you have young Thomas remove that musket from my back?" replied Brightman, who sighed a relieved breath when Thomas pulled back when his father nodded his head, "now, second, I am going to reach into my pocket. I have a letter from Mrs. Clarke for you and Daniel. That will explain why I'm here. I'll give you a few minutes to read and then we'll talk."

Daniel and Henry sat down with the letter spread out before them, both looking up at each other in surprise as they read. Henry folded it when they finished and put it in his pocket. "Well, that is full of surprises," he said looking over at his three nephews, "make no mistake about that. Why the change of heart, Mr. Brightman? Is it something to do with this formal inquiry Liza mentions?"

"Let's just say that was the tipping point. The way that they intended to use our friend Bert started the process, and that despicable display of power, hanging an innocent boy did much to further my defection. I suggest that you call in the rest of your men; they should all hear what I have to say. While we wait for them, is there any more of that coffee?" said Brightman, taking a seat, and smiling as Mrs. Lapley brought him a mug.

A few moments later Thomas returned with James, Bert, and Samuel. When Samuel saw who was sitting at the table, he rushed in pulling a knife from his belt, "You killed my brother!"

"Samuel, no!" screamed Daniel as he stepped in front of Brightman, grabbing Samuel's arm, "he had nothing to do with that. Now put that knife away, and listen to what he has to say."

Samuel relaxed shaking off Thomas, and Bert who had seized him from behind. He looked at Brightman with contempt and said, "Very well, I'll listen to what he has to say."

Brightman smiled at Samuel in an effort to calm him down, "Thank you, young Webb. I'm pretty sure you will change your opinion of me in a few moments." He then stood up, and began his tale.

****

One Day Earlier – Mallory Town

Major Whitby strode into the infirmary tent changing his smile into a snarl as he addressed Higgins. The knife wound was being stitched, his bare arse quivering with every stroke of the needle. Grantham and Brightman followed him in. "Private, you are a miserable excuse for a British soldier, and should be hung, but it is your lucky day. You have presented me with the perfect opportunity to squelch the Mallory family. Listen up, do as I say, and you will live." Higgins could only nod his head, and wince in pain as the surgeon poured some wine on the wound as he continued stitching. "The woman, she led you on. The harlot tempted you, wearing her nightclothes out in public, smiling at you, offering a glimpse as she bent over to help Mrs. Webb, mouthing enticements, whispering for you to come to her cabin. Whereupon you were brutally attacked, suffering these grievous wounds. That is all you have to say at the inquiry. I will take care of the rest."

Whitby left the tent and with Grantham went to the church with Brightman following behind. "What kind of lunacy is this?" Brightman asked as he entered the room, "you can't be serious about that bullshit story."

"Not that this is any of your concern, Mr. Brightman," replied Whitby, "but, yes, I am serious about that bullshit story. The inquiry will find Higgins innocent, the woman and the boys guilty of attacking a British soldier while he was in the, shall we say, performance of his duty. I would have thought you would understand how power and politics make pragmatic use of situations some would find distasteful. The point, Mr. Brightman, is that this gives us what we need to further our aims. Imagine how Daniel Mallory will react to the charge that his wife is an adulteress who along with his son, and nephews, will be flogged for their transgressions. He will act out of anger, and make the crucial mistake to try and retake this town; a task that he will find impossible. Besides, Mr. Brightman, it is entirely a military inquiry. The only part you need play is to help gather the good folks of this town. The inquiry will begin in an hour."

Whitby entered the church, stood at the podium, and gazed out at the filled pews. There was a murmur running through the townsfolk, gossip of the event having already started. As Deborah and the children were brought in a few of the more vocal among them could be heard making comments about that "Jezebel and whore." Private Higgins entered, slowly making his way to the front of the church where he was to be questioned by Whitby. He kept his eyes straight ahead not wanting to look at the woman, or the boys he was about to condemn. To the occasional cheer he told his story while Liza held Deborah's hand and stared daggers at Whitby. Having decided that if the inquiry took on an ominous tone she would not testify or dignify any questions with any answers, Deborah remained silent when she was brought to the front of the church. Repeatedly asking for her version of the story, Major Whitby, his patience finally running out, banged his hand down on the podium and said, "Mrs. Mallory, I have no choice but to find you guilty of attempting to corrupt the morals of a British soldier with your lewd behavior. I also find the three boys guilty of attacking a British soldier without cause. You will be held in your cabin along with the boys, the sentence of flogging to be carried out in two days."

****

Brightman approached Whitby's tent knowing that his efforts would most likely be fruitless, but he felt he had to try anyway. As he was talking to the sentry on duty, Private Higgins came out of the tent, and picked up a rucksack lying just outside the tent entrance. His face was a mass of bruises and he grimaced with every painful step. He was accompanied by three other soldiers, a guard, Brightman realized. The sentry announced Brightman, and held open the tent flap for him to enter. Whitby was sitting at his camp desk, a goblet of wine in his hand. "Ah, Brightman, come on in, have a seat. Would you like some wine?" he asked, "Quite the morning, wouldn't you say?

I've not had such a good stretch of days in recent memory. All that is missing is Daniel Mallory, and his band of outlaws and rebels, but I think I may have forced his hand today. He'll have to make the attempt to take back the town to save his wife and the boys. That Higgins did us a huge favor, too bad he won't be here to enjoy our eventual triumph. I'm having a camp built on the big island up river. One that will be big enough for a company of 150 men, and Private Higgins has just volunteered to be part of the building crew. He doesn't know it yet, but he has also volunteered to be on permanent latrine duty. Now, what is it you want to talk about?"

Brightman accepted a goblet of wine and took a sip before speaking. "This is an excellent vintage. I'm guessing it is some of Two Birds French stock. Yes, very fine indeed." He put the goblet down, "Maybe it's the fact that I used to be a pretty good preacher, and that I really thought God cared for us, especially for women and children. That has me wondering why you see the need to punish the boys for protecting a woman, their mother and aunt from a predator. Surely you don't mean to flog the innocent."

"I am surprised at your reticence, Mr. Brightman," Whitby replied, "Reverend Grantham has no such qualms, and he is currently the spiritual guide for this hamlet. In fact he wants me to go even further and flog the whole Mallory clan, and their followers. I've managed to placate him somewhat with the promise that if Daniel doesn't attack in the next two days, I will find cause to do what he desires. So, to answer your question, yes, I mean to flog the Mallory woman, and her would be rescuers, and I have sent a message to the Lapley farm informing them of my intent."

It was at that moment that Brightman knew he no longer wanted to be part of this madness, and that surprised him given that for the last ten years he had lived a life not dissimilar in its approach to human worth versus the ultimate goal of the enterprise. "An admirable plan," Brightman answered, "I know this is a military matter and all, but if the need arises for my help, just say the word."

"Why, thank you, Mr. Brightman. It may well be that your services will be required once I send the building crew to the island. Your assistance will not go unnoticed; I can assure you of that. Now, if you'll excuse me. It's been a busy day, and I still have more to do," Whitby said rising from his chair and offering his hand to Brightman.

Brightman took another sip of wine and took Whitby's hand. As they shook Brightman felt a sense of revulsion. Letting go of Whitby's hand, he turned, and hurried out of the tent, barely making it to his room in the church before vomiting up the contents of his stomach. When he stopped retching, he sat upon his bed, and began formulating a plan.

****

Liza, lost in thought about the alarming series of events, found herself, not for the first time, wishing Liam was there, stared at the plate of food she had no appetite for. Pushing it away she was startled by a knock on the back door. "Mrs. Clarke, it is me, Brightman." She opened the door noticing that he was carrying a satchel, and dressed for traveling. "I need you to do something before they decide not to let anyone near Deborah and the boys. Go over and have the boys readied to leave an hour after sunset. I will not stand by and see them hurt in order to further Whitby and Grantham's plans. I will take them across the river to the Lapley farm. I wish I could get Deborah out as well, but that may be impossible right now. Let me have that letter as well. Best that Henry and Daniel know what they are up against, and that it comes from you rather than just me."

Lapley Farm

"God's bollocks," screamed Henry, "those bastards need to be stopped."

"I agree, as do the rest of us I imagine,' replied Daniel, "but with what our new friend has told us, it would seem we would be playing right into their hands if we try an attack now."

"Mr. Brightman is that hidden gate still unknown to the British, and Grantham?" asked James Crane.

"Why yes, I do believe so," responded Brightman, "and I have been pondering how we can use that to our advantage. The obvious, and extremely risky, play is to have one of us go in and get Deborah, Liza, and probably Anne Webb out of there. It's my line of country, but by now they will have figured out who took the boys, and my appearance is rather hard to disguise." That brought a smattering of chuckles from around the table; even Samuel had a smile on his face.

James scratched the top of his head and looked around the table. "I think I may be the logical choice. I am the least recognizable member of this group, and since I helped build it, I know how the gate works. If there are no objections, I will go in tonight."

"If I may offer some suggestions," said Brightman, "I brought the boys out by way of the lumber mill and I think that would be the best way for James to get in. The less attention we draw to the gate by the Mallory's cabin the better. Take the canoe I used, but your return may have to be by the ferry depending on how many you manage to bring out. That will prove to be the most dangerous part of the plan, as the British will certainly see any activity in that area."

"I would stick to canoes," said Daniel, "however, instead of coming straight across the river, head upstream to the valley we use to keep hidden when scouting. Liza can handle a paddle as well as any man."

"I would feel a whole lot better if we got all of our children out," added Henry, "we know they have no misgivings about flogging youngsters. What if they decide to punish the others?"

The cabin, having been built for the Lapley family of four, proved to be too small for everyone to gather comfortably, so the discussion and planning took place around a fire outside. One other advantage to this was that they could illustrate their ideas by drawing in the dirt. It took some time to sort through the options, and the best way to pull this escape off, but in the end it was decided that it being obvious that the Lapley farm would be the first place the British looked, so Henry would take Samuel, their destination the Oneida village on Buffalo Creek to prepare for the arrival of everyone else. Jonas, Bert, and Brightman would go down to the river with James providing covering musket fire if it was needed. The rest would pack up what they needed to make the trek to the Oneida village some 30 miles to the north of Mallory Town. Most of the terrain was wooded with only a few game trails, none of them wide enough to enable passage for wagons, so it would be by horseback, and foot that they made the journey. The children with Daniel's group would make use of the horses. The children with James' group, however, would have to walk or be carried so Jonas and Brightman were going to rendezvous with James upriver in order to lend a hand. Bert was still too sore to carry a child, so he would join the group heading to Buffalo Creek once James and his charges were on their way up the river.

Fortunately for James the moon was a thin crescent that night as he paddled noiselessly across the river. He beached the vessel and keeping a low profile entered the lumber mill. The way to his first stop, Liza and Henry's cabin, was across an open space with no buildings to shield his movement. Pulling his hood down as far down as it would go and still leave him able to see where he was going, he sighed, took a deep breath, left the mill, and headed across the compound. Walking as normally as he could manage with his heart beating much faster than normal he went past Deborah and Daniel's cabin taking note of the sentry posted outside the front door. He would have to be distracted, or eliminated if the plan was going to work. When he reached Liza's he rapped softly on the door startling Anne Webb who was staying with Liza causing her to drop the mug of tea she was holding. James opened the door when he heard the noise. Liza looked up from the table and exclaimed, "James?"

"Yes ma'am," he replied, "we don't have much time. I've come to get you and the others out of here including the children and Mrs. Webb." He explained the plan while Liza and Anne woke up Meagan, Ethan, and Abigail. When they were dressed and had packed what they needed, Liza headed over to Deborah and Daniel's cabin. James followed her, and when she had drawn the attention of the sentry away from his approach, he came up from behind, knocked him unconscious and dragged him into the cabin.

Hearing the commotion, Deborah came out of the bedroom where she had been unsuccessfully trying to fall asleep, the prospect of being stripped, tied to a post, and suffering the pain of the lash weighing heavy on her mind. "Deborah," said Liza, "hurry and get dressed. Pack some essentials; we're leaving Mallory Town for the time being."

"Oh thank God," she replied, "I won't be but a few minutes."

While she was getting ready, James bound, gagged, and dragged the sentry into the bedroom, closing the door. "We will leave by the hidden gate behind the Trading Post," said James, "there are two canoes. I will take the three children with me. Liza will take you and Anne in the other one. We will not go straight across the river but head upstream to a spot we frequently use for scouting missions. If all goes well, Brightman and Jonas will meet us there. The rest will be on their way to Kariwase's village on Buffalo Creek."

They managed to make the short walk to the Trading Post without being seen. Liza gathered the three children making sure they understood what was going on, and that they needed to be absolutely quiet. James opened the back door taking a moment to see if there was anyone by the canoe landing. The way being clear he waved to Liza to bring everyone out and into their canoe. James and Liza pushed their respective canoes out into the river, clambered aboard, and began paddling.

Whitby, having drunk more wine than usual that night, stepped out of his tent to relieve himself. When he had finished he glanced over to the Mallory cabin wondering if Deborah found it hard to sleep. "Where the hell is the sentry?" he muttered heading over to the cabin to see what was going on vowing to clap the guard in irons if he wasn't on duty. He opened the door, and saw his man struggling to loosen the rope that tied his hands. Whitby pulled the gag out of his mouth, "Where is the woman?"

"Sorry Major, sir. I was hit from behind and knocked out cold. When I came to she was already gone."

"I'm going to the canoe landing," Whitby said, "I need you to get some of the men from the gate, and head over there."

Grabbing the sentry's musket, Whitby ran out of the cabin heading toward the river when he heard the sound of a paddle splashing in the water. "Damn it all! I can't see a thing in this dark," he said when he arrived at the landing, "of all the beetle-headed, cock ups." Putting the musket to his shoulder, he fired a shot in the direction of the splash.

James glanced back to the landing thinking they would be safe now that they were on the way. A muzzle flash caught his eyes, and then he heard someone scream from the other canoe. Jonas, Bert, and Brightman hidden behind some trees on the other side immediately fired back when they saw the flash. One bullet grazed Whitby leaving a shallow bleeding furrow across his upper arm. More soldiers rushed over returning fire, but Jonas, and Brightman had already left to meet up with James. Bert stayed crouched behind the tree, reloaded, fired back, and then began to slowly retreat toward the farm.

Deborah heard the shot, and then Anne screaming as she slumped forward, blood seeping through her clothing, the lucky shot having hit her in the back. "Liza!" shrieked Deborah, "Anne's been hit."

"I know, but we can't stop here," she replied, "tend to her as best you can."

Deborah, carefully as to not tip the canoe, turned around, and moved to the center of the craft where Anne had fallen. She could not see much because of the dark, but she could smell the blood, and when she pulled her hand off of Anne it was covered with it. "Anne? Can you hear me?" asked Deborah, but there was no reply. Deborah felt for Anne's neck, "I can't feel a pulse," she said to Liza, "I think she's dead."

****

The march to the Oneida village was arduous given the terrain, but Caleb, Bowie, and Jack thought it was the best adventure they could imagine. Despite the time of night, and the excitement they had already endured they managed to stay awake while alternately walking and riding every few miles. It was a few hours before dawn when the group stopped to take a breather before continuing on, the boys found it hard to fall asleep. "You boys stop your talking, and get some sleep," admonished Timothy, "we need you to be rested. The trek gets harder from here on out; lots of hills lie ahead." After a few more giggles, and the welcome embrace of Hannah Lapley, they were silent, and soon sleeping alongside Ruth and John.

Thomas and Bert sat huddled around the small campfire, Bert wincing from the exertion that had aggravated his sore ribs. Daniel and Timothy back tracked a short ways to see if anyone was following. "I imagine that if all goes well we should be at the village by dusk tonight," said Daniel, "and James should be there about the same time."

Timothy took a drink from his water skin passing it over to Daniel, "I wonder how long it will be before the British find out where we've gone?" asked Timothy.

"That depends on which group they want to find; us or James, though I think we'll be the target. Whitby wants us more than the women and children. One thing in our favor is that they will have to wait until daylight to find our trail."

"Yeah, the moon will not help them, and we know the country a lot better than they do," replied Timothy.

Daniel yawned, stretched out his arms, and said, "Get some shuteye. I'll watch for a bit, wake you in a couple hours, and then it'll be my turn to close my eyes. We'll resume our trip once the sun rises above those hills to the east."

****

James helped Liza carry Anne's body out of the canoe, laying her down on the ground, all of them shocked at the dreadful turn of events; tears on all their faces, the children crying, and clinging to Deborah. "First his father and little sister die from sickness, then his brother is hung, and now his mother killed by a lucky shot in the dark," said James, "Samuel was already intent on killing Whitby and Grantham."

"I fear this night's sadness may change that sweet boy," replied Liza, "though I pray he gets his revenge."

James rose from the ground, looking back into the woods in the direction of the Lapley farm. "I hear someone coming," he said grabbing his musket, "everyone get down behind those rocks over there." Liza and Deborah gathered the children, and scurried behind the boulders while James crouched behind a canoe, his musket at his shoulder ready to fire.

"James? Are you there?" said Jonas as he appeared out of the trees.

"Jonas, Brightman? Thank God it's you," answered James, "come on ahead. We've had some trouble. Anne was shot and killed."

While James and Jonas fashioned a litter out of fallen tree limbs and lashed them crossways to the canoe paddles in order to carry Anne, Brightman and Liza pulled the canoes out of the water, hiding them in the brush and rocks. "This means that Deborah and Liza will have to carry the two youngest," said Brightman, "the three of us will take turns carrying the litter with the one not occupied with that task carrying Meagan." "This is going to slow us down quite a bit," said Liza, "but I see no other way." So, with Ethan and Abigail clinging to Liza and Deborah and Meagan to Brightman, James and Jonas lifted the litter, and headed into the valley. The going, usually an easy hike along the creek bed, became much harder with the need for frequent stops. The children became tired quickly and even the adults were being worn down by the extra burdens they bore. Finally, too exhausted to go any further they settled among a grove of birch trees to rest until daylight.

****

Whitby stood in the Lapley's kitchen while his men formed up to begin their march having scoured the surrounding area with his Seneca scouts for the trail that would lead him to the long overdue reckoning with Daniel Mallory. They were pretty sure that not all of their foes left from here, as they could not locate any of the canoes used last night, and the trail they found led north though there was evidence that at least two of the outlaws did go upriver. Therefore, he split his force into two. He led the group following the northern trail, while a smaller contingent of eight soldiers and two scouts would take the river trail.

"I have too much at stake to sit idly by," Grantham said to Whitby, "and besides I have a score to settle with that traitorous bastard Brightman. So, if you don't mind, I will go with the patrol following our escapees upriver."

"Fine with me, but remember, my sergeant is in charge, not you." answered Whitby. "You do know that Brightman might not be with that group."

Grantham' face contorted into an angry grimace, "If he isn't, know this. I want him alive. Do you understand me Whitby?"

"Mr. Grantham, you have my word that I will do all I can to keep him for you, if possible. No guarantees though, mind you, anything can happen when bullets start flying." replied Whitby. "Now if you'll excuse me it is time to go. Good luck, and good hunting."

****

Daniel couldn't sleep. He stepped outside and noticed that Henry was also awake sitting by a cook fire. Henry handed him a mug of coffee, "You worried about James and the others too?"

"They should have been here two days ago," replied Daniel, "we best head out at first light."

"I agree," said Henry, "but, not us. We're getting old Daniel and we've been on the go for about a week straight."

Daniel sat down, a grunt escaping from his lips, "Not that old, but old enough to have youngsters who can do the job. You're right, we need to rest up, we'll be busy enough for a while more I reckon."

Henry stirred the fire sending sparks into the air, "So, we send Timothy and my Thomas. What about Samuel?"

Daniel shook his head, "No, not Samuel. I want him close by so we can keep an eye on him. If Bert is up to it, he can join Timothy and Thomas, and I'm sure Kariwase will spare a couple of his men."

"It'll be dawn soon," said Henry getting to his feet, "may as well wake them up now."

****

James waved the others on, stopping to wipe his brow. The noon sun and nary the breath of a breeze were causing a steady stream of sweat to run down his face. He'd had the feeling that they were being followed, as did Jonas. They were now crossing a clearing which meant they were visible to whoever was tracking them. He looked back to the edge of the woods they had just left, and then looked forward to the trees they were heading toward. At this pace it would take them at least an hour and he wasn't sure how long they could keep that pace as they would soon reach a series of rolling mounds that would tax their waning energy. The children could only go so fast, and needed frequent stops. He picked up his pack and started to follow, taking one more glance back. There was movement in the trees revealing the Seneca scouts followed by the soldiers. James hurried away quickly catching up with Jonas and Brightman who were carrying the litter. "British soldiers, and Seneca scouts just entered the clearing. They'll be upon us before we reach the woods yonder."

"Well, there's nothing for it," Jonas said putting his end of the litter down, "we cannot carry Anne any further if we're going to make it. I'll run ahead, and speed up the women and children. You and Brightman need to hold them off. I'll high tail it back here once the others are in the trees. Make your shots count. I'll leave my musket. I can grab Liza's to use when I come back."

****

Grantham made his way forward to where the sergeant was speaking with the Seneca scouts. "Ah, Sergeant Kelly, is it?"

"Kelleher, Mr. Grantham, uh Reverend Mr. Grantham, Sergeant Paul Kelleher of the Donegal Kelleher's. Finest Irish family the Good Lord ever graced this green earth with. Now, what's on your mind?"

Grantham pointed ahead, "What did the scout say? Have we spotted our prey?"

Sergeant Kelleher, a veteran of many years on the frontier, was feared by recruits, respected by his peers, and certainly not bothered by the prattling of civilians. He put his hands on Grantham's shoulders, their faces next to one another facing the trail left by the passage of the escapees, "We are not chasing prey, Reverend. We are in pursuit of women and children. The scout says they passed by here twenty, maybe thirty minutes ago, and appear to be slowing down. I'm going to have the boys take a breather before we continue in this heat."

Grantham shook himself out of the sergeant's grasp, a look of disbelief on his face, "Take a breather? Sergeant I insist we carry on immediately!"

"Aye, Reverend, but you see, as the good Major said, I am in charge of this mission. We will rest for half an hour, then we will be at the trot. I suggest you have a rest. I wouldn't want you to fall behind. We'll be up with them before nightfall."

Grantham turned to walk away, stopped and said, "Alright Sergeant Paul Kelleher, one thing I would ask, however. If Brightman is with this group, I want him alive."

"As the Major also said, we will do what we can to accommodate your wishes in this regard," replied Kelleher. "You know, this whole venture is rather strange, at least to me."

"And how is that, Sergeant?" asked Grantham.

"You may not know this, my good Reverend," continued Kelleher, "I was with both Braddock and Forbes in the late war. Served with the Mallory's during those campaigns; went on many a scout with 'em. Never saw anyone like Liam Mallory for woodcraft, not even our Seneca can match him, and I consider them top notch. His brother Daniel ain't no slouch neither."

"Oh please, spare me the praise of our enemy, Sergeant," said Grantham with a sneering look on his face, "besides neither of them is here. I'm almost positive that Daniel is being pursued by Major Whitby, and Liam is God knows where, but it won't be around here." Grantham gave a little chuckle, "You know? I heard a rumor that someone blew up a cache of munitions over at Fort Michilimackinac. I wouldn't be a bit surprised to find out that Liam had something to do with that."

Kelleher smiled, "I heard that too. And meaning no disrespect to yourself, but anyone who has been trained by either one of them is someone to be wary of. We are going to proceed assuming they know we are close, and that they will be taking measures to slow us down. So, please keep your wits about you, and as I will instruct the men, no one fires until I give the order."

****

Brightman lowered the telescope he was peering through, "They'll be within range in a few minutes. Grantham is with them."

"The others are still ten minutes from reaching the trees," James replied taking the telescope from Brightman, "you think the good reverend might be a mite sore with you?"

"Oh, you can be pretty sure he has issued orders that I be taken alive," said Brightman, "Grantham is a little shy in the turn the other cheek department." Brightman grabbed James pulling him down behind the boulder they were using for cover. "We've been spotted by their scouts. Remember the plan, we both fire at once. I'll reload while you fire Jonas' musket. I'll fire, and then while you reload, I'll start retreating. We keep moving back between shots until Jonas comes to join us."

"I suppose I should have inquired earlier," James said, "are you a good shot, Mr. Brightman?"

"Mediocre, I'd say. Always been more interested in close up work," replied Brightman chuckling, "and losing an eye certainly hasn't helped."

****

Pausing at a small creek to let their mounts drink, Bert was amazed at the stamina of the three Oneida braves. Even though afoot they were able to keep pace, and seemed no worse for it. "If I remember right, there's a clearing not too far ahead," said Timothy, "if James is caught out there, it'll be hard going. Let's load up now, and no heroics. We need to see what we're up against first." They remounted and rode ahead. Hearing the sound of musket fire, they spurred them into a gallop. They halted at the edge of the trees and watched as Liza and Deborah led the children toward them.

Jonas called out to them, "Come quick, Brightman and James are in a spot of trouble."

Timothy looked out over the meadow and saw ten soldiers, in two ranks; volley firing at the two figures crouched behind a boulder too small to do the job properly. He spoke to the Oneida sending them with Jonas. "Thomas, Bert, we're gonna flank them. We'll stay in the trees and ride until we can come at them from behind. Ride hard, ride fast, make your shot count, and then get your arse over to the others. Liza, stay here for now. If this little fracas goes to shite, keep going west along this trail. Daniel will be coming along behind if he can."

****

"Corporal, take three men and carefully edge closer to their right flank," ordered Kelleher, "when I give the word rush them, we'll give you a staggered volley."

As the corporal and the three chosen men, attached their bayonets, Grantham loaded his pistol and said to Kelleher, "I'm going with them. Brightman is there."

"Suit yourself, Reverend. Good luck sir," answered Kelleher. Kelleher watched as his men crawled in the tall grass keeping to the cover of a line of mounds. He glanced up at James and Brightman, judging when to give the word. Movement caught his eye and he spied Jonas and the three Oneida rushing to their aid, "Saint Patrick's hairy bollocks!" He gave a shrill whistle getting the attention of the corporal, and gave him the sign to attack. Turning to the musket crew he ordered, "Alright boys, first rank fire then reload. Second rank fire after the first, then reload, and fire at will. "Fire!" The burst of musket fire sent Jonas and the Oneida to the ground. Sergeant Kelleher fired and gazed at his attacking force as they made their way, as yet unseen. The jolt to his shoulder spun him around. It was then that he saw Timothy charging his position on horseback. Bert and Thomas barreled into the rear rank of soldiers scattering them, hooves flying into torso, limbs, and one unfortunate soldier's head. They continued into the front rank with the same effect, and without firing a shot made their escape. Sergeant Kelleher looked at what remained of his squad. Two men were unconscious; one of them was certainly dead. The other three were dazed, and he was struggling to tie his bandana around the wound to his shoulder.

Jonas and the Oneida ran up the hill towards James and Brightman, as yet unaware of the flank attack. As they crested it Jonas saw them and yelled, "Fire!" The air was suddenly filled with the smoke of many muskets as the attackers also fired. The sound of the thunderous report of the muskets was quickly replaced by screams. The corporal and one of his men were down, the other two were retreating. James staggered as a shot grazed the side of his head. Jonas was felled by one to his leg, and one of the Oneida was dead. Brightman was unscathed, and was tending to James when he heard the sound of a pistol being cocked by his ear.

"Well now, Mr. Brightman," hissed Grantham, "you have caused me great pain and misery. I had thought to kill you slowly, but given the circumstances, a summary execution, I think, is in order. Stand up and face me. I want to look in your eyes as you die."

Thomas and Bert still galloping to the scene, halted when they heard the muskets. Bert saw Grantham raising his pistol, pointing it at Brightman's head. He yelled to Thomas, and they both fired. One shot struck Grantham in the chest, the other in the arm causing his hand to lower the pistol. As he began to fall he managed to squeeze the trigger. Brightman stumbled backward, the spreading pool of blood soaking through his shirt.

Timothy, with his pistol out, and pointing at them, rode over to the British soldiers who raised their arms in surrender. "By all the saints if it isn't Timothy Winslow come to take me prisoner," remarked Sergeant Kelleher with a big grin on his face, "I warned Grantham we'd be in trouble if any of the Mallory Militia was around."

Timothy dismounted, and walked over to Kelleher, "If I'd known that Paul Kelleher of the Donegal Kelleher's was my foe, I'd've thought twice before pulling off that flanking maneuver. Are you hurt badly? I'm afraid that it was me what shot you. I can have Liza take a look."

"No need, my old friend. Tis a clean wound; went clear through without hitting a bone or artery. Besides, how would it sound at my court martial to have it told I was bandaged and cared for by the enemy?" laughed Kelleher, "Now if you'll give us some time to tend to our wounded and bury our dead, we'll be ready to be led away."

"Led away?" questioned Timothy, "Taking prisoners never entered my mind. You take care of your men, and then you're free to return to Mallory Town. I must warn you, however, that we will want our homes back. I hope I don't have to shoot you again."

"Aye, as to that, many of us have orders to go back to Fort Pitt as soon as the Major decides to send us. My guess, and that of my colleagues, is that when the island camp is complete, we'll be heading out," said Kelleher, "now if I'm of a mind to retake the town, I would wait until then, keeping my eyes on that island camp will tell me when to do the deed. But, I need not tell you that which you have already figured out. Perhaps next time I visit Mallory Town, you'll stand me a couple pints."

Timothy nodded his head, "I'll do better than that. Tell Two Birds I said to give you your own barrel. That should last you a day or two."

"You're a fine man to treat your enemies so," Kelleher replied, "you take care Timothy and may the Good Lord be kind to you."

****

Trying to lend some normalcy to the fact that they were separated from most of their families, and living in an Indian lodge, and to help take his mind off of his wife's plight, Daniel was reading to the three boys from a primer that Hannah Lapley had thoughtfully brought along. The Oneida chieftain, Kariwase stooped as he entered, the aged warrior and longtime friend of the Mallory's saw the children and smiled. "Little ones, I need to speak with your father."

Daniel saw the smile disappear and said, "Run along children. See if Hannah needs any help." Daniel stood and beckoned Kariwase to sit while he went to the fire retrieving the coffee pot. He poured two mugs, handed one to his guest and sat opposite him, "What news do you have?"

"My scouts have brought word that the British are on their way here. The Major is with them. They will soon be where the trail narrows. If we get there first, we can keep them from getting any further."

"Even there it will be a tough fight. I only have Henry and young Samuel with me. I am asking a lot of our friendship, Kariwase. I will understand if you decide to sit this one out. It's me they want."

Kariwase took a sip, shook slightly as the bitter brew slid down his throat, "When my old friend, Donehogawa, spoke to me of a white man he had come to respect as if he was a Mohawk, I said to him that I would like to meet this man. When I met Otetiani, I knew I had a friend for life. When I met his brother, I knew I had another friend for life. We will fight alongside of our friends."

****

James put his hand up to his bandaged ear wondering how he looked now without an earlobe, and how fortunate he was that that was all he lost. His other hand was helping to support Jonas as he limped along, a badly torn calf muscle the worst of the damage done by the musket ball. The women and children were trudging along behind them, tired, but in a much better mood. Timothy rode ahead to let everyone know what had taken place. He left Thomas and Bert behind to watch the bodies of Anne, Brightman and the Oneida brave, and to keep an eye on the British. Sergeant Kelleher may be a friend, but he was also a British soldier under orders.

Bert shifted around looking for a comfortable position against the base of an oak, "Tis a mighty shame bout Mr. Brightman," he said, "You know, he done told me he knew that I was going to escape that night. Told me that, and said he didn't like Reverend Grantham's plans for me. I feel I owe him for that."

Thomas looked at his friend, sitting next to him and said, "Well I'd say you paid him back somewhat. TWas your shot that killed Grantham, mine only winged him."

"I reckon I owed him too," Bert replied, "Man was evil, Thomas, evil."

****

Major Whitby halted his two platoons and turned to his adjutant, "Corporals Fuller and White if you please." He looked up at the hill, and the narrowing trail as it wound its way up an area of loose scree, brush, and scattered boulders. The contours effectively reduced the number of men who could advance in a line. His eyes scanned the slope above and knew in his heart that Daniel Mallory was up there waiting for him. The sound of boots on the gravelly surface announced the presence of the two corporals. "As you can see gentlemen, if you use the eyes God gave you, that we are in a precarious situation here," Whitby announced, "a frontal assault by itself is sure to fail. That's where you two come in. Fuller, take your section around to the left. It's well wooded over there; pick your way through, ready to attack their right flank. White, take your section to the right; you will have to be a bit more careful as the trees aren't as thick that close to the top of the hill. The sun is in a good position, so signal me when you are in position using a mirror or your bayonet. When I have seen both signals, I will order a volley and charge. You attack when you hear the volley. Right, off you go and good luck."

"Looks like the good Major has some sense," Henry said, "he's not just barging into our well planned ambush. We best send some of Kariwase's men out to watch our flanks. If Whitby is smart enough to recognize an ambush, then he's probably smart enough to try to find another way."

Daniel moved into a position next to Samuel behind a granite outcrop. Kariwase and five of his men were behind another one just below them. Henry was doing the same on the other side of the trail. He had Hannah next to him a she absolutely refused to stay behind. Four more of the Oneida were secluded behind the fallen remains of a pine tree that lay adjacent to the trail. As Henry had suggested two groups of three Oneida had scattered to the trees. "I reckon he at least thinks we're here. Might as well make him certain," Daniel said as he aimed downhill and fired. His shot kicked up dust and gravel as it landed about ten feet in front of Whitby. "Come on ahead Major," he yelled.

Whitby kept his eyes searching for his flankers. "At last," he said when he saw the flash from the group on the left and a moment later from the right. "Advance in groups of nine, in three ranks; staggered volleys. Our first objective is that lower ridge of boulders. First rank advance until fired upon, then fire your volleys, and get to that ridge." He looked upon the faces of the men first in line to advance knowing that some of them would be dead soon, but saw no cowardice in their eyes. He saluted them, "Ready, advance," he ordered.

"Here they come," yelled Henry, "Hold your fire until they get a little closer; make better targets for the bowmen." A few of the Oneida were armed with bow and arrow. They would keep up a steady barrage while the others with muskets fired and reloaded. Kariwase acknowledged Henry with a wave of his hand and told his warriors to wait. When the British had gotten to within fifty yards of their position the defenders opened fire, musket balls and arrows flying with deadly accuracy as four redcoats went down. The others knelt and hastily returned fire, racing ahead to the cover of the rocks while they only had arrows to face. Firing from that position, and by staggering their shots the five soldiers were able to provide enough cover for the second rank to advance with only two casualties. The third rank followed close behind, the major with them; the sounds of fighting on the flanks bringing a smile to his face.

"Mallory!" yelled Whitby, "Do you hear that? You're being flanked. If you surrender now, I promise not to kill your family, although I'm not sure about Liza or Deborah's well-being. I took a shot in the dark the other night, heard a woman scream, or it could have been a child. It really doesn't matter though, I've run out of patience, but I will give you five minutes."

Henry made his way over to Daniel, "I for one am not giving in to that bastard."

Daniel started to answer when he was distracted by Timothy coming down to join them. "I heard what he said. It's true that he did hit a woman. Anne Webb is dead. So are Brightman, and the good reverend. Everyone else is alive, and on their way. I sent Sergeant Paul Kelleher and his survivors back to Mallory Town."

"Whitby," answered Daniel, "you'll have our answer in lead. It was Anne Webb you killed, and your friend Grantham is also dead. Your other mission failed, major, as did your flank attack. The only sound I hear is the retreating of whoever survived. Perhaps you might want to reconsider your plans."

"My mother is dead?" snarled Samuel.

"Oh, Samuel, I am sorry to have blurted that without thinking," Daniel said reaching out to comfort him. Samuel pulled away, screamed and clambered up to the top of the boulder. He sighted down his musket barrel and fired.

When he heard the scream, and saw Samuel pointing a musket in his direction Whitby turned away but was hampered by the press of men as he tried to fall to the ground. The ball hit him high in his back, ricocheting off a rib and cracking his collarbone. "Get me the hell out of here," he ordered, grimacing from the pain, "retreat in an orderly fashion."

Seeing that Whitby was still alive, and was getting away Samuel went into a furious rage. Throwing down his musket and pulling the knife from his belt he charged after the British. As he passed them, four of the Oneida grabbed their tomahawks, and followed him. The British rear guard was overrun as Samuel, and the four Oneida slashed and stabbed their way through. Samuel was a whirlwind as his knife swept back and forth. His face became a mask of splotched blood and spittle as he screamed and stabbed. He stuck one foe so hard that he couldn't pull the knife out from behind the rib it had lodged against. He grabbed the fallen soldier's musket, bayonetting the next man in the throat, the warm gush drenching Samuel's face so that he spat blood as he screamed. The next group, however, was able to get off a volley killing two of the Oneida and wounding Samuel. Samuel slumped on the ground, blood pooling around him from the hole in his buttock. He managed to stuff some goose down from the pack he always carried into the hole before he passed out from shock and exhaustion.

Daniel and Henry carried Samuel up the hill and into the lodge. They laid him down on his stomach and were beginning to work his breeches down so they could look at the wound. The goose down had slowed down the flow of blood, but there was a musket ball that needed to be removed. They were startled by the sound of Bowie yelling, "Momma!" Daniel and Henry looked at each other, and then down at Samuel. He turned his head to look at them and said, "Well? Go on and see your wives. I guess I can lie here bare arsed with a bullet inside me for a few more minutes."

Tired beyond belief, Deborah found a last reserve, and ran to Daniel flinging herself into his outstretched arms. Liza just stood for a few seconds with Abigail at her side looking at her husband. "Well my daughter, we are back with our Handsome Henry," she said, "let's go get a hug and a kiss."

Abigail scampered over to her father, who picked her up, covering her face with kisses. He set her down as Liza came over and pulled him to her and kissed him so intently that Abigail said in a hushed voice, "Momma! You're out in front of God and everybody." Liza and Henry broke off their kiss, erupting into a fit of laughter. Soon everyone was gathered with their loved ones, but seeing Jonas was injured, Hannah reminded them there were wounded to care for. They led Jonas, and James into the lodge where Samuel was still bare arsed to the world. Liza, Hannah, Deborah, and Ruth Lapley all entered to see to the wounded. Ruth gasped when she saw Samuel, drawn not only to the bare buttocks, but by his blood covered face. Liza turned when she heard the gasp and exclaimed, "My goodness Samuel, you look like Caesar made up for a Triumph."

Samuel smiled, making his face appear even more gruesome and replied, "Why thank you ma'am, but I look like whom for a what?"

"I'll explain later," she chuckled, "first we have some work to do. Hannah? Please get some water to clean young Caesar's face, and some hot water for Caesar's butt." She then turned to Ruth and said, "Ruth honey, please go find my nephew Jack and ask him to fetch the medical bag Pierre gave us, and whatever herbal supplies he brought along."

****

Major Whitby took a sip of the wine infused with some poppy juice hoping it took effect quickly. The pain from a cracked rib, a fractured collarbone and the surgery to remove the flattened soft lead that had once been a round ball had lessened slightly, but it would be a few weeks before he would be able to leave this post for Boston.

A knock on his office door was followed by Sergeant Kelleher bearing a dispatch. "Major, sir," Kelleher said as he came to attention, "This just arrived from Fort Pitt, and I'm just guessing, mind you, but so did the gentleman officer that this dispatch is about."

"Thank you sergeant," said Whitby taking the note, "how is your shoulder? I see it is still in a sling."

Kelleher looked down at the sling, "Doc says I should be good as new, or at least as good as I can be at my age, in another week. I thank you kindly for inquiring, sir."

Whitby opened the dispatch and began reading, "So you think this Captain Ludlow, who it says here should be arriving to take command of the garrison at Mallory Town next week, is the gentleman who is here now?"

"He fits the description as has been told to me by some of the lads who know him," replied Kelleher with a look of contempt.

"I detect a note of dissatisfaction in this Ludlow, sergeant. Pray tell me why. I've not had the pleasure of meeting him," said Whitby gesturing for Kelleher to have a seat.

"Thank you, sir," Kelleher said as he sat down, "this is what I have heard. This Captain Ludlow is the youngest son of some Duke back home, and was involved in a scandal with another man's wife. The good Duke, to keep his boy from harm, and further embarrassing the family, bought him a commission in the army, and made arrangements to have him sent as far away as possible." Kelleher paused for a moment as he chuckled and continued, "I guess we're as far away as one could get, and so the captain arrived at Fort Pitt a few weeks ago, spent most of his time at Two Birds place, drunk; a very loud drunk as to hear tell. That's how the lads know his story, he would blubber it out every night."

"And why, Sergeant Kelleher, is he here now, a week early?" asked Whitby.

"Well you see sir, he has made himself unwelcome at Two Birds on account of he ran out of money, and ran up a large bill. He also got a little rough with one of the whores. Now I judge no man for needing a drink as long as he can pay for it, or is stood to by others, but any man who hits a woman is not worthy of my respect, officer or no."

"Thank you, sergeant for your report. I will endeavor to have as little to do with Captain Ludlow as I possibly can," Whitby replied, "You are dismissed. Show him in, please on your way out."

Kelleher stood turning to go but stopped and said, "Oh I almost forgot, and I thought you should know, William Crane returned from his journey back east. Arrived just before sundown yesterday and has been with his family ever since."

"Ah, yes, another of the Mallory lackeys" said Whitby, "well, be that as it may. I am tired of them. I hope to never cross paths again with any of them. Let Ludlow deal with it."

****

For the next few weeks, the exiles continued to live with Kariwase's people giving their wounded time to heal enough to travel. Although they hadn't decided their next move, they were keeping tabs on the town and the island camp. Anne Webb and Brightman were buried on the mound where he was killed. Samuel, well enough to make the few miles to the spot they now called Brightman's Meadow, shed not a tear as his mother was interred, staring silently at the horizon. His only thought at that moment was the vengeance he would bring upon Whitby.

Major Whitby, on the other hand had had enough of Captain Ludlow ordering sergeant Kelleher to inform the troops who were going to Fort Pitt to be ready in two days' time; a whole week before the surgeon suggested. Ludlow, meanwhile, was more than happy to see the over officious, and arrogant major leave. Sitting in the rear of the wagon as it trundled out of the gate heading north; Major Whitby looked back at Mallory Town, raised his poppy-wine concoction in a salute to his success, and drank it down.

Thomas and Bert were on patrol near the Lapley farm watching the progression of British troops march out of Mallory Town. "Looks like our time in the wilderness is about done," said Bert, "not many soldiers left to defend it."

Thomas pointed down to the gate as a wagon came out, "I believe that is Major Whitby in that wagon."

Bert pulled out the spyglass lent to him by Jonas focusing on the wagon, "Yes, that is the major. Samuel must have hurt him pretty good; his arm is still strapped to his body. He has a drink in his hand and looks as though he is toasting his farewell."

"Here's hoping we never meet again," Thomas answered the toast hoisting his water skin up taking a drink. "Ready for a few hours in the saddle Bert? It's time to report back to my Pa and Uncle Dan. They'll probably want to start moving back to the Lapley's right away."

"Take a look at the ferry, someone's coming across. We better check that out first," said Bert. They turned their horses back to the ferry landing, coming to a halt in the trees where they dismounted, grabbed their muskets, and approached the dock. "He's got a horse with him but I don't recognize the man."

Thomas broke into a grin, "Why, that's William Crane. He went east a while back with a letter to Colonel Washington." They walked out onto the dock and waited for the ferry to finish crossing the river. Thomas started waving, shouting, "William, over here."

William was leading his horse to the edge of the ferry when he heard his name called out. He peered over the neck of his horse and gave a gasp of surprise and recognition, "Thomas Clarke? Well I'll be damned."

Thomas shook William's hand and introduced him to Bert. "Ah, so this is the famous negro escapee. It's a pleasure to meet you, Mr. Sawyer," William said extending his hand to Bert, "heard tell of you from citizens and soldiers alike while I sat and enjoyed the ale in Timothy's tavern. Now, I take it you can get me to your pa and the others. The sooner the better, I have information that they will find useful for getting them damned lobsterbacks out of our homes."

They held a meeting in Kariwase's lodge with everyone present. Daniel stood and addressed the assembly, "William has returned, and has had a chance over the last few weeks to mingle with the soldiers, and more importantly with the captain who replaced Whitby. I'm going to let him tell you what he has learned."

William strolled into the middle of the circle and said, "When I first arrived I knew I had to keep a low profile as I was recognized as soon as I entered the town by Timothy's good friend, Sergeant Kelleher." He paused for a moment as a ripple of laughter went through the crowd.

Timothy, his face blushed, held up his hands and said, "I do apologize. I guess I should have arrested the fiend when I had the chance."

"No need to apologize my good innkeeper," William continued, "the good sergeant told me of the magnanimity of young Winslow. Indeed he drinks for free telling the tale nightly in the tavern. Now mind you, he wasn't the only tale teller. I became acquainted with Captain Ludlow, a nightly visitor to the tavern. I invited him to join me at my table and introduced myself as I poured him a mug of ale. He drained it in one pull, gesturing for a refill. He told me he knew of me, but could care less about the doings of anyone in this damned hell hole. Ludlow is a sorry excuse for a British officer, and I've known my share of sorry excuse officers. Most nights he just passes out in the tavern, and when he does wake up he grabs a pitcher of ale, a mug, and staggers to his bed. Order and discipline was only maintained by our Sergeant Kelleher as even Whitby had withdrawn from any affairs in the town, staying in his quarters. He's still in some considerable pain, and frequently has to drink a poppy laced drink. Now that he is headed to Boston, and Sergeant Kelleher is leading most of the garrison back to Fort Pitt, morale among the remaining troops is going to plummet, and I can guarantee they will take it out on the townsfolk. Now is the time for us to reclaim our home."

After a short discussion followed by a vote, the results of which were unanimous; they made the trek back to the Lapley's. Kariwase put on a big feast the night before, and everyone felt a bit sluggish, or in some cases, hungover, but the desire for home was stronger. Another result of the meeting was that Kariwase was going to maintain watch on the island camp. He was concerned about British interference with his people as they often used that stretch of the river. The first couple of days were spent putting things back together in and around the farm house. The British patrols used the place occasionally as a barracks, leaving behind trash and dirty linen strewn about. The barn needed a serious mucking out as it had been used for stabling the patrols' mounts. Regular watch on the ferry was continued, with the potential of any encounter being very low, Bowie, Caleb, and Jack were allowed to accompany the watch.

In one of his rare lucid moments, Captain Ludlow managed to set up a rotation of troops between the town and the island. Private Higgins smiled as he neared the gate, relishing the relief from the back breaking work of setting pylons in the river for the dock they constructed, or the task of building the two block house towers that gave the lookouts views of the river in both directions. On top of that had been the latrine duty ordered by Whitby. "Well Whitby is gone," muttered Higgins, "so is that bog trotting mick sergeant. Time for this trooper to get drunk."

Bowie, Caleb, and Jack came along with Timothy and James as they began their turn on duty watching the town. The boys were hoping for some kind of excitement, but after a couple hours of just sitting and seeing nothing, they began to get bored scattering into the woods; anything was better than sitting listening to Timothy talk about making beer. They chased each other around for a while coming to a spot where the trees met the river. From there they had a better view than James and Timothy of a troop of soldiers marching toward the main gate. Bowie's eyes were drawn to one of the soldiers who walked with a slight limp and exclaimed, "That's the bastard tried to force my ma."

****

Jonas Lapley and his three Oneida companions guided the canoe through the tall reeds and cattails bringing it to rest on the small beach that formed the eastern most part of the island. It was a perfect night for secrecy, the sky was overcast, and the cooling pre-dawn temperature caused a mist rising off of the river. Jonas helped unload the bundles of dried grass and kindling, enclosed in linen bags that had been smeared with pig fat. The three Oneida each took one; two of them headed to the newly constructed dock, while the other went to the base of the wall beneath the block house tower. Jonas, because of some loss of agility due to the tear in his calf muscle, was on this part of the two fold attack plan; all he was required to do was paddle a canoe, and guard the shielded vessel that contained a small fire. He picked it up from where he had it nestled between his booted feet and climbed out of the canoe. He was glad he only had to walk a few steps as his calf was aching from the extended time sitting, and with the extra strain of holding the firepot still. He advanced to a spot where the archers couldn't miss. The Oneida warriors returned to the canoe grabbing their bows, and an arrow wrapped in a strip of pig fat linen. They walked over to Jonas, each one lighting their arrows in the flame. When each arrow had been lit, they let fly, all three hitting their linen bag targets.

The misty condition was also a boon for William Crane as he guided the ferry back across the river. As he tied it off to the dock he heard the ripple of a canoe paddle as it glided through the water. Walking his horse off the ferry he glanced over to see the two canoes coming in, shielded from view of the town by the ferry and dock. For the prior couple of weeks while William was spending time in the tavern getting to know some of the soldiers, he was also letting it be known that he was fed up with the Mallory's and their high handed ways. He was so convincing that he even fooled his sister Lucy who after finishing work at the tavern one night berated William so vehemently on the walk to the Crane's cabin that she had him flinching from her pounding fists, and was the butt of many a joke the next night. He took a deep breath to calm his nerves, and walked his horse over to the river side gate.

The plan for the attack came together the day before. The troops coming to the town, after being worked hard on the island would undoubtedly be ready to relax, and a little off their guard. That plus the element of surprise would help negate the fact they were outnumbered about two to one. They also hoped to lower the odds by getting help from inside the town when the attack started, and by keeping the troops on the island occupied. For that reason James, snuck back into town the night before using the hidden gate, making his way to his father Richard who would rally the others. The signal for the attack was the sight of flames rising from the island, and the ringing of the town's warning bell.

"State your business," called a voice from the wall above the gate.

"Is that Private Miller?" asked William, "it's me, William Crane, back from negotiating with those damned Mallory's."

"Come on ahead," replied Miller, "didn't hardly recognize you in this fog." Miller then spoke to the soldier at the gate telling him to open it up. William glanced quickly behind him and saw that Liza had crept into position. He grinned, thinking of the argument that ensued when she decided that she was the best archer in the bunch, and was going to be part of the attack. Henry was set against the idea, but when Kariwase said that Liza had been practicing with him, and could do the job, he reluctantly relented. It was also decided that Samuel would be the other archer since he was a good one and his mobility, like Jonas', was limited.

William nodded to the sentry at the gate and said, "Come on down Miller. I may detest the Mallory clan but am still fond of Winslow's ale. Have a drink with me on my return." He left them with a skin full of ale, walked over to the front of Daniel and Deborah's cabin, and tied his horse to a hitching post. He peered into the window, and seeing that his father and brother were in position to exit out the back door of the cabin, gave them the go sign to subdue the two gate sentries. He then strolled over to the pole that held the warning bell, grasped the rope, kept his eyes to the east, and waited for the flames.

James and Richard crept out of the cabin, and keeping to the shadows made their way to the gate. The sentries were still passing the skin of ale when James said, "Easy now fellows and not a sound. That would make my partner angry." They dropped the skin and raised their hands when they saw Richard come out of the shadows. As one would expect in a blacksmith, Richard Crane stood six feet two inches with the broad shouldered build of a man who hammered steel for a living. He was carrying a large mallet as well as a musket, and as he approached he held the mallet high, daring them to move. James handed each a bandana, "Gag yourselves please, and then put your hands behind you." They did as requested and were soon propped up against a cabin wall, bound hand and foot.

****

It only took a few seconds after the arrows hit before the dock was erupting into flame, spreading even to the canoes tied to it. The fire by the block house wasn't as quick to engulf the wall and tower, but it still caused the sentry on top to scurry down making it easier for Jonas and the Oneida to make their escape down river where they beached on the opposite end of the island placing two bags of pig fat saturated kindling under the second block house and set them alight. Soon the ten man garrison busy fighting the fires on one end of the island, many of them using their helmets as buckets, were now faced with another flaming tower to deal with, and with the fact that without the canoes they were stranded.

****

William couldn't see the actual flames but the telltale glow in the distance was all he needed to start pulling on the rope. The glow also caught the attention of the two block house sentries in Mallory Town and they both were standing nice and tall when Liza and Samuel pulled back their bowstrings and loosed their arrows. Liza's target fell back with the shaft protruding from his chest. Samuel, however missed his man, but the sound of the arrow flying just past his ear startled the sentry, and losing his balance tumbled out of the tower, falling twelve feet to the ground, hitting with his back, and then his head, all the breath in his lungs escaping with a whoosh as he hit the hard earth.

Daniel rushed through the gate, Timothy on his heels. Meeting up with William, James, and Liza, the five of them headed out into the open. Richard, meanwhile, had gone into the tavern by the rear entrance, motioning for Lucy to get out. She went to Timothy and told him there were six drunken soldiers inside, but they all grabbed their muskets when they heard the bell. Daniel tapped William on the shoulder and said, "You and James come with me, we'll hit the main gate. Liza and Timothy watch the front of the tavern. Remember; shoot to kill only if we have to."

****

Henry, Thomas, and Bert entered through the hidden gate catching up with Samuel who had tied up the fallen sentry. "Find yourself a spot to cover the tavern area," Henry said to Samuel, "Bert and Thomas, we'll head through the saw mill and hit the gate behind the church. It won't be easy, they will be alert now. If they surrender to our challenge great, if not, then so be it."

Samuel limped over to the bell pole and knelt down, finding it difficult to feel comfortable. Whatever position he tried would pull at the still healing hole in his arse. All thought of his discomfort disappeared as the first two soldiers barreled out of the tavern and fired at Timothy and

Liza. He heard Timothy scream as he fell from the wound to his lower leg. The soldier who fired that shot was now charging Timothy, his bayonet thrusting forward. The second soldier fired and missed Liza, but was rushing at her as she fired, striking him point blank in the chest. Samuel fired his musket at the trooper charging Timothy, hitting him as he raised his arms to strike, the musket ball entering under his armpit, and straight to his heart. The tavern door was thrown open as three more of the soldiers ran out. Liza and Samuel, having no time to reload their muskets, had picked up their bows and each had an arrow nocked. They both drew back their drawstrings and sent the missiles at the attackers, both finding the intended targets; one in the hip and the other in the neck ripping apart his jugular. The third attacker soon found himself sprawled on the ground as he tripped over his fallen comrades, the pulsing artery spraying him with his friend's blood. The remaining soldier in the tavern wanted no part of the front door, and turned to head to the rear one not knowing that Richard was waiting. When the soldier entered the kitchen area, Richard stepped in front of him brandishing his blacksmith's mallet. He lurched to a halt, dropped his musket surrendering.

Liza went over to Timothy and knelt down to examine the damage to his leg. Struggling with the pain he managed through gritted teeth to say, "Shin bone is broken at the very least." Liza saw that the bone was more than broken; it was shattered beyond her ability to set. She managed a weak smile and replied, "Let's see if we can slow down the bleeding first. I'm not going to give you false hope, Timothy; the bone is crushed pretty badly." Timothy looked at Liza and nodded, "I reckon I can still manage to brew ale on one leg."

Samuel checked the fallen soldiers and tied up the two survivors, plugging the hole in the trooper's wounded hip with goose down and joined Liza. Together with Richard who had emerged from the tavern they managed to carry Timothy to Liza and Henry's cabin. He groaned as they set him down on the bed, the pain so intense he fell unconscious. Richard hefted his musket and headed to the door, "I will see what I can find in the garrison's infirmary. Who knows, maybe even find the garrison's surgeon."

As he left the cabin he noticed two of the men who volunteered to help retake the town. There were seven all together, these two were going to join Daniel at the main gate, three were headed to the church gate and the remaining duo proceeded to the cabin that served as the garrison's barracks. Since the weapons of the townsfolk disloyal to Grantham had been confiscated, only a couple of the men had firearms; one a musket, the other a one shot pistol. The others carried clubs, a butcher's cleaver, a hayfork, or anything else they could use as weapons. Daniel, William, and James approached the gate from the sentries left flank, the two volunteers ran at them straight on, one with a cleaver, one carrying an oak axe handle. Daniel shouted at the soldiers, "Lay down your weapons."

"Bugger me! I will not," shouted one of the sentries as he fired at the villager with the club killing him instantly. As the soldier made to attach his bayonet the other villager barged into him, chopping down severing the soldier's right arm at the elbow. The villager then turned toward the other sentry who backed up, stumbling into the advancing Daniel. "I ain't 'appy 'bout it," he said while dropping his musket to the ground, "but I reckon I'm surrenderin'."

On the other side of the compound, Henry, Bert, and Thomas made their way through the saw mill quickening their pace when they heard the sound of musket fire coming from the church gate. They rushed over to support the three volunteers, one of whom had fired at the sentries. He hurriedly reloaded as Henry and Bert fired a volley to keep the soldiers busy. "Throw down your weapons and you'll live to see the coming sunrise," ordered Henry. The sentries, now facing four muskets and two club wielding villagers, looked at each other and let their muskets fall. Henry tuned to the villagers, "Abner, tie these gentlemen up and take them to the barn. Bind their feet when you get there." "Thomas, Bert, go on over and try to convince the sentries in front of Ludlow's quarters to join their friends in the barn, but be wary. Don't hesitate if the situation gets ugly; shoot to kill."

Henry, a little out of breath after the run to the gate, took a moment to glance around the compound. Things were quiet at the moment, there was enough light now from the first glow of the pink dawn sky for him to see that Daniel was heading to the barn gate and that the fight at the tavern was over. Richard ran over and joined him, "Timothy's been hurt pretty bad, and may lose a leg. I'm going to the infirmary to get what supplies I can."

"Damn! Let's hope that's not the case," replied Henry, "I'll join you."

They entered the tent to find a portly gentleman filling a medical bag with surgical tools. "Ah, I take it my services are now required?" he asked putting out his hand, "Doctor Charles Godwin, the surgeon for this motley garrison. Are the wounded being held together, would make things easier, you know."

"Yes they are, Doctor," said Henry shaking Godwin's hand, "Henry Clarke here and this is Richard Crane. Now, if you'll follow us, we'll take you to the wounded."

"It sounds like there may be more soon," Godwin said as a fresh round of musket fire erupted close by.

****

The two sentries posted outside Captain Ludlow's quarters, raised their muskets pointing them at Bert and Thomas as they approached. Thomas held his right hand up and away from his musket and said, "The fight's over. Lower your arms and no harm will come to you."

"The fight is never over, there's always another one," answered the sergeant, "but you're too young to have learned that yet. Besides, we were charged with keeping our beloved Captain Ludlow safe, and while I find him repulsive as an officer, I will do my duty." With that he fired kicking up the dust between Thomas and Bert, "A warning, the only one you'll get." The two friends backed away, turned and ran toward the livestock paddock, ducking down behind a water trough. The sentries took cover, one behind a catch barrel; the other using the corner of the building to hide behind.

"I reckon that the situation just got ugly," Bert said as he rose up to take a shot, ducking back down quickly as he saw the troopers ready to fire.

Thomas looked at Bert, "Take off your hat and put it on your musket barrel, when I say go, raise it up. I'm going to go for the one standing by the corner if he takes the bait." Bert placed his hat over the muzzle while Thomas peered around the trough watching the corner of the building for movement; "Go!" he said. Both troopers fired when they saw what they thought was Bert, Thomas got to his knees quickly, sighted and fired.

"Bollocks, those kids just fooled us," said the trooper behind the barrel while reloading, "eh sergeant?" He turned when he didn't get an answer and seeing the sergeant lying on the ground called out, "Sergeant?" Crawling over he spotted the pool of blood and the hole in the sergeant's forehead. "Bloody Christ, they'll pay for this," he said turning to go back to his spot behind the barrel. He was only exposed for a second in the open, but that was enough for Bert. The shot hit the trooper just below his throat apple shattering his larynx before exiting the back of his skull.

Bert sat down shaking from the experience, "That's two men I've killed in battle. I hope this doesn't become a habit. Don't much like killing."

Thomas reached over tapping Bert on the shoulder, "Feel the same way, my friend. Let's go see if the good Captain Ludlow is of a mind to surrender."

"Oh God, I hope so. Seen enough ugliness today," replied Bert.

They reloaded and walked over to the church building trying not to look at the carnage resulting from the fight. They passed through the nave and carefully opened the door to the captain's room. "Come in, come on in and join me," beckoned Ludlow seated behind a desk, an ale barrel turned on its side dripping the last few drops onto the desk top. Ludlow raised a mug in greeting, but stopped before taking a drink, "What is this? They have sent two youngsters and one of them a darkie, to capture the famous captain of King George's army? What an illustrious end to a storied career."

"Will you come with us, sir? We'll take you to my pa and my uncle. You've no need to fear for yourself," said Thomas as he walked over to lend the obviously drunken captain a hand.

Ludlow waited until Thomas was within easy reach and quickly put down the mug grabbing his pistol out of an open drawer. He thrust his free arm out and grasped Thomas by the throat pulling him in front of his body and placed the pistol at Thomas' ear. "Well now, my darkie friend. Seems we have a bit of a problem here. I'm not so inclined to be captured, would be just another in a series of embarrassments I have caused my family," said Ludlow suddenly pointing the pistol at his own head, "and I'm too much of a coward to do the honorable thing and kill myself, so I guess it's down to this." He shoved Thomas out of the way and pointed the pistol at Bert. Both weapons fired at the same time, the pistol shot passing through Bert's hat, the musket shot from Bert, however, found its mark hitting Ludlow in the chest. He fell back and gestured to Thomas to come close. His breathing became labored and the punctured lung caused him to choke on the pink froth rising up his throat, but he still managed a kind of smile and said, "At least now I'll go down as being killed in action." He gasped one more time and died.

Bert fell back onto the floor and patted himself wondering where he was shot. When he reached up to check his head he discovered the hole in his hat where the musket ball had hit. "Lord amighty, that was too close," he said, his finger poking through the hole, "what did he say to you?"

"That he was killed in action," said Thomas.

"Killed in action, crazy drunken fool almost killed me in action," replied Bert, "reckon we outta go report what happened. Hope we don't run into any more trouble to report."

"Reckon you're right," said Thomas as he helped Bert up off the floor, "I figure that having a cocked pistol in your ear and having your hat shot full of holes is enough for one night."

****

James met up with the two villagers staking out the barracks. They managed a good look inside and found only two soldiers snoring 'like a herd of pigs' they told James. James hefted his musket and motioned for them to follow him. When he got to the door he kicked it open startling awake one of the soldiers, "What in hell is going on – oh, I see. Come back for the town, eh? Well you won't get a fight out of me or Abner over here. Ya see, we're both stinking drunk."

He turned to the still snoring Abner and shook him awake, "Seth? You bog trotting pig fucker, why you waking me up?"

Seth pointed at the door and said, "Seems the Mallory's want their town back, and we're prisoners."

Abner rolled back over and said, "Fine with me as long as I can go back to sleep."

Seth lay back down, "Abner I just want to set it straight. I never did fuck no pig; I ate a lot of 'em but that's it."

Abner opened one eye and growled back a reply, "Will you please just shut up? My head is pounding something fierce and your blabbering ain't helping."

"I'm sorry Abner, just thought it was important you know that I never fucked no pig."

James couldn't help but laugh at the exchange and said to the two villagers, "Make sure Seth and Abner stay put," and added as he headed out of the door, "and don't let any pigs get in here. Not sure I believe our pal Seth."

****

"There's two of them," William said to Daniel as they peered around the corner of the barracks building taking in the scene at the barn gate, "looks like they're having a bit of an argument. See the one with the limp? He's making fighting gestures; the other one's nodding his head."

They advanced, the barracks still in the shadow of the barn providing cover. Just before stepping into the open Daniel called out, "I suggest that the result of your disagreement is to surrender. If not, then you'll both be dead and none of us wants that to happen, now do we?" The sight of the two coming into the light with muskets raised created a slight panic as the two sentries who a moment ago were considering standing their ground, were now staring at death. After a quick glance at each other, they dropped their muskets and put their hands in the air. "Good choice, gentlemen," said Daniel, "now, if you will please sit down with your hands behind your back, my partner here will bind them."

William set his musket up against the log wall and picked up the rope he had brought along. Higgins waited until William had started tying up his fellow sentry, and then reached into his boot for his knife. Daniel turned to face the direction of the sound of musket fire over by the church, and did not see the movement. Higgins rose from the ground bringing the hilt of the knife down on William's head and then sprang towards Daniel.

The other sentry yelled out, "Higgins, don't be a fool!"

When Daniel heard the name Higgins, he turned back to the sentries raising his musket in time to block Higgins' stabbing attempt, but was knocked to the ground by the force of Higgins' charge, dropping his musket as he hit the ground. Higgins roared and dove on top of Daniel, the knife thrust headed for his chest. Daniel grabbed Higgins' wrist stopping the downward motion and with his knee, kicked up at Higgins. It wasn't a strong kick but he caught him in the balls with enough force to cause Higgins to yelp and to fall backwards. Daniel took advantage of the moment and took Higgins knife hand and turned it and plunged the knife into Higgins stomach. Higgins' scream was high pitched and terrible to hear but Daniel didn't care. He pulled the knife out, looked Higgins in the eyes and placed the knife up under the rib cage saying, "You tried to rape my wife, you son of a bitch!" as he thrust the knife in, piercing his heart.

Chapter 7 1772 - New Ventures

Mallory Town

The next few days were busy ones as the residents began repairing the damages to the town, and dealing with the wounded. Timothy's leg was beyond repair, and was amputated. The army doctor was keeping a close watch for any sign of infection in the stump created by the surgery. Timothy was still too groggy from the poppy juice being administered for the pain, to fully comprehend the extent of the damage done to his body. Hilda Crane and her youngest daughter, Marsha, took turns staying with him at night as he fought his way back from the fever that had set in.

Daniel and Henry met with the townsfolk who had sided with the British during the takeover. They were told they could stay, if they so chose to do so, with no repercussions, or they could make their way to Fort Pitt with the British soldiers captured during the battle to retake the town. Most stayed, but a few of the more vociferous packed up their belongings, and headed to Fort Pitt. It was the third day since the battle when Henry remembered that they still had not read the letter that Washington had sent with William, and decided it was time.

Henry sat down at the table; Liza and Thomas were busy in the kitchen while Deborah was reading to the rest of the children up in the loft. He took a sip of water and said, "Daniel? Don't you think it's about time we read that letter from Colonel Washington?"

Daniel looked up from the now empty bowl of stew, "I plum forgot about it, but you're right. Now, if I can remember where I put it."

Deborah climbed down from the loft and stood behind Daniel, ruffling his hair, "You didn't put it anywhere, my love. You gave it to me to put away. Top drawer of the bureau in the bedroom. Would you like me to fetch it?"

"I'll fetch it, Aunt Deborah," said Thomas coming into the room, "I'm anxious to hear what it says. William told me and Samuel that there's trouble back East with British troops and all, not that we would know anything about that," his comment eliciting a few chuckles.

"I think we all need to hear it," said Daniel, "Thomas, go and get Samuel, Bert, and William Crane. I'll get the letter."

When everyone had gathered, Daniel opened the letter, and started reading:

March 15

Dear Friends,

I trust all is going well in Mallory Town. I thank you for the information your man William brought. I suppose it was to be expected that there would still be trouble with the tribes. I fear that situation will never resolve peacefully, and someday, harsh decisions will have to be made.

Things here are not peaceful either. It has been almost four years since British troops were stationed in Boston, and other places as well. There had been isolated incidents of confrontation but now we have had violence resulting in deaths. I had hoped for reasonable men to come to the fore especially from the King and his Parliament, but that has not been the case, at least so far. I fully understand their need for monies to pay for the last war, but to treat us here as servants rather than partners; to enact laws without our consent, without our being represented in the decision making process; these things do not bode well for the future. I still think we can resolve our differences without resorting to bloodshed, but am not about to stand idle in case peaceful means are not successful. That brings me to the heart of the matter. I was hoping to convince Liam to come and take over the training of the militia I command. It was a grievous blow to hear what happened to Rebecca, and Liam's subsequent flight. However, my need still exists. I am asking a lot to be sure, but if there any among your acquaintances who might fulfill that role, I plead for their help. If war does come, we cannot defeat the British Army by conventional means alone. We need the skills of the irregulars, and I cannot think of any group who can do what you and your men can do. We are entering perilous times, gentlemen.

Yours,

George Washington

Daniel put the letter down, and looked around the room. He knew he needed every man, and woman to get Mallory Town back in shape. However, he also knew the very real threat posed by the British, and that they couldn't ignore the plea of their old commander; their old friend. "It appears we're not done yet, but I don't know how we can help. There's too much to do here for Henry or me to go."

Thomas nudged Samuel in the side to get his attention and whispered something to him. Liza furled her brow and said, "I agree that you and Henry cannot go. Damn, I wish Liam was still here."

Daniel smiled at his sister's cursing, "I doubt he would consent, even if he was still here. His fate is west, not east." He then turned to Thomas and Samuel who were still talking to each other. "Do you two have something to say?"

Thomas looked at Samuel, and then across to Bert, "What about us, me, Samuel, and Bert?"

Henry ran his hands through his hair and exclaimed, "Lord above, the pups think they can run with the pack. What do you think, dear wife, of our son going off to join Washington? If you recollect, my times with the colonel weren't exactly free from danger, and if he is right, then our boy will be in the thick of it."

"He'd be in the thick of it no matter where he is if it comes to war with the British," she replied, "and I think he's man enough, and skilled enough to do what the colonel asks." She smiled at her brother and Henry and continued, "after all, he learned from the best."

"What say you, Samuel, Bert?" asked Daniel, "you care for a little adventure?"

Samuel stared straight ahead, his answer was tinged with hate, "I still owe the British, and I aim to pay them back."

Bert fidgeted in his seat. He did not want to be seen as a coward to the people who had given him a new chance at life, but he did not relish the idea of going back east. "I surely appreciate that you think I could be of help. Fact is, I know I could, but the thought of being recognized, and thrust back into slavery scares me. I would rather stay, and be of service here."

Deborah was seated next to Bert, and with a gentle touch to his shoulder replied, "Oh Bert, you dear man, we will not ever ask you to put yourself in that position." She scanned the room, and fixing her stare at Daniel, said, "Will we, husband?"

Daniel laughed, "Well I guess that settles that. Bert stays with us in Mallory Town. I'm not sure that Thomas and Samuel should go alone, though. They may have what it takes woodcraft wise, but neither one has been to Philadelphia or Boston."

William Crane stood up and said, "I have, and I believe that Mallory Town will come to rights without me. It seems I've been at war most of my life, and to tell the truth, I enjoy the challenges. If you all agree, I will accompany the two pups, and see that they don't get lost in the big city."

Late Winter – Mandan Village

Liam pulled the fox fur hat down more snugly on his head, and wrapped the elk hide robe tightly against his body. Although winter was just about over, the equinox being only a week or so away, the wind was strong, and bitter coming down from the mountains to the north, and to the west. The vast prairie was still covered by deep snow making life hard for the herds of numberless buffalo. He had gone out to greet the rising sun from the top of a small knoll that looked out east over the wide expanse of the Missouri River. It was a habit he picked up while staying with the Ojibway. Wahta and Turtle were away from the village for a few days hunting elk with some Crow warriors who had traveled with a sizable portion of their village to the Mandan village to trade, and were in need of some time away from their wives. With them was a garrulous old mountain man named Gabe. Liam wanted to go with them, but a twisted knee he suffered a few weeks ago was still not ready for that kind of activity, as he was discovering from even this short hike to the knoll, and back to the lodge he shared with his two companions. The village was quiet except for the yapping of one of the camp dogs who was chasing some children playing in the snow. He entered the lodge and after warming up a little by the fire sat down at the small table he had traded a hand whittled flute for. He picked up the letter he had begun for Liza and Daniel. He needed to finish it today as the French trapper who said he would get it to Fort Pitt was leaving tomorrow at dawn. Smoothing it out over the surface of the table he began to read:

Liza and Daniel,

Time to bring you up to date on my travels. It is late March and I am camped with Wahta and Turtle in a Mandan village along the banks of the Missouri River. We left the Grand Traverse area a few weeks after Glyn died. We got word that a British patrol was sniffing around the area looking for us. So, with a group of Potawatomie heading west to trade with the tribes near the headwaters of the Mississippi we paddled across the big lake called Michigan, and after a couple weeks with the Lakota we started walking. At first it was a land teeming with lakes and deep woods of oak, birch, and pine, but it gradually gave way to grassland that reached to the horizon in the west. We took our time, rarely making more than twenty miles a day. There was no shortage of game, so we never went hungry, and you know how much Wahta can eat. I welcomed the slower than normal pace. I tell you I am beginning to feel my age, yes Daniel, I know you're older than me. It's just that I feel an ache in my joints that I never felt before, when we could run for miles, rest for two hours, and run some more. Well enough of that, was beginning to sound like Glyn there. One morning we came over the crest of a hill and watched in amazement as a group of mounted Indians, we found out later when we went to their camp that they were Kiowa, rode through the biggest herd of buffalo I've ever seen, or thought could be real. They were hunting them with arrow and spear and that meant getting real close. Not one of those riders went down, and they must have killed twenty buffalo. We stayed with them for two days, and finally by hand sign, and finding one old warrior who knew a little French, me and Turtle were told of the Mandan village. Wahta spent his time playing with the children. He never complains, but I know he misses his family. Turtle doesn't talk of his, but I have noticed that he goes back and forth between his British half and his Ojibway half. That's something I saw in Teeyeehogrow as well. How easy it was for him to be his old self, if only for the few moments he would be singing a song he said he learned from the field hands. I envy them. I feel torn as a Mohawk, and as a white man. Happy as neither. It's as if I am missing the parts that make me whole in both minds. The buffalo dreams have returned. They started again once I saw the vast herds that live here. They have always varied depending on what I was going through at the time. In this one I am watching the herd, so many animals that they take up the view from horizon to horizon. Suddenly, they vanish except for one lone bull, my bull, I can tell from the white patch on his shoulder. He is standing on a hillock, snorting, and I hear a voice saying, "follow me, it is time." He then ambles off, the wind picks up, and the knee deep grasses blow in the direction he is walking. It is then that I wake up. I have suspected for some time that this trip would be my last, now I am certain. If this is so, I have no regrets except for having to leave my boys, but it seems that was always my destiny. Remember what Pierre told us about the Vikings and their 'wyrd'? I guess this is my 'wyrd'.

He put the letter down, grateful for the fact that he was alone as the tears began to flow. The thought of not being around for his sons weighed on his mind, but knew they were being well cared for. Better than he could, he was certain. He wiped his eyes with his sleeve, dipped the quill pen in the ink pot and began writing.

We made our way to the Missouri, and followed it as it meandered steadily west and north. Near where it meets the Heart River we found the Mandan village. It sits on a high bluff looking out over a sandy beach. The beach is littered with the canoes of many different tribes, as the Mandan do a lively trading business that could rival our old friend, Two Birds. The village itself stretches for quite a ways filled with their lodges, a kind of longhouse but not as large, and is round. The one we are using belongs to a widow, and is smaller than most of the others. Winter arrived early, almost on the heels of a large band of Crow who had come to trade, and were now trapped by a succession of blizzards. Among them, and you are not going to believe this, was the almost spitting image of that trapper who was killed in Chogan's raid, Stump nose. Turns out that he had a twin brother, Gabe. He came out here, drawn by the sound of the mountains, as he puts it. He lived with a tribe called Shoshone who gave him the name Dainah-Weda. It means 'man bear' and it suits him. He wears a robe of bear hide, the head of the bear riding on his head and the bushiest beard I have ever seen. He lives with the Crow now, and has suggested we join him when they head back to their village.

So my dear family, I know not if I will write again, but will somehow make it known where I am when I have reached the end of my buffalo dream.

Liam

On the trail to Boston – Late Summer

After three months of nonstop repair work, hunting, and preparing for their journey, the three companions were finally on their way. They were accompanied by Jack Tomlinson who was transporting merchandise from Two Birds to his partner in Albany. Thomas was excited about going to Albany as his grandfather, Joseph Clarke was blacksmithing there. They left at dawn, the goodbyes between Thomas and his parents were tearful ones, and he was still wiping his eyes when they passed through the gate. William Crane, however, and due mostly to the fact that he was rarely home, had no tears shed, rather a clap on the back was all that was communicated between father and son. Samuel, his family dead, still smoldered though he kept it inside, maintaining a pleasant manner with everyone, though devoid of some of his quick wit. Deborah and Liza did their best to make him a part of the family, and he was genuinely appreciative, but they could never replace fully what he had lost.

They rode southeast following the well-worn path to the Kiski ford. Their first goal was the Iroquois camp on Mahoning Creek. Two Birds knew that some of the nations would be there hunting and trading, and couldn't pass up a good business opportunity. It was also in keeping with Two Birds relationship with Colonel Washington that Tomlinson would also be sounding out the tribes gathered for their current mood. William warned the two youngsters that it would be a long, hard journey, a warning that was reinforced by Tomlinson, "Reckon we'll be at the Mahoning on our third day; from there it's only about a month to Albany, that is if we don't run into any problems. That's about as likely as my mules sprouting wings."

The first couple of days passed without incident. The weather was agreeable, if a little cool at night, and the terrain was for the most part, flat, but the third morning brought a chilling rain making the sighting of the large temporary village that afternoon, all the more inviting. "I declare," exclaimed William, "that is the largest camp I've ever seen."

Jack clambered down from the wagon and joined William. Stretched out below them on the other side of the creek was a vast array of tents, wickiups, and long houses. Each tribe had their own spot with the area surrounding the more permanent long houses set aside for commerce, disputes adjudicated, and for just renewing old friendships. "Two Birds told me they would be gathering," Jack said, gesturing toward the camp, "but I don't think he had this in mind. This looks like almost the entire Iroquois League is represented, even the Tuscarora, and they don't have a vote in the council." "And look over there," he continued, pointing to a group on the edge of the camp, "those are Mingo; probably Logan's people. That is most unusual. This is more than the seasonal trade and gossip gathering."

They met no resistance, but there also weren't any overt signs of greeting except from their friend the Oneida chief Kariwase, so they set up camp close to his people. While William, Thomas, and Samuel sat and ate with Kariwase, Jack set out his trade goods, observing and listening, with some occasional haggling with potential customers. They decided to rest for one day before continuing on giving them the chance to completely dry out from the drenching from the prior day, and to wander about the encampment. The only time they felt threatened occurred when they came across a group of young Seneca warriors, but a stern command from Logan sent them on their way before anything happened. Jack joined them for the evening meal, but waited until Kariwase bid them good night, to tell them what he had learned. "There's a lot of grumbling about the number of white's moving onto their lands. Some want the British to step in and force the white's back across the Allegheny's. Others want to take matters into their own hands, and it appears that some other tribes already have. Huron and Delaware raiding parties are even now attacking white settlements."

"If that's the case," William said, "we need to take every precaution. Two of us will scout ahead; one will stay with the wagon. I want to leave at first light, so, no more ale tonight."

It was two days later that William and Samuel saw smoke, a black spiral wafting over the tree tops. "That ain't no campfire," exclaimed Samuel.

"Ride back to the others," said William, "I will go see what's causing the smoke."

The scene before William was one of complete devastation. The remains of a cabin and barn, flames still licking along the last of the log walls of the cabin, lay smoldering in mute confirmation that what Jack heard was true, there were tribes bent on violence. "Now, what have we here?" William muttered as he rode around the ruins. Three fresh graves had been dug by someone, but surely not by the Indians who attacked, and destroyed this place. He dismounted, checking the ground for any tracks that may have been left. Satisfied that he had learned all he could, William remounted, and headed back to the road.

They set up camp for the night by a small creek that flowed alongside the road. Samuel and Thomas brought in a turkey while Jack dangled a line in the creek, a couple of trout already caught. The discussion during their meal had the youngsters scanning the surrounding woods, certain that there were hostile forces ready to swoop down on them. "That is a puzzler," said Jack continuing his thoughts. "Somebody buried those poor unfortunates. I've been by this way plenty, and the nearest white settlement or farm is another day's travel."

"From what I could gather from the confusion created by the number of tracks, it looked like a raiding party of at least eight, maybe ten. The tracks near the graves were definitely boot made; maybe even army style boots, certainly not worn by any Indian. Two sets of tracks; they appeared to have headed southeast." William looked over at Thomas, "You take the first watch tonight."

They made their way down from a line of hills, the landscape before them a series of meadows interspersed with ponds and marshes. "Just a few miles and we'll come to a turn off leading to that settlement I mentioned," Jack said, "though calling it a settlement is a stretch. Two former soldiers trying their hand at raising horses. Still, a chance to sleep with a roof over our heads for one night."

There was a small cabin, a stable, a barn still under construction, and two paddocks holding a dozen horses, and a few mules. One man was at work chopping wood, the other came out of the cabin holding a musket but set it down when he saw that it was a group of white men. "Well, now, this is a pleasant surprise," he said, "climb on down and welcome. Name is Buxton, Corporal Charles Buxton, as was during the war. That over there is my partner, Stuart Laing, a surly Scot; also part of His Majesty's finest what wrested this land from the infernal French. You're probably looking for a place out of the rain that's coming tonight. Take your mounts over to the stable. We've plenty of fodder for your beasts, and we'll see about rustling up some grub. Don't get many guests out here."

William dismounted handing the reins to Thomas, "You and Samuel take care of the horses, and give Jack a hand with the wagon and mules." Turning to Buxton he said, "Thankee kindly for your hospitality. As to grub, we can help with that." He looked up at the sky, and saw the sun becoming obscured by a thick bank of gray clouds. "Looks like we will be getting rain tonight."

"I knew about the rain afore those clouds showed up. Got a pain in my leg tells me the weather," Buxton chuckled, "got kicked by a mule, broke my shinbone. Army doc didn't quite set it straight, couldn't march any more so I mustered out. Private Laing took a musket ball to his head, tore off one ear. His time was almost up so they let him go. Now we raise horses, mostly for farmers, hunters, hell, whoever needs them. Time's coming when these valleys will be filled with settlers."

Dinner was eaten outside; the small cabin was built for two or three at the most. William, Jack, and the two hosts occupied the two chairs and a roughhewn bench, while Thomas and Samuel made do sitting on the ground with a large log as a backrest. Introductions having been made earlier, Buxton looked over at Thomas and asked, "You any kin to Henry Clarke? I know him; well let's just say I fought with him. He was part of Liam Mallory's outfit what was with Braddock. I was part of Howe's command, so was in the thick of the fighting from the start. I tell you, those militia boys saved our hair that day."

Thomas beamed a huge smile, "Yes sir. He's my da."

"Now, ain't that something," Buxton responded, "course it does make one wonder why the son of a famous woodsman is out trekking in this wilderness?"

William saw a look of confusion on Thomas' face and said, "Learning the ways of the wilderness while we transport our goods to Albany."

"Splendid idea," said Buxton taking a sip of ale, wiping his mouth on his sleeve, "ah, we heard tell of some trouble over in Mallory Town. I 'spect your Da had something to do with driving out Colonel Whitby."

Samuel scrambled to his feet, the name of his enemy roused, once more, his rage, "I am going to kill that bastard," he growled as he walked away, heading into the woods.

Thomas called out after him, but Samuel ignored the cry and picked up his pace. Thomas shook his head, and sat back down, "He'll be all right in a bit, just needs a few minutes to calm down."

"I didn't intend no discomfort," said Buxton, "I was unaware that he has a complaint with the good colonel."

"More than a complaint I'd say," Tomlinson replied as he stood up, "'scuse me gentlemen but I need to piss, and then check on my mules."

"Speaking of troubles," said William who, uneasy with Buxton's questions, changed the subject away from Whitby and Mallory Town, "we came across a burnt out homestead a few miles back. You had any problems with Indian raiders?"

"Me and Stu saw the smoke. Knew what it was right away, so we rode over there to do what we could." Buxton sighed, and continued, "Only thing we could do was bury the victims. Saints be praised, those savage devils leave us alone."

"Pretty lucky, I'd say." William responded.

"Being former soldiers might have something to do with it," Stu replied, "and some luck, too, I s'pose."

"We keep on our toes, our eyes open." said Buxton after yawning, "We need to be up early, so I'll say goodnight now."

William watched until Buxton and Laing were behind the closed door of the cabin. He looked over, and seeing that Samuel was returning, waited before speaking. "Something doesn't add up, but I'll be damned if I can figure out why I feel that way."

Samuel poked at the fire watching the sparks dance, "I feel it too. For one thing how does that Buxton know that Whitby is a Colonel? That wasn't common knowledge as far as I know."

It was then that the rain started, sending the companions scurrying to the stable where they were bedding down for the night. Inside the cabin Buxton peered out of the door, his eyes on the stable, deciding that the travelers needed to be stopped. "We are still soldiers, Private Laing, and these gentlemen have all the makings of enemies of The King. I think they should meet our friends up the road."

Stu Laing cursed under his breath, as the rain was pelting down, and mounted the horse he had tied up behind the cabin. He headed into the woods, and once out of sight picked up speed. It was a good seven miles to the camp of the Delaware and Huron raiders. An excellent spot for an ambush, thought Laing.

Jack joined the others in the stable, and spread his blanket on a pile of clean straw, "There is treachery afoot unless I'm mistaken. This Buxton character said they were raising horses for farmers and hunters? The horses I just looked at are not plough or pack animals; they are cavalry mounts or I'm a barmy fool. This place isn't made for breeding; it's a way station or depot. On top of that, I just saw Laing mount up, and ride out. Now, why would he be going out this time of night, and in this pouring rain?"

William sat up, and scratched his head, and said to Jack, "How well do you know the trail ahead?"

"Been through this way many times," he responded, "a couple miles ahead there is a valley that steadily narrows as you go. If I understand your question, and if I was of a mind to plan an ambush, then the far end of the valley is a lovely spot."

The rain continued throughout the night, tapering off to a fine misty drizzle, shrouding the countryside in fog. There was no sign of either Buxton, or Laing as the companions saddled their mounts, and hitched the mules to the wagon. Breakfast was a meager affair as they were in a hurry to leave. They decided during their discussion after dinner to have two riders scout farther ahead than they had been doing given their concerns over possible treachery ahead. William and Samuel left the compound first, with Thomas and Jack following about a half hour later. The mules struggled in the muddied track climbing the many hills that were a prominent feature of the terrain slowing down their progress. Jack knew that they may have to leave the road if indeed there was trouble ahead, so when they reached a spot he had used as a camp in a previous trip, he called a halt. "We'll stop here," he said to Thomas, "William and Samuel are due to report back shortly. I have a plan to get around the trouble I feel is ahead. I've got an itch running down my neck, only feel that when I sense someone's looking to take my hair."

Just as Jack described, William and Samuel saw the valley tapering, and as they crested one of the hills, they looked down, and saw a culvert off to the right side of the road. A small creek ran at the bottom of it. It was enclosed on both sides by trees, but there was an area where an attacking force could easily climb out to the road while remaining hidden before they did. "Stay here," William said to Samuel as he dismounted, handing the reins to him, "I'm going to have a closer look." He left the road using the trees to screen his movement. When he was in direct sight of the creek he noticed the band of eight warriors waiting there. They weren't mounted, and the only horse he saw was Laing's, who was getting ready to ride, presumably to find out where their victims were. William scurried back to Samuel and said, "Bastards have set us up real good. Time to get back to the wagon."

Laing took another swig from the jug of whiskey he had tied to the pommel of his saddle. He swayed a little, the result of drinking since he left the cabin and uttered a curse as the jug was now empty. His senses dulled by the alcohol, he failed to notice the tracks of two horses that headed back the way they came, and deciding that this was a good spot to see the blasted wagon crew, dismounted to wait, but was soon dozing at the base of one the many elm trees that lined the road.

"Our suspicions were correct," William told the others, "there's too many of them for us to take on, and I'm not sure we can outrun them even if they're not mounted. The wagon is going to slow us down."

"That's a fact," said Jack, "if they have any sense, they'll shoot the mules first." He pointed into the woods, "When I've camped here before, I found a trail leading away from the road. It runs the same way we need to go, at least it starts out that way. I'm guessing it'll only be passable for the wagon for a few miles." He frowned and giving a sigh, continued, "I heard tell from an old friend of there being some caves in the hillsides hereabouts. I don't like it, but if we find one suitable, we could leave the wagon in one, and hope no one finds it afore I can come back. I'll ride one of the mules, use t'other to carry what we need."

Samuel, his face showing the anger building within, wheeled his horse around, and started heading back to Buxton's place. Thomas quickly caught him up, grabbing Samuel's reins. "Just what do you think you're going to accomplish going back there?" he said, "We have a more important job ahead of us."

Samuel tried to pull away, but by then William was on the other side of him. "Listen to him. This ain't no time for personal vengeance. I'm tasked with getting you two to Colonel Washington and I presume that the Colonel would prefer you being hale and hearty, not dead."

Samuel shook his head, but said in a voice tinged with bitterness, "Buxton and Laing are two more bloody curs I have to deal with along with Whitby, but if I have to wait, then so be it. They'll still be dead by my hand."

William wrapped the reins to his horse around an overhanging pine branch, and threaded through the trees back to the road. The others were heading down a trail that barely allowed passage of the wagon, but Jack was a skilled driver, so while the pace was slower than they liked, they were putting some distance between them, and the would be ambushing party. From his vantage point, William could make out the prone figure of Laing still sleeping against a tree. He gave a brief thought to putting Laing asleep permanently, but he didn't think they were at the point of killing men in cold blood, not yet, at least. "Sleep tight, and for as long as you like," he muttered while climbing back into the saddle. A few moments later he was back with the group, and after giving them the news that they were not being pursued yet, sent Thomas on ahead to find a way to a river Jack remembered.

"Not more than three or four miles ahead," Jack said, "this path crosses the river. But, the other side is a steep grade. Dunno if this here wagon could make it, even if my life depended on it." He chuckled, "and it just might." "Now, if you go downstream," he said to Thomas, "you'll find a big bend in the river where the water has washed out the rock. I seem to recall there is an overhang of rock. Could be a cave in there as well? I never took the time to look."

Four long hours later, they were leaving behind the wagon, and riding single file down the river. It wasn't a very deep cave, but they were able to hide it as best they could by concealing the cave's entrance with a pile of small boulders and bushes. Jack was mounted on one of the mules, using a saddle he always brings on his trips. "My momma done told me, many times, in fact," he said, "best to have what you need with you when you need it." The other mule was laden with food, and other supplies deemed necessary. They climbed out of the water a few hundred yards further along and headed north. They would have to cross the road at some point and while they hoped to have put off any pursuit, they didn't know for sure.

****

Buxton was perplexed, why didn't he hear any sounds of fighting up ahead? He had waited a couple hours, and then followed, hoping to find the colonial scum either dead, or about to be.

As he crested a hill he saw Laing , and galloped over to him. Laing looked up, rubbed his eyes and said, "I must've dozed off for a minute."

"You fool," replied Buxton, "where are the Mallory's? I imagine they didn't sneak by you, and they certainly aren't back that way. Go, get a couple of the boys, and backtrack. You check south. I'll take a few of them, and see if they're north of the road. Find them, Laing!"

William and Samuel bringing up the rear, stopped periodically, watching and listening. They were about to remount when they heard a horse nicker. They dropped to the ground, muskets at their shoulders. Laing came trotting, the two braves with him were scanning the ground, when one of them stopped and pointed in the direction of William and Samuel. Laing stood in his stirrups to get a better look. The last thing he saw was the muzzle flash from Samuel's musket. The lead ball hit him just under his left eye. By the time he hit the ground, he was dead. "Shite," cried a surprised William as he took aim and fired at one of the Huron, catching him in the abdomen. With no time to reload, Samuel pulled his tomahawk, and charged the remaining Huron who was preparing to fire his musket. While diving to the ground, Samuel threw the tomahawk, the sharp axe like blade turning end over end striking, and embedding in the warrior's upper chest, causing him to fire his musket into the air tearing through the branches of a pine tree, one of which landed on Samuel.

William ran over as Samuel threw the branch off, and jumped up, the adrenaline from the battle still coursing through him. "Jumping Jesus," he whooped, "did you see that, William?" He walked over to the stricken Huron, the blade of the tomahawk stuck in his heart. "I think I'll just leave that there," he said, "I have another one I sort of borrowed from Two Birds." He looked over to Laing's dead body, "That's one British bastard off my list."

William knelt down by the other Huron. The warrior was still alive, the musket ball passed through the lower left side of his abdomen and exited out his back, missing his kidney and spine. He looked up at William and in passable English said, "Wound will not kill me, so make my end quick, white man."

William reached into a pouch hanging on his belt and pulled out a handful of goose down. "I'm going to plug your wounds," he said, "when I'm done, go to Buxton, and tell him what happened. You can come back for the bodies."

The Huron grimaced as he stood up, but didn't utter a sound. He bent to pick up his musket, taking a quick glance at William. William nodded, and the warrior picked it up, and headed back down the trail.

"Grab Laing's horse," William said to Samuel, "that'll make a better mount for Jack. We may have to ditch the mules if we have to run."

The need to put distance between them, and their pursuers was balanced by the need to rest their horses. They found a secluded hollow to bed down for a few hours. The meal was a chilly, damp affair as a thick fog had settled over the hills and woods. They talked about the mules while eating their meal of dried venison, Jack being the one who brought it up. "I think there's a small farm near a river not too far from here," he said, "if we can find it in this fog. I'll see about making a deal with the farmer."

They made their way slowly through the strangely quiet woods, the blanket of fog starting to lighten as the morning wore on. Thomas was in the lead, and had somehow found a path leading in the right direction. Samuel remarked that the fog would also slow down Buxton, a statement that Jack didn't quite agree with. "Well, as to that, I reckon that unless Buxton is a fool, he's sticking to the road, and heading to the bridge that crosses that river up ahead, that being the only place for miles to cross. We'd best be wary when the time comes."

As the sun began to burn away the fog their pace quickened, and were soon looking down on the river valley. The steep sided banks gave credence to Jack's assessment of the terrain. They rode down, the valley floor festooned with long grass, and wildflowers, the fog's dewy residue coating the horses flanks and the riders legs. The smell of wood smoke drew them north along the river. William and Thomas trotted ahead, and were greeted by the farmer's dog, and then the farmer, his musket pointed at them. "Come ahead," he said, "My eyes ain't what they used to be, but I can tell you ain't them bloody Huron's I seen yesterday."

Randolph Giles lived alone, his brusque manner, and lack of regular bathing testifying as to why. The companions shifted the loads off the mules, each of them taking a portion, including an extra musket, and for Samuel, a new tomahawk. Giles agreed to keep the mules until Jack could come back for them, but promised he would work them hard for their fodder. He told them of seeing a party of Huron a ways north of his farm. "Don't rightly know if they stayed the night," he said, "but I followed them for a bit, afore the fog rolled in. You'll reach the road in a couple hours, but if you want to keep your hair, back track a few miles. There's a deer trail that'll get you to the road a mile or so west of the bridge. Might be, you'll come up behind them what's hunting you."

Without the need to post a guard, Giles' dog being well suited to the task, the companions enjoyed a well-deserved uninterrupted sleep. Taking Giles' advice the next morning, they found, and followed the deer trail, halting before reaching the road. Jack rode up to William, "I ain't no coward, but I ain't no fighter neither. If we cross the road, and continue cross country, we're bound to find another way east."

William looked at the others knowing that if they had to fight their way through that they might not all survive. "I agree with Jack. We can outrun them if it comes to that. I'll lead with Samuel. Thomas, watch our backs. Let's take a few minutes to get ready. Load both muskets, and oh, if you're smart, you'll take a piss while you can."

****

Buxton swore, and mounted his horse. He was tired of the waiting. "Damn fools should have been here by now." He told two of the braves to follow him, "Could be that they're trying to sneak behind us." They scoured the ground for any sign of anyone using or crossing the road. Buxton was in the lead; his head bent low along the horse's flank when his mount reared to avoid colliding with Samuel's horse as he came out of the woods. Somehow, both riders managed to stay mounted, the surprise now registering as they pulled their muskets up. Buxton fired first, but his shot went wide as his horse was still jittery, and moved while Buxton fired. Samuel's aim was also spoiled by Buxton's horse. Dropping the musket he pulled out his tomahawk, and kicked his steed to charge Buxton. Buxton tried to turn his horse to flee, but it was too late. The pipe end of the tomahawk crashed into Buxton's skull driving the broken bone into his brain. The two Huron rushed at Samuel, one of them grabbing at the reins of his horse, the other trying to pull him out of the saddle. Samuel lashed out, kicking the one by him in the face, the sound of his foe's nose breaking bringing a smile to Samuel's face. He turned the tomahawk so the axe blade was now pointing down and slashed the Huron across his neck. The Huron fell away clutching at the spurting artery. The one by the horse's head let go of the reins and turned to flee. The whirring sound of a thrown tomahawk was the last thing he heard as it slammed into his back severing his spine.

William emerged as the short battle ended, Jack and Thomas on his heels. They all stared at the carnage, and at the blood spattered figure of Samuel. He was smiling, and breathing heavily. He gulped in a lungful and said, "It all happened so fast. I don't rightly recall what I did." He paused, and looking at the fallen Huron with his tomahawk in his back, "Ah, it's coming back to me now. Guess I'll be needing another of Two Birds' hatchets. Gonna owe him a fortune, this keeps up." He rode back to Buxton's body, "That's two off my list, though they were the least of my concern." Feeling a bit nauseous as the battle lust wore off, he put his hand to his mouth in an effort to keep from retching. The urge passed and his smile returned, "We gonna sit here all day? There's still a few Huron left and I'm not looking forward to meeting them."

The terrain was a mixture of thick woods, face slapping branches a frequent nuisance, rolling hills, and an occasional open space where they could let their horses run for a while. William was in the front, and was currently stopped at a small creek. He wiped the sweat from his face and then plunged his head into the cool water. "That looks mighty refreshing," said Jack as he, and Samuel dismounted, "only a couple more hours of daylight. This here creek is running in the right direction. Reckon we just follow it for a while and then make camp."

Thomas caught up with them a few minutes later, having been watching to see if they were being followed. He slid out of the saddle and after cooling off in the water, said, "You remember that Huron what was shot yesterday? I just saw him and his two remaining companions 'bout five minutes back."

Samuel grabbed his musket, "Good Lord, I thought we were done with fighting today."

Thomas laughed, "Well, if we do have more fightin' to do, it won't be with them Huron. They were on top of a hill and they knew I could see them. The wounded one just raised his hand up, and then they all took off the other way. I guess they had enough of Samuel for one day."

"Still and all, it would behoove us to continue to scout ahead," replied Jack, "we still have three weeks at a steady pace til we reach Albany."

Crow Village on the Bighorn River

Liam, his gaze drawn by the starry expanse of the nighttime sky, tried to recognize stars he remembered from his youth. Back home the land was covered with trees. Out here on these endless grasslands, nothing blocked your view of the endless sky. "It would take Pierre months to teach me all the constellations we can see," he said to Wahta and Turtle. They were seated on the ground near the camp fire having just finished a meal of some kind of stew. They hadn't come to a conclusive agreement as to the identity of the critter that the elderly Crow widow used to make their meal. Her name, according to Gabe, was Morning Dew on the Buffalo Grass but that she would answer to Morning Dew. She had more or less adopted the three guests, moving in with her widowed sister so her boys could have her tipi. Liam put down his bowl, "Yep, Pierre would love this sky."

"This here Pierre fellow sounds interesting," said Gabe as he sauntered over to join them, "someone you could have a good talking with."

"Smartest man I know," replied Liam, "and a close friend." He looked over at Wahta who was struggling with a piece of the dubious meat, "Of course, not as close as my ravenous Mohawk brother," he said laughing.

Wahta finally swallowed and said, "Not even our friend the Black Robe is smart enough to know what this meat is."

Turtle nodded and replied, "I know it isn't buff," a huge belch later he continued, "buffalo. Probably one of those little rodent critters we see popping up from their many holes in the ground."

"I reckon you're right," said Gabe as he lit his pipe, "it won't be long though before we'll have buffalo, lots of buffalo, and elk. Starting to get colder up in the higher meadows, the buffalo and elk will be moving down soon. Then we'll have us a hunt. It's a lot easier now that most tribes use horses. The Crow got them from the Shoshone, and now are the biggest horse breeding tribe around. Trade mostly with the Shoshone and the Kiowa but will do business with Lakota, and Cheyenne either by trade or by raiding." He pulled a small burning branch out of the fire, and relit his pipe, the glow of the flame illuminating his eyes as he puffed the flame into the pipe's bowl. "Now, of course," he chuckled, "all them critters moving down the mountain will be followed by wolves, bears, and mountain lions. Not that you have anything to worry about. If this large Mohawk can handle Morning Dew's cooking, he can handle those beasts, I reckon."

Up at the crack of dawn, as befitting her name, Morning Dew rekindled the fire, and went into the tipi to retrieve her kettle. Just as she opened the flap, Turtle let loose with a gust of foul smelling wind. Morning Dew wrinkled her nose and promptly stepped back outside. Liam heard the stifled intake of breath of the old woman, and as he opened his eyes, he too smelled the fugue emanating from the prone form of Turtle. Holding his breath, he got up joining Morning Dew at the fire. She smiled at him, and began speaking in Crow, and gesturing at the tipi. Liam could understand some of what she said, and steeling himself for the onslaught to his nose, reentered the tipi, and brought out the kettle. He took it to the river, filling it for Morning Dew while she gathered what she needed to cook the morning meal. Liam, once again braving the elements went into the tipi. He nudged Turtle with his foot, "Wake up, and smell what you did," he said.

Turtle threw off the elk hide blanket, "Oh my lord a mighty," he said grabbing his nose, "now that's a proper way to digest rodent. I do apologize."

The village was in a bustle of activity as women tended fires, and cooking food while children, reenergized after a night's sleep, scampered about, chasing each other or one of the camp dogs. Gabe came over, dodging three laughing children, the puppy that ran between his legs, and a large Mohawk warrior who was chasing them. "Seems the young ones have a new playmate," he said as he sat down next to Liam.

Liam smiled, "It's the same everywhere we go, the children and Wahta. I sometime envy my brother his way with kids."

Gabe noticed a slight tremor in Liam's voice, "May be that I've been with Indians for such a long time, that I've learned to live with the sorrows that plague my heart. I'm not one who pokes his self into other's business, but I know you suffer. There's an old man lives just outside this camp, name of Takoda, which means, friend to everyone. He's half Pawnee, and half Lakota, but lives near the arch enemy of both. He's revered by most around here, but some scoff at his notions of peace. I'd like you to meet him."

Liam let out a sigh, "I don't talk about it much; the way my soul suffers. I've always been restless, always had the desire to explore; to test myself. My Mohawk father, Donehogawa recognized my spirit for what it is, the restless buffalo. Never been able to quiet that spirit completely; though when I was with Orenda, I was at peace." Liam paused for a moment; this sudden unburdening of his soul, the flooding back of memories had him gasping for air, tears forming in the corners of his eyes.

Gabe handed him a flask, "Now, go easy on this, tain't water." Liam took a drink, his head twitched as the burning liquid slid down his throat. "Irish whiskey, finest you'll find within 500 miles," Gabe chuckled.

"Thanks," Liam rasped. He handed the flask back to Gabe, cleared his throat, wiping his eyes as he continued, "After the attack by Chogan and Huritt, I was a rather surly sonofabitch. The restlessness took on a new quality, rage. Pure rage and hatred. Handy things to have during the war, but not so good otherwise." He looked up, a smile coming to his face, "My poor brother and Henry sure had to put up with a lot those days. I'm sure they weren't too unhappy when I took off with Wahta and Mulhern. I was probably at my lowest when I met Rebecca. Took some time but she gently forced herself into my heart." He stopped, "Better have that flask ready," he chuckled quietly, followed by a short sob. "During the battles in the war it was as if I was one of those heroes Homer wrote about. My senses at their highest, the sights, sounds, and smells of war arousing within me a beast craving death. Rebecca tamed that beast. Her death woke it up."

"I s'pose we all have something within us we don't understand," Gabe said, "the Almighty seems to delight in the unique qualities we all possess. The crosses we have to bear, in a manner of speaking. All we can do seems to me is to cope with it as best we can. Course now, living out here where every day is a struggle to survive, sorta takes your mind off other things." He stood, and gestured down the river, "C'mon Liam, Takoda lives just down the river. If I've learnt anything during my time on this earth, it's that sometimes you can't do the job alone."

Over the course of the next few weeks Liam spent a lot of time with Takoda. His initial meeting settled Liam's mind whether this holy man was a man to listen to. When Takoda came out of his dwelling he shouted out while pointing to Liam, "Bi-shee, Bi-shee." Liam knew enough of the Crow language by now to recognize the word for buffalo. Some days Takoda listened to Liam as he spoke of the ways of the white man. Other days he would talk to Liam about The One Who Has Made Everything, the Crow's name for god the creator. It was decided that Liam would undergo a sweat lodge ceremony after the coming buffalo hunt. The fasting required for the sweat lodge would not be beneficial to a hunter.

****

The young Crow, one of three chosen to wake the village when the scouts returned with the location of the herd, peered into the tipi. Liam was already awake, "Ahh, good morning Badger. I will awaken the others."

Badger grinned and replied, "This is my first hunt." He then yawned, "I did not sleep. I am both excited and afraid."

Liam walked over to Badger, putting his hands on the young brave's shoulders. He looked him in the eyes and said, "So am I. Stay close to me. Perhaps we can conquer our fears together."

Just then Morning Dew entered the tipi and gently shoved the smiling Badger out. "My sons are lazy," she yelled out, "why are you still lying down? Your poor Crow mother will not make it through the cold winter with sons too lazy to hunt." She turned and winked at Liam while prodding Wahta with her walking stick, "Is this the way of the Mohawk?" Moving to Turtle, her stick rapping off his backside, "Your Ojibway Father would be ashamed."

Turtle rolled away and stood up. He put his arms around Morning Dew and lifted her in a gentle hug, "My Crow mother complains too much. How many buffalo does she want her brave son to kill for her?" He kissed her forehead and set her down.

"You must kill many if I am to feed that giant Mohawk," she said opening the tent flap, "It is dangerous, do not get hurt." At the sound of Wahta's growling stomach she turned around, pointed her stick at him began cackling, a cross between a laugh and a cough.

"Is there any food ready my loving Crow mother?" asked Wahta.

"Of course there is," she replied, "your loving Crow mother is not lazy like her sons." She cackled again, and walked outside.

"Well, she's right about one thing," Liam said as Wahta's stomach let loose another wave of rumbling, "we need to kill a lot of buffalo."

While the rest of the villagers readied themselves, the hunters were checking their weapons, decorating their horses with painted symbols. The women, old men and, children gathered everything they would need as they prepared to follow the hunters to the kills. Liam was seated on a stool checking each arrow shaft while Morning Dew braided his hair. He decided to hunt with bow and arrow today; however, not leaving anything to chance, his musket would be loaded and strapped to his back, just in case.

Badger came over leading his pony. He had painted hand prints on the pony's front shoulders; the rear flanks were covered in multi-colored swirls. "This is his first hunt, too," Badger said as the pony pawed the ground nervously.

Liam stroked the pony's nose, and whispered quietly to it. The pony whickered softly, and calmed down. Liam was looking in its eyes and just for a split second he saw a buffalo reflected in those eyes but when the pony blinked, it was gone. A sense of foreboding, and caution filled Liam's mind. "He's a good pony," Liam said trying to mask his sudden nervousness, "he will serve you well today."

The hunters were ready, and gathered into a large circle into which Takoda entered. He carried a ceremonial pipe, reaching down to the fire he pulled out a glowing stick, and lit the pipe. First he smoked facing east then turned, and did the same in the other three directions, raising the pipe to the sky after each puff. He then prayed to Grandmother Earth thanking her for sacrificing her children the buffalo so her people could live. When he finished he looked at Liam and said, "Bi-shee."

Liam, Wahta, Turtle, and Badger rode together as part of the hunting group with the chief, and his best warriors. The scouts led them to the far end of a lush valley. The herd had been contentedly grazing at the other end for two days. They stayed downwind, and out of sight by riding below the ridge that bordered the valley. Stopping where the valley descended into a large gully, the chief signaled the leader of the second group of riders to begin their task. They wheeled around, and rode away, heading for the other end of the valley where they would drive the herd to the waiting hunters.

Liam and Wahta dismounted and crawled to the top of the ridge. The herd was mostly at the other end, though there were some frolicking youngsters just below them, and one old bull rolling in the dust. The sound of thunder reached their ears though there wasn't a cloud in the sky. The old bull stood up suddenly, obviously agitated. The calves ran to the protection of their mothers. Then the ground began to tremble as the enormous herd was startled into a stampede. In a flash, Liam and Wahta were up racing to where Turtle and Badger held their mounts. "Remember, Badger, stay on the edge of the herd," said Liam, "I'll be close by."

They rode down the ridge. Some of the group descended into the steep sided gully that spanned almost the entire width of the valley, and which presented an unavoidable obstacle, and then clambered up the other side to take up positions for firing arrows into the bogged down herd. The rest of the hunting group was racing to meet the herd. Wahta, Turtle, and some of the more adventurous Crow guided their mounts in and out of charging buffalo, firing arrows, or plunging their lances into the sides of their prey. Wahta held back, looking for a large bull to bring down. Spying one up ahead, he yelled for Turtle to follow him. When Turtle saw the bull he pulled alongside Wahta and yelled, "God's bollocks, Wahta. That's got to be the bloody largest, angriest one in the herd. Gonna take both of us to bring him down."

Liam settled in riding behind Badger, and watched as the young Crow let an arrow fly. "Too soon," thought Liam as the arrow fell harmlessly to the ground behind his target. Determined not to make the same mistake, Badger urged his pony to come alongside the shaggy beast. This time his arrow found the mark, the force of the blow taking the pointed head between ribs and into the lungs and heart. The buffalo went down creating chaos behind it sending two more to the ground, thrashing legs catching Liam's pony a glancing blow. The horse reeled sideways, but caught its balance before it, and Liam hit the ground. By the time Liam caught up with Badger, the young brave had another kill, but was now out of arrows. He motioned for Badger to pull off, feeling the need to check his mount.

Turtle guided his galloping mount, and came up on the opposite side of the large bull, plunging his lance into the buffalo's side, but lost his grip as the now enraged animal veered away. Wahta readied his lance for a strike just as the bull bumped his horse. Only Wahta's strength kept him from being knocked off of his mount as he gripped the horse's sides tight with his powerful legs. He pulled back his right arm, and threw his lance with as much force as he could, but watched incredulously as the bull shook it out of its body, and continued running, blood streaming from both wounds. The two hunters kept pace as they grabbed their bows, and began firing arrows into the bull until it finally succumbed, and tumbled to the ground spraying them with clods of turf as the massive creature tore the earth in its death throes. As if in one last act of defiance, the dying bull rolled into the path of Turtle's horse. The pony reared to avoid the collision throwing an unbalanced Turtle onto the slain bull, landing hard enough to have the breath knocked out of him. Wahta saw him fall, but was trapped in a group of buffalo making it impossible to come to a quick turnaround. Turtle gasped, and seeing his situation crawled over to the front of the bull and crouched down behind the massive head. In the distance he could see a Crow rider heading his way and when he was close, Turtle stood on the buffalo's head and grabbed the outstretched arms of the hunter, swinging up behind him, and galloped away from the stampeding herd.

When Liam saw Turtle go down he quickly remounted, turned to Badger told him to stay put, and began threading his way toward his fallen friend. He soon found an open path, and urged his mount into a gallop. The pony raced through the high grass, grass that hid the many prairie dog holes that dotted that part of the valley. With an audible snap, the pony's foreleg broke as it stepped into one of the holes throwing Liam forward over its head. He struck the ground, his left shoulder dislocating from the impact. Liam struggled to his feet, his upper body racked with pain. He looked up and saw Badger heading his way at a gallop. Liam tried to warn him to stop, but it was too late. Badger's pony reared when it saw Liam's horse thrashing on the ground catching the young rider by surprise. Badger fell off backwards, and was lying in the path of the last remnant of the herd as they charged towards him. Liam rushed over, and stood in front of Badger. Despite the agony caused by the movement, Liam raised his arms, his left one noticeably lower than his right. He then knelt on the ground, and watched as the herd split on either side of them. As the last of the buffalo passed by, the old bull Liam had seen earlier, stopped and looked at him. It bobbed its large shaggy head, snorted once, and then rejoined the herd.

Gabe and Takoda stood on the ridge, having ridden ahead of the butchering party, and watched in horror and then fascination as they saw the herd pass by Liam and Badger. "Bi-shee! Bi-shee!" screamed Takoda looking first at Liam and then to the heavens.

"I'll be a suck egged mule." uttered Gabe, "Like Moses parting the waters." Takoda looked at him questioningly, "Oh, sorry old friend," Gabe replied, "one of the white man's stories about The Great Spirit. I'll tell you it later."

Turtle and his Crow rescuer came over to Liam. "That was either the daftest thing I have ever seen, or the bravest," Turtle said.

Liam just looked at him, the sudden realization of what had happened, and the returning of the pain jolted Liam back to the present. He fell to the ground grabbing at his shoulder. "Ahh damnation, but this hurts," Liam said, "I must be getting old. Used to I'd reset this shoulder myself. Look at me now, weak as a kitten."

Turtle shook his head, "You have no idea what you just did, do you?"

Liam nodded, "It will come back to me eventually. I only remember pleading with Grandmother. I guess she heard me."

Suddenly the painful screams of Liam's pony ended. Wahta had finally reached them, and seeing Liam was apparently all right walked over to the stricken, frightened horse. Its leg was shattered beyond repair, so Wahta drew his knife, cradling the pony's head in his lap, speaking softly to it as he pulled the blade through the pony's throat, sending him on his way back to Grandmother.

Liam watched Wahta, and shuddered as his pony was put out of its misery, causing another spasm of pain. He fell back holding onto his damaged shoulder. Turtle looked down at him and said, "I guess I'll have to do the deed since you're in no shape to do it yourself." He gestured to Badger, and told him, "Set down on Liam's other arm." To Wahta he said, "Grab a hold of his legs." Turtle gently lifted Liam's left arm. He looked at Wahta and mouthed to him to talk to Liam. Wahta nodded his head and said to Liam, "Snake Slayer, or should I now call my brother, Bi-shee? What did you see when you were with your spirit brother?"

Liam smiled, "Last thing I remember is seeing Badger on the ground." He then turned toward his young friend, "I seem to recall telling you to stay back."

Badger looked down in shame, but then raised his head and said, "I am sorry, Bi-shee, and I am grateful as well."

"I reckon I should be proud that you came to my rescue," Liam replied, and then to Wahta he said, "After that I seem to remember calling out to Grandmother." He was about to say something else when Turtle, judging that Liam was distracted enough, yanked on the dislocated shoulder pulling it back into place. Liam bucked but was held down by Badger and Wahta. His eyes rolled back, and whimpering once fell unconscious.

"Best just leave him resting for a bit," said Turtle to Wahta, "Why don't you find Morning Dew, and bring her over to see what her sons did for her? Besides, she can help butcher the beast."

Albany

Joseph Clarke took off his heavy apron, hanging it on the peg near the door. It had been another long, hard day, but he was used to long, hard days. During his life he had labored as a seaman, carpenter, miller, farmer, and was now mostly a blacksmith. He had been settled in Albany for about ten years, and his business grew. He now employed three assistants, and a farrier for horseshoeing. He had dismissed his crew earlier than usual, but when he had a special commission piece to work on, he preferred to work alone. His skill with fashioning sharp and durable blades was in high demand from British officers looking for a good sword, and even from some common infantrymen seeking a good knife. It was through those skills that Joseph became acquainted with many of the officers. He would often be invited to join their table at the tavern. They would talk mainly about their lives in the army, battles they'd been in, wounds described, but there was also news, and opinions of the growing discord towards the Crown, especially in Philadelphia and Boston. It was Joseph's way to steer clear of politics deeming that a man's opinion of the governor wasn't relevant to that man's need to have a broken wheel fixed, or a plough blade remade. Now, however, he was beginning to think that the discord was unwarranted and possibly even treasonous against King George III.

Shivering as he stepped out of the heat of the smithy, and into the cold night air, he pulled the elk hide coat tighter, and trudged through yet another fresh layer of fallen snow. The calendar said it was March, but weather here in the Hudson River basin didn't care too much for calendars. Heavy snow and frigid temperatures had plagued the area for the last few weeks making travel difficult.

Joseph paused for a moment. He looked up at the now clear sky, and uttered another prayer for the safety of his grandson, Thomas, and his companions, as they made their way to Boston. He had not seen Thomas in many years, and it had gladdened his heart when the four bedraggled, travel weary companions staggered into the tavern asking for Joseph Clarke.

The first few weeks of the reunion were as pleasant as could be imagined. Thomas, Samuel, and William stayed at Joseph's home while Jack bunked with a fellow employee of Two Birds. The three boys, as Joseph thought of them, spent their time just relaxing, the luxury of not being in the saddle being felt daily as stiff and sore thigh muscles ceased their complaints. It was only when they gathered for supper in the tavern that any tension arose, and then only if there were any British soldiers present. Joseph caught Thomas more than once looking at the British with anger in his eyes, but that was nothing compared to Samuel's too loud utterances about his feelings concerning lobsterbacks. It was only William's calming demeanor, and forceful grip on Samuel's arm that kept things from escalating.

Further discussions with Thomas shed light on the situation but did nothing to stem the growing concern Joseph felt about his grandson's opinions of the British, and in his choice of friends. The rift between Joseph and Samuel widened daily, their talks had gone from pleasant exchanges to vehement vitriol, and resulted in Joseph demanding Samuel leave his house. It became apparent to William that they needed to get out of Albany as soon as the weather allowed. Still, it wasn't until a bout of warm weather that he, Thomas, and Samuel rode south to Boston unaware that the weather had played a cruel joke on them.

Chapter 8 1773 - Tea Party

Boston

April 1773

      Marguerite was startled into wakefulness by a sudden and very loud snore from the British colonel lying next to her in his bedroom. She wondered what had happened to the family who used to live in this rather affluent house. 'Probably a prominent merchant linked to the rebels, and had thus fled for his life along with his wife and family,' she thought, 'but now it houses four British officers.' Being set adrift with little or no prospects for the future was something she understood all too well. She was born in 1756 to Geoffrey Edgerton, a sergeant in the British army who was killed in the battle on the Plains of Abraham in 1759, and Claudia Marceau, a French-Canadian woman he met in Quebec. After her father's death, her mother, left with an infant, and no income other than Geoffrey's meager savings, gradually made her way to the city of Boston. Finding employment as a laundress, and seamstress for the officer corps stationed in Boston helped feed, and house her and Marguerite, but just barely. Marguerite tiptoed out of the room to go to the lavatory down the hall. Pausing by the colonel's coat, she reached inside, and pulled out a packet of official papers. Marguerite smiled at how easy it was for her to get information. Most of the officers who chose to keep her company had fallen prey to her charming smile, and her witty intellect. This colonel mentioned he had gotten new orders simply because Marguerite said how much she had missed him the last two weeks while he was on patrol, and now she had those orders in her hands. Marguerite quietly opened up the paper, and read its contents putting to memory the details. She slid the packet, now put back together, into the pocket, and proceeded to get dressed. The colonel woke slightly, and noticing that Marguerite was dressing mumbled, 'don't forget your money, love.'

      When Marguerite left the house, she smiled at the guard at the door, and gave him a naughty-like wink, it was all he could do to not abandon his post, and follow her swaying hips down the street. The sentry had been standing post outside the officer's quarters for five hours, and was glad for anything to shake the boredom, if only for a few minutes. The smile dissolved quickly on Marguerite's face when the ever present memory of a British soldier, much like the sentry, attempting to rape her mother intruded on her thoughts. For two years after her father's death, Marguerite and Claudia were mostly shunned by the other soldier's wives, as Claudia embraced the Catholicism of her youth. They eventually made their way to Casco Bay where, thanks to a kindly old priest, they found lodging, as well as work for Claudia. For three years they lived happy lives, but were soon and once again targets of scorn, and ridicule from a group of citizens being led by a frenzied anti-Papist preacher. It became a daily ritual for Claudia and Marguerite to run a gauntlet of cursing, shoving, rotten fruit throwing, by church going people, whose fear of the unknown was being fed with every evil calumny the preacher could invent about Catholics. Fearing that their lives were in danger, the priest encouraged them to take passage on a merchant ship bound for Boston. He gave them the name, and whereabouts of a silversmith he was acquainted with, having done business with him, and who might be able to help them get settled. While for eight year old Marguerite this was a frightening experience, it was also one of those leaps of faith, a favorite phrase of her mother's, where the potential for adventure was high. Deprived of any proper schooling, it took Marguerite a while to learn to read, but under the tutelage of the priest her thirst for knowledge was awakened, and she now devoured any book she could get her hands on. She was also a keen observer of nature, and also of human nature. Her effortless charm, and wit were her most notable traits, though as she grew into womanhood, her beauty added to her allure.

It hadn't taken long after their arrival in Boston before Marguerite became aware of the tension existing between the British, and many of the residents. She had found work, with the help of the silversmith Paul Revere, as a barmaid in one of the taverns frequented by like- minded men calling themselves The Sons of Liberty. Her natural inquisitiveness would have her lingering around the interesting conversations, much to the chagrin of other patrons waiting for another tankard of ale. One of the things she had heard frequently was the lament that they lacked someone close to the officers who could get them better inside information. One night, not being able to fall asleep, her thoughts kept returning to that awful day her mother was almost raped. The British were, in her mind, clearly in the wrong in their heavy handed approach to governing the colonies, and combined with the loathing she felt towards the soldiery had her wondering what she could do to help The Sons of Liberty. It had seemed to her that getting information from a British officer could be possible with guile and charm, and those qualities were perhaps more likely to be found in a woman. She sat up realizing that she may have a solution, but was she brave enough to go through with, or to even suggest it to Mr. Adams and Mr. Revere?

As she made her way to the Hanover Street house of Dr. Joseph Warren to deliver her report, she remembered the first time she had gone to this place. She had overheard that there was going to be a meeting of what they called The Committee of Safety at Warren's house, and having made the decision to go through with her idea, and with some trepidation, knocked on the doctor's door.

Telling the servant who answered the door that she needed to see Dr. Warren about an emergency medical need, she followed him, barging past him when he opened the parlor door. "Young lady," asked Warren rising from his chair, "what is the meaning of this intrusion?"

Marguerite gathered up her courage and replied with a smile on her face, "Gentlemen, please excuse my rather rude entrance, but I have been listening to your discussions at the tavern, and I believe I may have a possible solution to one of your biggest problems." She paused for a moment and glanced around the table seeing surprise and some amusement in their eyes, "I am here to offer myself to your cause, mind and body."

Warren stroked his chin as he chuckled but when he looked at Marguerite he saw courage, determination, and intelligence in her eyes, and the set of her jaw. "Do you know what you are suggesting Miss, ahh, what is your name?"

Giving him her best smile Marguerite replied, "Marguerite Edgerton, sir, and I do understand what I am suggesting. Wouldn't you agree that the wiles of a woman can be a potent weapon? As to your kind concerns about the lengths I will take to get what you seek, I thank you, but if my body is required to further your, our, cause, then so be it."

She smiled at the memory, then as she turned the corner, noticed three young men she had not seen before, enter Warren's house. Her first impression was that they weren't locals as they had the look of the frontier about them. "Well, wherever they're from," she mumbled, "I hope they're on our side."

Albany to Greenfield

They made good time the first few days out of Albany, crossing the Hudson River in the early morning, being the only travelers on the usually crowded ferryboat. Thomas stood at the rail looking back toward Albany. He felt bad about leaving his grandfather in such a hurry, and with hard feelings, but was anxious to get to Boston. He was about to turn away when he saw Joseph walk onto the quay they had just left. Thomas waved and saw Joseph cup his hands to his mouth, and shout in order to be heard above the noise of the river, "God be with you, Thomas."

The weather held for the first couple of days with temperatures above freezing, making for good traveling conditions, although the reminders of winter were evident by the snowcapped peaks looming ahead of them in the morning light as they awoke from their first night's camp. The sunrise was a brilliant color combination of yellow and red prompting Samuel to mention, "What's that saying about a red sky in the morning? Sailors take warning or something like that? I don't see much to be worried about. Sky is clear up ahead."

William paused as he placed his saddle on his horse's back, and looked at the sky behind them. "Yeah, well, it's clear up ahead, but I don't like the looks of what's coming up behind us." Their camp was on a mostly flat hilltop, and William could see the western sky as he looked back toward the Hudson. "We need to push hard today. About thirty miles to a village on the Connecticut River," he said pointing to the sky, "I want to get to Greenfield before those clouds get to us." The trail they were following was familiar to William having made this journey, and back again taking messages to their friend George Washington. They were riding down a valley that led to a pass through the mountains that lay between them and Greenfield. They were sheltered from the wind as it became gustier as the day went on. They could see puffs of snow smoke being blown by the wind on the higher peaks. With a couple brief rests for the horses, and their aching backsides they pushed on. Finally, just before dusk they could see the village smoke ahead. Their mounts seemed to realize the end of the day was near, and found one more burst of energy.

A night under a roof, a meal of venison stew, and passable ale did wonders for stiff muscles, and they woke refreshed the next morning. After a quick breakfast, they retrieved their mounts from the stable, and walked them to the ferry that would take them across the deep Connecticut River. They had met the owner of the ferry at the inn, and made arrangements with him to be off at dawn. He was reluctant at first, because of the storm he said was coming. The weather had just started to change with wind gusts creating choppy waves on the water. The ferry captain said he'd be lucky to get back across, but agreed to do it at double the fee. The horses were agitated by the wind and the choppy river and had to be manually coaxed, and shoved onto the barge, and even then it took a blindfold to calm Thomas' mount enough for her to go on board. Ironically it was the pack mule who presented the least trouble, ambling across the ramp on its own. While crossing, the craft was bounced around by the waves throwing up sprays of water across the deck, but the captain and his three sons kept it on course. The wind increased so that when they disembarked the waves were now white capped, causing the ferry crew to hurry them along knowing that it was only going to get worse. Walking their mounts to the top of the bank, they were met with the sight of storm clouds, heavy and dark, heading their way. "Mount up, and head to those trees yonder," said William pointing to the forest in the distance. They rode for a couple of miles looking for a spot they could hunker down, and ride out the storm. The temperature was dropping steadily, and soon the snow began to fall.

"Down there," yelled Samuel, gesturing down the slope to the boulder strewn gully below them. The old creek bed was wide enough for Thomas and William to set up one of their tents, but not without some difficulty, as a strong gust knocked Thomas down. Samuel picketed, and hobbled the horses, and mule, giving each a feedbag to tide them over. With no possibility of a fire in these conditions, they wrapped themselves up in as best they could, and ate a cold meal of pemmican, and slightly stale biscuits.

"My Grand Da will be worried about us," said Thomas during a lull in the howling wind.

Samuel poked his head out of the burrow he had made and said, "Worried about you, and probably William. Don't reckon he gives two hoots 'bout me."

Thomas laughed, "You're probably right about that." He stopped smiling, and looking at William said, "Here's what worries me. My Grand Da ain't the only one in Albany what thinks like he does, and I'm guessing that it's like that everywhere in the colonies."

William stood up, and opened the tent flap, "Damnation, but it's snowing hard, can't hardly see more than a few feet." He tied the flap closed, and settled himself into his bedroll. "More than likely you are correct, Thomas. This kind of thing will set families, friends, and neighbors at each other's throats. Naught we can do about it, especially while stuck in a blizzard. So, get what sleep you can. Tomorrow promises to be a chore."

Mallory Town

Mid-February

Life slowed down during the snowy winter. Everyone concentrated on keeping warm, so the busiest people in the town were Bert, keeping up with the demand for cut firewood, and Timothy, his tavern being a warm refuge, and where hot mulled cider was readily available. The sleepy attitude gave way as the weather turned warmer; soon there was a bustle of activity as repairs were made to the ravages of winter. The change also brought with it a steady influx of travelers, some intent on staying, some just stopping over before continuing west to Fort Pitt, and the Ohio River. Also arriving upon occasion were refugees from Indian raids. Whatever their motives, most of them were greeted by the unofficial gate guards, Bowie, Caleb, and Jack. Jack, being more of a conversationalist than his companions would answer the traveler's questions while Caleb and Bowie stood at attention.

Jack Tomlinson arrived back from Albany shortly after the New Year delivering a letter from Thomas to Liza and Henry. Knowing that it was also meant for the others they planned to read to the whole group when they could all be together, a difficult process since Daniel and Henry stepped up patrols due to the news from fleeing settlers. It had become a tradition for the families to gather on Sunday mornings at the grave sites. When it became clear that Mallory Town was going to grow, Daniel hired Richard and James Crane, and now the area was separated from the new homes by a stone wall. At one end of the cemetery were the graves of Stumpnose, Rob Carter, and Phil Burke. In the middle Thomas, Abigail, and Grace lie together. Next to them were Orenda and her unborn child. Rebecca was buried with her child; her father in the grave next to hers.

On this particular Sunday, Daniel, Deborah, Liza, Henry, and their children were joined by Timothy, Marsha Crane, the Lapley's, and Bert. They stopped first by the graves of the three traders. The girls, Meagan and Abigail, placed a wreath of wild flowers on each grave. Liza looked down at Phil Burke's marker, and smiled as she remembered the fastidious merchant. She wiped away the debris on top of his grave, and added a bouquet of lilacs to the wreath, the fragrance a soothing balm for her sadness. Soon all of the graves were adorned with spring time colors set alight by the rising sun's rays. At a signal from Liza everyone became quiet as each took a moment to reflect, and remember those whom they had lost. When Daniel deemed the time right, he cleared his throat, and intoned an 'amen', ending the brief ceremony.

The weather was warmer than normal, so rather than gather in someone's crowded cabin, the group was going to meet at the fire pit in the center of town, preparations having been made for a meal after reading the letter. Meagan and Abbie tended the fire, and had coffee, and tea heating up. Jonas and his son John set a freshly butchered pig on a spit. Tables and benches were brought out of cabins, and soon were laden with breads, and cakes straight from the ovens, venison stew, and kegs of ale, and wine. Once all that was done, and the children had a chance to run off pent up energy, Henry stood and got everyone's attention. The crowd was even larger now as some of the villagers were up and about, and hung at the edge of the circle of people gathered to hear the news. He held up the letter, and began to read:

Ma and Da,

We made it to Albany, though not without some difficulty, including a battle. We had come upon a burnt out farmstead, and the dead family. A party of Huron was responsible for the raid, but they had assistance from a couple ex-British soldiers.

Most of the crowd had already heard about the farmer and his family, and the coming fight with Buxton and the Huron. Jack Tomlinson, before he left to report to Two Birds in Fort Pitt, spent three days in Mallory Town regaling all who wanted to hear the tale. As Henry finished the description of the skirmish a rippling murmur went through the crowd including some comments extolling long life to King George. Daniel looked out over the still growing throng of onlookers, many of them newly settled in Mallory Town, and not necessarily tied to the history of the founders. He knew the full contents of the letter, and thought it best to make known the rest to a select few only. He went over to Henry, and whispered those thoughts prompting Henry to nod his agreement. He folded up the parchment, and put it in his pocket, "As the rest of Thomas' note is of a personal nature, I'll stop reading at this point. I see we've drawn quite a crowd. I reckon it wouldn't be neighborly not to invite the whole lot to our little feast. Come one, come all. Let us celebrate the end of winter together."

That pronouncement set off a cheer, and a flurry of activity as the residents rushed to and fro adding to the bounty to be consumed. Even the new preacher got into the act by proclaiming that since most of his congregation was partaking of the impromptu feast rather than attending his sermon, he would forego the service, and join in. In no time, a side of beef was spitted, and joined the pig turning over the fire. Sunday meals meant for family dinners were now to be shared. Ciders, ale, and wine were contributed, fiddles and pipes added to the festivities, an unexpected daylong party commenced.

Daniel made his way over to where Henry was speaking to one of the new settlers. He listened to the conversation for a moment, his attention drawn by the settler's story. When the man excused himself, and returned to his family, Daniel asked Henry for the letter wanting to read again the concerns raised by Thomas. He sat on a bench and read:

I know I've not had the experience in battle that you and my uncles have had, but what I witnessed from Samuel had to be something out of the ordinary. He seemed to be possessed and without fear. He told me later that he was so focused on killing the enemy that he was unaware of anything else around him. It was frightening and amazing at the same time. I hope that I will never see the likes of it again though Samuel says that his battle beast is always with him. I worry about him. He has changed a lot since Josiah and his Ma died. He seems to think of nothing else but revenge on the British and especially Whitby, although when we were gone from home for a few days his old self returned and he was once again joking around; that is until we met Buxton.

Daniel shook his head in amazement. He had seen Liam in battle, had seen the awful carnage, had seen the enemy's blood and gore spattered all over his brother. He knew what Thomas felt. He knew the revulsion, and if he was honest with himself, the thrill of watching a warrior in the throes of battle lust. He returned to the letter. The part about Samuel was important, but what Thomas wrote of their time in Albany, and the reason for leaving sooner than anticipated seemed to Daniel to be even more important. Important for the words now struck a nerve about the changing times in Mallory Town.

Crow Village on the banks of the Bighorn River

May 1773

Liam waded out into the pool created by a bend in the river, and ducked his head into the water. As he emerged from the water, he noticed his reflection among the ripples created by the drops falling off his hair and beard, and was startled by his appearance. His hair was now mostly gray, his face was weather beaten, and creased with lines and scars. He was momentarily shaken by a memory of Rebecca, and the way she would tease him whenever she found a new gray hair on his head. He looked over to Wahta who was standing on the shore, and seemingly for the first time saw how his Mohawk brother had aged. "Wahta," he called, "When did we become gray hairs?" He chuckled, "I thought that one became wise when that happened."

Wahta grinned and pointed to Morning Dew as she was beating one of Liam's shirts on a rock, "We are wise enough to let our Crow mother care for us. Come, my brother, Turtle and Takoda are waiting. You are as clean as that shirt our mother is washing."

Liam nodded and headed back to the shore. He was going to start building a sweat lodge with Takoda today while Turtle and Wahta left to travel to the Mandan village for trading. He was saddened that his friends were leaving for a while, but realized that this was the perfect time to focus on what Takoda was teaching him. The sweat lodge would be on the bluff overlooking the river. Takoda felt that the cleansing ritual of the sweat was vital to learning what The Great Spirit was teaching.

Gabe was also going away before winter set in. He intended to spend some time with the Shoshone, hunting elk along the Snake River. For now, though, he was cutting wood and brush for Liam and Takoda to use for the sweat lodge fire. He dropped an armful on the ground, and while surveying the progress made, listened to Takoda telling Liam about a dream he has been having. "I am standing on a high bluff looking down at a roaring river with powerful waterfalls. There is smoke rising from pools and holes in the earth along the prairie floor, and water shooting out of the ground."

Liam nodded at the description saying, "I too dream of a place like that. In mine, I see buffalo warming themselves by the smoking waters."

Gabe chuckled, "I'll be a suck egg mule. I know that place, or at least one like it. Along the Yellowstone River there are many hot springs, and I have seen the buffalo doing just like Liam's dream. If you two are of a mind to join me, I wouldn't mind going back there when Wahta and Turtle return in the spring?"

The twelve poles were now up, the door of the lodge facing the rising sun, and the pit had been dug. Liam was now filling the pit with rocks that would be heated during the ceremony. He had placed the first four in a cross shape to represent the four directions, the rest would line the walls of the pit. A gourd filled with water, and a smaller one to use as a dipper, sat next to the blanket Liam would sit upon. Gabe brought in brush and wood for the fire and after arranging them in the pit stood, and said, "This is where I say farewell for the time being. They say the elk are plentiful along the Snake, don't want to keep them waiting." He turned to Takoda and continued, "You take care of our buffalo man."

Liam watched Gabe walk away. He took the lit brand, and set the brush and kindling to burning. They would continue feeding this fire for the three days Liam would spend fasting. He then would enter the lodge to pour the 'uncounted dips of April Showers' onto the rocks, producing the sweat inducing heat. The ceremony was divided into four parts; the first quarter, four dips are placed upon the rocks, the second seven, the third ten, and then the fourth an uncounted 'quarter of a million'. With the fire now going, Takoda finished wrapping the self-painted buffalo hide around the lodge frame closing the door flap. The paintings were scenes and animals from Takoda's past, a past that he was now revealing to Liam as he explained each character or event. The most prominent part of his tale was depicted as a crowd appeared to be shoving one man away from them. "I was a young warrior," he said pointing to the figure being expelled, "This happened because I had shamed my family and tribe with what is considered a weakness. As befitted a young Pawnee warrior, I took part in many raids and witnessed captives being tortured. One day the Great Spirit appeared to me in the eyes of a young captive Blackfeet woman. Her gaze triggered a voice in my head; the Great Spirit told me that torturing captives did not please him. I then stood up to my fellow Pawnee, and rescued the woman. I took her back to her people, and was banished by my tribe."

As interesting as the pictures of Takoda's life were, it was the scene painted on the door flap that had Liam staring the longest. The figure of a white man stood in the midst of a stampeding buffalo herd, his hands touching the head of a large bull while the rest of the herd gallops around him. From that picture, Liam felt a strong connection; his thoughts turning to the coming sweat ceremony, and knew that it would be a transforming point in his life.

They headed back to the village to eat, the last food Liam would have before his fast began in the morning. Takoda was going to sleep by the sweat lodge to keep the fire going. Liam stopped, and shaded his eyes, glancing back across the river he thought he saw a dust cloud like what would be raised from the hooves of a galloping horse. It disappeared quickly making Liam think he was seeing things. "Blasted old age. Eyes playing tricks on me," he muttered as he caught up with Takoda.

The Pawnee scout kept his mount hidden in the dip in the landscape until he was sure that the white man known as Snake Slayer was no longer looking his way. The rest of his band of raiders was camped five miles away awaiting his report. He had seen the large group of warriors, and families head south, and then just a little while ago the white hunter, Bear Man left with the Shoshone visitors. He was not concerned that Snake Slayer was still in the camp. He had watched him build a sweat lodge. Having been through the sweat ceremony many times, he knew that by the third day, Snake Slayer would be too weak to be a threat. He patted his horse's neck, and gently kicked it into motion. In three days, he would return with his brothers, and enrich themselves on the thinly guarded Crow horse herd.

Greenfield to Boston

Early April

The dawn sky was still dark and foreboding though the rate of snowfall had dwindled to flurries. William carefully pushed open the snow laden flap to the tent. He stuck his head out noticing how much snow had fallen, and how much was piled up against the front of the tent. "We'll have to dig ourselves out," he said. As he turned back, a tent slide of snow rolled down and onto his neck and head. "Damnation!" he shrieked, "By God, that's a rude way to awaken."

Samuel sat up, "So, William, has it stopped snowing?" he asked with a chuckle.

Thomas took one look at William's face and burst out laughing, "I swear, William, you look a little put out."

"Ha ha! Come on laughing boys," he said after shaking the snow off of his head, "Grab your shovels, you two, and dig us out of here. We need to check our mounts."

An hour later, Thomas and Samuel had cleared out the space in front of the tent and then trudged through the knee deep snow to the tree line where their mounts were tethered and hobbled. The snow in that area wasn't as deep as by the tent. The trees acted as shields, sheltering the horses and mule from the full brunt of the storm. Among the tools and supplies carried by the mule were some dry blankets that were now being used to dry the wet and cold animals, after which they refilled their nosebags with some more oats.

One thing the tent did besides providing a dry place to sleep was to act as a barrier to the west wind leaving a space on the east side of the tent relatively free of deep snow; a space that was large enough for William to clear and dig a pit for a fire. William then headed into the woods looking for fallen tree limbs in the more exposed parts of the forest. Finding a spot that yielded what he needed, he made four trips back and forth from the camp. Leaving Thomas and Samuel to split the wood thereby exposing the drier wood inside the logs, he went into the tent to retrieve the supply of dry kindling material he always carried, knowing that it might make a difference in survival, or death, the next few days. Fortunately, the wind had died down considerably, so after a few strikes of his flint he had a small flame going in the pit. Carefully he fed more of the kindling into the flame, watching it slowly grow. Soon he was placing small pieces of the split wood onto the fire. By the time Thomas and Samuel returned with another load each of firewood, the fire was a roaring, welcoming blaze.

They warmed themselves while waiting for the coffee to get hot, and the bacon to sizzle. They had moved the picket line for the horses and mule to a spot closer to the fire having decided that travel on this day would not be a good idea. After breaking their fast, the plan was to dry out the tent they used last night, and to put up a different one for tonight. The hope was that the weather would cooperate, and perhaps get a little warmer.

For what seemed like the hundredth time, William glanced up at the western sky. "Finally," he said to himself. "Thomas, Samuel, take a look at this," he called while pointing to the sky. The end of the clouds could be seen and the blessed, clear blue sky behind. "We leave at first light tomorrow. In the meantime, I am tired of pemmican. Why don't you two go hunting?"

The next two days were more reminiscent of May, warm and sunny, and with only a gentle breeze. Though the quickly melting snow slowed them down somewhat, they made good time. The area was dominated by forested hills, boggy meadows, and numerous streams. They were camped alongside one of the small rivers, Samuel trying his luck fishing. Thomas was building the fire when he felt a gust of wind coming out of the northwest. "William, I think our spot of good weather is gonna be over soon. Take a look at that sky."

William sighed, "Aye that it does. Go get Samuel, and make sure the horses are hobbled well. I'll double check the tent stakes."

Though the wind increased during the night, it was only snowing lightly as they prepared for the days ride. Except for the wind, the forest was quiet, even the early spring arrivals, and yearlong resident birds refused to sing on this gray, foreboding morning. They had ridden for a couple hours, the snow not much of a bother, but then the snow was replaced with a stinging, icy sleet. With no option but to continue they rode on, thankful at least that the wind was at their backs. In a matter of a couple hours, the frozen rain had left the newly budding trees encased, the weight of the ice bowing limbs, some cracking under the strain, a resounding bang startling men and beasts. The ice was also beginning to make the trail treacherous. "We need shelter," said William, "keep your eyes open for anything we can use. I seem to remember that there were farms scattered about in this area."

They grew more miserable as the day wore on, the ice now coating their horse's manes and tails. They straggled up another hill and paused at the top. It was hard to be sure in the gloomy light but they thought they could make out the shadowy form of a building down in the meadow below. Samuel pointed, "I don't rightly know for sure, but I see movement down there, and it ain't people."

"I smell smoke," said Thomas as they picked their way carefully down the slippery slope approaching what they hoped was a place out of the weather. A howl from up ahead, followed by another frightened the horses, and surprised the men.

"Damnation!" said William, "just what we need, wolves. Well, gentlemen, unstrap those muskets. We are going to carry on to whatever that building is. In the meantime, we make ourselves as unappetizing as we can. Shoot to kill if they venture too close."

The wolf pack scattered when the men entered the farmstead compound. The remains of mangled and bloody pig carcasses stained the ice and snow red. The building turned out to be a small barn. Beyond that stood the smoldering ashes of the farm house. "First things first, gentlemen," said William, "check out the barn. See if anyone is in there. I'll take a quick look over by the house."

Thomas and Samuel led their mounts and the mule to the barn. Peering inside, they waited until their eyes adjusted to the low light, and then entered, muskets at the ready. The barn was sectioned off, the larger section was storage for hay and tools; the door to the smaller room, a lean-to open to the outside, was ajar. Thomas entered cautiously but slipped on the spilled entrails of the large sow he was now kneeling on. "Looks like we know what them wolves were feasting on," said Samuel helping Thomas to his feet, "let's get our poor beasts inside."

They tethered the animals to the far wall. Thomas picked up a shovel and handed it to Samuel. "We need heat. Dig a pit for a fire. I'll tend to the beasts."

Samuel kicked at the dirt floor of the barn, "At least the ground in here is a little less frozen."

Thomas removed saddles, and wiped the horses and mule dry while Samuel took the shovel and began digging. He dragged over a pile of hay, and was looking for a vessel he could use for water. "I wonder what's taking William so long?" he asked.

"Dunno," replied Samuel, "the pit is ready. There's plenty of kindling what with that stack of hay. Think I saw some cut wood out in the lean-to. Should be a fire going and coffee brewing in a few minutes."

They continued with their tasks, and soon the animals were contentedly browsing, and the fire was ablaze. Thomas warmed his hands over the flames; the aroma from the brewing coffee heightened his anticipation of that hot, bitter drink warming his insides. His revelry was broken as William came in leading his horse and carrying a squealing piglet. "Anyone fancy fresh bacon? I take it this little one is the only survivor, porcine or human?" he asked, "I found the owner out back of the house. Three arrows sticking out of him. Delaware arrows. Saw their tracks; this only happened a few hours ago. I don't think they'll be back, but to be prudent, we will keep a watch tonight. I'll take the first, then Thomas. Samuel will welcome the morning sun. The best spot is in the corner of the lean-to. It'll be cold but dry." He handed the reins to Thomas, and took a steaming cup of coffee from Samuel, the piglet under his other arm had ceased its agitation. "As for this little guy, he'll die anyway from the elements, or more likely from a wolf. I think he'd rather die in a nobler manner. Bring out the fry pan. I'll take care of the butchering."

Thomas was shaken out of his dream of home, opening his eyes to see William grinning down at him. "Your watch, Mr. Clarke. Colder than the devil's heart out there. Skies have cleared. There's good moonlight to see by. Stay alert, I didn't see them but I could hear the wolf pack rustling about in the woods."

Thomas wrapped his blanket around his shoulders, picked up his musket, and headed to the lean-to. Making himself as comfortable as possible propped up against a stack of firewood, he pulled the blanket tighter, his musket lying across his lap. To stay awake, Thomas tried to identify the stars he could see; when that stopped working he concentrated on keeping his eyes moving. He scanned the area in front of him stopping when he thought he saw movement. Three wolves materialized, and began searching the compound for the meal they knew was there. As Thomas shifted slightly, a piece of firewood fell to the ground. The pack leader looked over, and started walking toward the sound. Thomas raised the musket to his shoulder, the wolf, seeing the movement, snarled; his companions joined him, and they all advanced. Thomas tensed, willing them to stop, but when the leader went into a running leap, Thomas pulled the trigger. The musket ball tore through the exposed chest of the wolf, dropping it to the ground just a few feet from where Thomas stood. The other wolves yelped at the sound, and ran back into the woods.

William and Samuel rushed into the lean-to. "Thomas?" yelled William, "what happened?"

Thomas turned to his friends, "Wolf ventured too close, so I shot to kill, as ordered." All three erupted into laughter releasing the tension they all had felt, especially Thomas, his hands still shaking from the experience.

The morning saw the world in a dazzling display of sunlight reflecting off the ice encased trees, but soon the ice began to melt, the trail now mud slicked. The frequent drops of cold water that fell from the trees seemed to hit Samuel right where his neck was exposed, soaking his shirt. "I swear, even when it ain't raining, I'm getting pelted."

The weather stayed pleasant until the second day after the burnt out farm. The dawn sky that morning was one of those that sailors took warning to, and true to form it was starting to look nasty again.

They broke camp quickly, skipping a hot meal, in order to try to get ahead of the weather they could see coming their way. The air was cool, and frequently made cooler by the brisk, easterly gusts prevalent this time of year close to the Atlantic. William guessed that they were no more than fifteen miles from the village of Worcester.

They had ridden about five miles, and were giving the horses a breather before climbing out of the meadowlands and into the rolling hills ahead. "Best break out the rain slickers," William said, "rain for sure up there."

Just as he predicted it was only moments after reaching the top of the hill when the rain began. It wasn't a hard rain, more of a persistent mist. Samuel pulled the hood to his poncho over his head, "My Da used to tell me that back home in Ireland they would call this 'a fine soft morning'."

"Aye, that it is," replied William. "But I'm certain that at the end of this day, we will be three fine, soaked Irishmen."

They were certainly that upon reaching the gate into the village. While the rain did abate at times, it would always start up again, giving them no time to even attempt to dry off.

A farmer, driving his team and wagon through the gate, stopped and hailed them. "Well met, strangers. Looks like you've been through some inclement circumstances."

"At the least," said William as pulled back his hood smiling, "aye, at the very least. Between blizzards and unrelenting rain and wind, we are bone soaked and weary. Could you be telling us where we might find bed and board?"

The farmer grinned, "As to that my three bone soaked friends, The Harp and Fiddle is just up the road on the right. As fine an Irish tavern you won't find west of Boston. You'll find stabling for your beasts in back of the pub. Tell old Archie O'Keefe that Donal the fiddler said to treat you well."

"Thank you, Donal the fiddler," replied William, "we will mention your name."

Donal slapped his knee, "Hah, might do some good, and then it might not. Archie is a fine man, but he's only half Irish. It's the Welsh part that makes him so ornery. Now, Agnes Rose, his wife is all Irish, fiery red hair, and green eyes that sparkle like emeralds in the moon light. My advice, young men is to not get her riled. That woman does not take kindly to guff, puts her in a crosswise mood. I just left there, and she was cursing me to the heavens, and my only crime was to tell her about her eyes in the moon light. Ah, now come to think of it, that may be why Archie was threatening me with a bolloxing."

The Harp and Fiddle met their every need, a hot bath, a hot meal, strong ale and a reasonably comfortable bed. Archie was accommodating, and once he finished cursing Donal for flirting with Agnes, was a cheerful host. He even supplied them with some bread and cheese for the road. Agnes, taking advantage of the slow night sat at a harp and played for the guests.

Having been given directions to the Wayside Inn in the village of Sudbury and from there to Buckman's Tavern in Lexington, the three companions set out at first light. As they prepared to leave William kissed Agnes' hand, prompting Archie to threaten William with a bolloxing.

The day promised to be perfect for traveling, and so they did not anticipate anything that would prevent them from making the 25 miles to Sudbury. Indeed the ride was pleasant, the woods and meadows alive with birds in flight, and birds perched and singing. At one point they stopped and stared at an immense flock of pigeons passing by overhead. The flock was so large it almost blotted out the light of the sun. "You could bring down two or three with one shot," said Samuel mimicking a shot, "can't hardly miss with all those targets."

As the afternoon drew on, it became overcast, and the wind was now coming out of the east. The temperature dropped, and the chilled wind had the travelers reaching for their heavier outerwear, bundling themselves up to ward off the biting gusts. Three hours later they were seated as close to the fire they could manage in the busy Wayside Inn. Fortunately, the inn's clientele were mostly locals so the companions had no trouble procuring beds for the night. Their bellies full, and their minds slightly fogged by the warm, mulled wine, they bade their host good night.

The next day played out in similar fashion to yesterday, a warm sunny morning followed by the bone chilling easterly wind in the afternoon. As they rode past Lexington Green, they could see a militia group practicing. They were running and loading their muskets, the sight bringing a smile to Thomas, "Now, that's exactly the type of thing I would do. Learning to load on the run ain't easy, but sure comes in handy."

"I should say so," replied a stranger who had ridden up to the companions, "and have you mastered the skill, young man?"

A surprised Thomas turned to the stranger, "I have indeed, and so have my friends here," he said with a slight tone of defiance.

"I meant no offence," replied the stranger chuckling, "let me introduce myself, I am Dr. Samuel Prescott, and my companion here is the Reverend Jonas Clarke. The gaggle of men you see there is the beginnings of our militia." He paused, rode closer to the drilling field and yelled out, "Sergeant that will be all for today thank you. Dismiss the men." Prescott returned to the travelers, and pointed over to a building on the other side of the Green, "You three seem as you could use some refreshment. Head over to Buckman's Tavern, and tell that old rascal that I said to seat you at my table. I will join you shortly. Ah, Reverend Clarke, would you care to join us?"

"I would indeed," replied the reverend, "these young men interest me for some reason."

Two stable hands took their mounts and the mule. Rubbing sore backsides, and shivering at a gust they entered Buckman's. They inquired about rooms, and were directed upstairs to a room that had three beds. After changing they went downstairs to find that the inn was starting to fill up now that the militia drill was over. William hailed the innkeeper mentioning Prescott's name, "Prescott, eh?" replied Buckman, "you don't happen to be more of those hotheads what disagree with good King George, are ye? If'n you are, then God be praised, and welcome to my humble establishment."

The night passed in pleasant conversation about doings on the frontier, and the current, and increasingly volatile situation with London. After Prescott and Clarke arrived, and been properly introduced to the three travelers, Samuel mentioned that they were going to help Colonel Washington, sparking a flurry of questions and comments. The other matter of debate, and conjecture was whether Thomas was related to Reverend Jonas Clarke. In the end they decided it was possible though Jonas' forebears were from Sligo in the northern portion of Ireland, while Thomas' hailed from Waterford in the south.

As they were saying good night Dr. Prescott pulled William aside, "I need to get word to John Hancock and Dr. Warren about our preparations. If I leave a letter with Buckman for the morning, can you take it to Warren?"

William shook Prescott's hand, "Of course, will be a pleasure, and an honor, sir."

With an early start they reached the outskirts of Boston in the late afternoon. They crossed over Boston Neck which was a hive of activity with farmers heading out of town after their day's business. They were detained only for a few minutes at the British guard post while the sentries dealt with a testy colonial farmer. "Cantankerous gentleman, eh, corporal?" said William to the approaching guard.

"There's always one or two who feel that we poor lowly servants of the King are the cause of all of their griefs and complaints," replied the guard, "state your names and business."

Following William they entered Boston. Thomas and Samuel both rode with their mouths agape in amazement at the first city either had ever been in. The sheer number of people on the streets, the size and variety of the buildings, the smell of the ocean mixed with the odors emanating from the daily lives and businesses threatened to overload their senses. Thomas felt lost in this forestless wilderness, "Uh, William, do you know where you're going?"

"I was here once," William replied, "of course, I know where we're going. We're heading to Boston Common, and from there I will ask somebody where to go next."

Samuel laughed, "An excellent plan."

Dr. Joseph Warren was well known in Boston, so it didn't take William long to learn how to get to his home on Hanover Street. The doorman led them in, and announced them. Dr. Warren rose from his seat, "Gentlemen, how may I be of service?"

While Warren read over the introductory letter from Daniel and Henry, and the note from Dr. Prescott, Thomas glanced around the table at the other two men they had been introduced to a minute ago. He had heard of them from William during the course of the trip. Sam Adams, Paul Revere, and Dr. Warren were the leaders of the resistance to the King. His thoughts were interrupted by the arrival of a young woman.

"Marguerite," said Revere, "How lovely to see you, as always. Pray be seated. We're just about to discuss the future of these fine gentlemen. Ah, my dear doctor, that is, if what you have read is the cause for that smile on your face."

Warren nodded as he passed the letter over to Adams, "Very impressive. It is true that I do not know the authors of this letter, but I do know that Colonel Washington does, and not only knows them, but holds them in very high esteem. If I understand correctly, Thomas and Samuel will remain here for the time being. We are expecting Colonel Washington within the next week or so. We'll leave it up to him as to where you go from there. William, will you be going back to Mallory Town?" Dr. Warren stopped suddenly, "Oh where are my manners? Marguerite Edgerton, this is William Crane, Samuel Webb, and Thomas Clarke. They come to us from the wild frontier near Fort Pitt."

The three visitors stood, and bowed while Marguerite did a little curtsey, smiled and said, "Bienvenue. Welcome to Boston my three wild men from the frontier." She walked around the table, and shook each of their hands, "Dr. Warren, I believe these gentlemen could do with some refreshment, perhaps in the kitchen while we talk?"

"Yes, certainly," he replied, "excuse us gentlemen, my servant will show you to the kitchen, and set you up. Enjoy, we'll talk some more after you eat."

Fresh bread, butter, honey, and cheese, washed down with ale almost as good as Timothy's had satisfied their hunger. "Seems they like us well enough," said Samuel following a belch.

"That it does," replied William, "and that Marguerite is very pleasing to the eyes. Don't you think so, Thomas? I noticed you couldn't take yours off of her."

Thomas sputtered while swallowing a mouthful of ale, "What? I hardly gave her a notice. I am puzzled though as to what her role is? Why is she still in there with those distinguished men? What could a young girl like her possibly offer to their cause?"

"I suppose," said Samuel, pouring himself another mug of ale, "she gathers information for them."

"Well fed I see," said Revere as he entered the kitchen. He filled a pitcher from a cask of ale, "If you would follow me, we have some thirsty work ahead."

As they entered the parlor, Marguerite was saying goodbye. She was in need of some sleep and was heading to the room she shared with her mother. "I hope I will see you gentlemen at the Green Dragon," she said as she walked out of the door.

They were bid to enter and be seated. "After some deliberation," began Warren, "we have altered the plans slightly. I'll leave it to Mr. Adams to explain."

"Lads, these are uncertain times, and it is very likely to become dangerous, even violent, in the near future. Colonel Washington has been advocating, rightly so, that we need to be prepared, we need to train our militias, stockpile weapons, and ammunition. There is always the hope that King George will see the sense of solving our differences peacefully, but that hope dwindles quickly. The news brought by Marguerite is a sure sign that England intends to enforce the blasted tax on tea. If they do, we will not have many options to choose from. It is either acquiesce, or fight back. If we fight back, we are one more step towards full rebellion. Time is running out. That is why we have decided that William will extend his journey, and take Samuel to Colonel Washington. There he will help the Colonel train his militia. I say this, if we do go to war, I and many others agree, that Washington is the man to lead us. Thomas will stay here with us, and work with the local militia groups."

"Are there any questions or concerns?" asked Dr. Warren, "if not, I am sure you all need to get some rest. We have made arrangements for you to stay over at the Green Dragon. The owner is a particular friend to our cause. Our Marguerite works there most nights, and you'll find us there quite often as well. Take a few days to recuperate."

"I'll be asking our merchant friend, John Hancock, to book passage for William and Samuel as soon as may be," said Revere, "he'll be more than happy to accommodate you two, and have you dropped off in Virginia."

Three days later, Thomas was standing on the wharf saying goodbye to William and Samuel. "Take care of your selves," he said as he shook their hands. Pulling William close, he whispered, "Keep an eye on Samuel."

William nodded, "I will, though it seems that you'll be more likely to encounter the British here than we will while we're in Virginia."

For the first time in his life, Thomas was now alone. He spent the morning wandering the streets barely registering the activity around him as merchants opened their businesses, dock workers unloaded cargo, wagons laden with produce rolled to the markets. He eventually found himself turning the corner to the Green Dragon almost colliding with two clergymen who were engaged in a rather heated discussion regarding the merits of the colony's governor. "Oh, excuse me," he said stepping to the side allowing them to pass by.

"Not used to walking crowded streets, my wild man from Fort Pitt?" Marguerite smiled at a startled Thomas.

"Umm," he stuttered in reply, "good morning Mistress Edgerton. I suppose I was a little lost in thought. I didn't see the vicars, and I certainly didn't see you. Not much good as a wild man if I cannot see things in broad daylight."

Marguerite threw back her head laughing. She put her arm through Thomas' right arm and began walking with him. "No need to be so formal, Mr. Clarke. Please call me Marguerite. I take it your friends are on their way to meet Colonel Washington, and you are all alone in the big city feeling a little sorry for yourself. I understand that feeling, so very well in fact. Come; let us cheer each other with some coffee and fresh baked bread. I know just the place."

The next morning he was awakened by someone pounding on his door. Running his hand through his hair as he pulled it open, he looked down noticing that he had answered the knock, naked. "Oh my stars," said Marguerite quickly looking away.

Thomas stepped away from the door covering himself with his hands, "Give me a moment." He pulled on his buckskin breeches and a linen tunic, "You can come in now."

Marguerite entered the room smiling noticed the embarrassed blush on Thomas' face. "I am sorry to have intruded. I have a message for you from Revere. They have set up a meeting at Dr. Warren's house with some of the militia officers. Come on down when you're ready and I'll walk over with you."

Thomas thought back to the time he first looked over the men gathered on the Boston Common, the men who comprised the local militia. Many were dressed in their farming clothes, a few in the smock of a hunter, and even some in the dress of merchants, and lawyers. The two lieutenants he met with were impressed enough to have given him responsibility over the training in woodcraft and stealth. They also assigned Sergeant Martin Lake, one of the few militiamen with a military background, to assist and advise Thomas. Together with Lake, Thomas put together a plan to meet three days a week with the whole group, eventually culling from the militia a specialized unit of scouts and trackers. Once the scouting group was chosen, they began to learn from Thomas the secrets of tracking, and how to negotiate any type of terrain quickly, and quietly. Thomas threw himself into the task, confident that he could teach the skills he had learned. He relied on Sergeant Lake to provide the leadership and discipline required. The training regimen afforded Thomas the chance to get to know the lay of the land from Boston, north to Medford, west to Menotony, and south to Roxbury.

Knowledge that could be necessary for a fighting force keen on avoiding an open battle with the organized, experienced, and lethal British Regulars. Knowing where to find the best cover was the principle aim of these exploratory exercises, other than the training itself, and the fastest way to get there, a close second.

Thomas attended a weekly meeting with Lieutenants Abe Hunt and John Hinckley, apprising them of the progress of the scouts, and gleaning from them the workings of the militia, the logistics of supplies, and the communication links to the neighboring towns, but it was from Sergeant Lake that he learned more about his father and his uncles, Daniel and Liam. Lake, as a corporal assigned to work with the militia, had served with both the Braddock and Forbes campaigns to take Fort Duquesne from the French, and would regale young Thomas with the tales of the battles over pints of ale in the tavern. One of the tales he liked to tell was when Thomas' father, Henry, saved Lake's life after Lake had taken a musket ball to his arm, shattering the upper bone, and of which his empty left sleeve still bore witness.

Crow Village on the Bighorn River

October 1773

To prepare for the sweat ceremony, Liam had been fasting for three days. The rumbling of his empty stomach had subsided, now he only felt a dull ache and a little light headed. Takoda peered into Liam's lodge, "It is time, Bishee."

Liam sat up, waiting a few seconds for the fainting like feeling to subside before standing, groaning as he did so. "It is good the time has come. This fasting seems to have made my joints a bit more stiff and cranky than usual."

Takoda chuckled, "Maybe it is the way of the Great Spirit to remind his children that they are mortal. Come, my son, let us go."

Liam stood outside the sweat lodge after having entered to pour water over the heated stones. He stripped down, around his waist a loosely tied breech cloth the only clothing he would wear during the various phases of the sweat. Takoda faced the rising sun, "Great Spirit, bless this child with your thoughts. May his seeking be aided by the Grandmother; the sounds of her gentle breezes, the rush of waters, the songs of the air?" He opened the buffalo hide flap for Liam to enter, closing it tightly. Liam could already feel the heat as he sat on the elk hide blanket. Reaching over to the water bucket he pulled out the gourd dipper. Four dippers full were poured over the stones creating a thick swirling fog, a fog that settled on Liam. Sweat began to slide down his forehead and torso. He sat back, closed his eyes, and as best he could, he emptied his mind.

The scene before him was that of him and Orenda living on the banks of the Mohawk River. It awakened in him a feeling of happiness; of contentment. The scene then shifted to Mallory Town, and the cabin he shared with Rebecca. Again he was overtaken by the same peaceful feelings. That vision soon faded, and he found himself surrounded by enemies. All of his foes were dead. His body drenched in the blood of the vanquished.

He opened his eyes when the visions retreated from his mind. His body, though sweat soaked, was beginning to feel a little chilled. It was time to pour more water on the stones. This time it was a series of seven full dippers, but first he spoke with Takoda who was seated just outside the tent flap about the first session. Takoda listened to Liam, nodding his head at various points. "I have seen this many times," he said, "the first visions are of a time in your past, and reveal who you are. The scenes with Orenda and Rebecca remind you of that part of you that you give over to love and peace. The battle shows clearly that you are also a man of war. The fact that you vanquished so many foes shows that your skills are not to be shunned or denied. It would not surprise me if the Great Spirit now brings you visions of the present time."

Takoda left the front of the sweat lodge leaving Liam to pour out the seven dippers. He went over to sit under a tree, and was soon snoring softly, his head bobbing up and down. He was startled by the sound of horses splashing across the river.

Liam let the haze, and the heat once again overtake his senses; the sweat was now pouring down his body. In his mind he was confronted with a vision of a raiding party preying upon a poorly defended village. He watched frenzied, painted warriors slaughtering the old men trying to protect their village; the women, young and old, rounded up as captives, and the pony herd stolen. One man, naked and alone faced the invaders.

The trance like state he was in was shattered as Takoda flung back the door flap, "Pawnee raiders have crossed the river."

Liam's sweat drenched hair hung down over his forehead, salty droplets interfering with his sight. "How many are there?" he asked pulling off the breech cloth, and using it to wipe his face and neck.

"I saw five," Takoda replied, "but now I only see four. They probably left one warrior to hold their horses."

Liam started running to the village, Takoda coming on more slowly. "There's the fifth one," Liam yelled back over his shoulder, "like you said, holding the horses." Liam paused when he reached the bottom of the bluff to survey the situation grabbing two lances he found lying up against the wall of a lodge. He saw the four Pawnee rushing up from the river. One Pawnee split off, and headed toward the corral, the others ran to the village to round up captives. Liam could see the few old men, and the young boys prepare to stand their ground to protect the women and children. Seeing Morning Dew among the women, he turned to Takoda, and tossed him one of the lances. "It is time to be warriors again, my friend. Go and protect Morning Dew. I will protect the herd."

The Pawnee was just lifting the rope that held the gate closed when he noticed the naked white man coming at him with a war lance. With a snarl he stepped inside the corral, and began to hurriedly herd the horses to the open gate. He stopped one dappled gray mare, and jumped up onto its back. With one hand he grabbed a handful of mane, with the other, his tomahawk, kicking the mare forward to meet his foe.

That old feeling of intense focus hit Liam as he ran to the corral, that battle frenzy, a temporary reprieve from pain and fatigue. Although he knew what to expect, there was something different this time, not in the sense of fighting skills, but the motive for fighting was not the same. Here he was fighting to protect others, not for his own survival. A brief thought, one that had lain hidden in the deep recesses of his mind came to the fore. It was guilt at not being able to save Orenda; it was guilt at not being able to save Rebecca. This was the core to his inability to be at peace with himself.

The agitated herd was milling about the corral rather than stampeding as Liam entered, closing the gate behind him. The Pawnee rushed forward through a gap and came at Liam. Liam, not wanting to injure the mount turned the lance so the butt end faced out. He jabbed it at the chest of the horse, stopping its forward progress, bucking and rearing, the rider was thrown to the ground. He rolled out from under the thrashing hooves, managing to get clear enough to stand up. Liam charged, the Pawnee waited, and at the last second sidestepped the lunging lance, wincing as the lance head scored across his ribs. Liam's momentum carried him by the Pawnee, but not enough to keep a swinging tomahawk from gashing his shoulder. The bloodied combatants stared at each other looking for an opening, a weakness to exploit. Liam knew he had to end this quickly if he was going to be of any help to Takoda and the others. Letting his experience, and instincts take over he feinted with the lance, and when the Pawnee reacted, Liam pretended he lost his balance, falling to the ground, coming to a rolling stop behind his foe. The Pawnee began to turn to meet the new threat but as he did, the lance darted upward, and into the exposed torso, past the ribs, and right to his heart. The now dead Pawnee fell against Liam adding to his bloody appearance. He let the warrior fall to the ground, and picked up the tomahawk. His own horse came over to him, and pawed at the ground, eager to join the fight. Liam grabbed the halter rope, and led the horse to the gate, opening, and then closing it. Mounting, he could see that speed was of the essence. Takoda and the young brave, Badger seemed to be okay for now, but the group defending the other women and children was quickly being whittled down, many of them too wounded to continue.

Liam hit one of the two Pawnee with the full force of his charging warhorse, sending him flying, the impact of his landing taking his breath away. Unable to turn the horse quickly enough to do the same to the remaining warrior, Liam vaulted off his steed and landed on top of the Pawnee. The startled brave had no time to react as the pipe end of the tomahawk smashed into his face, breaking his nose and a few teeth. Liam reversed his grip and made a quick swipe, jumping back to avoid most of the now blood spurting jugular.

He located the fallen Pawnee who scrambled to his feet, and started to run to the river, and the waiting horses. Liam started to run after him but he was quickly coming out of the battle lust and knew he wouldn't catch him. The Pawnee smiled when he saw Liam stop. Turning away he slowed to catch his breath but was thrown to the ground again; this time by a tomahawk striking him in the right buttock. There would be no escaping this time. A group of enraged women carrying clubs, and knives soon filled his sight.

Liam knelt after throwing the tomahawk, the pain of the gash in his shoulder and the fatigued result of the extended exertion had him gasping for breath. He turned his head at the sound of Morning Dew's scream, and with a notable groan stood. He reached down, picked up a discarded lance, and noticeably limping, started to trot, his legs rebelling against this renewed activity.

Takoda was lying on the ground, clearly overmatched. The Pawnee managed to break away from Takoda's hold as they grappled face to face, and as he pushed the old warrior away, his knife sliced across Takoda's forehead, the wound shallow, but very bloody. He stood, picking up his war lance, to finish off Takoda. Badger recovered from an earlier blow, and ran at the Pawnee, his lance snaking out, striking his unsuspecting foe in the back of the thigh. With a howl of rage, he grabbed the shaft of Badger's lance, pulling the head out of his leg, and then yanked it forward. Badger was met with a forearm to his head, knocking him down, dazed.

The Pawnee paused in his attack on Badger, being distracted by the appearance of a haunted looking specter, a blood drenched demon, running at him. Weakened by the torn muscle in his leg, the Pawnee couldn't move quickly enough to avoid Liam's charge.

Liam was visibly exhausted physically, but his mind was clear and focused. As he forced his body forward, Liam sensed, and then saw the opening he needed to win this contest, the weakness to be exploited. Liam screamed and charged, changing direction slightly at the last second and slammed into the Pawnee's injured leg. Toppling back, the Pawnee fell, a surprised look on his face as he stared in horror at the lance protruding from his chest. Badger, his face bloodied, and bruised grinned at Liam who was on his knees once again gasping for breath. Takoda sat up, and with Morning Dew's help came over to Liam. Liam looked up at his friend, and shook his head, "Time to be warriors, hah! We did well, old friend. I must confess though that fasting before a battle does leave one a bit peckish at the end."

Takoda smiled up at Morning Dew as the old woman wiped away the blood from his forehead. The gash wasn't deep but like wounds of this type, bled profusely. "We may not be finished yet, Bishee," he said pointing at the young Pawnee riding towards them, "but, I see a young brave fighting his fear. I will speak with him." Takoda walked out to meet the Pawnee. The brave circled around the old man yelling that he would have revenge for the killings. Takoda held up his hand, pointed to Liam, and after a few minutes of explanation, the Pawnee rode off, stopping to grab the reins to the other horses, and crossed back over the river.

Takoda made his way back to the others. Morning Dew was now tending to Liam's shoulder wound muttering about having to sew it closed. Liam flinched as she wiped it clean and looking up at Takoda said, "My Pawnee's a little rusty. What did you say to him?"

Feeling a little woozy Takoda sat down, and grinning replied, "I just impressed upon him the fact that this village is protected by The Great Spirit in the person of his son, Bishee, and to go back to his people, and tell them. When I pointed at you, I told him that Bishee would haunt his dreams. I guess your appearance frightened him enough."

Boston

December 1773

Thomas shook off the cold as he dismounted, handing the reins to the stable boy. He had spent the day in the saddle delivering dispatches for Dr. Warren, and was looking forward to a warm fire, and mulled cider. He entered the Green Dragon, and sat at his favorite table by the fire. There were only a few customers, so when Marguerite brought his cider, she sat down with him. "You look pretty bedraggled," she said reaching over to remove his cap, "your hair is a frightful mess." Thomas yelped as she tugged her fingers through a nasty knot of hair. Standing up, Marguerite reached into her apron and pulled out a comb, "I'm going to try and fix this mess, young Thomas. You stay still now. After all, you want to look good for the ladies, don't you?"

Thomas flinched as the comb worked its way through his hair, "Ouch and damnation, that hurts," he said, "and what ladies do I need to look good for?"

"Oh Thomas," she replied, "I've seen the way you turn heads out in the street. How such a notable scout and tracker could be so unaware is simply amazing."

Not knowing how to respond, Thomas just sat back, and let Marguerite, and her comb do their work. Once he grew comfortable with the decreasing number of tugs, he began to feel quite content. He was pretty naïve and innocent when it came to women. By the time he began noticing girls in Mallory Town, he was too busy defending the town, and learning woodcraft to have any type of relationship. He kissed one girl, or rather she kissed him, but it was hurried and totally unexpected, so had no real memory value. He was suddenly aware of Marguerite's body as she leaned into his back and a rush of warmth surged through him causing some discomfort below. As stealthily as he could Thomas dropped his hands to his lap. "So do I turn your head, Marguerite?" he asked.

Marguerite stopped combing, and was about to answer when a British soldier entered the inn. He paused in the doorway, and looked around the room. Spying Marguerite he smiled, "Mistress Marguerite, Colonel Whitby sends his compliments, and asks that you join him immediately for dinner. I will escort you."

Marguerite felt Thomas begin to rise from his chair. She pressed down on his shoulders, and as he turned to look at her, she saw anger and then disappointment in his eyes. "I am sorry Thomas, but I must go. I wish you would understand." She then bent down, and kissed his cheek, grabbed her coat from behind the bar, and walked to the waiting soldier. She knew she was falling in love with Thomas, but also knew how much he hated what she did. If he could only realize how much she hated it too, but she was determined to do what she could for the cause, even at the cost of love.

"Damn that colonel to hell," muttered Thomas a sly smile creeping on his face, "if Samuel doesn't hurry and kill Whitby, then I'll kill the bastard." The pleasantness of the evening having been shattered, Thomas took a mug of ale, and retired to his room. He sat at his desk with the intent of continuing a letter home, but after ten minutes he realized he hadn't even looked at the parchment let alone written anything. He just couldn't get his mind off of Marguerite, and the way he felt when she touched him. He was frustrated that she didn't answer his question, "but," he said aloud as he drained the last of the ale, "she probably would have answered in such a way as to make things more confusing."

****

"So did you enjoy your dinner, my dear?" asked Whitby as he wiped his mouth with a napkin, "I do hope the wine was satisfactory."

Marguerite smiled, and raised her glass, "A most excellent choice, my dear Colonel." She put her glass down, and started to rise, but Whitby hurried over to slide her chair out of the way. Marguerite turned to thank him, and saw the envelope with General Gage's seal in the pocket of his uniform jacket. "I'm feeling a little flushed and giddy," she said with a big grin, "I think I shall lie down."

Whitby followed her into the bedroom and watched as Marguerite slid out of her dress, and into the bed wearing only her linen shift. Her beauty was a constant source of joy to the colonel. He removed his jacket, and hung it over the back of a dressing table chair. Sitting next to her on the bed he cupped her chin to better gaze into her eyes and said, "My dear Marguerite, how I have missed you. I find myself thinking of you often, and would really love to have you all to myself," Whitby said, his hand playing with a lock of her hair, "You know, when this business with the colonists is settled I expect to return to England covered in glory, and suitably promoted. How would you like to come to England with me?"

 Marguerite sat up, a look of surprise on her face, "Oh my stars," she replied, "surely you cannot mean to take me home as your wife. Even I know that."

"Ahh, yes, I'm afraid the difference in our social stations would preclude our being man and wife, but keeping a mistress, well, that is something else again."

"It is true that I long for a more settled life," Marguerite said, "but to become a kept woman; there is something unsettling about that." She took his hands into hers replying, "Though I have to admit that if I were to be a mistress, then I would have it be with you."

"You need not worry about your well-being as long as you are with me," continued Whitby, "I'm already a pretty wealthy man, and expect to profit more as I rise through the ranks."

Marguerite paused untying the top to her shift, and in a voice tinged with regret said, "Though my heart bids me say yes, I cannot give you my answer until I am sure that we have a future together.

With all of the strife, and tension between those foolish turncoats and King George, how can I know what to answer? What if this tension turns violent? What if you are killed?"

Whitby laughed, "Oh my poor love. Even if those foolish turncoats, that rabble of farmers and shopkeepers take the rebellious path, do you think for one moment that they could defeat the might of the British Empire? No, if it does get violent, it will be a short war; I can assure you of that. And since it will be a short one, I suppose, to ease your worries, I will wait for your answer." He finished undressing, and climbed into bed, kissing her forehead, then her nose and then a quick peck on her lips. He sat up, an excited look in his eye that had nothing to do with Marguerite's languorous pose, "I've just had a brilliant thought. You spend time at the Green Dragon. I'm sure you hear the men talk, perhaps what they might be planning. How would you like to spy for me?"

Marguerite caught her breath, "My, you are full of surprises. What an intriguing proposition. It's no secret to you that I loathe those people. People with no shame, turning against their own. They besmirch their King, and the memory of my father who was killed in the King's service. Yes, I will do what you ask, though I don't know if I'll come up with anything of any real value. Most of what I hear is politically charged rants against Parliament, not what they plan to do about their complaints."

"Nevertheless," Whitby replied, "even the tiniest thing could at the very least corroborate information we get from another source. Don't look so surprised. We have someone on the inside of these so called Sons of Liberty. Now, enough of this talk; I believe I was about to make love to my mistress the spy."

****

It was one of those rare occasions when Thomas stayed abed late into the morning. He had slept fitfully, tossing and turning, his dreams always returning to Marguerite spurning his embrace as Whitby enters. He seemed as though he had just fallen asleep when a pounding at his door woke him up. Checking to make sure he wasn't naked this time, Thomas ran his fingers through his hair, and with a smile opened the door. "Good morning, Marguer. Sergeant Lake?"

"Sorry to disappoint you, lad. Just a crusty, one-armed old soldier, not the lovely lass," said Lake. Standing at attention, Lake continued, "With Dr. Warren's compliments, he requests your presence. Something big is happening. I don't know much, but apparently Marguerite has news, and Warren says he has a job for our scout group."

For security reasons, the meeting was held in a back room of the Green Dragon. Already in attendance were, Adams, Dr. Warren, Marguerite, and the militia commanders. Thomas and Lake entered, and sat down, graciously accepting a mug of hot coffee. "While we wait for Revere and Hancock," began Warren, "let me bring Thomas up to date on what we know. Marguerite has brought us new information regarding the tea tax. It seems the British are intent on enforcing our compliance." Warren paused for a moment to refill his mug.

Thomas looked up from his coffee, glancing at Marguerite, a pang of grief at the thought of how she acquired that information. With a slight shake of his head, he turned away at the sound of Revere and Hancock entering the room. "It's true," said Hancock taking off his gloves to warm his hands by the fire, "we just verified Marguerite's information through a contact I have in the Port Authority. They expect four tea ships to arrive here any day now."

Revere sat down, and reached for the coffee, "The Dartmouth will be the first to arrive. When they all arrive, they will have to be unloaded, and the tax paid. A tax that is unjust; oh I know, I repeat myself, but damnation, if we are not represented in Parliament, then to hell with this infernal tax."

Hancock nodded his head, "And not only that, but the rumor we heard is also confirmed. The East India Company is exempt from paying this tax on tea; meaning they have an unfair advantage over the rest of us merchants who deal with tea."

Sam Adams drummed his fingers on the table, finally standing up, he said, "Gentlemen, the first thing we need to do is to call a meeting for the public. I will send out an announcement to meet tomorrow evening at sunset in Faneuil Hall. The second thing we need to do is to petition the Governor to send the ships back, with their cargo. The third thing and this depends on the first two, concerns Thomas and his militia group. If we find it necessary to take some action, then I want your group involved. If there are four ships, we'll need at least 100 men to do what I think we will have to do." He paused to take a sip of his coffee, "So, Thomas, I need you and your men to head up this expedition. Divide them up into four groups to lead the boarding parties. What I am going to suggest to the assembly, if our petition falls on deaf ears, is to dump the tea into the harbor."

Hancock spluttered, coffee spewing out of his mouth, "You can't do that. You can't mean that. That would be, ahh, that would be..."

"Yes, we can, and I do mean it," said Adams, interrupting the still gasping Hancock. "Drastic? Yes it is, but also a sure means to get our message across." He paused, and hoping to placate his businessman friend added, "Well, let us have hope that the governor sees the light, and grants our petition. Now, before we go I have one other bit of information. It has transpired that our Marguerite has captured the heart of Colonel Whitby. Not only has he asked her to accompany her back to England, but he also asked her to spy on us, for him."

Thomas stood so fast that his chair fell over backward. "Excuse me gentlemen," he said while looking at Marguerite, "I feel the need for some air."

As he left the room, Marguerite started to follow, but Dr. Warren gently stopped her, "Let him go. His sensibilities have been given a rude shock. I take it that you are growing fond of him. We all are. He's a remarkable young man. Give him time."

****

Whitby woke up, the sweet, lingering smell of Marguerite's perfume on the pillow bringing a smile to his face. "To think, Whitby, old boy," he said to himself, "how envious the other officers will be when she is on my arm strolling around London." He completed his morning ablutions, and was putting on his uniform jacket when he noticed something odd. Last night when he took off the jacket, the seal of General Gage on the envelope was facing out, now it was facing the other way. He thought for a moment, but kept coming to the same conclusion; somebody had removed, and replaced the letter. "Oh Marguerite, what game are you playing? Whose side are you on?"

****

Faneuil Hall was packed. Soon the heat from the fireplace, and the huddled masses, mixed with the smoke of the many lit pipes, and the whale oil lanterns, made the place somewhat uncomfortable. Thomas removed his outer jacket, and found a place to stand, off to the side of the platform where Adams, Warren, and Revere would be addressing the crowd. Adams was incensed at the unwillingness of Governor Hutchinson to even consider the petition to send the ships back to where they came. A hush fell over the crowd as Adams stood, and held his hands up for quiet. As he began speaking, bringing everyone up to date on the latest developments, Marguerite sidled over to stand next to Thomas. He glanced at her briefly, but then returned his attention to Adams speech.

"Oh Thomas," she said taking his reluctant hand, "don't ignore me and please don't judge me. You have no idea what I have been through in my life, no idea of the horrors that visit me at night. My world and my life have been forever stained by what the mighty British Army has done to my family. If I choose to retaliate in a manner that is unseemly, then so be it. All I ask is that you try to understand."

Thomas looked at her, saw the tears beginning to form, and was reaching to wipe them away when the crowd erupted into a frenzied clamor. Adams had just announced that The East India Company was exempt from the tax, followed quickly by the Governor's refusal to send the ships away. The hall was filled with the sound of many angry voices. Warren pleaded with the crowd to calm down, slowly the noise lessened, when one voice shouted out, "It is time for action."

Adams repeated, "It is time for action. It is the time for The Sons of Liberty to show the British the seriousness of our resolve." With that pronouncement many of the men began to head to the exits, including Thomas.

He squeezed her hand, "I've got to go." He put on his coat, saw Sergeant Lake waiting for him, and together they headed to Griffins Wharf where the three ships full of tea were docked. The fourth ship had been lost in a storm, so Thomas rearranged the boarding parties into groups of thirty men; each group led by members of his scout team. At the suggestion of Hancock, the tea raiders disguised themselves; this being a criminal offense. Some came dressed as Mohawk warriors, but most, like Thomas, simply covered their faces with a kerchief. They also all came armed with an axe or hatchet; a few had pistols but as there was no opposition, they remained tucked into belts.

On the Dartmouth, Thomas directed a chain of men, starting in the hold, and up the ladder to the deck where Sergeant Lake and a couple others hacked opened the wooden chests while others dumped the tea into the harbor. The same scene was being played out on the other two ships, The Eleanor and The Beaver. Three hours later, 342 chests of tea had been destroyed, and as the tea leaves floated away on the current, so did any chance of peace.

Chapter 9 1773/1774 - Response and Resolve

Boston

The Green Dragon – night of tea raid

The Green Dragon became alive with celebrating, the excitement still coursing through the men of Thomas' scout group. The owner of the tavern announced that the ale was "on the house" drawing an even more enthusiastic huzzah from the happy throng. Soon even more of the raiders came in, as well as Dr. Warren, Sam Adams, and Paul Revere. Sergeant Lake led them to a table where he convinced the occupants to vacate, but to leave the jug of ale. Warren poured four mugs and gesturing to Lake, "Sergeant, have a seat. You look as though you need a pint or two."

The noise made it hard for them to talk, but Lake managed to replay his part in the raid, adding that he was surprised that there was no resistance from the British, "I believe we caught them napping," he said while wiping the ale foam from his mouth, "a proper surprise it was."

Adams nodded, "Aye, that it was Sergeant. However," he continued, the grin on his face turning into a frown, "the Governor and General Gage are sure to retaliate in some fashion. That's a fair amount of money floating in the harbor. We need to step up our preparations for the response."

Revere reached over, and clapped Adams on the back, "Enough of the gloom and doom, Sam, my friend, at least for tonight. Look around you. I do believe you'll need to wait until this lot sobers up to remind them that this was just the beginning."

A loud squeal and much laughter came from the other side of the room. "Looks like our Thomas is enjoying the evening," said Warren pointing to Thomas twirling Marguerite around.

Thomas, mug raised in a toast, laughed at the antics of one of his men. Marguerite walked over with a fresh jug of ale, placing it on the bar. "Oh Thomas," she said, putting her arms around him, "what a glorious night. I wish I could've been there."

The sound of a fiddle broke over the cacophony, the lively tune prompting Thomas to pick Marguerite up and spin her around. When he put her down their eyes met. Marguerite pulled his face closer, and kissed him. Thomas was caught off guard and started to pull back but found he was unable to do so, and returned the kiss. Marguerite sighed as they finally broke apart, and started to speak, but stopped as the door to the Green Dragon opened, and three British soldiers entered, led by Colonel Whitby.

The tavern became silent as Adams stood, "Ah, colonel, to what do we owe the pleasure of your company? Care to join our little celebration? It seems that someone mistook the harbor for a teapot."

Whitby started to reply but hesitated as the laughter at Adams teapot comment echoed around the room. "Silence!" screamed Whitby, "I should have the lot of you arrested."

"Arrested for what, my dear colonel?" a smirking Adams replied, "having a party?"

"Joke all you want. I know you are responsible for tonight's blatant act against the Crown," he said pointing at Adams, "you and the rest of your so called Sons of Liberty."

"I suppose you have proof of this?" inquired Adams, "for if not, I suggest, rather I advise you to leave. You are dampening our spirits with your ridiculous talk of arrest. We have been here all night, just ask anyone," he said sweeping his arm around the room.

Whitby scanned the crowd, quickly deciding that he was outnumbered even with the squad he had stationed outside the tavern. He turned to leave, but then saw Marguerite in the arms of Thomas. He stared at them for a moment, but knowing that in the current mood it would be foolish for him to call her to his side, stepped out into the cold December night.

Spring 1774

The hue and cry was varied throughout the colonies in response to the destruction of the tea. Many, like John Adams, felt it was a bold, daring act bound to have positive consequences. Others, including Ben Franklin and George Washington were appalled at the wanton destruction of private property, and demanded reparations be made. In London it served to galvanize Parliament into a sterner approach to her recalcitrant children, especially the colony of Massachusetts, even to the point of refusing repayment for the loss. Instead, harsher laws were enacted. Governor Hutchinson was replaced with a military governor, the position having been given to General Gage who wasted no time in closing off the Port of Boston, and working towards curbing the activities of the Sons of Liberty. However, the lessons of obedience to the crown went unlearned. Samuel Adams, instead of being silenced, used the tea event and the British response as a springboard for forming The Continental Congress with representatives from each of the thirteen colonies.

Thomas and Sergeant Lake continued the training of the scout unit three days a week. The other days Thomas rode the countryside either learning the various routes, and forest trails, or acting as courier for Adams and Revere. When time allowed he would sit with other members of the Sons of

Liberty either in committee meetings, or at the almost nightly gatherings at the Green Dragon. It was a heady experience for Thomas, and he was often struck by the sheer intelligence of the men he was now associating with. He remembered his Uncle Liam telling him how he felt being taught by Pierre Baptist and the awe he would feel, and now Thomas understood what his uncle meant. His feelings for Marguerite remained muddled and confused. He found her to be intelligent, witty, and certainly beautiful, but could not stomach what she did for the cause. It puzzled him that the others like Adams and Warren accepted the fact that she whored herself. He tried not to dwell on it, though it was hard not to on those occasions when she would be summoned to attend to Whitby.

Mallory Town

Early August 1774

The stranger's face was covered in road dust and grime, evidence of long days in the saddle, his horse lathered in sweat. He was met at the gate by the three boys, Caleb, Bowie, and Jack. Cal and Bo took him to Timothy's tavern where Daniel and Henry were currently enjoying a break from the day's routine, while Jack took the stranger's horse for a walk to cool it down. The stranger held out his hand, "Mr. Mallory and Mr. Clarke, my name is David Rollins," he paused, overtaken by a coughing spell from his dust dried throat.

Daniel stood and motioned to Marsha to bring another tankard of ale. "Please have a seat and quench your thirst, Mr. Rollins."

Rollins cleared his throat, "Thank you, my mouth does seem to need reviving." He took a long drink, wiping the foam from his moustache. "He raised the mug in salute to Timothy, "Very nice, I compliment you on your brewing skills, sir." He then turned to Daniel and Henry, "No doubt you have heard about what happened to Logan's family?"

Henry nodded, "Yes, word came to us that a group of whites attacked a peaceful settlement on Yellow Creek and murdered the inhabitants; including some members of Logan's family. We know he has sworn vengeance, and that he has turned away from his peaceful ways with the white settlers."

"Precisely why I am here," replied Rollins, "a band of mixed Mingo and Shawnee have surrounded and cutoff my village on Whitely Creek. Your friend Two Birds is trapped there as well.

When it was decided that someone needed to try and get through, I volunteered. Two Birds suggested I come here. He wrote you this note."

Daniel took the note and began reading it out loud.

My Dear Friends,

I managed to find myself in a bit of trouble. Came here to Whitely Creek to do some trading, but it seems the Mingo have come to do some raiding at the same time. The garrison at Fort Pitt will not be of use as they are entangled in some business with the Delaware further north, so I am asking you to do what you can to relieve us.

Oh, rest assured that this is not an attempt to lure you away like with that distasteful episode with Grantham and Whitby.

Two Birds

"Well, it seems we're headed back into battle," said Henry, "I had hoped we had seen our last of that. We're getting a little long in the tooth for this."

Daniel refilled his mug, "Aye that we are, but duty calls." Turning to Rollins, he said, "What reason, other than hate, would Logan raid Whitely Creek? You've been established there for quite a few years and according to what I've heard from Two Birds, have enjoyed particularly good relations with the Mingo and Shawnee."

Rollins grimaced, "Was afraid you'd ask that." He took a drink followed by a deep breath, "One of the men involved with the Greathouse brothers' raid on Yellow Creek is from Whitely Creek and is there now. Logan somehow found out."

"God's balls, man!" cried Henry thumping his mug down on the table, "Why don't you just give him up? If he rode with Greathouse, he deserves whatever he gets from Logan."

Shaking his head despondently Rollins said, "I and many others in the town share that opinion. The problem lies in the fact that his family is rich, powerful, and has a lot of influence with the British. As long as they're determined to hold out, then we have no choice. Things will come to head soon though. Water is running short, as is the food supply. If not relieved soon, it will get ugly in the village."

Timothy set his wooden leg back onto the floor from the chair he had propped it up on and stood, "You do realize that the longer Logan has to wait, the less chance he will have to rein in his followers. Giving this man up may not suffice to quench their thirst for vengeance and loot."

Daniel looked at Henry; Henry nodded in resigned acceptance. "Timothy's right," said Daniel looking for and finding his son, Bowie, trying to remain hidden while listening to the adults, "Bo, go out and ring the meeting bell. We'll wait a few minutes, and then see who we can get to volunteer. While we wait, I think it would be wise if we talked to our wives first. They're even more firm in the belief that we are too old for this kind of mission."

Liza had always been somewhat selfish, not overtly so, but as an only daughter and the youngest child in the family, she was used to getting her way. As she grew older, she was less likely to feel slighted when things ran counter to her wants. However, little by little, those incidents built up, so when once she would not have argued with Henry about the mission, this time she was furious. "How many times have I heard you complain about all the aches and pains you feel in the morning, and that's after sleeping in a bed? There are plenty of others who can go, why you?"

Henry had been expecting resistance so wasn't too surprised at Liza's reaction. He had seen a change in his wife, especially after the taking back of Mallory Town from Grantham. She was still cheerful and very diligent in her position as a healer, but her temper was much shorter these days; a condition Henry felt was due to the increasing opposition between the older residents of the town, and some of the newer arrivals. It was too early to know if the colonies and Britain would clash, but it wasn't hard to know on what side most of the new arrivals were on given that many of them were retired British soldiers. Henry walked over to the fireplace, and poured himself a cup of coffee, the ale, plus an angry wife, had started his head pounding. "You know as well as I that I cannot stay out of the rescue. We need experience, and common sense on this mission, not a bunch of hot heads looking for trouble. Besides, chances are that we won't have to fight. We've known Logan for years. I know we can come to a peaceable solution."

Liza put her arms around Henry, "Yes, I know all that. It's just that things are changing around here; more tension. Hardly a day goes by without one of our nephews brawling with one of the new settler's boys." She sighed, taking Henry's mug to refill it, "Sometimes, I just wish that we had remained a small outpost. How long do you think you'll be gone?"

Henry shuddered as he swallowed the bitter liquid, "We'll be going by canoe, so that will save time. Shouldn't be gone more than a week or ten days, if all goes well." He put down his cup, walked over to Liza and kissed her. "Wouldn't want to stay away too long," he whispered.

At the meeting there was very little opposition voiced, mainly out of concern for the safety of Mallory Town. There was no shortage of volunteers as 37 men and boys put themselves forth. After discussing it over, the number of canoes available was the deciding factor in determining the size of the party. In addition to Daniel, Henry, and Rollins, 22 men were chosen. The remaining 15, including the three boys, were given the task of maintaining patrols of the area.

While everyone made preparations to leave, Jonas Lapley and Rollins combined their knowledge of the area around Whitely Creek, and came up with a plan that would get them between the village and Logan's followers. The village was set on a bluff overlooking the creek, a short way upstream from where the creek empties into the Monongahela. The Mingo-Shawnee were spread out covering the waterfront of the creek and the river, as well as the heavily forested western approach. To the south of the village a marsh meandered at the foot of a series of rolling hills. Logan believed that the terrain there was sufficient to deter anyone from getting in or out of the village, and not willing to thin out his warriors any more than he already had, left that approach mostly unguarded leaving only one young warrior there at night. Rollins knew better, and used his knowledge of the marsh to escape, and would take them back the same way for the rescue.

They stopped for the night near the confluence of the Monongahela and Ohio rivers. There was time to make it to the spot Rollins had chosen to disembark, but that meant spending the night near the Mingo-Shawnee camp. This way, they decided, gave them a better chance to arrive undetected. Daniel climbed up the bluff to get a view of the Ohio. Liam had told them of the wonderful country that lay down the Ohio, the bountiful game, the salt licks, the fertile grasslands. Daniel turned at the sound of Henry climbing the bluff; his heavy breathing making Daniel chuckle. "Getting to old to climb, Henry?" he said.

Henry stopped and put his hands out on the ground ahead and above him, to catch his breath. "Saint's above but this is a steep climb," he replied, "I suppose you made it without any problems."

"Nary a one," Daniel laughed, "unless you count the burning sensation in my thighs, and the little coughing fit when I reached the top. Come sit, but I must warn you, the view is making me think of taking a journey when this mission is done."

"What is it with you Mallory's?" asked Henry as he sat down, "Liam is off God knows where, probably somewhere no white man has ever been, now you spouting off about traveling down a river you know nothing about. Hells bells, even Liza is starting to complain about it being too crowded at home."

"I reckon we all take after our Da," Daniel replied, "Liam got it the most, but as I get along in years, I've been thinking I got one more journey to do before I get too old. Not surprised 'bout Liza. I sometimes see that faraway look in her eyes, same as Liam used to get afore heading out."

Henry gazed out at the sunset reflecting off of the Ohio and said, "Now, it's not that I'm against the idea. I just think it would be smart to find out more of what we'll be getting into. Talk to someone who knows what's going on."

"Two Birds!" they both said at once, chuckling as they made their way back down the slope to camp.

By the light of the almost full moon, the canoes glided up the Monongahela with Rollins in the lead canoe. The eastern sky was just beginning to brighten when he beached his canoe, and motioned for the others to do the same. They hid the canoes among the scrub brush covered dunes, and then followed Rollins up a small creek screened from view by a line of hills. Where the hills ended lay a boggy marsh. The cry of the red wing blackbirds perched among the cattails competed with the early morning chorus of frogs.

Daniel looked at Rollins and said, "I sure do hope you know what you're doing. Otherwise we're gonna get pretty wet."

Rollins laughed, "I reckon I know my way, but I never said it wasn't wet. Just be sure to step where I step." He led them along a meandering path through the bog. While it wasn't completely dry, it was a lot drier on the path than off of it, as a few of the men discovered if they missed a step. It took until late afternoon to reach the bottom of the hills that overlooked the village. They stayed out of sight in a thicket of oak, taking the time to dry off their sodden feet, and to enjoy the relief from the clouds of insects encountered on the march. Rollins sat next to Daniel and Henry, "If Logan holds true to form, there'll be one sentry posted atop the furthest hill. We'll need to take care of him."

"I agree," said Henry, "but we'll have a better chance negotiating with Logan if we deliver his sentry alive."

Daniel nodded, "All right, this is what we'll do. Jonas and Rollins will take care of the sentry, alive if at all possible. When he is secured, the rest of us will head down to the village gate in groups of two.

An hour later Rollins returned to the rest of the men, "Jonas has the sentry all trussed up. Time to head to the village."

Rollins led Daniel to the gate and called out, "Open the gate. It's Rollins, and I've brought help."

A face appeared over the stockade, "David Rollins? By God, you're alive. We'd given up hope." A moment later the gate opened, and soon the last of the rescue party, and one unconscious Mingo, were inside. They distributed the food and water they had carried with them, and then succumbed to fatigue, getting some needed rest as they awaited an uncertain dawn.

Logan heard a commotion from his warriors stationed by the creek and hurried over. As he topped the bluff, he was greeted with the sight of twenty extra muskets lining the walls of the village. Surprising as that was, he was even more surprised by three men sitting on the opposite bluff under a white flag. He smiled for a moment and yelled out, "Ah, my old friends, Daniel and Henry, and I see my young brave with you as well. His mother, my wife, will be very cross with me if he has been harmed."

Daniel cupped his hands, "No harm, excepting a headache, I reckon. As you can see, we want to talk. Come across, we are unarmed. We'll get a tent setup here. It promises to be a hot day."

Logan silenced the vocal dissenters among his warriors and replied, "If it were anyone else, I would attack, but I know you to be honorable men. I will come across to talk."

Later that day, a weary Daniel and Henry returned to a village anxiously awaiting the results of the negotiation. Upon hearing that Logan had lifted the siege in exchange for the promise that the culprit, Edward Tilton, would be delivered to the colonial authorities at Fort Pitt, the residents immediately began preparing a feast, sending out hunting and foraging parties to supplement what they had left in the village to eat. The only uproar of disagreement came from the Tilton's, but faced with an armed mob, they had no choice but to surrender Edward to them. They did take solace in the fact that it would be the British, not Logan, who would determine Edward's fate.

It had been a hot day both from the sun, and from the heated discussion, but in the end Logan came to trust the word of his friends, but promised dire consequences if justice wasn't served. Daniel was a little puzzled that Logan finally agreed, and that he only did so after a private conversation with Henry, a conversation that Henry said was nothing more than pleasant inquiries about Mallory Town, but Daniel wasn't sure he believed that. Nevertheless, he let it pass. He was too tired to delve into it any further.

They rested the next day, the only activity being the retrieval of their canoes. The following morning the entire village turned out to say farewell to the rescue team and to Two Birds who was returning to Fort Pitt with them. They set a leisurely pace stopping at noon for a long break. Daniel had the sense that there was someone watching them, but could not spot anything out of the ordinary, finally giving up, chiding himself for his over tired imagination. That night after a meal of fresh venison, Daniel and Henry sat with Two Birds, and told him of their idea to travel down the Ohio.

Two Birds reached out and sliced off another piece of the venison spitted over the fire, "It is a fine country. There can be no denying that." He took a bite, and after swallowing let out a loud belch, "Perhaps I should stop eating now," he chuckled. Turning serious he looked at both of his friends and said, "I would strongly advise against making that journey at the present time for a couple reasons. It is true that there are new settlements south of the Ohio, Harrodsburg and Boonsboro to name two, but the Shawnee aren't too happy about that, and are sure to cause trouble. The other reason is the current state of affairs with the British. If I were you I would stay close to Mallory Town until things sort themselves out. You know as well as I that if things turn ugly, then most of the tribes will side with the British. I don't believe Mallory Town will be a target, they know how well defended it is, but answer me this, how sure are you that the new settlers can be trusted? Also, if there are raids in your area, will you be content to stay in your walled town, or will you venture out on another rescue mission? Knowing you as I do, the thought of abandoning anyone to that fate doesn't enter your minds. So, just another reason to stay put for the time being."

"I reckon you have the right of it," Daniel replied, "it's no secret that we have many in the town who might side with the British, and while I may have started to feel my age, I will not fail to answer a call for help. I suppose our little trip will have to be postponed."

"Aye," agreed Henry, "though if I'm thinking right, Boonsboro might be a good place to start. Be nice to see our old companion, Boone, again." He stood up and yawned, "Well I'm off to check on our prisoner and then to bed." He walked over to where Tilton was tied to a tree. Henry pulled out his knife causing Tilton to flinch. "Rest easy Tilton," Henry whispered, "there are those among us who can't stand the thought of a white man being tried for an act against any savage. If I were you I'd disappear, maybe join up with your pal Greathouse." Henry cut through the rope around the tree and then freed Tilton's hands and feet. "Go," Henry said. As Tilton vanished into the forest Henry said to himself, "He's all yours, Logan."

"I feel so stupid." said Henry the next morning to the group gathered at the now empty tree, "He said he needed to piss but couldn't with his hands bound up. I untied them, but wasn't ready for him to strike. He hit me over the head, and that's all I remember."

Daniel took Henry aside, "What about Logan? Do you think he will be overjoyed with this turn of events?" Henry didn't say anything but only smiled. "You know," Daniel continued, "I have a sneaking suspicion that there is more to this than you're letting on. Poor Tilton, I imagine he's already suffering, or I'm a doddering fool. Well done, my friend."

Boston

Late August 1774

Revere looked over at Dr. Warren who nodded his head. For security reasons, they were meeting in the house of a friend of John Hancock. Since General Gage became Governor of the colony, it was harder than ever for the Sons of Liberty to function. Increased patrols, the occasional random arrest, and the ever present feeling that you were being followed meant more devious means were required in order to meet. Sam Adams bore much of the attention from Gage's agents, so for today's meeting he was on the other side of town with Thomas, playing the part of decoy. The reason for today's gathering was to supply Marguerite with information she could give to Whitby. They had known for a while that Gage had an agent placed in the Sons of Liberty, and now they knew who it was, and more importantly, they knew what he had told Gage. There was a weapons cache in Somerville, and the British were privy to that information. Giving that information to Marguerite would corroborate what the British already knew, but would also help solidify Whitby's confidence in her as a spy.

The effect of the British crackdown was felt sharply at the Green Dragon. Marguerite counted four patrons and they were regular customers who weren't shy about going behind the bar and refilling their ale jugs, meaning she could relax for a while. She sat near the hearth, and pulled out the note Revere had given her with instructions to memorize it, and relay it onto Whitby, as soon as could be arranged. That could be a problem, she thought, as Whitby summoned her to him, she had never gone to him without that summons. She stood up having determined that she would initiate the contact this time, after all, it might convince him of her eagerness to spy for him. Just then Thomas walked into the Dragon. Marguerite sat back down, her resolve regarding Whitby disappearing, replaced by the renewed longing she felt for Thomas.

"Thomas," Marguerite called, "come sit. Are you hungry? Can I get you a drink?"

"I'm in need of sleep," Thomas replied as he sat down, "has been a long day having to listen to Adams all day. I mean, he's a brilliant man and all that, and we're in a perilous time, but there are other things in life other than politics, and the British."

Marguerite smiled and moved over to sit next to Thomas, "Surely there was some worthwhile conversation."

Thomas thought that Marguerite's smile was the loveliest one he had ever seen. He took her hands into his briefly but let go to cover his mouth to stifle a yawn. "Gods, I'm tired. Yes, he's an excellent teacher, but a hard taskmaster. I'm off with the sunrise to deliver messages to the militia commanders in Marblehead and Salem. Seems the British have gotten word about our weapons and powder cache in Somerville. Adams and the others are making arrangements to move some of our supplies to Salem before Gage raids the place."

Marguerite sighed, and thought it better not to mention her part in the scheme, "Drat that Adams, I was hoping to spend some time with you."

"Huh?" Thomas replied, "You mean go on a picnic or something like that?"

Marguerite shook her head slightly, his naiveté bringing a sly grin to her face, answered, "Something like that."

"I should be back tomorrow, we could go then or the day after," he said. He stood up, yawning once again, "I'm off to bed before I fall asleep on the table."

"I'll make sure there's something to break your fast in the morning, and to take for your ride." She watched him walk up the stairs wondering when, if ever, he was going to see past her role; a sordid one, no question about that, and see her as just a woman. She went into the kitchen, and gathered bread, cheese, and apples. She also filled a water skin from the rain barrel outside the rear door. With every passing moment her determination to make her feelings known to Thomas grew until at last she decided tonight was the time.

Thomas blew out the candle and lay down. He had been going over the message for the militia commanders in Salem making sure he had it memorized, burning the note as a precaution. As he lay there, his mind went from the message to the feeling of Marguerite's hand in his, and the time they kissed. 'Can it be that she is genuinely fond of me? I am certainly growing fond of her.' With that thought, Thomas closed his eyes and was asleep.

Marguerite stood poised to knock on Thomas' door; taking one last deep breath she raised her hand. The sound of the tavern door opening drew her attention, and she quickly pulled her hand down as Whitby's adjutant walked in. Glancing around the room he finally caught sight of Marguerite as she made her way to the top of the stairs. "Ahh, Mistress Edgerton," said the aide, "Colonel Whitby sends his compliments, and asks if you would please join him?"

Mallory Town

September 1774

Daniel stared across the table at Stanley Murdock, the spokesman for the newest group of settlers. He was a former Sergeant Major and could be intimidating, but Daniel wasn't in the mood for any sort of extended argument. "I understand your frustration," he said, "let me think about your request, talk it over with the others. In the meantime, just do the best you can."

Murdock was about to keep arguing but was interrupted by Deborah coming into the cabin, "Husband," she said, "Bert has just returned, and has some disturbing news. He's over with Henry and Liza."

While Daniel, Henry, and the others had been away to Whitely Creek a pair of Oneida warriors came to Mallory Town with news of a large band of Seneca and Delaware warriors preparing to raid the settlements along the Allegheny east and north of Mallory Town. Bert had gone with them to see how large the raiding party was, and had returned and was quenching his thirst from the long run back. "They mean business and that's a fact," he said, "I counted thirty but it could be more by now."

"Two Birds warned us that this could happen," said Henry, "I'm guessing that the British are behind this."

"That may be true," Bert answered, "we saw one white man with them. He wasn't in the uniform of a soldier, but he acted like one."

"British involvement or no, we need to respond," Daniel said looking up in the loft, "well boys, go out and ring the bell."

As the three boys left the cabin, Murdock entered, "I apologize but I overheard the news. I volunteer for the mission, and so will most of the men in our group."

Daniel nodded, "Just remember Sergeant Major that you, and your men are under our command. If you can agree to that, then we welcome you whole heartedly."

Murdock straightened into attention, "Sir, you can count on us."

Two days later they beached their canoes and made their way through the forested hills; each of the forty men soaked with sweat from the effort needed to traverse a pathless wilderness. Bert and the two Oneida ran ahead to locate the raiders, but discovered that they were too late for at least one farm, and its occupants; the charred remains of the cabin sending a spiral of smoke into the air. The man, his wife, and three children butchered, their bodies left as carrion for the crows, and other scavengers.

Urging the men on, Daniel and Henry knew they had to catch up with the raiders before they reached the next settlement. The Oneida scouts found the raiders trail, and led them to a spot overlooking a small valley dotted with the buildings and fields of the three families who lived there. The Seneca and Delaware had caught the inhabitants by surprise coming through a corn field, the tall stalks of corn masking their approach, and attacking the cabin closest to that field. Henry could see at least one dead settler; the rest appeared to be clustered in the other two cabins. "I recognize the white man," he said pointing to the figure standing off to the side, "that there is Simon Girty." Girty was a well-known advocate for keeping the land west of the Appalachian mountain range free of settlers, but it was still a shock to Daniel and Henry that he would be part of a massacre.

Daniel hastily made his plans for their counterattack. They filed down the hill keeping to the cover of the trees following a small creek that eventually flowed into the Allegheny. The forest stretched from the creek all the way down the south side of the settlement. He directed Murdock to take his dozen men and make their way through the trees, and to come up behind the two cabins. Henry was going to lead an assault to the rear of the raiding group. Daniel was taking the rest of the men to the corn field to take on the group of raiders that were ransacking, and setting fire to the first cabin.

The first group that Girty saw was Murdock's men as they came charging out of the woods to the rear of the two cabins. He yelled to the leader of the raiding warriors but the noise of sporadic musket fire from the cabins, and the shrieking of the Seneca and Delaware drowned out his warning. Murdock ordered his men into two ranks, the first kneeling, and the second standing behind them. "Front rank, fire," he cried. The volley startled the attackers who wheeled around to face the new threat. "Rear rank, fire. Both ranks reload and fire at will." The second volley tore through the warriors, leaving four of them dead or wounded. They returned fire, wounding two of Murdock's men and killing one.

Henry and Daniel began their attacks when Murdock's men fired the second volley. The warriors were fully engaged with Murdock when musket fire from Henry's men hit them from behind. Girty realized that they were out maneuvered, and gave the signal to withdraw. The Seneca and Delaware under fire from Henry and Murdock disengaged, and began running back to the cornfield, but were met with a withering blast of muskets from Daniel's men. The panicked raiders changed direction again, leaving the precarious safety of the cornfield. One more volley from Henry and Murdock, and the warriors finally reached the woods, leaving nine of their dead and wounded behind. Henry halted his men, some of whom were eager to keep up the pursuit. He looked over to Daniel, and saw that he had done the same. As Murdock came over to join Henry, a last gasp shot from the retreating raiders hit Henry, knocking him to the ground. The lead ball hit him just behind his hip, exiting out of his right buttock. Daniel saw him go down and ran over.

"Somebody plug these holes," Henry said through gritted teeth. Daniel reached into the pouch hanging from his belt and pulled out a handful of goose down, and carefully placed some in each of the holes caused by the bullet. Fortunately for Henry, the wounds, while painful, were not fatal having missed the vital organs and femoral artery.

"By God," said Daniel, "I'm sure lucky that ball didn't kill you Henry. Liza would never forgive me if I returned with a dead handsome Henry."

"Your concern is admirable, if a little selfish," replied Henry, "did you happen to notice which way Girty went? He has a lot to answer for."

"Is that the name of the white man who was with the savages who attacked our home?" asked one of the settlers, "I saw him follow the bastards into the woods, but not before he took one last shot."

Henry looked up at the farmer, "You mean to tell me, I was shot by Girty?" A spasm of pain caused Henry to groan. "Jesus, Mary, and Joseph, but this hurts. I could use some ale or whisky about now."

"You can have all the ale you can drink," said the farmer, "whisky might be a problem, not much of that on hand."

Murdock reached into a pocket on the inside of his jacket, and pulled out a flask. "Here you go," he said handing it to Henry, "I got this from a trader in Fort Pitt. Can't vouch for the flavor, but it will deaden the pain."

The settlers treated their rescuers to a feast that night to thank them, and to also pay tribute to those who died in the fight. The next morning the group from Mallory Town began their trek back to their canoes. Henry, his head pounding even more than the wound to his hip, limped along stoically, his thoughts centered on what retribution he could bring to Girty if they ever met again.

Yellowstone River

September 1774

The scent of the bear caused Gabe's horse to twitch nervously. He held his hand up signaling a halt. Liam rode up next to Gabe and gazed to where he was pointing. There was movement in a meadow of tall grass, two grizzly bear cubs came into view as they chased each other about. The cubs were downwind of the riders, and were unaware of their presence so close to their playground; that is, until one of the horses whinnied. Suddenly the cubs stopped their frolicking; standing on hind legs they looked at the group of men and horses. Gabe immediately raised his musket. He knew that the real danger was still hidden from view. The mother bear, invisible in the long grass, had been grazing on blueberries when she sensed danger to her cubs. Standing now, she caught sight of them, and the intruders. "I suggest we keep on riding," Gabe said, "that momma won't take too kindly to our lingering around her babies." As if to impress that fact upon them, she roared her disapproval, and lumbered over to her cubs. Urging their mounts forward, the riders moved ahead, muskets at the ready. Gabe kept them moving for another mile before pausing for the break they had meant to take a few moments earlier. "The Shoshone usually have a hunting camp not too far from here," Gabe said, "course, so do the Blackfeet, and they ain't as accommodating as the Shoshone. We should reach it before sundown."

Liam reached his hands out to the fire, the chill of the mountain air having more of an effect on him as the years have passed. He looked across the fire and saw Wahta grinning at him. It had been three weeks now since they left the Crow village, traveling with Turtle, Gabe, and Takoda. Once across the Bighorn River they gradually left the plains steadily climbing toward the looming mountain ranges ahead. The plan was to winter somewhere along the Snake River. Gabe had been there once before, but was talking to the Shoshone about having a guide from their village. Wahta put down the bowl he'd been eating from, "Our Crow mother makes better elk stew," he said followed by a loud belch. "Does my brother feel the weather more as we climb?" he asked, the grin replaced with a look of concern.

"Aye, that it does," Liam replied, "and yet I am looking forward to wintering this high up." He then chuckled, "May have to wear three elk robes to keep warm, but if this place is as Gabe tells us, then it will be worth it."

Turtle pointed over at the sleeping Takoda, "I know our Pawnee friend is anxious to see the places from his dream. I don't quite know what to expect, though I have a feeling we'll see a lot of snow, and soon. I was talking to a Shoshone elder, and he said the snow will start tomorrow. I indicated to him the clear, starlit sky. He just shook his head and laughed."

Indeed, when they awoke at dawn, the sky was gray and threatening. Snow was already falling in the higher peaks, and it wouldn't be long before it reached the camp. They made ready to leave as quickly as they could, their plan was to reach the Snake River, and the forested plateau where they would camp for the winter. Two Shoshone hunters, Tohopka and Makya, were joining them as guides, and to help them setting up their camp.

The Blackfeet hunting party approached the northern end of Yellowstone Lake; a spot they used frequently when the elk started to gather for the rutting season. One of them had gone ahead;

their enemies, the Shoshone also hunted in the area. He raced back to his companions, and told them of the approaching Shoshone party.

Gabe and the two Shoshone rode ahead of the others, following the shoreline of the lake. They rounded a bend, and were met with musket fire from the Blackfeet. Tohopka was thrown from his horse, the musket ball smashing into his face, killing him instantly. Gabe and Makya wheeled their mounts, and raced from the beach into the woods to take cover.

Liam and the others heard the shots. "Head into the woods," he ordered, "Wahta, come with me." They kicked their mounts, and sped ahead. Three of the Blackfeet, thinking to get behind Gabe, emerged out from behind a sand dune right into the path of galloping mounts of Liam and Wahta. Taken by surprise the horses reared, Wahta managed to hang on but Liam was thrown, the sand cushioning his fall. One of the Blackfeet was down, having been struck by the flailing hooves of Liam's horse. Wahta grabbed his tomahawk, and chased down one of the remaining two, the pipe end of his weapon crushing the Blackfeet's skull. Liam quickly recovered from the fall, crawling over to retrieve his musket. The third Blackfeet charged him, tomahawk in hand as he took a running leap at his foe. Liam, with no time to spare fired his musket; the momentum of the now dead Blackfeet warrior propelled him into Liam. The tomahawk flew out of the Blackfeet's hand. Liam heard the whirring sound it made as it just missed his ear.

Wahta led Liam's horse to him, "Snake Slayer my brother," he said handing him the reins, "we must hurry. More Blackfeet are coming." Liam mounted, and the two of them rode to where Takoda was keeping the horses. Gabe, Turtle, and Makya were crouched behind fallen logs exchanging fire with the Blackfeet. Liam and Wahta joined them, Liam taking the time to reload while he glanced around forming a plan.

"We need to get them out into the open," Liam told the others, "Otherwise we'll be stuck here with neither side having any advantage. This is what we we're going to do." He then relayed his plan to the others. After the next volley from the Blackfeet, they all rose up and fired then fled to their horses, riding slowly back the way they had come. As Liam had hoped, the Blackfeet were following on foot, thinking they had chased their enemies away. Liam led them back to the beach, and headed for one the taller dunes. Halting the group when they were hidden from view they all reloaded, and waited for the Blackfeet to come closer. Turtle dismounted, and crawled up the side of the dune. Peering through the clump of beach grass at the top, he signaled Liam when the time was ripe for the surprise. He clambered down the dune and remounted, and joined the others as they flew out from behind the dune, and charged into the Blackfeet.

Liam, Wahta, and Makya led the attack with Turtle, Gabe, and Takoda close behind leading the three pack horses. The six Blackfeet were spread out in a ragged line when they saw the group they were chasing come galloping around the dune, and straight for them. With no time to aim properly two of the Blackfeet fired wildly, the lead balls flying harmlessly over the heads of everyone. Liam and Wahta rode them down, Makya taking coup on both of the warriors, knocking them out with his tomahawk. The remaining four Blackfeet had scrambled out of the way of the leading horses, but found themselves in the paths of the trailing riders and pack animals. Two of the Blackfeet managed to avoid being rammed or trampled; the two unfortunate ones did not.

Liam's group kept galloping, anxious to be on their way. The last of the Blackfeet warriors had their six horses on a lead, bringing them up to the sound of the fight. Makya saw him first, breaking away from the others he charged the Blackfeet. Taking coup for the third time in the battle, the Shoshone swung his tomahawk striking his foe on the hand holding the reins of the other horses breaking it causing him to let go of the lead rope. With a cry of defiance, the Blackfeet urged his mount away from the fray, and made his escape. Makya yelped a victory cry as he gathered up the six horses, four of which he would give to the widow of the fallen Tohopka.

****

The open meadow started on the banks of the Snake River, and stretched out for hundreds of yards, eventually giving way to a jack pine dominated forest. Off in the distance they could see an immense herd of elk that had come down from higher ground, and were grazing on the lush grass of the meadow. "Seems we won't go hungry this winter," said Turtle looking over at Wahta, "I reckon we can even keep our giant friend here from going hungry."

Wahta laughing, replied, "Turtle speaks like our old friend, the little Irishman."

Boston

November 1, 1774

Sam Adams arrived back in Boston after attending The First Continental Congress in Philadelphia, riding straight to the home of Dr. Warren. The doctor's servant showed him in, and ushered him to the study, returning a few moments later with a cup of coffee. "The doctor will be here shortly," he said as he set the cup down, "he is finishing up with a patient." Adams sank into the comfort of an expensive chair, his backside tender from uncomfortable carriage benches and the last day spent in the saddle.

"Sam, how good it is to see you again," said Warren refilling Adam's cup from the pot he carried with him. "What news from congress?"

"I reckon it turned out about as we thought it would," he replied, "still a lot of folks want to see a reconciliation with Parliament. There aren't many of us calling for independence, not yet, though if Patrick Henry had his way, we'd be fighting already. What we did accomplish after all those days of debate was to put into motion a boycott of all British goods beginning in December. Each colony will have a committee to oversee it. If that doesn't work, we will institute a policy of no colonial goods being traded to Britain starting in September of next year." Adams stopped for a moment to sip his coffee, "Naturally, a petition was drawn up to be given to the King, but no one aside from a few die-hards thinks it will do any good. I think that given time to experience what more Britain can do to us, and to realize that Parliament is not going to go back on any of their proclamations, we'll see more and more turn to open rebellion. We'll certainly know more next May when the Congress meets again."

Chapter 10 1775 - Leslie's Retreat

Salem

February 1775

With tension between the colonies and King George rising steadily, it was decided to stockpile weapons, and munitions throughout the colonies. One such depot was located about twenty miles north of Boston in Salem in a warehouse on the North River. The owner, Dan Sinclair, Big Dan, as he was known to his friends, stood on the dock in the pre-dawn mist, and supervised the offloading of a barge containing barrels of gunpowder. "Quietly as can be, Mr. Hogan.", whispered Sinclair to his assistant, "We don't want to wake any Tories this fine morning." Hiding cannons, and barrels of powder and lead right under the noses of the British, and the loyalists, was not an easy task, so deliveries were carried out in the early hours of the day, and particularly when there was a fog encasing the area in a deep gloom, and a sound dampening mist. It was but a short distance from the wharf to the warehouse, so the crew used carts rather than a noisier wagon pulled by horse or oxen. The exception to this was the muscular Sinclair who possessed the strength of four men, and was even now carrying a barrel upon each shoulder as he clambered up the short slope from the river. "This is the last of them, Mr. Hogan. I want a guard posted inside as well as out." said Sinclair, "Word from Boston is that General Gage is getting a bit annoyed with our rebellious attitudes."

"Begging your pardon, Big Dan, but bollocks to the general." replied Hogan.

Boston

February 23

Lieutenant Colonel Charles Whitby considered himself to be a lucky man on this glorious spring like morning. He had just spent the night with his future mistress, and yesterday had been selected by General Gage to accompany Colonel Leslie and a squad of British Regulars to Salem on a warehouse raid, and it seemed that even the birds were chirruping just for him as he strolled through the town common. He was on his way to headquarters to pick up his orders when he spotted Marguerite up ahead. She was speaking to a young man dressed in buckskin. It looked to be a heated discussion, so Whitby, feeling a bit jealous that his favorite was talking to another man, and appeared to be in trouble, decided to intervene.

Marguerite saw the British officer looking their way, and recognizing him quickly said to Thomas, "Damn, Whitby's coming this way. He's pretty besotted with me, jealous even of any one who looks my way let alone spends the night with me, including his senior officers, and if he recognizes you from the Dragon our plans could be in trouble. Before he gets too close, I am going to slap you and walk away."

"Is he the one who bragged about his new assignment to you last night?" asked Thomas.

"Yes, he is, and here he comes," replied Marguerite as she raised her hand and slapped Thomas, staggering him backwards, "and stay away from me, you filthy creature. Go back to the woods with your stinking body, and vile suggestions." Thomas recoiled from the blow to his face thinking that she struck harder than necessary, and heard her whisper before she turned and walked away toward Lieutenant Colonel Whitby, "I'll find out what I can about his orders, and report to Mr. Revere tomorrow."

Thomas turned away from Whitby, pulled his cap down to hide his face as best he could, and turned back to watch as Marguerite approached Whitby, and saw him wrap his arms around her while he kept his gaze on Thomas.

Marguerite blocked Whitby's view of Thomas slightly making it hard for him to recognize Thomas. "I have seen that woodsman somewhere before but I cannot recall who he is. Ahh, that isn't important now. What is important is how you, my dear Marguerite are? I hope that colonial backwoodsman didn't upset you too much."

Marguerite was touched by Whitby's concern, though she was well aware of the danger she was in, not only for herself, but for the men she worked for should her treachery be discovered. "Thank you Lieutenant Colonel, but I am quite recovered," she answered, "your gallantry speaks well of you. Are all the men in England as gallant? Surely England must be a wonderful place. These colonials can be so uncouth, so vulgar. I am glad to be in the company of one so civilized." Marguerite put her arm through Whitby's and gently turned him away from the retreating Thomas.

"My dear, I would love nothing more than to have your company," replied Whitby tracing his finger along her cheek, "but I am on duty, indeed I am on my way to headquarters for my orders. I shall be away for a few days I'm afraid, but I am certainly free tonight. I do hope you can join me. We shall dine in, I think, and the finest wine, of course."

"That does sound lovely, my dear Lieutenant Colonel," Marguerite whispered in his ear and then kissed him passionately on the mouth, "until tonight, then." She walked away with a big smile, thinking that the danger was worth it.

****

On the road to Salem

February 24

Marguerite had indeed been successful in finding out Whitby's orders, at least enough of them to know that Salem was his destination, and that he was leaving on the 26th. Thomas reined in the horse, a fine beast from Paul Revere's stable, and pulled his scarf further up on his face. The wind blowing in from the ocean put a definite chill in the air despite the promised warmth of the noonday sun. He had been dispatched as soon as Marguerite gave her report to Revere and Sam Adams, carrying their warning message to be delivered to Salem's militia commanders, Colonel Mason and Captain Felt. He patted the horse's neck saying, "Come on then. Next stop is Marblehead." The one thing Marguerite was unable to provide was the method Leslie and Whitby were using to get to Salem; marching overland, or by ship, and if by ship, where would they land? Therefore, Thomas was making arrangements among the coastal villages to send a warning if the British landed near them. Marblehead was the last town south of Salem. He would also alert Beverly, the nearest town north.

Marblehead Neck

February 26

Jonas Glover shivered against the chill wind that seemed to be always blowing along this exposed stretch of Homan Cove. He sat on a rocky outcrop that overlooked the bay watching in case the British landed here, his hand resting atop the drum he used when he drilled with the militia. Most of the other Marblehead villagers were attending church while he stood watch. In an effort to warm up, he stood with his back to the breeze, stamped his feet and rubbed his hands together resulting in a moment's reprieve. He had been on duty since before dawn, and a few minutes after he was seated again, was finding it harder to stifle the urge to close his eyes.

Shouted commands to 'ship oars' and 'form up on the beach' reached Jonas' ears from the bottom of the cliff and startled him awake. He had somehow slid off his rocky perch and was lying on the ground, his neck and head propped up against the front of the rock. He rubbed his stiff neck then peered over the edge of the cliff. The sight of British troops wading through the shallows startled him into action. He did a quick count of the number of soldiers, and began drumming the alarm signal.

Within a few minutes a horseman came up alongside Jonas, "How many, son?"

"Two hundred forty, father," answered the proud young man. With that, Robert Glover raced off to Salem.

Lieutenant Colonel Whitby along with Colonel Leslie had been the first to disembark. The Colonel was busy organizing the march so Whitby lingered off to the side; his mind in some turmoil as his thoughts kept returning to Marguerite, and the unexpected longing he was experiencing. Not just the humping, though there was no denying that it was exquisite, but a fervent desire to just be with her. Whitby knew that he could never marry a woman such as Marguerite; his social standing demanded a much better match. However, having her as a mistress was certainly possible, and he dearly hoped she would say yes to that proposition. His reverie was interrupted by the sound of a drum coming from the top of the cliff. "Ahh, the natives are restless," said Whitby as he walked over to Colonel Leslie.

"Let them beat their drums. We'll be in possession of those weapons before the sun sets," replied Leslie, "I don't expect much resistance but we will keep our composure at all times. Is that clear, Lieutenant Colonel?"

Whitby saluted and answered, "Yes Sir, Colonel. Colonials with pitchforks and rude tongues will be tolerated with all decorum."

Salem

Morning of the 26th

Big Dan entered Jedidiah Kenelm Winslow's tavern looking forward to finally being able to relax. For two straight days he had supervised the moving of 19 cannon, 50 barrels of gunpowder, and the many crates and barrels of muskets, and lead for shot from the various locations in Salem, and dispersed them throughout the nearby countryside. Some weaponry went to outlying farm buildings, some, in the case of crates of muskets, were buried in the woods. The last of the cannons was now being loaded for transport to a farm in nearby Danvers. Leaving Hogan in charge of the last shipment, his only thought was for food and ale. "Whatever you have and plenty of it," shouted Dan to Jedidiah as he wandered over to sit with Colonel Pickering, "and a mug of that swill you call ale."

"Swill, he calls it," muttered Winslow to his daughter, Bethany, who was helping her father while the regular serving girl took Sunday off.

"Aye, but sure enough he drinks more of it than any other man," she said loud enough for all to hear, smiling as she plopped the mug down in front of him.

"Meaning no disrespect, young miss Winslow," Dan responded after taking a drink and belching, "it is damn fine swill, and I'll have another, if you please."

"So, Colonel, we've done our job. How's the militia?" said Dan turning his attention to Colonel Timothy Pickering.

Before Pickering could answer the tavern door swung open revealing a slightly breathless Robert Glover. "Colonel Pickering, 240 British troops landed at Homan Cove, and are on their way here," said Glover taking a mug from Dan, "I reckon we have two hours before they arrive."

"Sneaking bastards, thinking a Sunday morning would find us unprepared, eh? Well they've a surprise or two ahead of them," replied Pickering, "now if you'll excuse me, I have militia to call out. I'll head over to North Church; Colonel Mason and Captain Felt will be there. The Reverend Barnard will excuse the congregation, I'm sure. It seems he no longer supports the local Tories. Big Dan, if you would, head over to the drawbridge and see that our side of it is raised? That's one of the surprises."

On the road to Salem

The first part of the march was uneventful, Colonel Leslie's men making good time once they reached the well-traveled and well-kept Bay Road. Leslie and Lieutenant Colonel Whitby led the column maintaining the pace being set by the squad drummers. A rotten apple fell at their feet, seemingly coming from out of nowhere, followed by dozens more as a group of locals rose up from their concealment on top of the ridge that paralleled this stretch of the road. The apple barrage continued, and the men being pelted flinched causing the whole column to fall out of rhythm. "Steady on, men," exhorted Colonel Leslie, "show this rabble the quality of His Majesty's finest."

Lieutenant Colonel Whitby shaded his eyes and glanced ahead, "Looks like quite the gauntlet we'll be running. The road is lined as far as I can see with pitchforks and rude tongues."

The last four miles were indeed a gauntlet, one comprised of angry farmers, merchants, fishermen, and their wives and children. Many were armed with nothing more than a basket of offal to toss at the passing soldiers. Others contributed verbally, cries of "Lobster back, go home" and "Down with King George" were among the least rude. An occasional cry like, "King George can kiss my rebel arse" would filter out of the crowd. Leslie's column proceeded, seeming to be undaunted by the abuse, though at a slower pace than before. The calm exuded by Colonel Leslie was echoed by his men, but Leslie was anything but calm on the inside. Seething with a building hatred for this disgraceful, embarrassing situation, he resolved to complete this mission whatever the cost, even at the risk of fanning the flames of another Boston Massacre.

Salem – North River Drawbridge

The taunting continued, though most of it was verbal now that Leslie had reached the village center. The crowd lined both sides of the road, unarmed men from Pickering's militia kept them back while barking their own coarse slogans at the passing column. Shouts from upper story windows and some from those perched on rooftops added to the chaos that welcomed Colonel Leslie, and the 64th Regiment of Foot to Salem. It was a rather crude remark from a woman sitting in her window that brought Leslie's eyes up. It was then he noticed that the drawbridge, the only way to get to the weapons cache, was raised, and was manned on the other side by militia officers. "Lieutenant Colonel Whitby, have the men fix bayonets," Leslie ordered with a barely concealed look of frustration, "if these treasonous rebels want to play games, then, let's show them how serious we are about winning."

Whitby saluted and turned to face the troops, "Fix! Bayonets!" he shouted. As one, the men of the 64th pulled their bayonets, and mounted them on their muskets.

"Forward! Advance!" yelled Colonel Leslie.

Leslie halted the troops at the bottom of the lowered end of the drawbridge while he and Lieutenant Colonel Whitby continued on to where their half of the bridge ended. On the other side, Colonel Mason was gesturing to Leslie, drawing his attention to a canoe coming to rest next to the bridge. Captain John Felt and Reverend Barnard clambered out of the canoe, and up the bridge way to meet with Colonel Leslie. Thomas Clarke and Big Dan pulled the canoe out of the water and remained below.

"Let's keep our wits about us," Dan said to Thomas, "I don't trust that Colonel."

"Well I certainly don't trust that Lieutenant Colonel," snarled Thomas, "that's Whitby. He's the officer I was talking about last night at the tavern who handed Mallory Town over to Reverend Grantham and the Tories."

When they reached the British, Captain Felt addressed Colonel Leslie, "I am Captain John Felt and this is Reverend Barnard. To what do we owe the honor of a visit from a company of the King's finest to our quiet little village?"

"You know damn well why I am here," exclaimed Leslie, "and I demand that the bridge be lowered immediately. You and your rabble, Captain, are interfering with the King's business, and I have full authority from General Gage to use whatever methods I deem necessary to confiscate any contraband weaponry I find in this quiet little village. Now, send your people home; lower that bridge and get out of my way."

Somewhat taken aback by the ferocity of Leslie's edict Captain Felt nonetheless was determined not to be intimidated. "I can assure you, my good Colonel that I am unable to disperse the crowd that has gathered solely to pay respects to your fine troops. Nor, I'm afraid, will you find any contraband. Now, if you would"…

Leslie shook his fist in Felt's face, "No more of this useless banter." Turning to Lieutenant Colonel Whitby, his face flushed red and said, "Have the men up here on the double and prepare to fire a volley." Whitby quickly walked back toward the column, and informed the sergeant to march double quick, and get ready to fire.

The Reverend Mr. Thomas Barnard had until recently been a supporter of the Crown; his sermons geared toward keeping his flock loyal. However, he was also an astute observer of the nature of mankind, and seeing the effects of the British taxation policies on the people in his care, he came to the conclusion that rendering unto Caesar may not always be the right thing to do, that God was more concerned with the welfare of His people than He was with those who were abusing the power He had entrusted to them. Barnard's change of heart was reflected in the sermons he now preached, though he was careful not to condone violent action. Colonel Mason now saw Reverend Barnard as a welcome option in case he was needed to smooth the negotiations.

Reverend Barnard knew this was the time that Colonel Mason alluded to, and he stepped in between Felt and Leslie, his hands held out gesturing for peace. "Colonel Leslie, I pray you reconsider. Do you want to be responsible for innocent blood being shed? Does General Gage? Does the King? Please rescind that order."

Colonel Leslie took a step back and glanced out and noticed the arrival of a sizeable contingent of armed and ready militia; more than enough to outnumber him by two or three to one. "Yes, Colonel, your command would most certainly be wiped out," said Felt, "stand your men down. For God's sake man, this does not have to happen."

Leslie nodded; the situation did not demand his death, "Stand the men down, Lieutenant Colonel Whitby."

The negotiations continued on during the afternoon in which time the North River, being subject to the tides, began to recede, leaving a slick, and thick muddy beach. While the crowd's attention had been drawn to the confrontation on the bridge, three rowboats were beached just west of the bridge on the south side of the river. The six Tory crewmen disappeared into the marsh reeds; their job completed. Whitby was lost in thought, trying to arrive at a solution when he caught a whiff of the low tide's smell of salt, mud, and seaweed. He looked upriver catching the sight of the three boats, and saw a possible solution. Taking charge of the first twenty men in the column he raced down the bridge, and was soon floundering in the boot sucking mud heading toward the beached rowboats. With them Whitby could get across the river and force the issue.

"Thomas! Quick, grab the canoe. We'll make better time than those mud stained redcoats," said Dan, "we need to scuttle them boats. I'll paddle. You get the attention of some of those good folk along the way. We could use some help."

Whitby and his men, their red uniforms now indistinguishable from the mud they struggled through, had almost reached the first boat when they were set upon by an equally mud coated group of locals. The soldiers were careful not to impale anyone as they warded off the weak, and off balanced, flailing blows. Thomas was in the second boat using an oar to pound a hole in the deck, while Dan hefted a large rock and dropped it into the deck of the third boat. Two men with axes were rendering the first boat into kindling so Whitby focused his attention on the next one, and saw Thomas. With a roar Whitby sped through the shallows nimbly leaping into the boat, knocking Thomas off balance, and onto the deck. Whitby stood over Thomas, lowered his musket so that the bayonet was just inches from Thomas's heart.

Big Dan was not normally a master of stealthy movement, but with Whitby so focused on the prone and vulnerable Thomas, he caught Whitby by surprise, picking up Thomas with one hand and tossed him out of the boat assuming that the mud would cushion his fall.

"Care to point that thing at me?" Dan sneered at Whitby, "Here, I'll make it easy for you." Dan opened up his shirt, thrust out his massive chest, and pointed to a spot just below his rib cage. "There you go mate, stick it right there, angle it up, and to the right, and you can't miss."

Whitby was momentarily shaken by the sudden appearance of this very brave and very large man. He looked over at Thomas who had just extracted his face from the muddy hole it had landed in, and laughed. He then, in a swift, fluid motion, flicked his bayonet up and grazed Dan's chest, drawing blood from a shallow four inch gash. "There, let that be the last of the bloodshed, eh, mate?" Whitby said. Dan looked down at the rivulet of blood streaming down his abdomen, and balled his fists to retaliate, but Whitby turned, and was quickly away, gathering his men for the embarrassing trudge back to the bridge.

"I say, Thomas me lad, are you quite all right? I'm sorry for the toss, twas the only thing I could think of under the circumstances." Dan grinned at Thomas and asked, "You wouldn't have a bit of clean cloth I can use on this terrible wound? Ah, but no, you're nothing but a stinking mud pile yourself. Come on then, I need some doctoring and you, lad, need a bath."

"You know," Dan continued as they canoed back across the river, "this terrible wound will make quite an impression on the ladies. They'll think I'm a bloody hero, they will." Thomas looked back at Dan and saw a large man with a tiny wound and began laughing, and for good measure splashed his paddle catching Dan full face with water. That soon escalated and both of them were soaked by the time they reached the other side. They were met by a throng of cheering townsfolk who had witnessed the scuffle, including Bethany Winslow who handed each a mug of heated wine, and who made much of Dan's terrible wound as he played up the pain and agony, winking at Thomas, "See? A bloody hero."

Colonel Leslie grimaced as he saw his last hope of reaching the other side of the river sinking in the mud and shallows, and as he watched Whitby and his men climb out of the stinking mess. "It was a close run thing Colonel," said Whitby as he rejoined his commander, "if only our Tory friends had brought the boats around before the tide receded."

"It was a gallant effort, Lieutenant Colonel, and one that will not go unnoticed in my report to General Gage," observed Leslie, his nose scrunching at the smell of the tidal mud coating Whitby's uniform, "however we have yet to reach our objective. One thing I find odd is the rapidity in which the villagers responded to our approach. I'm beginning to think they were forewarned, and that means we may have a spy in our midst."

"That thought has crossed my mind, as well," responded Whitby, "If it pleases the colonel, I would like to investigate that possibility."

"Very well, Whitby," replied Leslie, "There were only a few on the General's staff who knew the plan, but I don't think any of them would play at treason, not directly, of course. But if one includes the people our staff members meet with, and I'm thinking of whores and the like, among them we are likely to find our spy."

Colonel Mason, having been informed by Hogan that the last of the cannons was safely hidden, saw the dejected manner in which Colonel Leslie now held himself, his shoulders were stooped, and his steps were more of a shuffle than what one would normally see in a military man. Grabbing his orderly, he made his way to Dan's canoe and shoved off to join Captain Felt and Reverend Barnard on the bridge with Colonel Leslie. This was the time to be a little more conciliating with the sullen Leslie.

"So, you came all this way just to cross a bridge?" asked Mason after saluting and extending his hand to a somewhat bemused Leslie.

"Well yes," chuckled Leslie, "and to get the guns."

"I can assure you my dear Colonel Leslie that we've hidden them where you can't find them," replied Mason.

Colonel Leslie, the smile disappearing from his face, sighed and said, "Well how can I tell General Gage that I found no guns if he learns that I never even got across the bloody bridge?" Mason, an idea forming as he stroked his chin replied, "Do you want to tell the General that you crossed the bridge but discovered no guns?"

Nodding his head, Leslie answered, "Considering the circumstances, methinks that will suffice."

An hour later, with the drawbridge lowered, and with the crowd moved further from the road, Colonel Leslie led the 64th Regiment of Foot across the North River. They marched the predetermined 275 yards, and turned around in the yard in front of Winslow's Inn and Tavern.

Bethany and Big Dan were perched on the second floor window ledge of the room where Thomas was staying. He entered the room after taking a bath, still smelling the muck that lingered in his hair. "Ah, Thomas me lad, looking a sight better," said Dan lifting his shirt, "just take a look at how nice my terrible wound is now that young miss Winslow has took care of me."

Bethany smiled at the comment, but her attention was drawn back to the British as the command to "advance" was shouted by Lieutenant Colonel Whitby.

"Go on back, the blooming lot of ya. Tell your master twas a fool's errand he ordered you on," she hollered.

Big Dan took her hand and said, "You sure are something, young Miss Winslow and make no mistake."

When the last of the troops had crossed back over the bridge, Captain Felt seeing Thomas in the window yelled up to him, "Thomas, please prepare to ride back to Boston. Mr. Revere and Mr. Adams need to hear the outcome of today's events as soon as maybe."

"Certainly, Captain," said Thomas, already missing what was sure to be a lively celebration.

Bethany saw the dejected look on his face, touched his arm, kissed him on the cheek, and told him, "I will fix up some food, and a skin of ale for the road."

As she was leaving the room, Dan said to Thomas, chuckling, "Now you ain't aiming to steal my girl, are you young lad?"

Thomas trotted off to the cheering of the crowd, putting his steed in full gallop once he crossed the bridge and the crowd had thinned out. Bethany was standing in the doorway of the tavern and said to Dan with a mischievous grin on her face, "So, you think I'm your girl, eh, Big Dan?"

Chapter 11 1775 - One by Land – Two by Water

Boston - March 1 1775

Upon returning to Boston, and after a rather tempestuous meeting with Colonel Leslie and General Gage, Lieutenant Colonel Whitby began his plan to root out the source of the apparent leak of information to the rebels. His first item of business was to confront Marguerite in a somewhat roundabout fashion. His feelings towards her was such that he didn't really want to find out that she was the source, and he was determined to protect her, if he could, and so tonight he would supply her with false information, hoping against hope that this bit of information would not be acted on by the rebels.

Marguerite pulled the blanket up to cover her now chilly body. Whitby had rolled away and was breathlessly content, smiling at her, and admiring her form before the blanket concealed her intoxicating beauty. Whitby rose off of the bed, walked over to his desk, and held up a sheet of paper that he handed to Marguerite. "See my dear? Already my fortunes are on the ascent. I have been given the command of another weapons raid. There is a supply being stored in a warehouse belonging to John Hancock, that miserable rebel cur. A supply of cannon and munitions that ironically came from Salem, so it seems I will get my hands on those at last."

Marguerite read the orders and smiled, "Saints alive, I will be waiting for your successful return."

****

"A cache of weapons from Salem, being stored by Hancock?" inquired a doubting Revere, "The only weapons being stored by Hancock are in Lexington, not Cambridge, and could not have come from Salem, as your friend Whitby's orders indicate."

Taking a sip of coffee, tea was being shunned by many colonials, Sam Adams responded, "This smells of treachery. I think our British friends are trying to flush out a leak. It would seem that you, Marguerite, are a suspect."

Revere nodded in agreement, "The best course of action is to ignore this ploy, and let this Lieutenant Colonel Whitby carry out his raid. We will do nothing to stop him, after all, there is nothing for him to find."

Adams held his cup out for a refill and said, "However, to make this look real, we cannot even tell Hancock about the coming raid on his property. That'll make his anger and surprise that more believable to the British."

Revere broke out in a hearty laugh, "yes that will surely piss off our dear colleague."

Thomas came in the room and announced, "I believe that Marguerite was followed here. I noticed two men come down the street who appeared to pay too much attention to this house. One of them is still across the street lying in the alley pretending to be sleeping off the previous night's drink. The other one headed back in the direction of Gage's headquarters."

Marguerite looked at her mother sitting in the corner repairing a rip in one of Revere's shirts, "Tis a lucky thing that me mum works for Mr. Revere, and I have occasion to visit, and help her with her duties."

Thomas flashed an angry look at her and said, "This is too dangerous for you to be so unconcerned."

"Why, Mr. Clarke, I do believe you are underestimating me. I am well aware of the danger, but am willing to risk it. I have hated the British for too long, ever since my Pa died, and the cursed British military abandoned us to a life of destitution, and that after an officer tried to rape my mother. So, no, Mr. Clarke, I will not back away from this."

"Even so," responded Revere, "Gage will undoubtedly have my house watched even more diligently now that he suspects your involvement. I think it would be wise to limit your visits here to times when I am not at home, thereby giving more credence to the visiting your mother aspect. We will, of course, continue to meet, but not here."

Thomas took hold of Marguerite's hands, gazed into those captivating eyes, smiled and said, "Do take care. I do not want anything to happen to you."

"I thank you for your concern, Thomas," she replied, "I will be careful. I will survive this conflict and hopefully so will you." She then gave him a hug, and headed out to continue her part of the plan by getting closer to Whitby.

Two nights later, Whitby returned to his room, and found Marguerite lying seductively on the bed, a glass of wine in her hand. "Did you surprise that miserable cur Hancock, and arrest him for hoarding weapons?" she asked.

"We surprised him all right. Even now, I suppose, he is drafting a lengthy letter of complaint to General Gage demanding my head, and reimbursement for the damage done to his warehouse doors, where we found not even a bullet, or cannonball," said Whitby, "and you my dear have surprised me in a most tantalizing way. I did not expect you tonight, but I am so glad you are here."

"No weapons?" she replied, "Could the rebels have moved them like they did in Salem?"

"Not this time," he answered. "I've had the place constantly watched," he continued, lying now in order to cover his deceit, "it appears our information was incorrect."

April 17, 1775

Margaret Kemble Gage, the wife of General Thomas Gage, was born in Massachusetts, and was torn between her marriage to the commanding General, and the love she felt for her fellow colonists, and the land she had known all her life. When her husband revealed to her his plans to march on Concord she was torn even more. She knew she had to act in some way, and so that morning she found herself at the door of Dr. Joseph Warren, a man whom she admired and who was one of the leaders of the rebel cause.

The plan was also made known by talkative British sailors to some of the whores who plied their trade along Boston's waterfront, some of whom in turn relayed this information to Paul Revere and Dr. Warren. However, as is the way in human nature, the dissemination of the facts became somewhat enhanced, and now it was feared that the plot not only included the capture of the military stores in Concord, but also the arrest of John Hancock and Sam Adams, both of whom were now heading to Lexington, not only as a precaution, but to also take part in a meeting of The Committee for Safety, an underground, shadowy group of rebels which was basically the governing body tasked with resisting British control of the colony.

Thomas reined in his horse as he surveyed the rushing water of Mill Creek. It had been a snowy winter, and even this usually benign tributary of the Mystic River was a noticeably wider, roiling cascade of snow melt. With rumors spreading of a possible mission to Lexington by His Majesty's troops, he had been sent by Revere to scout the woods and fields west of Charlestown to see if it could be traversed in case the roads were patrolled by the British. He patted the horse on the neck, and turned the mare around so he would have room to gain speed for the jump across the creek. The mare didn't hesitate, and landed on the far side though her hind legs did land on the far bank, sliding a bit before she gained purchase, and scrambled up the side to the soggy ground and safety. "Well done girl. Time to head back, and make our report," he told the mare.

Morning - April 18, 1775

"Gage will have stationed troops along all of the ways out of Boston," counseled Dr. Warren as he and Revere looked out over the harbor where they watched the early morning activity aboard the warship HMS Somerset.

"Aye and by the looks of all those longboats being lowered from that warship, they plan on ferrying troops, probably to Cambridge," replied Revere, "from there straight north up the road to Lexington. Unless the target is Concord. We have considerable munitions stored there."

"I agree, but I still think Hancock and Adams are the primary targets," said Warren, "Has Marguerite received any more information from that Lieutenant Colonel?"

"Surprisingly very little, though he did tell her that he would not be seeing her tonight. Perhaps he doesn't know the full plan yet. Gage will want to keep this close to the vest," replied Revere.

Dr. Warren thought for a moment and said, "Let's go to my office. We have some planning to do."

Dr. Warren's office was agreeably empty of patients as he and Revere entered. He instructed his aide to bring refreshments and then dismissed him for the day. "We cannot be sure that they intend to use those boats for all or even part of his force," Warren said to Revere, taking a sip of the coffee his aide had brought, "Gage is no dummy. He has to know that we will have noticed the unusual activity aboard that ship."

Revere nodded and went to the window. His eyes eventually came to rest on the steeple of Christ Church, recently closed as the parishioners grew tired of the current minister's Loyalist preaching, and refused to pay him. He turned back to Warren, and replied while pointing to the church, "I know the sexton of that church. He's loyal to our cause, and that bell tower is tall enough for a lantern to be seen from Charlestown. I suggest that he light one if the troops are heading along the road to Boston Neck. If they are boarding those longboats, then two lanterns will be the signal."

"Excellent idea," replied Warren, "we should send Thomas over to Charlestown. He can relay our signal plans to Colonel Conant, the militia commander there. The colonel can arrange to have a horse ready for you so you can get the message to Hancock and Adams in Lexington. You'll have to cross the bay at night, and within sight of that warship. Do you know some boatmen who can row you across without being seen?"

Revere chuckled, "Aye, I may know a few who have become adept at avoiding unwanted interference. However, it seems prudent that we have more than one rider out given the patrols that we know will be on the roads. I will talk with the tanner, William Dawes. He frequently uses the road on Boston Neck for his business. We can also take advantage of the fact that Thomas will already be in Charlestown and knows the countryside."

Dr. Warren rose from his seat and shook Revere's hand, "Go my friend, and make the necessary arrangements. I will draft three copies of the note we will send to our fellows in Lexington. Please ask Thomas, and Mr. Dawes to come by here this afternoon to pick them up."

Revere left Dr. Warren's office. His first stop was to William Dawes' tannery, and then to a tavern he knew would be frequented by the type of boatmen he needed. Next he met with Robert Newman the sexton of Christ Church explaining what he required him to do, and finally to his home to send Thomas on his way, and to get some sleep. It promised to be a long night ahead.

Afternoon - April 18, 1775

Thomas left Revere's home, and headed to Dr. Warren's office to pick up a copy of the note for Hancock and Adams. From there he headed to the wharf where he kept a canoe for the short paddle across the bay to Charlestown. As he turned a corner he collided with Marguerite who was on her way to see her mother, grabbing her before she fell to the pavement, the movement resulting is an unintended embrace. They locked eyes for a few seconds before she gently pulled away. "Well good morning Thomas," she said with a smile, "I was hoping to see you today, but wasn't expecting to literally run into you."

Thomas grinned sheepishly, "A very pleasant surprise indeed." He then turned serious and asked, "And how is your Lieutenant Colonel Whitby?"

Marguerite, her smile receding as she spoke, "He is not mine, good sir, nor am I his, despite his overtures of love. Now if you will excuse me, I have to go."

Thomas backed up, and watched her walk away wondering how that fleeting moment of closeness turned so sour so quickly. After all, she did say she was hoping to see him. He was still confused as to his feelings about Marguerite but had to admit to himself that if the embrace had lasted a few seconds longer, he would have attempted a kiss.

William Dawes closed up his tannery early, saddled his horse, and rode to Dr. Warren's as requested by Revere. His route took him past Boston Neck, and he was surprised that the sentry post was manned by more than the usual number of Redcoats. He had decided that he would not change out of his normal work clothes, using the attendant odor of the tanning process as a means to get through the check point later that evening, knowing that the usual sentries were used to seeing him on that stretch of road. However, as a courtesy to Dr. Warren, and his patients, he waited on the street outside the Doctor's office while he was being announced. Dr. Warren brought him up to date on the plan, and it was decided that Dawes would linger down by the waterfront a few blocks away until he was summoned to begin his ride.

Evening - April 18, 1775

Robert Newman and another member of the Sons of Liberty, John Pullings, made their way to the church barely avoiding a group of soldiers; soldiers bearing knapsacks, something that was unusual in itself. They carried one lantern each, and the necessary means to light them. Unseen, they entered the church, and began the climb up the 154 steps to the tower, and took a position that gave them a view of the waterfront, and of the road that led over Boston Neck. Shortly after 9:00 they saw 20 longboats leave, heading in the direction of Back Bay. "There they go," said Robert, "it's time to light both lanterns."

General Thomas Gage was under no illusion that this mission was of the utmost importance. The debacle in Salem a month prior had done much to damage his standing with his masters in London. He stood in the window of his office glancing out at the almost silent movement of his troops as they began to make their way to rendezvous with the longboats that would carry them to Cambridge, and then to Concord. He had chosen a remote beach along what was called Back Bay for the embarkation process so as to keep their intentions secret for as long as possible. He then sat at his desk, and went over the meticulous plans that were now being carried out. Twenty-one companies of handpicked troops, the finest soldiers he had at his disposal, had been roused from their bunks, and were told to go to the boats in small groups making as little noise as possible, though keeping 800 troops unnoticed would be a challenge. He had also dispatched mounted patrols along the various routes any rebel messengers might take to spread a warning. The companies were comprised of eleven squads of Grenadiers, the shock and assault troops, and ten light infantry as flankers and skirmishers. Among them were elements of The Royal Welch Fusiliers, and the King's Own 4th Foot regiment. He was sure that the rebels could not withstand such a force. The only thing that niggled in the back of his mind was that many of the men would be commanded by unfamiliar officers due to the handpicked nature of the force. He dismissed that worrying thought, counting on the professionalism of the British Regulars, and the officers in charge. At any rate it was now 10:00 p.m. and things were in motion, too late to be worrying whether the plan was a good one, it was all up to his men to execute it.

Dr. Warren and Revere had been watching the church tower ever since dusk from Warren's office window, when the sudden glow of two lanterns galvanized them into action. "It is time, my friend," said Warren as he shook Revere's hand, "send Mr. Dawes on his way, and take care." Revere took a last sip of coffee, walked out the door, and headed to the waterfront.

William Dawes was sat at a table outside one of the many coffeehouses that had sprung up in the colony after the Tea Party two years ago. His horse was tethered to a hitching post a few feet away, her ears perking up at Revere's approach. "Well William, it is a good night for a ride, don't you think?" Revere said with a smile, "The Redcoats are on the move, and so it is time for us to move as well."

Dawes put down his cup, stood up, and untied his mount, "See you in Lexington," Dawes replied, "my mare has been chomping at the bit to get going." He mounted, and rode off giving Revere a last wave as he disappeared down the street.

In Charlestown, Colonel Conant and Thomas shared a look when the lights appeared from the church tower. Two horses were saddled and ready, the mount Thomas had used during his reconnaissance, and the other, a mare of Spanish descent named Brown Beauty, was bred for endurance and speed, and would wait for Revere to arrive. "Be on your way young man. May fortune guide you tonight," said Conant.

Thomas pulled on his hat, climbed aboard the mare he called Becky after his deceased Aunt Rebecca and crooned, "Time to go Becky." She nickered once and took off at a trot.

****

Lieutenant Colonel Whitby approached the two mounted troopers patrolling the road that connected Cambridge and Charlestown. He had been given the command of two of the British patrols meaning he would be riding back and forth between this patrol, and the one guarding the road from Cambridge to Menotony. He was somewhat disappointed with the assignment for two reasons, he hadn't been doing much riding the previous few weeks, and he would be in the saddle all night; he was already starting to feel the soreness creeping into his legs and arse. The other reason was that he had hoped to be part of the force moving on Concord, thinking there was more of a chance for glory in that role. Sergeant Bishop and Corporal Miller saluted as he came up to him. "Anything to report?" Whitby asked, returning their salutes while unconsciously rubbing his left leg.

"No sir," replied Sergeant Bishop, "only one old, slightly drunk farmer with an empty wagon returning home from a delivery to Charlestown."

"Very well," Whitby answered, noticing the moon had just appeared from behind a cloud, and was lighting up the road, "though I think we should pull off the road into the shadows. That full moon will give us away before anyone reaches this spot."

****

The skiff glided over the agreeably calm water, the oars were wrapped in cloth to muffle as much of the splashing noise as possible. The two boatmen pulled in unison while Revere kept his eyes on the warship that loomed above them, a dark ghostly presence, the creaking of its wooden planks matching the slight rocking motion of the outgoing tide. These next few minutes would be the most dangerous; the full moon was thankfully behind a cloud bank otherwise they would be visible to anyone looking down from the bow of the ship. Revere found he was gripping the sides of the skiff such that it was becoming painful. Finally they found themselves beyond HMS Somerset, just a short pull from the shore off Charlestown. Revere helped pull the boat up on the beach and jogged toward where he saw Colonel Conant.

"We saw the signal," Conant greeted Revere, "I took the liberty of sending young Thomas on his way."

"Many thanks," replied Revere, "I see you also procured me the use of Brown Beauty. I doubt the Regulars have any mounts that can keep pace with her."

"She is the finest horse in the colony, and that's a fact," Conant added, "but we've had word of patrols on the road to Lexington, so, you need to be on the alert."

Revere nodded his head, grabbed Brown Beauty's mane, and hauled himself up in the saddle. He gave a wave of his hand to Conant, his spurs goading the mare into action, and soon he was at a full gallop heading north toward Medford. It was just a short distance to the junction with the road that led west, and Revere gave Brown Beauty her head, the mare eating up the distance while Revere settled into the smooth, rhythmic gait.

Thomas had reached that junction about a half an hour before Revere, and was now heading west. The moon had cleared the cloud bank, lighting the road ahead of him. The noise of the mare's hooves caught the attention of Whitby and the two sentries. Without a word they left the shadow of the woods, and spread out across the road. Thomas couldn't see them yet but the mare's ears perked up, alerting him to the three horsemen now blocking his way a few hundred yards ahead. He pulled hard on the reins, and came to a stop. Thomas took a quick glance at the patrol, moonlight revealing the faces of the three waiting British troopers. He was stunned to recognize Whitby among them. "A fine night for a gallop," Thomas yelled to the sentries, "don't you think so, Mr. Whitby?"

The Lieutenant Colonel was certain he knew that voice, and ordered his men to stand to, "I'll deal with this," he told them. "Stay where you are, Mr. Clarke," he shouted to Thomas, "your time for galloping has ended." He urged his mount forward, pulling his pistol, cocking it as he drew closer.

Thomas patted Becky on her neck, pulled her hard to the right, and headed into the woods. This stretch of land was heavily wooded so he kept Becky at a trot knowing from his previous reconnaissance that there was a clear meadow up ahead where he could pick up speed. Whitby, unfamiliar with the ground, cautiously followed him into the trees, firing a shot at his fleeing foe. Thomas flinched at the sound of the gunfire, hearing the bullet strike a tree behind him. Becky needed no command from her rider, and she gained speed immediately. In the space of a few heartbeats she was in the clearing, going down a gentle slope; the sound of Mill Brook just ahead. Whitby could now clearly see his quarry, digging his spurs into the sides of his gelding; he raced out of the trees. Thomas, with no hesitation on his part, or that of Becky, drove toward the rushing water. Becky gathered herself, and in full stride made the leap. Her back legs caught the far bank causing Thomas to have a moment of panic, but the mare soon found her footing, scrambling up the bank. Thomas, the exhilaration of the jump made him whoop for joy. He directed Becky slightly to the east, and was soon following the Mystic River north to where it met the road to Menotony.

Whitby, though unfamiliar with the terrain, would not let his mount slow down. He was soon going down the slope at a full gallop. His mount was a fine horse, but was not much of a jumper, so when it reached the brook it balked, and reared, catching Whitby by surprise. He found himself on the wet ground, and had to roll away from the horses front hooves as they came down almost catching him in the back. Unfortunately for him his motion carried him into the creek, and to make it worse the gelding bounded away, back up the way it had just come.

****

William Dawes was aware that speed was of the utmost importance, and was frustrated that he was being delayed by a queue of travelers, some of whom were backing away from him because of the unsavory odor emitting from his clothing. They were being stopped, and questioned by the sentry detail posted on the causeway, that linked Boston to the mainland called Boston Neck.

When he was close enough to the sentries he recognized one of them and called out, "What gives, Corporal Malone?"

"Ah, Mr. Dawes, bloody orders to detain suspicious characters what might be carrying messages to some of the rebel leaders," replied the corporal, "and on me night off. Would sooner be in a tavern drinking and wenching. What brings you out so late and smelling something awful?"

"I do apologize for that. Working late when I remembered I needed to go to one of my hide suppliers over in Roxbury. Will this take long? It is, as you say, getting late, and this odor is starting to bother even me," said Dawes with a smile.

"Come on through Mr. Dawes. I'll vouch for you with the sergeant," answered Malone, "and I hope you have a pleasant night."

"I thank you, Corporal Malone," said Dawes, "here's hoping you get to that tavern soon."

Once over the Neck, Dawes put his mare through her paces, and was soon racing west to Roxbury where he would turn north toward the Charles River, Cambridge, Menotony, and finally Lexington. His route was longer than the one taken by Revere, but he still expected to arrive around the same time if not a bit before.

****

Corporal Miller saw Whitby's rider less horse emerge from the trees, and trotted over to investigate. He grabbed the reins, and led the gelding back to Sergeant Bishop. Bishop was about to start searching the woodland when Lieutenant Colonel Whitby, shivering from the unplanned plunge, and sputtering oaths against Thomas Clarke, appeared. Corporal Miller reached around back of his saddle, and untied, and then unfolded a blanket, handing it to the visibly enraged Lieutenant Colonel.

"Gentlemen, mark my words," Whitby began, when I get through with that...." The sound of an approaching rider halted Whitby in mid-sentence. "Get after that rider," he ordered the two troopers, "one of you head cross country. There's a clearing a few hundred yards in, just be aware of that damn creek."

Revere yanked hard on the reins when he heard, and then saw the two sentries headed his way. Brown Beauty skidded to a halt, spraying bits of dirt and stones before coming to a complete stop. Unlike Thomas, Revere did not know the terrain, so he turned the mare around, and headed back the way he came.

Sergeant Bishop entered the woods and sought to head the rider off, sending Miller to follow the road in case the rebel turned south at the next junction. Just as Whitby said, the woods thinned and Bishop was able to gain speed. The difference, however, in the direction Bishop took, meant he was not heading directly toward Mill Brook; instead he aimed north east to find the road that went north toward the town of Medford. It was a good plan, except for the open clay pit that the local potters used for raw material, and that his horse was soon floundering in. "Bloody, fuckin' hell," screamed Bishop, as he dismounted, sinking shin deep in the mire, "bugger all, this trip has gone all to pot."

Corporal Miller was mounted on a good horse, but it was no match for Brown Beauty, and was losing ground rapidly. Revere continued at a gallop until he reached the bridge that re-crossed the Mystic. He glanced back over his shoulder, and was glad to see his tail had stopped. He didn't know exactly where the other sentry was, but he thought he heard someone scream from the woods, giving him hope that he had lost all pursuing Regulars. He slowed Brown Beauty down to a trot, giving the mare a breather, thinking to advance to a canter in a mile or so, leaving gallop speed for any unforeseen company on the road. It was about twelve miles from the town of Medford to the Hancock-Clarke house in Lexington. "Well Beauty, only about an hour to go," remarked Revere to the mare as he spurred her into a mile eating lope.

****

Once Thomas and Becky cleared the sodden ground around Mill Brook, they turned east to meet the road to Lexington. From there it was only four miles or so to his destination. Thomas put her at a canter after climbing up the slope and on to the road, but after a couple miles, Becky began to lag, and was favoring her right hind leg. Thomas dismounted and examined the leg and hoof, "Becky, old girl, you have lost a shoe," he softly told the mare, "Buckman's Tavern is just a short ways up yonder. There's a stable there as well, as I recall." He pulled the reins over Becky's head, leading her as he began the walk to Buckman's.

Revere and Thomas reached the home of Jonas Clarke almost at the same time. Thomas arriving a few moments prior to Revere, and was engaged in conversation with a militia sergeant, unsuccessfully attempting to gain entry to the house. "Everyone is bloody well asleep," exclaimed the sergeant. "Now what in blazes is this?" he asked, as a lathered horse stopped just a few feet away.

Ignoring Thomas for the moment, Revere shouted, "Let us in, sergeant."

Sergeant Munroe replied, "Stop making so much noise. Everyone's asleep."

"Noise?" exclaimed Revere, "You'll have noise enough before long! The Regulars are coming out."

"Now listen you cheeky bugger," retorted Munroe, but was unable to continue as Revere dismounted, and shoved the sergeant into the arms of Thomas, clearing the way for him to reach the door. After a few hard bangs, Jonas Clarke appeared in an upstairs window, and seeing it was Revere, shouted down to the first floor to get John Hancock and Samuel Adams' attention. They rushed to the door, opening it, Hancock exclaiming, "Revere, get on in here, and stop scaring everyone."

Hancock and Adams read the message from Dr. Warren, but were uncertain that they were the targets of the Regulars. While they were discussing this, Dawes arrived and added to the conversation that he had witnessed the Regulars being offloaded as he crossed the Charles River into Cambridge. It was decided that the force sent out by Gage was too large for an arresting party, and that they were in no danger for now.

Jonas Clarke glanced over at the three riders, noticing that they were a bit knackered from the night's events, and could do with some refreshment. Soon they were all seated around a table in a tavern just down the road. Over tankards of ale and cups of coffee they talked, coming to the conclusion that the weapons store in Concord was the real target of the Regulars. It happened that there were several militia men lodging there, and it was agreed that Thomas, since he was horse less for now, would join with the militia, and head to Concord. In order to get the warning out quickly so that the rest of the militia could form, Revere and Dawes along with Dr. Samuel Prescott, a local member of the Committee for Safety, mounted up, weary backsides and stiffening legs forgotten, and rode for Concord, the sound of a warning bell echoing off the hills urging them on.

Chapter 12 1775 - The Shot

Concord

      Thomas joined with the Concord militia led by Colonel Barrett. A messenger had arrived from Lexington with news of shots being fired by the British Regulars. The Lexington militia was badly outnumbered, and was retreating. The Regulars were now on their way to Concord. Barrett looked around, his contingent now numbered around four hundred, having been joined by the militia from nearby Lincoln. Deciding to wait and see what develops he ordered his men into formation with muskets loaded. The British split into smaller units as they marched to the buildings they intended to search for weapons. The main force continued on, approaching the North Bridge, and to a better location for a fight. Barrett knew that if the British crossed the river, he would be in the open, not the kind of battle he could win. He led his men down to the bridge, and formed up so that the first few rows had a clear line of fire. The British arrived in somewhat of a disarrayed fashion owing to confusion over the orders given. A warning shot rang out from the British side, and then more muskets followed striking the ranks of the militia. Major Buttrick yelled out to his men, "Fire, for God's sake, fellow soldiers, fire."

      The effect of their fire was devastating. Four British officers and a few privates were wounded or killed. The remaining officers were unsuccessful in maintaining order, and the startled Regulars began to pull back, leaving the bridge in the hands of the rebels. Some of the rebels were ready to pursue, but Colonel Barrett managed to keep control, splitting his force into two defensive positions; one behind a stone wall on the other side of the bridge, the other he moved back to the hill top they started from. The British withdrew slowly, gathering the groups back from weapons search, and began their march back to Lexington. The number of militia men continued to increase, near 1000 of them now converged. Not surprising, the British were stunned at the speed at which the colonials gathered, and that they were prepared to fight.

      "Ya see, young Thomas, thing is that we've been a planning this for quite some time," said Corporal Steven McKay as they threaded their way through the dense undergrowth. Thomas led the way, his abilities as a woodsman became evident early on as the gathered militia groups now paralleled the British retreat back to Boston by racing through open meadows and farmland occasionally struggling in the thick undergrowth and densely packed trees. More groups were arriving from the east, north and south of Lexington and were being positioned along the road side in the cover of stone and wood.

He was being followed by a group from the town of Woburn led by two Corporals, both of Scottish descent; Corporal McKay was the larger of the two carpenters, though Corporal Robbie Bayliss was no small man himself. "Aye," added Bayliss, "every town and village has been directed by The Committee for Safety to train and prepare. The towns also prepared ways to communicate, by church bells, bonfires, and messengers."

"One would think we're a bunch of sneaky bastards," continued McKay, "being able to bring woe and misery to the bloody lobsterbacks so quickly."

Bayliss chuckled, "Aye, and right they would be."

The sound of musket fire could be heard in the distance; the smoke and smell rolling through the forest, an eerie fog in dappled sunlight floating over the meadows. Bayliss stopped, and after consulting with the Woburn commander turned to McKay, "That fighting is at Merriam's Corner. We won't get there in time, but do you remember where the road veers sharply to the left? If we get in front of the Regulars, we can surprise them from both sides of the road. That spot is perfect for a cross fire ambush."

"Aye, tis a lovely place," replied McKay, "I've an idea that will make it even lovelier. Have the boys hurry on, but you, and me, and Thomas here are gonna slow down the British a little." He then led the other two on a more direct course to the road. It was mostly open meadow so they raced ahead at a good clip, the only obstacle was a small pond they decided to cross rather than go around.

Thomas crept out from behind the trees at the edge of the road, "I don't see anyone coming yet, and there's no dust cloud. I believe we beat them." Looking around, McKay and Bayliss found three manageable, but good sized trees. They pulled axes from their kit, and immediately began to bring them down. Thomas found a couple weather or age felled logs, and dragged them out to the road. Within ten minutes, they had constructed a barricade across the road, McKay and Bayliss each carrying the last two pieces.

"Ah, this here log would make a fine caber for tossing," said McKay as he balanced the pole into a throwing position.

"You were always the best tosser in the village, and that's a fact," answered Bayliss, "but on this occasion you best just lay that log down, and quickly. The Regulars are almost here."

The first of the British troops were just beginning to appear from around the bend in the road. Thomas and the others ducked behind the barricade. "You two fire a volley," Thomas said, "then high tail it out of here. I'll fire, and be right behind you." McKay and Bayliss rose and fired, their shots flew high but it stopped the advance. They then turned and ran while Thomas rose and fired. One British soldier returned fire hitting Thomas in the shoulder as he turned to run. He cried out and spun to the ground. McKay and Bayliss ran back and helped Thomas to his feet, and after an agonizing sprint to the safety of the woods, Thomas collapsed at the foot of an oak tree. The musket ball that hit Thomas was trapped between his buckskin jacket and his right shoulder. The leather kit bag that Thomas carried over that shoulder took the brunt of the blow, enough to stop the ball from drawing blood but not enough to keep it from cracking his shoulder blade just below the collarbone.

While the British dismantled the barricade, the Woburn militia set themselves up on the southeast side of the road. Contingents from the battle at Miriam's Corner, and from nearby Lincoln and Bedford formed up on both the northwest corner, and along an angle in the wall that had them facing the oncoming troops practically head on. Thomas had made his way so that he was behind the force waiting for the British. The doctor from the Woburn militia fashioned a sling for his right arm, his shoulder now restricted, brought some relief from the pain. McKay and Bayliss rejoined their mates and were crouched behind the stone wall. The sound of marching boots was the only thing they could hear, and then the muskets opened up from the Concord position. Repeated volleys and the return fire followed by the screams of the wounded and dying gave proof to the carnage being so cruelly enacted. Soon the British were in a confused trot only to escape one trap and fall into another. The Woburn militia fired from their side of the road immediately followed by a blast from those behind the angled wall. The Regulars could only keep running the gauntlet of an increasing number of angry militia, leaving their fallen comrades where they lay.

Brigadier General William Heath arrived at the scene of the battle having taken command of the militia. He looked out over the blood soaked road dust and the number of Redcoats lying along the way. Not all of them were dead but were too injured to keep the pace their retreating comrades were setting. As there were only a few casualties among the militia, the few doctors and some willing to help them, went among the British, tending to those who they thought would survive their wounds. "Let me know if there are any surviving officers," Heath ordered, "I would have them questioned before we attempt to return them."

Tired but still determined, the Woburn militia melted into the trees and headed toward another bend in the road. Thomas kept up as best he could, but it was clear that he couldn't keep a steady pace for long. McKay and Bayliss stayed with him as he took a break. He took a drink of water and was about to say he was ready when he saw a flash of red coming their way. The British had sent out flankers and a group of six were about to come face to face with three colonials. Thomas knew he couldn't fight or outrun them so he turned to his friends and quickly said, "Get out of here. It'll be a few minutes before they find me." McKay started to argue but Bayliss shook his head, "The lad is right, Steven." Thomas shook their hands, "Get word to Revere or Adams about my capture."

Thomas watched his two comrades head east, and leaving a trail for the British to follow, headed south. When he knew that the Redcoats were following him and he had lured them far enough away, he sat down and leaned up against a boulder. He carefully took his musket from around his left shoulder and placed it on the ground in front of him. When he saw the first soldier appear, he raised his left arm in surrender.

Thomas felt remarkably calm considering he was now staring at five bayoneted muskets. "Let's just skewer the rat," said one of the soldiers, "bastard led us away from the others." A chorus of "ayes" and they advanced on Thomas. Thomas tried to back away but was pinned against the rock. He closed his eyes and waited.

"Hold!" ordered the sergeant in command of the flanking group. The five soldiers pulled back, but kept their muskets pointed at Thomas. The sergeant came up to him, "I know this lad. He's from that little town Colonel Whitby took over."

Thomas glared at him and replied, "We took it back."

"Yes, I know. I was there," the sergeant snarled back, "lost a few of my mates in that fight." He then reared back with his right hand and landed a punch to Thomas' stomach, knocking the breath out of him and to the ground in pain. "Bring him along, boys. I'm sure Colonel Whitby would love to get reacquainted."

Robbie Bayliss peered out through the trees and saw Thomas being dragged to his feet. He and McKay had backtracked with McKay staying further back on a wooded mound keeping an eye out for any more British. Bayliss was close enough to hear the conversation between the sergeant and his men. When the British moved out with Thomas in the middle, Bayliss rejoined McKay. "He's in a bad way, Steven," he said, "they're going to deliver him to some colonel, Whitby, I think he said."

McKay nodded and replied, "We better head back to the others. Bound to be another fight when the Regulars start making the climb at Fiske Hill. Maybe we'll get a chance to rescue the lad."

****

Colonel Whitby led the charge against the militia group wreaking the most havoc on the retreating British troops. His was the lead group of reinforcements under the command of Brigadier General Hugh Percy. The British now had 1000 fresh troops taking up a position on Fiske Hill to cover their battered retreating comrades. Whitby's charge drove the colonials back into the woods, giving the British time for a quick breather before facing another gauntlet of musket fire. The militia continued its merciless fire, but now they were now under a more intense fire themselves.

McKay and Bayliss could only watch helplessly as Thomas was taken up the hill to where Whitby was waiting. "Come on, we can do naught to help him now," said McKay, "Let's go find those gentlemen Thomas mentioned."

Thomas was shoved in the back knocking him to the ground in front of Whitby. The pain from the shove and from hitting the hard packed dirt had him cry out. He looked up to see Whitby grinning at him. "Well, well, look at who we have here," he said, "it is so nice to see you again, Mr. Clarke."

Thomas struggled to his feet and retorted, "I wish I could say the same. I do see, though that you've had time to change from your wet clothes. Was your bath to your satisfaction?"

"I'd be a little less spirited, if I were you." snarled Whitby, "Do you have any idea what's in store for you, my young rebel? Well, I'll tell you. First, if we make it alive out of this chaos, I will see that you are settled in the hold of that nice prison ship we have in the harbor. The perfect place for you to heal up, if that's possible in that noisome, rat infested hole. Then at General Gage's orders you will be hanged as a traitor. Not right away, of course, a little time for you to think on things while you rot. I know you'll want to think about that lovely lass Marguerite. Oh yes, don't look so surprised, Thomas. I've seen the way you look at her. Think long and hard about her, my dear boy, long and hard about how she will be in my arms, in England."

The need to get the reinforcements to the scene of the fighting as quickly as possible caused General Percy to get on the road without much of his artillery and the ammunition for it. With only two pieces and limited ammo, he used them sparingly but effectively to keep the rebel militia pinned down, buying the nearly exhausted British soldiers' time to reach Charlestown Neck. General Heath ordered a charge to try and reach the Neck before all of the Regulars made it across, but Percy drove him back, firing the cannon one last time.

General Artemus Ward, the commander of the Massachusetts militia, arrived and took overall command from General Heath. Upon Heath's advice concerning the defensive preparations made by the British, well placed along the heights above Charlestown, and supported by the HMS Dartmouth's forty guns, Ward decided to lay siege to Boston. Soon 15,000 militia troops surrounded the Boston and Charlestown peninsulas from Chelsea in the northeast to Roxbury to the southwest. Fortunately for the rebels most of their leadership had left Boston prior to the events of the previous few days. Warren, Revere, Hancock, and Adams were all safe, and able to continue their roles, though they all knew that the chance for a peaceful resolution had disappeared like the smoke from the deadly muskets, having now fired the first shots of war.

There was one ship in the harbor set apart from the others. An aging war ship, the HMS Jersey had been stripped of all its former weaponry, and its glory. The hull and decks were weather worn. It had been months since any type of maintenance had been done; the only signs of any recent work were a new shelter on the deck for the guard crews, and a ramp used for the disposal of dead prisoners. The hold of the ship was now the home for the diseases, human waste, and rats that infested a hell on earth. Prisoners lay crowded together, manacled feet bleeding from open sores, rats scurrying among them, communal slop buckets overflowing with feces. Those too sick to fend the rats away were literally being eaten alive. Food, when they did receive any, consisted of moldy bread crawling with weevils. Water was often clouded with dirt and sediment. The only fresh air and light came from the stairwell leading to the deck, the hold being covered most of the time. At midday, the sun had turned the dank and dismal jail into a sweltering nightmare.

The rowboat came alongside the Jersey, the swell from the incoming tide rocking it gently against the side of the ship. A rope ladder was let down and Thomas was instructed to climb up to his new home. After the nerve wracking retreat into Boston, Whitby had Thomas confined in the cellar of the home he was living in. He stayed there for three days, seeing no one until that morning. Whitby entered, accompanied by one of the cruelest looking men Thomas had ever seen. Marguerite was also with Whitby standing arm in arm with him. She looked at Thomas and then at Whitby, "He doesn't look so proud and defiant now, my love. A shame, really, that one so young will have to die for his foolishness. Will the hanging be soon?"

Whitby patted her hands and answered, "Not right away. I've asked General Gage to wait on that for a while. I want Mr. Clarke here to enjoy the full experience of our harbor accommodations. Not to mention the pleasure of spending some time with the good sergeant here." He let go of Marguerite, and walked over to Thomas, "Sergeant Jack Collard is one his majesties worst soldiers, but oft times, the worst soldiers make the best jailers. And Collard is living proof, aren't you, Sergeant?"

Collard snapped to attention, raising himself to his full 6 foot, three inch height. His face was pockmarked, the result of a childhood bout with smallpox. There was a knife scar that ran from under his right eye to his right ear, the missing lobe a victim to the slash. His nose had been broken many times in the numerous fights he had endured. His mouth seemed locked in a permanent sneer, his breath reeking of onion and bad teeth. "Yes sir, colonel sir. A more wretched soldier you'll not find in the King's ranks. Bit of a temper as being a constant worry." He walked over to Thomas, reared back with his huge right hand, and punched him in his wounded shoulder. Thomas fell to the floor screaming. Collard kicked him once in the ribs, and then picked him up, "Come on scum. Time to see the nice place we made just for you."

Marguerite winced as Collard led Thomas away. Whitby left her side and went over to Thomas. Grasping Thomas by the chin, Whitby turned Thomas to face Marguerite, "One last look, Thomas me lad. By the time you reach your new home, she will be in my arms." He let go of Thomas to say something to Sergeant Collard. In that brief moment Marguerite winked at Thomas, and mouthed quickly, "Keep hope. I love you."

Epilogue

Mallory Town

October 1775

James Crane was increasingly frustrated with the divisiveness in Mallory Town between those who remained loyal to the Crown, and those who felt mistreated by the Crown. It had been kept in check, for the most part, by Daniel and Henry, but now they, along with Deborah and Liza were away exploring down the Ohio. Adding to his frustration was his need for action. It had become apparent to him that Mallory Town was safe, and well protected. Even the regular patrols had become boring and tedious affairs. When he heard the news and rumors from back East, he knew he had to go. The latest news brought by the Oneida chief was of a lot of activity around Fort Ticonderoga. That made up his mind that it was time to go.

He made camp that first night building a fire that was larger than he needed. He wanted to be sure that the three young men following him knew where he was. He had been aware of Bo, Cal, and Jack most of the day. They tried to remain unseen, but as good as they were becoming at woodcraft, James was better. He placed another log on the fire and yelled, "Come on in boys. No sense you being more uncomfortable than you have to tonight. We've an early start, and a long way to go to get to Ticonderoga."

Aboard HMS Jersey

Boston Harbor - November 1775

Thomas opened his eyes; the dream was disturbing, vivid, and bordering on frightening, even more so because it was the nightmare he was living. For seven months now he had been held captive in the bowels of the prison ship. He pulled back the tattered sail cloth that separated him from the other prisoners, some of whom had been there longer than him. The vividness of the dream became reality as rats scurried away at the sound, groans and flailing arms added to the nightmare sight. His eyes focused in on two bodies lying oddly on the floor having fallen from their sleeping space during the night. "Two more deaths," Thomas muttered, "how much longer before I join them?" While he was spared some of the agony by not being cheek by jowl with the others, he still suffered from the lack of nourishment, the never ending screams, and the pain from the frequent visits from Sergeant Collard. He doubted he would ever recover from the beatings, his arms and torso covered in an almost continuous bruise. Through all of this misery he would cast his mind back to the last sight he had of Marguerite, and the words she said. Right now hope was all he had, however, that was fading.

Snake River Valley

December 1775

Takoda quickly pulled shut the buffalo robe that served as a door for the oversized teepee. It was bitterly cold, and he had to use his tomahawk to chop through the ice that formed overnight near the shoreline of the river. He poured the water into the caldron sitting on the fire. Wahta was outside carving hunks of elk off of the carcass hanging from a tree, high enough to keep any scavengers from it, while Turtle and Gabe were tending to the horses. They were as ready for their second winter in the shadow of the Teewinot Mountains as they could be. The encampment now included a covered stable for the six remaining horses, Makya having returned to his Shoshone village with the Blackfeet ponies he captured. During the past year the group had traveled quite extensively in the area bounded by the Teewinot range and the Yellowstone River. It was a hunter's paradise; elk, mule deer, bighorn sheep and buffalo existed in such abundance that there was very little in the way of confrontation between the many tribes hunting there.

Liam lingered under the elk blanket, not wanting to let go of the warmth encompassing his body. It had been a hard day yesterday, the hunt lasting longer than anticipated due to a brief, but fierce snow squall that appeared suddenly. Blizzard like wind, and heavy snow made the trek back to camp a trial. The camp was protected from the worst of the alpine winter being situated in the lee of the Teewinot range, but diminished or not, winter was still brutal 6000 feet up. Liam started coughing, a reminder that something wasn't right. The others had adjusted to the higher altitude, but Liam found he was short of breath often, and needed to rest frequently.

Takoda brought him a cup of tea, "No need to hurry today Bishee. Old Gabe says another storm is coming; the higher peaks are already hidden beneath the clouds. Stay warm under the elk hide."

Liam shivered as he flung off the blanket, "If there's a storm coming there's bound to be work to be done." He picked up the blanket, using it as a robe, and made his way to the door. "I'll be fine, I reckon." Pausing for a moment he looked back at Takoda, "I'll know when it's my time, old friend."

THE END

Of book two of The Mallory Saga

Book three, The Crucible of Rebellion – coming soon.

Acknowledgements

Writing a novel is hard work. Writing a family saga, in some ways, is even harder. A lot of tidbits to keep track of as the family grows and disperses to their respective places in the historical part of the narrative. Relying on my notes, or even rereading parts of Clash of Empires, does help keep me on the straight and narrow, but my expert team of beta readers ensure that the path is clear. So a big thank you and a shout out to three excellent authors who took time away from their own work to read mine – Glen Craney, Adam Lofthouse, and Martin Lake. I highly recommend their books.

Writing a novel is also a time consuming process. Time is a precious commodity in our household what with two grandchildren living with us, working full time, and just the ordinary mundane tasks of living. I've been able to cut one of those out of the equation as I have finally retired from my 50 years of gainful employment. Though I must admit that there are mixed results from my retirement. I am still captive to the many years of 12 hour night shifts, so I am wired to be up in the middle of the night, meaning I am awake when the house is quiet. Good for writing, not so amenable to good sleep habits. My family is to be praised for putting up with my odd writing arrangements, and the occasional temper burst brought on by sleep deprivation. ☺

Writing a novel can be a bit nerve wracking. You finish a section, a paragraph, or even just a change of one word in a sentence, and you read it over and over; each time it seems less brilliant than you first thought. That's when a good support group comes in handy. The Facebook Group, The Review, is one such group. With #PromoFriday and #SnippetSunday, I had outlets for those bits; a place to test the waters, so to speak. More often than not they calmed my frayed nerves, reaffirming that my Muse was on the right track. Thanks to all you lovely people for the support and love.

Writing a novel, for me at least, is not only an outlet for my creativity, but is also a chance, albeit a small one, to enhance my financial situation. There are so many good authors; so many good books to read, that my chances at a "best seller" are slim despite how well I write. Therefore, my peeps and fellow travelers, I need you to help me out...actually to help out any author whose books you enjoy. It doesn't take much to leave a review on Amazon, Goodreads, etc., etc. Just a few words are all that is needed to make an author's day. Reviews drive sales, making for a happy author, and a happy author is more likely to write more novels. Thanks.

Writing a novel is not solely accomplished by the author alone. This author could not be all he could be without the ministrations, gentle or otherwise, of my friend, editor, and colleague,

Marguerite Walker II. Thanks again for the advice, wisdom, and for laughing at my attempts to brighten your day. I still owe you dinner in Greektown.

Many thanks also to Dave Slaney for another great cover. You make my life easier. If I ever make it back to the U.K., the pints are on me.

Author's Note

Most of the historical events in Paths to Freedom take place in and around Boston. The events in and around Mallory Town are fictional. Their main functions, other than making for an exciting tale, are as vehicles to get my characters where they need to be. As in Clash of Empires my aim in Paths is to remain as faithful to the history as possible while allowing my fictional characters some leeway as they play their parts. For example while the incident known as Leslie's Retreat did take place in Salem a month before Lexington and Concord, my use of Thomas as the courier bearing the message to Salem that the British were planning a raid is strictly my own invention. In the same vein the famous 'midnight ride of Paul Revere' is an historical event, though it is not true that he was the only rider that night, and he was not screaming 'the Redcoats are coming' as he traversed the countryside. He and William Dawes are probably the more famous of the riders that fateful night, but there were others as well; a perfect spot for Thomas.

The Revolutionary War, like all wars, was a very divisive event pitting rebels against the Crown, colonists against colonists, and Iroquois against Iroquois. With The Oneida siding with the colonists, The Iroquois Confederation came apart. The resulting victory of the colonies will have disastrous effects on all of the native tribes. This is, and will be, a prevailing theme or topic throughout The Mallory Saga. Perhaps it's just my meager attempt at shedding some light on this part of America's history. Not just the glossed over, the victors write story version, but also an attempt to show a more balanced look at the various tribal cultures.

The Tea Party is another example of myth sometimes superseding truth. Not all of the participants dressed as Indians, though there were many who did their best to disguise themselves. One of the more fascinating things I learned about the aftermath of the dumping of the tea is that there was some very vocal opposition to the tea raid from prominent members of the Sons of Liberty, most especially John Hancock and George Washington.

I decided to end Paths with the Lexington and Concord affair and the capture of Thomas. In the next book in the saga, The Crucible of Rebellion, I'll continue to follow the lives of the Mallory clan as they meet new challenges brought on by The Revolutionary War, and their own personal quests and dreams.

About the Author

Paul was born in Detroit when the Big Three ruled the automobile industry, and The Korean Conflict was in full swing. A lifelong interest in history and a love of reading eventually led him to Wayne State University where he majored in Ancient History, with a minor in Physical Anthropology. However, to make ends meet, those studies were left to the realm of dreams, and Paul found himself accidentally embarking on a 50 year career in computers. A career that he has recently retired from in order to spend more time with those dreams....7 grandchildren will help fill the time as well.

He now resides in the quaint New England town of Salem, Massachusetts with his wife Daryl, just a few minutes' walk from the North River, and the site where the Revolution almost began.

The Mallory Saga is the culmination of Paul's love of history, and his creative drive to write stories. With Nightwish and Bruce Cockburn coming through his headphones, and many cups of excellent coffee, Paul hopes to carry the Saga into the late 19th century, bringing American History to life through the eyes and actions of the Mallory family.

Follow Paul and the Mallory Saga:

On Facebook https://www.facebook.com/mallorysaga/

On Twitter https://twitter.com/hooverbkreview

Turn off the TV, read a book, write a review - an author's best friend. 😎

Made in the USA
Middletown, DE
14 January 2020